LOVE SLAVE FOR TWO: FAMILY MATTERS

Tymber Dalton

MENAGE AMOUR

Siren Publishing, Inc.
www.SirenPublishing.com

A SIREN PUBLISHING BOOK
IMPRINT: Ménage Amour

LOVE SLAVE FOR TWO: FAMILY MATTERS
Copyright © 2009 by Tymber Dalton

ISBN-10: 1-60601-471-4
ISBN-13: 978-1-60601-471-4

First Printing: June 2009

Cover design by Jinger Heaston
All cover art and logo copyright © 2009 by Siren Publishing, Inc.

Printed in the U.S.A.

PUBLISHER
Siren Publishing, Inc.
www.SirenPublishing.com

DEDICATION

Thanks to all the readers who loved Tyler, Nevvie, and Thomas the first time around! I hope you enjoy this one just as much.

LOVE SLAVE FOR TWO: FAMILY MATTERS

TYMBER DALTON
Copyright © 2009

Chapter One

Mail run. Argh. Nevvie didn't mind it so much before the baby, but maybe this chore she'd slough off on Tyler. At least it was on the way home from the pediatrician's office.

Nevvie pulled into the post office parking lot and parked away from the building, in one of the few shaded spots. The baby still slept. Hopefully he wouldn't wake up. She'd bought the car seat specifically because it had the detachable base.

After Tyler had, of course, carefully researched to make sure it was safe.

She climbed into the back seat. Carefully unhooking the baby carrier, Nevvie held her breath when baby Adam stirred. After a moment he settled and stayed asleep.

Whew.

She backed out of the Acura with the carrier in her arms, locked the doors and tried not to jostle the baby. Then she grabbed her tote bag from the trunk and headed for the lobby.

Tyler always received a ton of mail. It never failed that somehow fans managed to get the PO Box address to send fan mail directly to him instead of to his publicist or the publishers. She shouldn't complain too much, she supposed. That was a pitfall of being married to a famous novelist.

Well, married not being the legally correct term. By law, they couldn't be married. Thomas and Tyler were devoted life-partners for eleven years when Nevvie went to work for them as their cleaning girl. She'd always had the hots for the two cuties, but thinking they were gay, never imagined she'd be more than just friends with them. She jumped at the chance to move in with them as their full-time assistant, and then...

Then they saved her life when her asshole ex-boyfriend attacked her.

When months later the men finally admitted to her how they felt, she'd been happily relieved to find out they were bi-sexual. Even happier to learn they loved her as much as she loved them.

Now, five years after she first moved in, they were parents to a beautiful two week-old baby boy.

She sat Adam's carrier on the floor in front of her and opened the large PO drawer. Sure enough, mail nearly filled it even though she'd checked it two days earlier. Only a few things for Tommy, bills, a couple of architectural journals, and even fewer for her. Yep, the bulk of today's take was Tyler's.

Maybe she shouldn't feel guilty about asking Tyler to take over this chore. Tommy would back her up.

The contents of the drawer filled the tote bag. She locked the drawer, slung the tote bag over her shoulder, and carefully lifted Adam—still sleeping, thank goodness.

Back in the car with the baby safely buckled in, Nevvie cranked the engine and turned the air up. Florida summers didn't take long to heat a car, even in the shade. Tommy wanted her to trade the Acura sedan in for a larger car, or even swap him out and drive his Ridgeline truck, but she liked the Acura. The first new car she'd ever owned, the boys—*her* boys—had bought for her when she first moved in with them, before their relationship changed from friends to lovers to family.

* * * *

The drive home was short and the sight of Tommy's truck still parked in the driveway surprised her. She knew Ty would be home, but Thomas usually worked at his office all day.

She gathered the baby and the mail and walked inside. Thomas stood in the kitchen, was about to head to the back of the house to his home office.

"What are you doing home?" she asked, kissing him.

He leaned over and kissed the baby. "The afternoon meeting got cancelled, client had an emergency. I decided to stay home and bug the crap out of you two today."

"He's not kidding, Nev," Tyler hollered from his study.

"Quiet, you. You've got line edits due to your editor in three days, buddy," she playfully shot back.

Thomas grinned, his sweet brown eyes playfully gleaming. "That's it, baby girl. Ride his ass. Keep him in line." At six feet, he stood taller than both her and Tyler. Their sweet Georgia boy, his dark, wavy brown hair barely touched by grey.

Tyler appeared, carrying his coffee mug. "You're ganging up on me," he grumped. He kissed the baby, then Nevvie. "It's not fair, I tell you." Four years older than Thomas, he looked younger, and his boyish face and British accent never failed to make Nevvie's heart pleasantly thump.

"Yeah, like you mind," Nevvie said.

"I didn't say I minded, pet." Tyler smiled, his spooky blue eyes drawing her in. God, how she loved these men.

Thomas retreated down the hall. "I'm going to do a little work."

"I thought you were playing hooky today," Nevvie said.

"No, I said I was staying home and bugging the crap out of you two," he playfully called over his shoulder.

Tyler laughed. "How's the mail haul today, love?"

Nevvie gently poked him. "You've got mail duty from now on,

sweetie." She set the carrier on the counter and unfastened Adam's harness, then carefully picked him up. "Tommy and I only get bills. You get luuuurrrrv letters."

He grinned and kissed her again. "Ah, sweet, you know I only have eyes for you and our dear Thomas."

"You'd better." She knew the truth. Neither man would ever cheat on her or each other.

Tyler put his mug in the sink. "I'll take him for a while, love." He reached for the baby and she handed him over. While she didn't find out which man was the father—as far as she was concerned they both were—Adam's deep, spooky blue eyes were unmistakably Tyler's.

"Thanks." Nevvie handed the baby off to Tyler. He returned to his study with the baby while Nevvie dumped the mail on the counter. She really needed a cup of coffee, but knew she should settle for hot tea since she was nursing. While her water heated in the microwave she sorted through the mail and found an envelope from the Bureau of Vital Statistics.

Oh, must be Adam's birth certificate.

She opened the envelope, glanced at the paper, and then started to lay it on the counter when something caught her eye.

Disbelieving, she screamed. "Tyler, Thomas!"

Both men appeared, worried. She shook the paper in their faces. "What the hell is this shit?"

Tyler, with Adam in his arms, couldn't grab the paper but suspected what it was. "Nevvie, darling—"

"Don't you Nevvie darling me. What the hell did you two do?"

Thomas snagged the paper from her flailing hand. He read it. "Sugar, we talked to Bob and—"

"Don't you sugar me, Tommy! I specifically remember telling y'all I wanted *both* your names on the birth certificate!"

Tyler still hoped to calm her. "Nevvie, Bob told you they couldn't do that. It either had to be one of us or neither of us."

Red faced and enraged beyond further speech, Nevvie stalked out of the kitchen. When she slammed their bedroom door it startled the baby. He flinched in Tyler's arms and woke up crying.

Thomas sighed. "You want me to talk to her?"

"No, I'll do it. Here, you take him." Tyler handed off Adam and fortunately Nevvie hadn't locked the bedroom door. He found her crying face down in the middle of their bed.

He sat next to her and gently placed his hand in the middle of her back. "It's the way the laws are set up. There's only so much we can do. You know that. That's one of the drawbacks of our situation."

"It fucking sucks! You're both his father!"

Tyler stretched out next to her and gathered her into his arms. "Technically, no. Biologically, no. In heart and spirit, yes, of course we are."

She met his gaze and softly asked, "How did your name end up as father?"

"It was Thomas' suggestion."

"You didn't play Odds and Evens, right? Please tell me you didn't do that." It was a common way for the men to settle disputes.

Tyler laughed. "No, love. Even we're not that gauche." He hesitated. "Thomas said if we have another then we can list him. Age before beauty I think were his words." That finally drew a smile out of her. He stroked her cheek. "There's my beautiful angel. Why are you so upset about this?"

"Because you're both my husbands and it sucks that we can't do it legally, and it sucks that you can't both be on the birth certificate."

"It's the law as it is. Bob has only so many tricks up his sleeve." Bob was not only their personal friend but their long-time attorney as well. "We knew if we talked about this with you it would simply upset you."

"Darn right. Is it too much to ask that I want to be able to marry the men I love?"

"No, sweet. No more than wanting to be able to marry the man—and woman—that I love."

She snuggled close to his side, drawing comfort from him. "This sucks."

"It's just a piece of paper. That's all."

"A piece of paper that legally cuts Tommy out of Adam's life."

"Bob is working on that. He's drawing up papers so it's as legal as we can make it. His name is still Adam Ryan Kinsey-Paulson."

She fell quiet for several long minutes. "I wish he could grow up and not have to deal with bullshit like this. I wish he could say, 'This is my mom, and these are my dads.'"

"Maybe one day he will. It doesn't matter." He kissed her. "Please don't be upset about this. We have a good life, do we not?"

"Yes."

He was about to say something else when the phone rang. Tyler glanced at the bedside table before picking up the handset. "Hello, Mom." The way he pronounced it sounded like "mum."

Tyler listened, then smiled and handed the phone to Nevvie. "She'd like to talk to you, love." He gave her a quick kiss on the nose as Nevvie took the handset.

"Hi, Mom."

"Hello, sugar. How y'all doin'?" Peggy Kinsey was actually Tommy's mother, but all three of them called her Mom. She still lived in Savannah. Her thick southern accent made Tom's soft drawl almost sound like a New York native by comparison.

"I'm okay."

"Y'all don't sound okay."

Tyler rose from their bed, leaving the door open behind him as he went to help Tom settle the baby.

"I received Adam's birth certificate in the mail today and had a little bit of a meltdown. The boys didn't bother to tell me they listed Ty as his father."

"Well, sugar, it doesn't really matter, does it?"

"It's the principle." They chatted for a few minutes before Nevvie found Tommy in the kitchen and swapped him the phone for the baby.

Tyler looked at her. "Are you all right, love?"

She sighed. "I will be." She spotted the birth certificate on the counter and pointed at it. "Go put that away, please, so I don't have to look at it."

"All right." He kissed her and went to do it.

Nevvie took the baby to the nursery and put him down for his nap. Thomas caught up with her there, wrapping his arms around her from behind as she stood next to the crib.

"If it doesn't bother me, sugar, it shouldn't bother you."

Nevvie leaned against him. "It bothers me, Tommy. You're both his fathers. It's not fair. I love both of you, you both love me, and it's not fair."

He turned her to face him, kissing her. "Ty and I have dealt with this for, what, over sixteen years now. Give it some time, you'll get used to it, baby girl. It didn't bother you so much before."

"It was just the three of us before."

He guided her out the door, softly closing it behind them. "You're our wife. He's our son. What the rest of the world thinks doesn't matter. It's just a piece of paper. We're a family, and that's all that matters."

* * * *

Nevvie was still in a funk that night when they went to bed. The men held her.

"Love," Tyler softly said, "life is perfect."

"Listen to the evil genius," Thomas echoed. That had been Tom's nickname for Tyler since before Nevvie ever joined their lives, a humorous endearment that fit him well. "We've got a great life, baby girl. We've got money, we've got a great house, and we've got a great family."

"Except Emily," Nevvie grumped. Tom's eldest sister had been a vocal opponent to their union. When she found out her baby brother had made her an aunt she'd gone strangely silent, having no contact with Peggy or any of Tom's other four older sisters—all of whom had either immediately welcomed Nevvie to the family or grown to like her over time.

"I don't give a rat's ass about Em," Tommy said. "I keep telling you that. She's a nutcase. She's my sister, but she's still a nutcase."

Tyler pulled her snugly against him while Thomas draped his arm around them both.

"Go to sleep, love," Tyler soothed. "You'll feel better in the morning."

Chapter Two

Nevvie didn't feel better the next morning. Once the baby finished nursing, Tyler took Adam to the nursery to get him settled. Nevvie curled up against Thomas and was already drifting back to sleep in his arms. She'd gotten up several times during the night and felt exhausted.

"You worn out, baby girl?"

"Mmm hmm."

"Why don't you sleep in? Let Ty take care of Adam this morning."

"Mmm hmm..." It was an easy suggestion to take. He kissed her forehead. After a few minutes she'd fallen asleep again.

He looked at the clock, ten till six, might as well get up. Thomas shut the alarm off so it wouldn't wake Nevvie and went to make coffee without bothering to put any clothes on.

In the kitchen, Thomas jumped when he felt Tyler's arms encircle his waist. "You startled me, sugar. I didn't hear you."

"Sorry, love." He kissed Tom's back. The other man turned, encircling his lover in his arms. "She's totally shattered this morning, isn't she?"

"Yep."

"I knew I should have gotten up at three."

Tom laughed. "Ty, she's a mom now. There are a lot of things we can do to help, but nursing the baby isn't one of them."

Ty swatted Tom's ass. "You know what I mean. At least I could have brought him in for her and then gotten him settled again."

"Give her some time. She's still recovering physically, too." Tom made Tyler look at him. "Let her be a mom. Let her have this. You're a great dad but don't try to out-mom her, Evil Genius."

"Out-mom her?"

"You know how you get." He kissed Tyler, long and gentle. "Besides, if you have an overwhelming urge to take care of someone you can always take care of me." His cock hardened against his lover's hip. He felt Tyler stiffen in response.

"Oh, is that so, sweet?" Tyler gently ground his hips against Tom, making the other man moan.

"You know what you do to me, buddy."

"Do we have time this morning?"

Thomas glanced at the clock. "Yeah. I don't have a meeting until nine."

Tyler kissed him again, passionate, eager, his tongue parting his lover's lips and exploring.

Thomas' hungry moans punctuated the slow rhythm of his hips rocking against Tyler. "Jesus," he finally panted, "we'd better do something fast or you're gonna have me coming right here."

"Shower?"

"Mmm. What'd you have in mind?"

Tyler grinned. "Not in my mind, love."

Thomas groaned again. He grabbed Tyler's hand and practically dragged him back to their bedroom. "Let's go," he growled, his cock rigidly bobbing in the air.

They checked on Nevvie and found her still asleep. They quietly closed the bathroom door and embraced while the shower warmed.

"I want to feel that sweet cock of yours in my arse," Tyler hoarsely whispered in Tom's ear.

"Yeah, well I want a little bottom action myself, sugar. You'd better save me some energy."

Tyler moaned against Tom's neck. Tom stood five inches taller than Ty, but they fit together perfectly. "Get your arse in there so you can fuck me, love."

Tom grabbed a bottle of lube and followed Tyler under the spray. They never realized how fortuitous it was that they'd had the shower built as large as they did until Nevvie joined their family. The three of them had spent plenty of hours in there together engaged in much more than bathing.

Tyler nipped Tom's earlobe. "How do you want me, sweet?"

"Against the wall," he growled, his erection almost painfully throbbing with anticipation.

Tyler's blue eyes mirrored his own passion as he turned and faced the back wall, where he rested his palms and forehead against the cool tile.

* * * *

Nevvie registered the sound of the bathroom door shutting, then the shower starting. She cracked an eyelid and realized both men were missing from the bed. Tom's familiar low, hungry moan instantly awakened her.

Oh, no they don't. Not without me.

She got out of bed and slipped into the bathroom. The men were too distracted to notice her entrance. Through the opaque shower curtain she spied Tyler against the wall, Thomas slicking his shaft in preparation.

Nevvie stripped as Thomas lubed his fingers and carefully prepared Tyler, who groaned with need, starting an almost uncomfortable throbbing between her own legs. It was too soon for her to fully participate in their activities, but if one of them didn't do something for her soon she would explode. It'd been over a month for her and she was climbing the walls. Watching her men preparing to fuck only intensified her aching need.

Before she met them she never thought she'd be turned on by the sight of two guys doing it, but these were *her* men. They loved her and each other. Watching and listening to their passion was sexier than anything she could have ever imagined.

"Oh, yeah!" Tyler grunted, feeling Tom's fingers in him.

"You okay, sugar?" Tom asked.

Tyler nodded. "Damn, that feels good," he gasped.

"It's going to feel a lot better here in just a second."

Nevvie struggled not to laugh. It sure would! They still hadn't noticed her.

Tom withdrew his fingers and replaced them with his cock. "Ready?"

"Do it," Tyler begged. "Fuck me, love. Fuck that sweet cock into my arse."

Nevvie's knees weakened at his passionate growl. She reached out to the wall for support. Dammit, they were *hot!*

And they were *all* hers.

Tom gripped Tyler's hips and slid his cock into his lover. Both men groaned. Tom paused, waiting until Tyler ground his hips against him in encouragement to continue. When he was fully seated inside the other man, Tom covered Tyler's hands with his, their fingers laced, and stretched his body against his lover.

"How's that feel," Thomas gasped against Tyler's neck.

"Fuck me, love."

"I'm gonna fuck you real good, sugar."

She watched Tom's hips as he slowly, gently thrust into Tyler. She put a hand to her mouth to muffle her own passionate moan. He was always very gentle with Tyler, not wanting to hurt him, which was just one of the things she desperately loved about him.

Moving slowly, Nevvie slipped into the other end of the shower. Tom's ass tensed and flexed as he carefully stroked into Tyler. Both men's eyes were closed. They took their time, enjoying the sensations. She picked up the bottle of lube, generously slicked two of her fingers, and stepped behind Tom.

He yelled and jumped, startled, then laughed when he felt Nevvie's fingers press against his rim.

Tyler jumped in response to Tom's reaction. "What?"

Tom laughed. "Our girl snuck up on us—oh!"

Tyler tried to turn his head but he was still pinned to the wall by Thomas' hands and the larger man's body. "What?"

"She's having a little fun back there."

Nevvie pressed her body against the men and reached around with her other hand, found Tyler's stiff shaft. "You didn't think I'd let the two of you get away with having all the fun, did you?"

Thomas had stopped thrusting and gasped as Nevvie's fingers pushed deeper into his ass. "Oh, Jesus, sugar, that's good."

Tyler moaned as Nevvie slowly stroked him, running her fingers over the tip of his cock to gather some of the drops already forming there and slicking him with it.

"God, I love watching you two like this."

Tyler kissed her. "We didn't mean to leave you out, sweetheart. We thought you were asleep."

"I *was* asleep. If you want to invent an alarm clock that will wake me up instantly, record you two moaning."

Thomas laughed then kissed her. "If we'd known you wanted to play we would have waited for you, sugar."

"Yeah, well, when the two of you are done, you'd better take care of me."

Tyler frowned. "The doctor said you shouldn't—"

"Yeah," she interrupted, "I know. It's too soon for intercourse, but he didn't say you couldn't use your fingers on me."

Tyler kissed her again. "Need a little release, love?"

"More than a little." She nudged Tom's ass. "Who said you could stop?"

He laughed and resumed his slow, gentle strokes. Soon, both men groaned with need. She wanted to time Tyler's climax to Tom's, if possible. She knew all Tom needed was her to hit his button and he'd explode.

"Look at me, Ty," she softly said.

He turned his head, his eyes locking on hers as she slid her hand up and down his smooth shaft.

"I want you to come for me, baby," she murmured.

Thomas groaned behind him. She knew he was trying to hold back.

Tyler's gaze never wavered from hers and she increased her tempo, matching Tom's strokes.

"Are you close?" she whispered.

Tyler nodded, beyond speech, straining to make it over, desperate for release.

Time to play a little dirty. "Master, you need to come for your little slave—"

"Ah!" His eyes squeezed shut and she felt him throb in her hand as he exploded. She brushed a finger inside Tom against his gland and he groaned, his hips bucking against Tyler, his hands tightening around the other man's fingers.

She pressed her body tightly against them, holding them, loving them, feeling the last vibrations of their orgasms against her skin. When they could all speak again they separated briefly to rejoin under the spray, the men holding Nevvie between them, her back against Thomas and Tyler pressed against her in front, kissing her.

"Exquisite, sweet. Simply breathtaking," he murmured against the base of her throat.

Thomas explored her neck and shoulders with his lips. "Jesus, Nev, you're so fucking sexy. You don't know what you do to us."

She closed her eyes and relaxed against him. "I have an idea."

Thomas carefully cupped her breasts, knowing they were tender, simply holding her while Tyler's hand drifted between her legs. "Your turn to show us what we do to you, love," Tyler murmured. His fingers gently parted her as his fingers circled her clit, hitting the spot he knew would make her moan.

She threw her head back against Thomas' sturdy shoulder while he slid one arm lower, around her waist, holding her up. "Come for us, baby girl," he softly encouraged. "We want to hear you moan for us."

Tyler's skilled and knowing fingers rolled her clit. She exploded, her knees unhinging as her climax hit. Thomas supported her until she could stand again. When Tyler knew she'd finished he withdrew his hand, stood, and kissed her.

"How was that, love?"

She nodded, her eyes still closed.

"I think we wore her out, Ty," Thomas chuckled.

She smiled. "Not totally. You just wait. A few more weeks, I'll be giving you guys a run for your money."

One of her greatest fears during her pregnancy was that the baby's birth would fundamentally alter their well-balanced triad in a bad way. So far, those fears proved unfounded. If anything the men had been even more attentive than usual. More importantly, they were both great dads. Tyler had easily settled into caretaker mode, and Thomas, while at first a little nervous holding their son, didn't hesitate to change diapers or get up to bring the baby in to Nevvie for late night feedings.

Nevvie turned and hugged Thomas. She felt Tyler press against her back, his arms encircling them both. Her boys, her husbands. And in play, her masters.

"You were right. Life is perfect," she whispered against Tom's chest.

Tyler kissed the back of her neck. "Yes, sweet, it certainly seems that way, doesn't it?"

Thomas nuzzled the top of her head. "I love you two so much."

They stood under the spray for a few minutes longer before finally taking their shower.

Chapter Three

By the time Adam turned six weeks old, Nevvie was in agony when nursing. Despite repeated trips to the doctor, nothing she tried helped. Tyler drove her to her doctor once again, who told her she should probably switch to bottle feeding.

She burst into tears. "That makes me a horrible mother!"

He shook his head. "No, Nevaeh, it doesn't. It makes you just one of many women who've had the same issues you've had."

Tyler placed a call to Adam's pediatrician, who agreed to see them immediately and was able to calm Nevvie's worries. He examined Adam and smiled at Nevvie.

"He'll be fine bottle-fed. It's all right. My nurse will give you some information. He'll be just fine."

She sobbed, holding the baby in her lap. The doctor gave them a minute alone while Tyler tried to comfort her.

"Love, you're perfectly normal."

"No I'm not, Tyler! I can't be married, I can't be a good mom, I can't do anything right."

He knelt, his heart breaking for her. "Love, there is nothing wrong with you. You are a wonderful, beautiful mother. And you are our wonderful, beautiful wife."

Nevvie was inconsolable. "Let's face it. My birth parents didn't want me. My adopted mother dumped me. The state won't let me get married to both of you, and they're denying my son legal recognition for one of his fathers."

He let her cry for a few minutes. When she calmed down he kissed her hand. "Love, you are a fantastic mother."

The doctor returned and kindly smiled. "The nurse will be here shortly. Trust me, your son will do just fine, and there's nothing wrong with you."

They stopped by the store on the way home. Nevvie waited in the car with the baby. Tyler, in typical fashion, apparently bought out half the formula in stock. He returned with a large cart full of baby supplies, the sight of which was enough to lift Nevvie's funk a little.

She looked at him when he got behind the wheel, simply staring at him after he spent several minutes loading the full cart into the trunk.

He grinned. "Well, love, we don't know what kind he'll like, do we?"

Finally, a smile from her. He'd probably bought enough baby supplies to take care of a small Latin American country. Tyler was, if nothing else, thorough.

He was also sneaky. When they returned home, Tommy's Ridgeline sat in the driveway.

"What is he doing home?" she asked as she knelt on the back seat to unfasten the baby. When Tom walked out the front door to join them she spotted the concerned look on his face and realized what happened.

"You called him," she said to Tyler.

"Love, you acted rather upset."

"I don't need a babysitter."

Tom leaned in the back door of Tyler's Lexus. "Listen, baby girl. You need to get your head on straight. You're a damn good mother. The only one who doesn't think you're a good mother is you. Are you going to listen to the majority who sees you the way you are, or are you going to give those other thoughts rent-free space in your head?"

She didn't say anything, walked past him into the house without comment.

Tom helped Tyler unload the supplies and take them inside. Tyler immediately started washing bottles and nipples, read through the brochures from the doctor's office and picked one of the formulas to start with.

When the baby was ready to eat a half-hour later, Nevvie sat on the sofa and tried to control her tears again.

Tommy brought the bottle in and settled on the couch next to her. "Let me have him, sugar," he softly said.

She tearfully handed Adam over.

He looked at her, his brown eyes earnest. "Listen to me. You're missing something important here."

"What?" she asked. Tyler walked into the room and settled on Tom's other side.

"If we're bottle feeding, now we get to take care of him, too," Tom patiently explained.

Tom held Adam and the baby immediately latched on to the bottle. He hesitated only a second at the new taste and sensation, then promptly proceeded to greedily drain the bottle

Nevvie watched the men, Tyler's arm draped around Tom's shoulder as he leaned in and stroked the baby's cheek. Tom smiled at her. "Now we get to have some fun."

Another wave of guilt swept through her. Not only was she a bad mother, she was selfish, too. Of course they should get to feed the baby. She'd tried using a breast pump early on but it hurt nearly as much as nursing, so the men weren't able to bottle feed until now.

Jesus, she felt like she was losing her mind. Usually she was a very level headed, rational person, her personality a good mix of Tyler's passion and Tom's steadiness. Now she felt like an alien in her own skin.

She retreated to their bedroom and curled up on the bed. Before Adam's birth she'd felt worried, anxious, nervous. Then several weeks of bliss and now…

Back to craziness. Was this post-partum depression?

Nevvie awoke from her nap to find Tommy curled around her.

"You feeling better, baby girl?"

"No." She tried to roll away from him. He wouldn't let her go.

"Stop it. We're going to talk about this. You're not a horrible mother." He took a deep breath. "Momma wants me to have you call her."

"Why? Is she going to chew me out, too?"

He kissed her cheek. "She wants to talk to you. She loves you, and she's as worried about you as we are." Peggy Kinsey, a retired nurse, had been a wealth of information for Nevvie early on, between her medical and mothering skills.

Tom reached over, grabbed the phone and dialed his mom's house in Savannah before Nevvie could object.

"Hi, Momma. She's awake. Here she is." He handed her the phone and at first Nevvie tried to resist, then she took the receiver with a sigh.

"Hi, Mom."

"Nevvie, sugar, what's wrong?"

"You mean with me or life in general?"

Peggy's soft chuckle reminded Nevvie of Tommy. "Listen to me, the boys already called and told me what's going on. I want you to know that with all six of my beasties, Tommy is the only one who got breastfed. And I only breastfed him for six weeks until I went back to work. Then he was bottle-fed. Back then, we just didn't breastfeed very often. While Emily's a bitch that had nothing to do with the fact that she was bottle-fed."

Nevvie smiled, barely aware of Tom slipping out of bed and leaving her alone.

She spent over an hour on the phone with Peggy, laughing, crying, and finally feeling a little better. It amazed Nevvie early on that Peggy readily accepted her son's choice first to bring Tyler home as his partner, then to add her to their family years later.

"Sugar, let the boys have their fun. You're lucky enough to have not one, but two men who are practically tripping all over each other to take turns changing diapers and preparing bottles. A lot of women don't even have one who does that. Seriously, I think you're just going through the baby blues. If this keeps up, you need to talk to your doctor. It can make you feel crazy. I wanted to castrate Tom's father after Karen was born, and I still had two more with him."

Having her thoughts vocalized by Peggy helped more than anything. "I hate feeling like this."

"I know you do. I can't come this weekend, but do you want me to come down next week, spend a little time, give you a break?"

She didn't really need the break, but she could use the company. Peggy was more of a mother to her than her own adopted mother had been. Maybe a weekend with her would help even out her emotions and get her back on track.

"I'd appreciate it if you could."

When she finished talking to Peggy, Nevvie walked out to the kitchen. The boys leaned against the counter and watched her.

"Feeling better, love?" Tyler asked.

She reluctantly nodded. Both men walked to her, enveloping her in their arms. "We love you, Nevvie," Thomas assured her. "You're a great mom.

*   *   *   *

The next Tuesday, Nevvie had another OB-Gyn appointment. Her decreasing pain had at least helped improve her mood. Seeing how the men enjoyed taking part in feeding Adam helped soothe her wounded psyche. However, Tyler's blunt question to the doctor startled her.

"When can we resume sex?"

Shocked, Nevvie choked back her startled gasp.

The doctor shrugged. "As long as she's comfortable, anytime she wishes. I would suggest using birth control. Might want to avoid oral contraceptives for a few months though." They discussed options. When they left, Nevvie had a new vaginal ring she wasn't entirely sure of. The doctor showed her how to use them, gave her enough samples for two months, and wrote a prescription for three more months.

Tyler had paid entirely too much attention to how they were inserted, Nevvie thought. Then again, maybe she shouldn't complain. One or both men went with her to all her doctor appointments, knowing she hated them with a passion due to an incident years before she ever met them.

Tyler beamed. "You looked like you were going to crawl under the table," he said with an evil grin.

"Yeah, well, you just wait until your next annual exam, buster," she grumped. She realized they'd turned away from the house. "Where are we going?"

"To pay our sweet Thomas a visit."

She looked at her watch. "He'll be home in a couple of hours."

"Let's go show Adam off."

She eyed Tyler, but settled back in her seat. He was up to something, she just didn't know what yet. "All right, fine."

When Thomas left that morning on the Harley, she felt a melancholy pang. Before she was pregnant they used to ride the bike to work during good weather, sometimes several times a week. It was their special thing to do together, just like she had ballroom dancing with Tyler. Something they shared and enjoyed.

Thomas was Aerosmith—Tyler was Air Supply. Her playful tough-guy biker and her sweet, gentle brain.

Tommy didn't like to ride alone and rarely rode without her. Once she was pregnant, neither man would let her on the bike despite her protests and the doctor assuring the men it was safe in the early months.

The Harley sat in Tom's covered parking spot. Tyler pulled in next to the bike, in Nevvie's marked space. She had worked up until her last month, then focused more on helping Tyler. Before the baby her time had been nearly evenly split between the office with Tommy, and working at home with Tyler. Now she debated whether she wanted to return to work at all. The men assured her she could stay home if she wanted—they certainly could afford it—but she knew she'd miss her time spent with Tommy if she did that.

Not to mention she enjoyed working.

Maggie, their friend and Tom's long-time assistant before Nevvie went to work for him, swooped when they walked in.

"Oooh! Let me see him. I haven't seen him in a week! He's so cute! Almost makes me want to have another."

Tom heard the commotion and walked out to greet them. He kissed Nevvie and Tyler, then the baby. "Hey, what's up?"

She hooked her thumb at Tyler. "He insisted on dropping by." The mischievous gleam in Tyler's eyes could only mean one thing, that he was planning something.

What exactly, Nevvie still didn't know.

Tom's instincts matched Nevvie's. "What *are* you planning, sugar?" he asked Ty.

"Why do the two of you assume I'm planning something?"

Nevvie and Tom both replied, "Because you've got the look."

Tyler laughed. "My, aren't we the suspicious ones?"

Nevvie spent time visiting her friends and co-workers and showing off the baby. Maggie cornered her again to take her upstairs to meet a new employee while Tyler took Adam from her.

"I'll go change him, love."

When Nevvie returned to Tom's office on the first floor twenty minutes later, Tyler was nowhere to be seen.

"Where's the evil genius?" Nevvie asked.

Tom looked up from his computer. "What? I thought he was with you. I was in Kenny's office until about five minutes ago."

Nevvie realized the diaper bag wasn't on the large sofa where she'd left it. When she stuck her head out the back door, Tyler's Lexus was gone.

She stalked back to Tom's office and found her cell phone. Tyler answered immediately.

"Yes?"

"Did you forget someone?"

"Go look in the bathroom, love."

Puzzled, she opened the door to Tom's private bathroom. Her motorcycle helmet and jacket were laying on the counter.

Tommy's eyebrow shot up questioningly when she stepped out carrying them. "So is that why you suggested Tommy take the bike this morning? Did you engineer something?"

"Well, it has been a while since you got to ride. I thought the two of you might enjoy a little alone time, as it were. Let me speak to our sweet boy, right?"

She handed her phone to Thomas, who leaned back in his chair. "What did you do, Ty?" He listened for a minute, then laughed and shook his head. "All right." He looked at Nevvie. "Go lock my door, sugar."

Her heart raced, but she did. One of the benefits of being married, so to speak, to the boss was the freedom to engage in extracurricular activities with him.

"Okay," Tom said. "Hold on." He fumbled her phone for a moment, then figured out the speakerphone setting and turned the volume down. "All right, Ty. What is it?"

"Can you hear me, loves?" Ty asked.

Thomas pulled Nevvie into his lap. "Loud and clear," he said.

"Nevvie, love?"

"Yes, Ty?"

"Don't you mean Master?"

She froze, erotic heat immediately washing through her. They hadn't played this game in a while. "Yes, Master," she whispered.

Tom's sudden and hard erection poked her in the ass. "Goddamn," he muttered, his arms encircling her waist. "That's playing dirty, Ty," he rumbled in a low voice.

Tyler chuckled. "My sweet little slave, I want you to spend a couple of hours servicing Master Thomas. Then he'll bring you home and by that time I'm sure I'll have more fun waiting for you."

She gasped, her lower belly clenching in a pleasant way. "Yes, Master," she said, finding her little slave girl voice that got both men instantly fuck ready.

Tom's hands tightened on her. "Holy fuck, Ty. You could have given me a warning."

"Ah, but it is so much better this way, is it not?"

Tom slid his hands between her legs. "I guess you're right, it is."

"And the two of you haven't been able to ride together in a long time. In more ways than one."

Nevvie leaned back against Tom's firm chest and closed her eyes. No, she hadn't been rode in what felt like forever, and after their hot shower a few weeks prior, she wanted it more than ever before.

"Have fun, you two. I'm afraid I neglected to get condoms, but I'm sure you can improvise. Love to you both. Be a good girl, my sweet little slave, and I'll have something special for you later."

"Yes, Master," she said, enjoying the pleasant throbbing between her legs.

Tyler hung up. Thomas leaned back in the chair, pulling her against him. "Well, sugar. I guess we've got our orders, don't we?" He nuzzled the back of her neck.

This wasn't expected, but it damn sure was fun.

"Does my master have anything he'd like me to do?"

"Goddamn, girl!" he growled. "I fucking do." He stood, scooped her into his arms and carried her to the leather sofa. "You bet your sweet ass I do." He knelt over her, kissing her, then sat up again. "No condoms, huh?"

She groaned. "The doctor gave me something, but it takes a week to be effective."

He looked at her. "Damn I want to fuck you, baby. You have no idea how much."

She pulled him down to her. "How's your timing?"

He grinned. "You want to risk it?"

"Hell yes."

"Your wish is my command, sweetie."

He yanked his shirt off, the sight of his firm torso sending another ripple of heat through Nevvie's core. Both men were handsome. Tom's tall, lanky body was built from harder angles and leaner muscle, while Tyler's trim, shorter frame, softer and more compact, still hinted at his years of playing soccer in school. Both men were nearly equally well endowed.

"You have that backwards, Master. Your little slave will fulfill your every wish."

He paused, his jaw gaped. "Fuck, I forgot how damn hot you are when you talk like that!" He kissed her, his lips greedily crushing hers.

She wrapped her arms around him and ground her hips against him. The men were as different in their lovemaking styles as in their appearances. Tommy was her rowdy, passionate biker—Tyler her sensual brain. Both men could be either playful or passionate as their mood and hers dictated. Neither failed to please.

He lifted her shirt, remembering to be very gentle with her still-tender breasts, and kissed his way down her belly. "Baby girl, I'm gonna fuck you so good. Been thinking about this for so long."

"You ain't the only one!"

He laughed and worked on her jeans, sliding them and her underwear down her legs. Over the past couple of days Nevvie had been relieved to see the last of her post-pregnancy healing seemed complete. Tommy glanced up at her.

She nodded, smiling. "Go ahead."

Nevvie had to clamp down on her lower lip to stifle her moan as his tongue caressed her throbbing clit. He was sooo good, both men were. Tyler homed in on her most sensitive areas with precision while Tommy went for the scattershot approach, overwhelming her with the strength of his passion and exquisitely skilled mouth.

Closing her eyes, she jammed a pillow into her mouth and bit down to muffle her screams as he quickly and mercilessly brought her over once. When she tried to wiggle free he grabbed her hips and held on, not letting her go until he'd coaxed a second climax out of her.

Then he sat up, smiling. "Good?"

Nodding because she was too out of breath to speak, she couldn't resist him when he pulled her off the sofa. He rolled her onto her knees, ass in the air.

His favorite position.

He slid out of his jeans, pressed his body against hers. "Baby girl," he hoarsely whispered, "I've been dying to have you back like this."

He pressed his cock against her drenched opening, slowly, carefully sliding in, afraid of hurting her.

Nevvie moaned, pushing back against him.

"You okay?" he asked.

"Don't stop!" she gasped.

He chuckled. "Believe me, I'm not."

He wrapped his arms around her waist and slowly thrust, trying to prolong the sensation. He loved to fuck her hard and fast but not in this position, and not when he was afraid of hurting her. He was more than content to savor the feel of her hot, slick muscles grabbing at him, trying to keep him inside her every time he pulled out to thrust again.

Sitting up, he slowed his strokes and caressed her back, firmly gripped her hips. "I love you so much, baby. God, you have no idea."

"Shut up and fuck me, Tommy!"

He stopped. "What did you say, little slave?"

Nevvie laughed then cast a sultry glance over her shoulder. "I meant to say, 'Shut up and fuck me, *Master*.'"

He grinned and carefully bumped his hips against her, making her moan. "Like that?"

"Yeah. Like that."

He couldn't hold back much longer. He growled, "Get ready,"

then pulled out and rolled her over again. She greedily sucked his cock into her mouth, moaning with him as his hot seed pumped into her. He had to force her to let go. He collapsed onto the couch and scooped her into his arms.

"Ah, baby girl." He kissed her shoulder, gently nipped her. "You are so fantastic."

"You're not so bad yourself, Master."

"Goddamn!" he growled. "Keep talking like that, you're going to get yourself fucked again."

"I certainly hope so." She loved playing this with them, an ongoing game that started the night they made her promise to go with them to Pete and Eddie's Halloween party, dressed as their little slave girl. She'd been more than happy to play along at the time, without any idea they were trying to finally make their feelings known to her.

He was already stiffening against her backside. She rolled over and wiggled until his cock pressed against her entrance. "This time, Master, maybe you can last a little longer," she purred.

He grabbed her hips and buried his cock deep inside her, kissing her as he did. She could barely wait to see what Tyler had in store. Tyler had been petrified of hurting her during her pregnancy. She'd barely been able to get him to make love to her. She'd had plenty of trysts with Tommy here in their office or at home while Tyler was out running errands.

Moaning, running his lips over her neck, he took his time, eventually slowing and holding still as his hand slipped between their bodies. "All right, sugar," he hoarsely whispered. "I'm gonna play with you and make you come again, and you're gonna scream for me." He pressed his lips to hers.

With her fingers wrapped in his hair, she fucked him with her tongue while his fingers strummed her sensitive clit. Having his huge cock buried inside her only intensified the sensation. As she climbed toward release she hooked her leg around one of his and ground her hips against him.

He got his scream, muffled by his mouth on hers. Knowing she was finished he grabbed her hips again and thrust. He dropped his head to her shoulder and she sensed he was close. When he suddenly pulled out she grabbed his cock, stroking it as Tom moaned against her flesh, his juices coating her hand and belly as he climaxed.

Spent, she relaxed on the couch, tightly snuggled in Tom's arms. She loved having both of them in bed with her, hated it when one of them had to be away on business, but it was nice having a couple of hours alone with one of them.

"Did I please my master?" she coyly asked.

Thomas laughed, loud and hearty. He grabbed her hand and kissed it. "Ah, you know you always do, baby girl." He sighed. "Let's lie here for a couple of minutes and then grab a quick shower before we head home. I don't want to keep his royal slyness waiting."

Nevvie glanced at the clock. They'd already been there over an hour. *Wow.*

They took their time in the shower, playful and teasing. By the time they finished and dressed it was nearly six o'clock. The first floor was empty when they left, although she knew from the cars in the lot that some of the other employees were still upstairs. She tucked her purse and phone into the saddlebag and pulled on her jacket, helmet and gloves. Thomas backed the bike out and started it, waited for her to climb on behind him.

She wrapped her arms tightly around his firm abs. "Ready to go home, baby girl?" he asked over the bike's engine.

"I sure am, Master."

The engine's rev swallowed his, "Goddamn!" as they pulled out of the parking lot onto US 301.

* * * *

Tyler had dinner ready for them when they returned. Thomas pulled him into his arms and kissed him, long and deep. "Dammit I love you, mister."

"Mmm. That makes two of us, love." Tyler released him with a pat on his rump, then turned and kissed Nevvie. "And how is my sweet little slave?"

With her arms around his neck, she did a sensuous bump and grind against him, his stiff cock pressing through his slacks.

"I'm ready to play, Master," she said in her sultry slave voice.

Tyler's smile reached his eyes. "Ah, you shall have ample time to show me how ready you are after dinner." His hands settled on her ass, pulling her tight against him. He looked over her shoulder at Thomas. "You didn't wear her out, did you?"

Thomas grinned. "Does it look like I wore her out?"

"No, apparently not."

Dinner was, as always when Tyler cooked, fantastic. Thomas checked on the baby, found him sleeping, then kissed Tyler and Nevvie. "I'm going to go catch up on my email. Don't play too long or I might come join you."

"I'll save you some energy," Tyler teased. "If you wish."

Tommy's low, hungry growl did what it always did to Nevvie, made her soaking wet between her legs.

"Dammit," he whispered, "don't fucking tease me, Ty."

Tyler pulled his lover to him and kissed him. "Who says I'm teasing, sweet?" He stepped away. "But first, I need to take care of our naughty little slave here." He took her hand and led her to their bedroom, closing the door behind them.

Inside she tried to jump him but he laughed, caught her arms and pulled her over to the bed. "Ah, not quite so fast. You get your arse in bed like a good little slave."

She quickly stripped, lying on the bed with her legs spread. "Like this, Master?" she asked, her silky voice drawing a needy moan from him.

He shed his clothes. "Exactly. You've been very, very naughty." He stood at the end of the bed and stared at her, his cock at attention. "Very naughty indeed."

Nevvie felt the lower muscles of her belly contract in a pleasantly erotic way under his deep, blue gaze. "What did I do, Master?"

He grinned, kneeling on the bed between her legs. "The very thought of having you tonight has kept me like this—" he pointed to his stiff cock, "—all afternoon with no relief."

"I'm sorry, Master. What can your little slave do to make it up to you?" She licked her lips in anticipation. Anything, whatever he wanted, she'd do it and he knew it. If Tyler turned the full force of his blue eyes on her, she'd do anything at all.

He shook his head. "First of all, I'm going to make you scream and get you nice and wet. Then I'm going to fuck you for a little while, because I'm positive that Master Thomas made sure you were nice and ready for me. Then, if you're a good little slave and you please me, I'll turn you over and give you something you haven't had in a very long time."

She gasped, grinning, wiggling her hips at him. "Then we'd better get started, Master."

He lowered his lips between her legs, his tongue gently tracing every fold and curve of her sex, drawing a long, needy moan from her.

"Oh, Master, that's so good!"

"And I've barely done anything, my sweet." He loved teasing her, drawing it out, making her beg for release. She'd missed this so much with them, this aspect of their relationship.

After several long, sultry minutes he lifted his head again, chuckling at her disappointed moan. "What's the matter, love?"

"Don't stop, please!"

"How many times did Master Thomas make you come earlier?"

"Three."

"Hmm. That might be a challenge. I'm certainly up to it." He lowered his head to her mound again and swirled his tongue around her sensitive nub. She soon cried out as hot explosions went off in her belly.

"Oh, love, that was beautiful," he whispered, kissing her inner thigh.

Nevvie had learned years ago to never doubt her men's ability to make her climax even when she didn't think she could. They'd taken great pride in unlocking every secret and nuance of her body, enjoyed wringing every last drop of pleasure out of her that they could. On more than one occasion she'd been convinced there was no way she'd have another orgasm, just to have them pull one or more out of her beyond what she thought her body was capable of.

She relaxed, waiting, knowing Tyler had much more in store for her and that she was certain to enjoy it.

He kissed her as his cock rubbed up and down her slick cleft. "Did that feel good, love?"

Nevvie nodded, trying to find her voice.

His smile twisted her heart in a pleasant way. "I wanted to make sure we had at least a little playtime before Mom comes to visit." He nuzzled her between her breasts, being careful not to hurt her. "I would imagine in another few weeks you'll be giving Master Thomas and myself a run for our money."

"I hope so."

He kissed his way down her tummy again, settling between her legs. "Ready for seconds?"

"Like I could stop you anyway."

His warm, seductive laugh sent pulsations straight to her clit. "No, my love. You couldn't."

He changed tactics, using the lightest of touches, gently flicking his tongue over her clit, slowly bringing her back up to a rolling boil again. Then he teased her with two fingers at the entrance to her wet heat.

He kept her holding like this for several minutes until she thrust her hips against him. "Please," she begged. "Do it."

"Do what love?"

She lifted his head to look at him. "Please, baby. Please make me come."

"Ah, I think my sweet little slave is getting pushy."

She laughed then moaned as he pushed two fingers into her slick passage.

"So tell me, my love," he said as he stroked her with his hand. "What did you do with Master Thomas after I left?"

Nevvie swallowed hard. Christ he knew how to perfectly push her buttons. "He made me come twice," she whispered as he continued teasing her.

"How, love? Give me details."

"He went down on me."

"Ah, very nice. Then what?"

"He bent me over the sofa and fucked me from behind."

From Tyler's sudden, sharp intake of breath she knew he was rock hard, his cock throbbing. "His favorite position. And then? How did he come, love? Tell me everything."

She wiggled her hips against Tyler's hand. "He pulled out and told me to turn over and I sucked him down my throat."

"Mmm. And we both know how delicious our sweet Thomas is, don't we?"

"Yes."

"Yes what, pet?"

She sighed. "Yes, Master."

"Continue."

She wanted to grind her hips against his face but knew he'd keep her aroused until he was ready to make her come. He got as much pleasure out of keeping her like this as she got out of being kept like this. "Then we curled up on the couch together and in a few minutes he fucked me again."

"When did he make you come again?"

"When he fucked me. He used his hand."

"Very good, love. And I'm guessing he pulled out and you used your hand on him?"

"Mmm hmm."

He dipped his mouth to her clit and gently laved his tongue over it, triggering her climax. "That's two," he whispered, moving up the bed to lie next to her. He rested one hand on her tummy and cradled her with his other arm.

"How was that?" he asked with a playful smile.

Nevvie snuggled close. "Wonderful," she sighed. "But what about you?" Her hand drifted south between his legs, her fingers wrapping around his throbbing cock.

"You're on the right track, love."

She laughed and sat up, then went down on him. He gently fisted his hands in her hair. "Oh, yes. You know what I want, don't you, angel?" He sighed as she worked her tongue over his shaft and balls. "I'm far too excited to fuck you right now. I'm going to let you take a little edge off my tension, as it were. Then I'm going to enjoy fucking my sweet little slave."

She moaned around his shaft, already feeling a sensual tingle building between her legs. With the lightest of touches she stroked his sac with one hand, using her other on his cock while she sucked him.

He tensed, his hips bucking against her. "Get ready, pet."

Nevvie deep-throated him, not losing a single drop as he came, staying with him until certain he had finished. She looked up, his playful, content smile warming her.

"That was, as usual, amazing."

She climbed up the bed to lie next to him. "Only the best for my sweet masters."

He rolled on top of her, kissing her, his shaft already beginning to stiffen against her leg again. "I love you so much, darling." He caressed her cheek. "We love you so much."

The slave game was just that—a playful game, not any serious delving into an alternate lifestyle. As if their polyamorous triad wasn't alternative enough already. It was only one small part of their rich relationship, a little spice all three enjoyed. They had never asked her to do anything she wasn't comfortable with, and they certainly played closer to the vanilla end of the scale. Over the years she found as she gave herself to them, trusting them, that they took her to heights she never imagined possible. They loved her and would never hurt her.

It didn't take long for him to be ready enough to thrust inside her, both of them softly moaning as he held still, enjoying the feel of her slick heat.

"Oh, darling, that's wonderful," he murmured, resting his head on her shoulder, slowly working his hips against her.

Nevvie wrapped her legs around him. "Fuck me, baby. Fuck me good."

"Mmm. I will do that, certainly." His content sigh warmed her heart. "I'd love to take you in my favorite position but I don't want to try that too soon." She loved it when he put her legs over his shoulders, driving deep into her.

"Aww." She wiggled her hips against him. "Please?"

He laughed. "You sweet, cheeky thing. Not yet. Let's wait a week or so, at least, right? Because I get you like that, I damn sure don't want to stop."

Nevvie's hands stroked his back as she enjoyed the feel of him inside her. Then Tyler sat up and withdrew, making her moan with disappointment.

He chuckled. "Don't worry, love. I'm not going anywhere. Roll over."

She did, knowing what he wanted. She drew her knees under her and Nevvie felt him lean over to the bedside table. Then his fingers and cool wetness pressed against her rim.

"Are you all right, love?" he asked.

"Mmm hmm."

She felt his large cockhead press against her and relaxed as he pushed forward.

He paused, letting her adjust to him before slowly thrusting as he felt her hips work against him, urging him on.

Tyler folded his body around hers, wrapping an arm around her waist, his hand slipping between her legs. "How's that, love?"

"Wonderful."

He buried two fingers in her pussy, stroked her clit with his thumb. "Not as good as having Master Thomas' sweet cock there, I know, but you're still mine for a little while."

She closed her eyes, enjoying the feel of his body against hers. He would bring her over one more time, she knew, then he wouldn't have to pull out before he came taking her like this.

His lips brushed against the back of her neck. "I want one more from you, sweetheart. I want to feel you come with my cock deep inside you."

His words and tone made her heart thump in a pleasant way. She felt her climb, giving over to it, letting go.

"That's it, give it to me," he encouraged, reading her body, knowing she was close.

When it slammed into her she cried out against the pillow, pushing her hips against him, wanting his cock as deep inside her as she could get it. He waited until he knew she'd finished then grabbed her hips as his climax soon followed.

They collapsed to the bed, on their sides, Tyler's cock still inside her and his arms around her. "Amazing, love," he murmured against her flesh, kissing her shoulder. "Simply wonderful."

Nevvie basked in the warmth of his body, not wanting to doze off but then waking up when she felt him move, wincing slightly as he carefully withdrew.

"Are you all right, sweetheart?" he asked, concerned.

She smiled. "Ooohhh yeah."

He laughed, gently patting her hip. "I'll be right back." She heard him in the bathroom. He returned a moment later with a warm, damp washcloth, carefully swabbing her. Then he curled up against her again, taking her into his arms.

He nuzzled the back of her neck. "I love you so much. I am so blessed to have both of you." The bedroom door opened. "Ah, right on cue," Tyler joked. He turned toward the door. "Yes?"

Thomas winked at them. "All clear?"

Nevvie held her hand out to him and he quickly strode across their bedroom, sliding in beside her.

Their triad complete.

Thomas leaned over Nevvie and kissed Tyler, then her. "Fun?"

Tyler and Nevvie nodded. "I like being alone with one of you sometimes," she said, "but it's a lot more fun together."

"We've thoroughly spoiled her, Ty."

"Hey," she mumbled, already sleepy. "You told me early on that was your plan. I think the words 'kept woman' were invoked."

"Very true, love," Tyler agreed. "We'll keep you as long as you'll have the two of us. Hopefully forever."

"You just try to get away from me. I'll hunt you down and bring you back," she joked.

Thomas laced his fingers through hers, brought her hand to his lips and kissed it. "Did Master Tyler finally wear you out?"

"Mmm hmm."

He looked at Tyler. "Save any energy for me?"

Tyler laughed. "You've had time to recover from earlier, I take it?"

"Damn right."

"Well then, love, I suggest you rid yourself of those clothes and get over here so I can take care of you.

"Ooh, I get a show," Nevvie teased.

Tyler laughed. "You do so love to watch, you naughty thing."

Thomas was already pulling his clothes off. He knelt on the bed, his stiff cock ready for action. "What do you want to do, sugar?" he hoarsely asked.

Tyler sat up and kissed him. "The question is, what do *you* want, love? Do you want me to go down on you, or would you rather fuck that sweet cock up my arse?"

Nevvie moaned. "You're going to get me all horny again you keep that up."

The men laughed and looked at her. "Good heavens," Ty quipped. "Six isn't enough for you?"

Thomas snickered. "Holy crap, girl. Getting greedy, aren't you?"

"What part of spoiled rotten don't you understand? It's y'all's fault you two are good in bed."

The men leaned over and kissed her. Thomas looked at Tyler, his brown eyes smoky with passion. "I think I want to fuck your sweet ass," he said.

"Then by all means, love," Tyler said, reaching for the lube.

Nevvie shivered with anticipation, snuggling close to Tyler as he knelt on the bed next to her. He closed his eyes, moaning with need as Thomas knelt behind him, carefully lubed him and entered.

"Dammit, I love this," Thomas grunted. "No offense, Nevvie. I love your ass, but his is just…damn good."

With his eyes still closed, Tyler smiled. "Talk about spoiled."

Nevvie laced the fingers of one hand through Tyler's and gripped his stiffening shaft with her free hand. "I don't mind, Tommy," she said. "Because I know what both of my sweet masters love."

The men groaned. "Dammit, sugar. You talk like that, I'm gonna come too quick."

Tyler looked at her, his eyes holding her heart and soul captive. "Don't torment him, pet. You can torment me."

She grinned, stroking his shaft. "You mean like that?"

"You bloody well know what I mean."

Thomas caressed Tyler's back, taking his time, his long, slow strokes making Tyler's cock throb in her hand. "You feel so good, Ty," he hoarsely moaned. "God, I love you so much."

Nevvie loved this, loved them. This triad they shared never would have worked if the men hadn't had such a strong, solid relationship for over a decade before they met her. She knew this in the depths of her soul. They'd been inseparable from when they first met, always faithful, deeply in love with each other. It was her good luck they had room in their hearts—and bed—for her, too.

Tyler could melt her and Thomas, literally putty in his talented, sensual hands. But Thomas was their strength, their tough guy. Nevvie and Tyler always eagerly gave themselves over to him. Tyler might be four years older than Thomas, but Thomas was their rock. And the men treated her like more than just a beloved wife—she felt like a goddess in their arms and hearts.

While she sometimes enjoyed a rough and tumble sexual relationship with Tommy he was always very gentle and tender with Tyler, not wanting to hurt him. Their blended dynamic never failed to amaze her.

"Come for us, Ty," she whispered, her tongue lightly flicking his earlobe. "Squeeze his cock, baby."

Tyler gasped, his lower lip caught beneath his teeth. He was close, she felt it. They normally didn't have this much energy and knew after today they'd most likely settle back into a normal routine.

But it sure was fun.

Tom's hands tightened around Tyler's hips. "Come on, sugar," he grunted. "I can't hold it much longer. You're too good."

Nevvie shifted her hand, palmed Tyler's cock, her fingers brushing against his sac. "Look at me, Master," she murmured, playing dirty.

Tyler's eyes popped open, locking on hers.

"Come for your sweet little slave, Master," she begged. "Please. I want to feel Master Thomas make you come—"

"Ah!" Tyler's hips bucked against her hand and she felt his hot juices coat her palm. She looked at Thomas and nodded. He closed his eyes, thrusting, letting go as his climax hit him.

The men tumbled to the bed together, gasping. Nevvie wrapped her arm around them.

"You played dirty, love," Ty mumbled from somewhere at the bottom of the pile. "I was thoroughly enjoying that."

She grinned. "Hey, you loved it and you know it."

"Of course I did. I never said I didn't."

Thomas carefully untangled himself from them and walked to the bathroom, returning a moment later with another warm, wet washcloth for Tyler. Then the three of them snuggled together in their familiar way and drifted off to sleep.

Chapter Four

Nevvie finally settled into a routine. Eventually her hormones evened out, allowing her mood to stabilize. Peggy stayed for over a week to help and console Nevvie before returning to Savannah.

Life would go on.

Adam turned five months old. Nevvie and Tyler were home one Tuesday afternoon when their doorbell rang. Looking through the peephole, Nevvie first assumed the woman on their front step was a Jehovah's Witness or trying to sell something. When Nevvie opened the door, the woman held up an official ID.

"Nevaeh Kinsey-Paulson?"

Nevvie immediately froze, old fears crippling her. "Yes?"

"I'm Louise Jameson, from the Florida Department of Children and Family Services."

"Who is it, love?" Tyler called from his study.

Nevvie struggled to find her voice. "Tyler, can you please come here?"

Her tone must have clued him in. He ran into the foyer, pulling up short at the sight of the woman. "What's wrong?"

The woman eyed him. "I'm here to investigate a report our office received."

Tyler frowned. "What sort of report?"

"If I may come in, please?" She held up her ID so he could look at it. He finally stepped to the side, took Nevvie's hand and gently pulled her out of the way.

With Nevvie in tow he led the woman to the kitchen table and indicated for her to take a seat. Louise Jameson looked around on her way in, obviously scoping out the house.

Once they were seated, Tyler spoke. "All right, what exactly is going on?"

The woman opened a portfolio and notepad. "And you are?"

"I'm Tyler Paulson."

"You're Ms. Paulson's husband?"

Nevvie focused on Tyler, too nervous to say anything.

"In a manner of speaking. What is this in regards to?"

"We received a report alleging child abuse—"

"What?" Nevvie had found her voice. "My son is *not* abused!"

Apparently used to outbursts, Ms. Jameson didn't flinch. "That is what I'm here to investigate, Mrs. Paulson."

Tyler clenched his jaw. "And what exactly are these allegations?"

Ms. Jameson consulted her paperwork. "The main allegation is that the home is an immoral environment for him to be raised in." She frowned. "Frankly, there are no allegations of physical abuse or neglect. Apparently the caller was concerned about the family situation." She looked at Nevvie. "Ma'am, please don't assume I'm here to take your child. I'm here to follow up on an allegation, compile a report, and then go from there. We're required to investigate all reports."

Nevvie's hands shook. "Who reported this? Who would say something so horrible about us?"

"I'm afraid that's not information I could give out even if I had it."

Tyler unclipped his BlackBerry from his belt. "Hold on just a moment, please." He placed a call. "Bob? Tyler. This is an emergency. We have a CFS investigator sitting at our kitchen table... Yes... Right. Thank you." He hung up. "Our attorney is on his way. He said he'll be here in twenty minutes."

Ms. Jameson sat back. "Attorney?"

"I would prefer to let him explain our situation to you." He immediately placed another call to Thomas and told him to return home immediately, but not why.

Ms. Jameson looked unflappable. "While we're waiting I'd like to see your son," she said to Nevvie.

She felt too numb to stand. "He's asleep."

Tyler stood. "I'll show you to the nursery. Please do not wake him. He usually sleeps until around four."

Nevvie remained at the table while Tyler led the woman down the hall. Who would call on them? They barely knew their neighbors, and the ones they did they were on good terms with. None of their friends would do this...

Nevvie had a hunch.

When Tyler and Ms. Jameson returned to the kitchen ten minutes later, the investigator was filling out a form, checking things off as Tyler answered her questions. By the time they finished, Bob had arrived.

"What's going on?" he asked.

The four of them sat at the table and Tyler gave him the quick run-down. Bob turned to Ms. Jameson. "What is the exact allegation?"

The investigator shook her head. "There weren't specific allegations made, which is the problem. The caller stated that the child was being raised in an immoral environment. Frankly, I haven't seen anything here so far that concerns me. I'm not sure why Mr. Paulson called you."

That's when Tommy raced in, slamming the front door behind him. He slid to a stop in the kitchen. "What's going on? What's wrong? Bob, why are you here?"

The investigator frowned. "And you are?"

"This is *my* house and you're asking me who the hell I am? Who the hell are you?"

"Thomas," Tyler interrupted. "Sit down."

Tommy looked from Tyler to Bob to Nevvie and took a seat on Nevvie's other side, found her hand under the table and squeezed it.

Bob looked at Ms. Jameson. "This is the situation. The three of them are in a relationship. They live here together."

The investigator tried to make sense of that, then her eyes widened slightly as she realized what he meant. "They live...together?"

Bob nodded. "I have paperwork at my office, I didn't have time to run back and get it. Tyler is listed as Adam's father on his birth certificate, but we have filed custody papers giving Thomas joint guardianship. They also have powers of attorney for each other. They are not married, so they are not breaking any bigamy laws. They are polyamorous."

Nevvie lost her battle against her tears. "Please don't take my son away. They're good fathers, they love me and they love him and we have a good life..." She dropped her head to the table and sobbed. Thomas put his arm around her shoulders, comforting her.

The investigator shook her head. "I'm not making any decisions right now. And as I've stated, I haven't seen anything yet that would make me think any kind of intervention is necessary. But I have to follow procedure." She looked at Bob. "I need to talk to the baby's pediatrician."

He nodded. "No problem. I'm sure he'll back up everything they've told you. They're good parents, no child is as loved as Adam is. He doesn't have just one dad, but two, and a mother. A lot of kids don't even have two parents and he's got three."

Tyler gave her the doctor's information and she gave Bob her card. "I'll return in a day or so. I'll call to set up an appointment."

Bob escorted her out of the house. Tyler stood and put his arms around Nevvie and Thomas. "This will be okay. Bob will take care of it for us."

Nevvie sobbed. "Who would do this to us?"

Thomas glared. "I have an idea."

Tyler frowned. "Emily?"

"Probably. I'd be willing to bet." He reached for the phone, called his mother, and told her what happened. A few minutes later, he hung up. "She's packing to fly down right now, said she'll leave immediately so she can be here."

Bob returned, running his hand through his red hair. "Well, this will be an interesting couple of days."

Thomas snorted in disgust. "This is fucking ridiculous."

"I know it is," Bob agreed. "Technically y'all are breaking the law by cohabitating. Not that anyone's usually prosecuted for it. In a sticky case like this it has been brought into play. Let's just hope that woman doesn't have a chip on her shoulder or is out to score points." He leveled his gaze at Nevvie. "I'm warning you now, you might have to marry Tyler to make this go away."

She shook her head. "No! They can't force me to pick one of them over the other, that's not fair!"

Thomas laid a gentle hand on her shoulder. "Baby girl, if it means getting the state off our backs, we'll do whatever it takes."

"You can't mean that."

"I didn't say I liked it. Bob's right. If it turns out that's the easiest way to make this go away, we might have to do something."

Nevvie jumped up from the table and ran, crying, to their bedroom.

Tyler looked at Bob. "Is that going to be our only answer?"

He shrugged. "Hopefully they'll let this die. And hopefully it won't hit the tabloids. We'll deal with whatever they throw at us when they throw it. For now, we'll have to wait and see. Do you really think Emily did this?"

Thomas looked grim. "I'd be willing to bet on it. She actually showed up at Momma's house a few weeks ago, and in the process of catching up she was asking questions about us. Momma said Emily then ranted about our 'situation' at a family dinner the other night. Karen was gushing about Adam. Em laid into her like a chainsaw, yelling that what we're doing is wrong and an abomination."

Bob laughed. "Abomination, huh? Good grief. I know you said

she's a head case but this takes the cake. What does she think she's going to accomplish?"

"I don't know."

* * * *

Nevvie had cried herself to sleep by the time the airport taxi dropped Peggy off a little before three that morning. She sat at the table with the men and listened to the full version of the story.

"Well, as much as I hate to say it, sugar, I agree with you. It probably was Emily. Your other sisters got over their shock years ago and are fine with it. They were all happy for you when Adam was born."

Tyler nodded. "Come to think of it, Em is the only one who didn't send us a card or gift for the baby."

"I'd like to wring her neck," Tommy growled.

Peggy patted him on the hand. "You leave that to me, honey. I've got an idea."

* * * *

The wait proved agony for them all, especially Nevvie. She barely spoke to anyone, her silence punctuated by long crying jags with Adam cradled in her arms. Tyler felt her distress as if it was his own, his chest tight with crushing anxiety and worry. Life had been so perfect for them, and then this.

When Nevvie was eighteen, she was raped by a former classmate. After being dragged through hospital exams and police interrogations, the perpetrator was never charged because it was his word against hers, Nevvie was essentially alone with no family, and the rapist's father was rich. To this day, Nevvie had never gotten over her fear of being treated unjustly by authorities despite her later win in court against an ex-boyfriend who stabbed her. And now their legal limbo only served to bring those old feelings and worries back to the surface.

When Ms. Jameson returned two days later, she carried more paperwork and spoke in the same neutral tone. Bob and Peggy joined everyone at the table while Nevvie clutched Adam in her arms.

"I talked to Adam's doctor. He stated very adamantly that he believes Adam is in a fit home. I'll be honest that I haven't taken this to my supervisor yet because, frankly, I'm not sure how to approach it. Left up to me to make the decision alone, I would close this case immediately."

Peggy jumped in. "I'm Thomas' mother. If I don't have a problem with the three of them being together, no one else should either, not that it's anyone's business. It's not like they go parading around naked. They're just like anyone else except there's three of them. I've seen worse public displays of affection from my married daughters than I have from these three. They're very modest when it comes to that. They're good parents. I'd be willing to bet it was my oldest daughter who started all this mess, wasn't it?"

"Ma'am, as I told them, I can't give out that information. We are required to investigate every claim. Unfortunately, too much of my time is wasted on false accusations by vengeful family members. However, if we didn't investigate and there was a real problem, a child could die."

"I bet I can prove she's behind this. If I can get her to admit she did it and why, would it help you close this out sooner?"

The investigator nodded. "It would certainly give me a stronger position with my boss."

Peggy whipped out her cell phone and dialed. "Everyone, just stay quiet." She hit the speakerphone button then laid the phone on the table. On the other end a phone rang. Emily answered.

Peggy's face looked grim. "Emily, it's your mother."

Emily sounded nervous. "Hi, Momma. What's up?"

"I'm going to ask you something. You'd best be honest with me, missy. Did you call in a report about Adam to the state?"

Emily remained quiet for a long moment. "Momma, I'd rather not discuss this with you."

"You answer me right now, young lady."

Young lady wasn't exactly the right term to describe Emily, considering how much older she was than Tommy. Apparently, Peggy's angry tone cowed her. "Momma, it's not right what they're doing. You know that."

Thomas' face transformed into an angry mask. Peggy held up a staying hand to her son. "Emily, how could you call the state and tell them your brother is abusing that baby?"

"I didn't tell them he was abused! I told them they needed to remove him from the home because of how they're living."

"So what happens if they take Adam away from them and put him in foster care?"

Emily's voice quickened, her words tumbling together in her anxiety. "Momma, I told them I'd take him, that I'd drive down and pick him up and be his foster mother because I'm his aunt. Listen, Momma, this is a chance for us to get Tommy away from them for good. He can move in with you. I'll raise Adam, and Tommy can live up here. You know it's what's best for him! I talked to my minister and I know he could help make Tommy see reason!"

Nevvie suspected if Peggy could reach through the phone she'd strangle her daughter herself. "Have you finally lost your pea-pickin' mind? What makes you a moral expert? You've lied and accused your brother of being an unfit father!"

"No, I never did that, Momma. I swear! I just want a chance to save that baby from doing what they're doing."

"So this was some sort of scheme on your part? You don't think Adam's being abused?"

"Not abused. I'm sure he's well cared for but do you want him raised seeing the way they live? It's disgusting."

"And what if I tell you your plan won't work?"

"How can it not work? I looked up the law. They'll take him away from them." She sounded triumphant. "They're living together and not married. That's against the law."

"Emily, for one thing that's most likely not grounds for him to be removed. For another, Tyler is listed on the birth certificate as Adam's father."

Emily fell quiet for a moment. "What?"

"You heard me. You have no rights to that boy regardless. They would put him in foster care locally, not with you."

No longer as sure of herself as she had been, Emily tried to backpedal. "But the other night Karen said—"

"Karen has no problem seeing Thomas and Tyler both as Adam's daddies. I've seen his birth certificate. You haven't even laid eyes on Adam. How dare you assume you're going to steal him from them and try to raise him?"

"I just want what's best for him!"

Peggy's voice dropped to a momma bear growl. "So let me get this straight. You've never seen Adam, yet you put him at risk of being sent into foster care with strangers who might not be able to take care of him as good as his own parents? You do realize your brother probably won't forgive you for this."

"Momma! You can't tell him!"

Thomas had all he could stand. "She didn't have to, Emily. We all heard it. Including our attorney and the CFS investigator."

Emily's horrified gasp was unmistakable. "Momma! What did you do?"

"I had you on speaker phone. Ms. Jameson needed one last clear reason to take this to her supervisor to have it dropped, and I think you just gave it to her."

"Tommy, please, you have to understand—"

"The only thing I understand is that I don't ever want to see you again. Momma's right that I will never forgive you for this."

Emily loudly sobbed. Peggy hit end and looked at the investigator.

"Enough?"

Ms. Jameson had been taking notes. She nodded. "More than. As far as I'm concerned, everything's fine. Yes, it's unusual. Frankly, I have serious cases to deal with, legitimate incidents of abuse and children at risk. Do I agree with this arrangement? Personally, no, but my feelings on that have no place in my decision. There are no signs of abuse or neglect, the home is fine, and they are fit parents. I wish all the homes I visited were half as clean as this one."

She made another note and looked at them. "Obviously you're financially able to take care of him and he's in no danger that I can see. I doubt my supervisor will dig deeper into this. I can't promise you anything, but I'm planning on telling her this is a case of a vengeful sibling trying to cause her brother trouble, while keeping as many details out of it as possible. There are God only knows how many unmarried couples living together who are technically breaking the law. I'm not wasting my time going after people who are fit parents regardless of their marital status."

Thomas grimly nodded. "Fine with me."

Nevvie remained at the table, crying with relief as the men escorted Ms. Jameson to the door. Peggy stayed behind and put her hands on Nevvie's shoulders. "It's okay, sugar. It's over."

"No, it's not. You heard her. She still has to take it to her supervisor."

"It'll be okay."

The men returned. Tyler rubbed his chest. "Well, thank goodness that's over. Bloody hell, my stomach's upset."

"No, it's not okay!" Nevvie cried. "It's not over now, it won't ever be over. What happens when she tries again?"

"She won't try again," Peggy said, "Because I'm talking to all her sisters and telling her if she ever tries it again she's out of this family for good. Her sisters will skewer her when they find out what she did."

Tommy snorted. "I'd love to be a fly on that wall when Karen gets her hands on her. She'll kill her."

"No, it's not officially over yet," Bob said. "Considering the workload these people have, I'd be willing to bet they sign off on it and close the case. Try to relax, Nevvie. The worst really is over."

Chapter Five

Thomas and Tyler asked Peggy to stay with them for at least a week. Until they heard back from the CFS investigator, Nevvie wouldn't relax no matter how many assurances they gave her. Two days later, Nevvie was outside doing yard work with the men when Peggy stepped to the back door, Adam cradled in one arm, the phone in her other hand.

"Tyler."

He looked up and nodded, flexing and stretching his left arm and shoulder as he walked over and took the phone from her. It'd been bothering him off and on for a couple of days, probably aggravated by the yard work.

"It's Bob. Good news, I just heard from Ms. Jameson. The case is officially closed."

Tyler breathed a deep sigh of relief and flashed an okay sign at Thomas and Nevvie. Nevvie burst into relieved tears. Thomas reached for her, holding her. "Excellent. Thank you for calling."

"She told me she'd note the file about Emily in case there's ever another call. They might still have to investigate future allegations, if there are any. At least with that in the case file, it'll hopefully be resolved immediately."

"Very good. What would we do without you, Bob?"

"Hey," he laughed, "it's just billable hours."

Tyler grinned. "Right. Milking the cash cow, are we?"

"My most famous client. Take care. Try to relax now."

"Will do." Tyler hung up and looked at the others. "I say we celebrate."

The timing couldn't be better. Tommy had to leave for Ft. Myers in two days to be on-site at a construction project. Peggy and the men knew it would take Nevvie several days to emotionally recover from the traumatic experience.

Peggy went to the grocery store and cooked a full southern feast for dinner. They all laughed and relaxed for the first time in several days. Their best friends, Pete and Eddie, ate dinner with them. While Nevvie tried to enjoy herself, she still felt on edge.

Too exhausted to do anything but cuddle that night, she curled between her men and closed her eyes, breathing in their scent. Her boys. She didn't ever want to choose, how could she?

The next morning she felt a little better. Peggy had already called the other sisters and told them what happened. Even Kate, the other sister almost as reluctant to accept Nevvie into the family as Emily, felt outraged that her sister had put the three through such hell.

Nevvie noticed Tyler seemed unusually quiet. "I thought you said the worst was over? What's wrong?"

"I'm all right, love. Just tired. I think all the stress has caught up with me." He pulled her to him, hugging her.

"Are you feeling okay?" Nevvie asked.

Tyler forced a smile. "Just worn down, I'm sure."

Tommy looked concerned. "Do you want me to postpone my trip, Ty?"

"No, no. Not necessary. I'll be fine."

Nevvie helped Tommy pack. He'd be gone three days, and after some deliberation decided to take the bike. "You don't mind if I ride it, do you sugar?" he asked her.

"Why would I mind?"

Peggy chimed in. "*I* mind. I hate that thing. I wish you'd get rid of it. They're dangerous."

"It's okay, Mom," Nevvie reassured her. "I don't mind if he rides the bike."

Tommy decided to stand his ground against his mom. She never had liked him riding a motorcycle, had forbid him to own one when he lived at home. "It would do it some good to go on a long trip. And it's easier on gas than the truck."

That night they curled together in bed and made love. Nevvie straddled Tyler and kissed him, rubbing herself along his stiff shaft.

He rested his hands on her hips. "You know what I love, pet."

Thomas grabbed Tyler's hands and slid them down to her ass. "You know what I want too, don't you?" He held a bottle of lube.

She wiggled her ass as Tyler spread her cheeks. "I sure do. Why don't you get busy?"

Thomas froze for a moment, then softly said, "Dammit, you know what that does to me!"

He slicked his shaft then gently worked lube into her. She impaled herself on Tyler with a satisfied moan as Thomas gently pressed his cockhead against her tight ring of muscle.

"You ready for it, baby girl?" he softly asked.

She wiggled her hips at him again. "You'd better believe it."

He carefully pressed home and held still for a moment, letting her get used to him. He caressed her back as Tyler moved his hands to her hips. "You okay?" Tom asked her.

"Mmm hmm!"

Tyler snickered. "I suspect she's more than okay."

Nevvie rolled her hips, drawing soft moans from both men. "Don't keep me hanging, boys."

Once he was fully seated inside her, Thomas pulled her up against his chest and played with her nipples. Tyler stroked her clit. The feeling...amazing. This wasn't something they did all the time, but when they did she never failed to enjoy it. Something about the way their two large cocks stretched and filled her added an extra measure to her orgasm.

"Look at me, love," Tyler whispered.

She did.

"You're so beautiful like this, with both of us inside you. You enjoy this, don't you?"

She nodded, not trusting her voice. She wanted to loudly moan but couldn't make too much noise with Peggy in the house.

"I want you to come for us, angel. Give it to us, let us feel you squeezing our cocks."

Thomas gently nipped her shoulder as his fingers tweaked her nipples into hard peaks. "Do it, babe," he coaxed. "You know we love feeling you come."

Between the men's persistent fingers and gentle encouragements, within minutes she felt the familiar explosion start deep within her. Unable to keep her eyes open she threw her head back against Tom's shoulder as he kissed her, muffling her moans while Tyler relentlessly stroked her clit.

She finished, gasping for breath. Thomas lowered her to Tyler's chest. He grabbed her hips and slowly fucked her. "Dammit, sugar," he said, "you're so good."

Nevvie tried to help but felt too exhausted. Tyler cradled her against him and thrust into her from below.

"I'm close, Ty," Tom hoarsely said.

"Go ahead, love."

With a final groan he buried himself deep inside her as he came. He leaned over, gasping for breath, and kissed her between her shoulders. "You okay, sweetie?"

"Oh yeah."

He carefully withdrew and walked into the bathroom. A moment later he returned with a damp washcloth for Nevvie. "You're a slowpoke, Ty," he teased.

"I didn't know this was a race." He rolled her over and kissed her as he lifted her legs to his shoulders. "You don't mind if I take my time, do you, angel?"

Nevvie stroked his arms. "Of course not."

Thomas knelt behind Tyler and Nevvie wondered what he was doing until Tyler jumped, then laughed. "Ah, you're cheating again."

Thomas didn't respond. Nevvie could easily imagine what he was doing as Tyler's eyes closed and the pace of his thrusts increased, grew more jerky. After a few moments he gasped, softly crying out as he buried his cock deep inside Nevvie when he came.

He carefully lowered her legs and curled next to her. Thomas stretched out on Tyler's other side.

"How was that, buddy?" Thomas asked.

Tyler nodded, his eyes closed, and snuggled against Nevvie. He pulled Tom's arm around him. "It was bloody wonderful and you damn well know it."

"What'd you do?"

"Played with his balls."

"No, he licked them."

Nevvie giggled. "You play dirty, Tommy."

He winked. "I know how to motivate him."

* * * *

The next morning they gathered around Thomas in the driveway after he wheeled the bike out of the garage. He hugged and kissed Peggy and the baby, then Nevvie, and then Ty.

Peggy looked worried. "Tommy, I wish you'd drive your truck. I don't like you riding that bike."

"It's okay, Momma." He turned to Tyler. "I'll call when I get checked in tonight."

"You do that, love," Ty said. "Be careful. Stay safe. Come back to us." Then he patted him on the ass and all three smiled. It was their good luck ritual before either man had to leave on a trip, and so far had not failed them.

Nevvie leaned in for one last kiss before Tommy slipped his helmet on. "I love you."

"I love you too, sugar." He smiled. "Keep our boy safe for me." Yet another old ritual between them, "our boy" referring to Tyler, not

Adam.

They watched as Tommy cranked the bike. Then he waved as he pulled out of the driveway.

"I wish you two would make him sell that thing," Peggy groused.

Nevvie took Adam from her. "It's okay. He's safe on it. He'll be fine."

* * * *

That night, Tyler and Nevvie curled together and fell asleep after talking to Thomas on the phone. Nevvie suspected Tyler still didn't feel well from the way he'd been acting, although he hadn't said anything. The next morning, Nevvie stood in the kitchen and thumbed through the newspaper while the coffee brewed. Adam and Tyler were both still asleep. She heard the shower in the guest bathroom and knew Peggy, normally an early riser, was up and about.

She poured herself a mug of coffee when it finished brewing. A few minutes later, Peggy appeared, ready for her day.

"Mornin', sugar," the older woman said. "How'd you sleep?"

"Like a rock! Did the baby even wake up last night?"

"If he did, he didn't fuss. That means he'll wake up screaming for breakfast."

"Like the other men in this house," Nevvie said with a smile.

Peggy laughed. "Tommy could eat his weight in groceries when he was growing up. I had to shop for the girls and then shop for him. I swear he had hollow legs."

"I can believe it." Adam's keening cry from the bedroom drew her attention. "Ah, perfect timing."

"I'll go change him if you want to fix his breakfast," Peggy offered.

"Thanks, Mom." Peggy disappeared down the hall while Nevvie got it ready.

By the time Nevvie had Adam's breakfast ready, Peggy

reappeared with him. "Here's the hungry guy."

Nevvie took him and fed him, watching his blue eyes while he ate. It wouldn't be long before he was eating solid food. He looked more like Tyler every day, the spitting image of him. Speaking of...

She glanced at the clock. It was nearly seven-thirty and Ty hadn't emerged yet. *Very odd.*

As if sensing her thoughts, Peggy spoke. "Is Tyler feeling all right this morning? He's been acting a little off lately."

"I was just wondering that myself. He hasn't felt good the past couple of days. Then again, with all that crap, none of us did. Maybe he's coming down with something. I'll check on him when this one's done chowing down."

Twenty minutes later, Ty still hadn't appeared. Nevvie handed Adam to his grandmother. "I'll go check on sleeping beauty, see how he is."

Nevvie walked to their bedroom and found Tyler in the shower, where she quickly joined him. "Good morning, handsome." She wrapped her arms around him and kissed him.

He offered her a half-hearted smile. "Good morning, sweetheart." His color looked bad. "I'm sorry I slept so late."

"I think I need to make you an appointment with Dr. Aston today."

"No, I'm just worn down. Too much excitement, that's all. I'm sure I'll feel better in a day or two."

She studied his face. "This doesn't feel right, Ty. I think we need to get you checked out. If it was me you'd hogtie me and drag me down to her office."

He attempted a smile. "At least the hogtie part."

She laughed. He couldn't feel too bad if he was trying to crack jokes. "All right. If you're still out of it tomorrow, you're going."

"Agreed, love. I promise."

She kissed him. "I love you."

"Love you too, pet. I'll be along shortly."

She stepped out of the shower, dressed, and returned to the kitchen.

* * * *

Must be a bug. Tyler didn't feel at all well, but he didn't want to worry Nevvie. Maybe he should ask Peggy about it. He would go see Dr. Aston tomorrow if he woke up feeling like this again.

He finished his shower and sat on the bed to catch his breath, rubbing his chest. His left shoulder was really bothering him. Maybe he overdid it out in the yard with Thomas. He should leave the landscaping chores to him and Nevvie, but he'd wanted to help.

He wiped a hand across his forehead. *The A/C must be turned up high.* He was sweating, even though he felt clammy.

He dressed and walked out to the kitchen. Nevvie started preparing their breakfast and had the newspaper spread out on the counter.

Nevvie didn't care what Tyler said, he would go see Dr. Aston today, like it or not. His skin looked grey under the bright kitchen lights.

She turned to mix their scrambled eggs, and then something made her turn back to him. "Are you okay?" she asked.

Tyler started to speak to her and lost his train of thought. She looked at him and said something. He realized he couldn't hear her.

That's when the crushing pain enveloped his chest, driving the breath from him. He had enough time to register this as his eyes locked on Nevvie's before his world went black.

Nevvie watched as Tyler swayed on his feet, looked at her, and then collapsed.

"Tyler!" She dropped to his side, trying to wake him. "Tyler!" He didn't respond. "Mom!" she screamed. "Mom, come quick!"

Peggy raced into the kitchen. "What—oh my God!" She dropped to her knees next to Nevvie. "What happened?"

"He just collapsed!"

Peggy leaned in close, listened, then checked his pulse. She ripped his shirt open down the front, popping the buttons off, and leaned over him. "Nevvie, call 911." She started chest compressions, then tipped his head back and blew into his mouth.

"What?"

She resumed chest compressions. "Dammit, call 911! Get an ambulance!"

Nevvie scrabbled backward, in shock, trying to get out of the way and process what happened. *911?* "What's wrong—"

"Nevvie!" Peggy screamed. "Call *now*, dammit!"

The older woman's frantic tone finally broke through Nevvie's shock and spurred her into action. Nevvie dove for the phone, her fingers shaking as she made the call, trying to relay Peggy's answers to the operator's questions without crying.

Heart attack? Not her Tyler! Please, no!

"Nevvie, go open the front door," Peggy panted between compressions and breaths. "Then go get your shoes, your purse, his wallet, and your cell phones."

Nevvie's feet felt anchored to the floor. Peggy glanced away from Tyler for a second. "Dammit sugar, *go!*" she screamed. That shattered Nevvie's paralysis and she started moving.

Peggy tried to focus on her task, her arms and shoulders killing her. She was too old for this shit. Nevvie looked close to panic. Peggy knew she had to keep her head at least until the paramedics arrived.

"Dammit, Tyler," she muttered under her breath. "You can't leave them. C'mon, sugar. You can make it. Goddammit, don't you leave that boy without a father."

She paused to take his pulse, didn't feel one, and immediately resumed CPR.

Nevvie heard the sirens as she opened the front door and left it standing open. She then ran to the bedroom to do as Peggy ordered, returning to the kitchen as the first EMT rushed into the house.

Peggy was sweating and red in the face, trying to update the EMT as she maintained a rhythm. In a carefully choreographed swap, she rolled away from Tyler while the EMT took her place without missing a beat.

Nevvie felt numb, frozen. This couldn't be happening. This had to be a bad dream.

Peggy caught her breath on the kitchen floor and then looked at Nevvie. "I'll take care of the baby. You ride in the ambulance with him."

Nevvie nodded, still not comprehending. More paramedics rushed into the house, two with a gurney. Nevvie tried to stay out of the way, but as the severity of the situation sank in it was hard to remain calm as she watched the events unfold before her. Tyler was lying unconscious on the floor, the EMT still giving him CPR as the others worked on him. They put a tube down his throat, applied chest leads and prepared a defibrillator. Peggy answered questions and gave them information about Tyler.

When they had what they needed from Peggy, she stood, walked over to Nevvie and put her arm around her.

"Do y'all have your paperwork here?"

"Huh?"

Peggy gently shook her. "Paperwork. Insurance, medical power of attorney, that stuff?"

"Tommy's office. Top file drawer. Red folder in the front."

"That's real good, sugar. Give me your keys."

Nevvie numbly handed them over.

"I'll bring Adam to the hospital after I get the paperwork and get him ready, okay?"

"Okay." Nevvie couldn't pull her attention from Tyler. She willed him to open his sweet blue eyes and look at her.

The paramedics were ready. One of them looked at the defibrillator unit. "Clear," he ordered.

The EMT giving chest compressions sat back and held his hands up, waiting. Tyler's body jumped. That's when Nevvie's composure shattered and she sobbed.

The men working on Tyler watched the screen for a moment. One said, "Okay, let's get ready to transport." Another prepared an IV and inserted it in Tyler's arm.

Peggy kept an arm around Nevvie's waist. "Go with them. We'll call Tommy once I'm there."

Oh God, Thomas!

Nevvie stared. Peggy's voice grew stern, breaking through her foggy haze. "Nevvie, sugar, I know you're upset but you have to hold it together for him. They've got him back—"

Back?

"—and they'll take good care of him."

She glanced at the clock. Only ten minutes had passed from when he collapsed. *Only?*

"Mom, is he going to die?"

"Don't you *dare* think like that, missy," Peggy scolded. "He's young and he's got a family he loves more than life, every reason to fight. Do you think he's going to up and leave you three like that?"

Nevvie shook her head. The EMTs had Tyler loaded on the gurney and were rushing him out the door.

"Go," Peggy shoved Nevvie toward the door. "I'll be there soon."

With leaden feet, Nevvie followed the gurney. She climbed into the back of the ambulance when she was told, tried to hold back her tears. When the paramedics asked her questions she nodded or shook her head, unable to speak. Her eyes never left Tyler and she prayed, silently begging him to open his eyes.

* * * *

Peggy grabbed one of the firemen, who'd responded in a truck with the ambulance. "Where y'all taking him?"

"Tampa Community. Do you know where that is?" She shook her

head and he gave her quick instructions.

"Thanks, I'll find it." After the ambulance pulled away, Peggy raced inside. Adam lay crying in his crib, his face red and fists balled up.

"I'm sorry, sweetie," she said, her composure finally shattering as she picked up her grandson and cradled him. Her momma hadn't raised no fool. If Tyler wasn't Adam's father, she was George W. Bush.

"Daddy'll be okay, darlin'," she whispered, rocking him. "He'll be okay." She cried, praying it would prove true.

She allowed herself five minutes to be upset before gathering enough things to take care of the baby for the day. Nevvie would need her to be strong, and so would Thomas. She located the folder in the file drawer and found a sweater in Nevvie's closet to take to her. She might need it in the hospital waiting room. With a final check of the kitchen to turn off the coffee pot and make sure the stove was off, she pulled out of the driveway in Nevvie's car fifteen minutes after the ambulance had left.

Please let him live, she prayed. *Please don't take that boy from us.*

Chapter Six

Nevvie tried to stay out of the way, tried not to cry. Peggy's words echoed in her ears. She had to be strong.

At Tampa Community, the ambulance pulled into the ER entrance. When they opened the back doors, Nevvie climbed out and stood to the side. She tried to follow Tyler's gurney into the bowels of the ER when a nurse intercepted her.

"Please, let me go with my husband."

"Ma'am, you can't go back there with him. The doctors have to get a look at him. We need you to fill out paperwork. They'll probably take him to the cath lab."

"What's that?"

"Well, they'll check him to see what's wrong with his heart, to see if he needs surgery—"

"Surgery?" Nevvie gasped. That's when she lost it. Her knees buckled. Sobbing, she sank to the floor as the nurse tried to get her to her feet and into a chair.

She couldn't even tell him she loved him.

Another nurse and an orderly came over to help. They steered Nevvie into the admitting cubicle. Through her tears she fumbled with Tyler's wallet, trying to choke back her sobs as she struggled to get the requested items out. She finally handed it to the nurse to pull out his driver's license and insurance cards.

"You're his wife, ma'am?"

"Yes. My mother-in-law is bringing all our other paperwork with her, and our son..." Nevvie sobbed again. The nurse, obviously used to dealing with upset family, handed Nevvie a box of tissues and let her cry for a few minutes. They finished the admissions paperwork and Nevvie had almost composed herself again when another nurse poked her head around the corner.

"Mrs. Paulson?"

Nevvie nodded, her soul chilled, certain the nurse would break the worst news possible.

"We're taking your husband to the heart cath lab. You can see him for just a minute if we go back right now, but he's not conscious."

Nevvie leaped from her seat, clutching the admissions paperwork she'd been given, and followed the nurse. She caught sight of a clock—she'd already been there a half-hour. That long? Time seemed to fold and twist. It felt like five minutes ago she'd been standing in the shower with him, and yet hours since Peggy jumped on him to perform CPR.

The nurse spoke to her on the way and Nevvie didn't understand a word of it. EKG. Echocardiogram. Blood work. Cath lab. Stents. She might as well have been speaking Latin. Inside the room, several nurses and doctors worked on Tyler. He was hooked up to monitors and on a ventilator.

Her tears ran unabated as she leaned over him and kissed his forehead.

"I love you, Ty. Baby, please, you've got to pull through for Tommy and me and Adam. You can't leave us, you stubborn evil genius." She softly whispered in his ear, "Please, come back to me, come back to your angel. I love you."

One of the doctors spoke. "I'm sorry, we need to move him."

"Hold on," one of the nurses said. She removed Tyler's wedding band and watch. "Here, ma'am, hold onto these for him. You can give them back to him once he's in recovery." She said it kindly, apparently hoping to calm Nevvie's nerves. It didn't help.

Nevvie took them, nodding, noting the warmth in the gold band. She slipped it on her left hand and had to put it on her middle finger because of the size. She slipped his watch into her pocket.

They wheeled him out and the nurse guided her back to the ER waiting room. Peggy waited with Adam in his carrier.

"How is he, sugar?" She took the paperwork from Nevvie's numb hands and looked through it.

Nevvie burst into tears. Peggy turned to the nurse, who filled her in. "He's going to the cath lab right now, ma'am. I'll take you to the surgical waiting room."

Peggy nodded and tried to manage the baby carrier and the bag. Nevvie unfastened Adam and picked him up, carried him in her arms. Nevvie trailed behind while Peggy toted the empty carrier and asked the nurse questions. The nurse brought Peggy up to speed during the walk. Once they were settled in the waiting room, Peggy turned to Nevvie.

"Sugar, do you understand what's going on, what the nurse said?"

Nevvie cradled Adam and shook her head.

Peggy took a deep breath and put a hand on Nevvie's leg. "Tyler had a cardiac arrest. His heart stopped beating. I was right there and started CPR immediately so I'd be willing to bet he's going to be fine. They've got to find out why his heart stopped because he had a heart attack. They've got him on medication that will help, but they've got to do a heart cath on him so they can see what's going on. Depending on what they find they might do what's called a stent, or they might have to do surgery. We won't know for a while."

Nevvie squeezed her eyes tightly shut and nodded.

Peggy worried more about Nevvie's state of mind at that moment than she did Tyler's health. At least if Tommy was here she'd have a solid rock to lean on. Without him, she was a wreck.

"We're gonna call Tommy in a few minutes," Peggy said. "But not yet. We need to make a couple of other calls first. I need you to get Bob on the phone for me, okay?"

Nevvie fumbled Tyler's BlackBerry with one hand. She finally found Bob's number in the contact list and hit the send button before handing the phone to Peggy.

Peggy stepped out to the hall to talk to him. She briefly explained the situation.

"Oh, no. How's Nevvie and Thomas?"

"Nevvie's near collapse. Tommy's out of town, doesn't know. We haven't had any problems with the hospital yet. If we do, Nevvie's in no state of mind to handle them. Can you come?"

"Where are you? I'll be right there."

When Peggy finished with him, she found Pete's number and called him next. Pete met her news with a brief stunned silence.

"Is he gonna make it?"

"I don't know. Can you and Eddie get over here? Right now? I've still got to call Thomas and tell him. Nevvie's not doing good." Peggy peeked around the corner and watched as Nevvie stared at the floor, rocking in her chair, the baby in her arms and a stunned look on her face.

"We'll be right there."

"Thank you."

One more call, dialed from memory. Karen answered her cell on the third ring. "Momma? Why are you calling from Tyler's cell phone?"

More shock once she broke the news. "Can you come down?" Peggy asked.

Karen's stunned voice nearly finished Peggy. "Yeah. I'll call the airlines and see if I can get a flight to Tampa. Otherwise I'll drive. Momma, is he going to be okay?"

"I don't know, sugar. If we lose him, Nevvie and Thomas are gonna need all the support they can get." She gave Karen the hospital information.

"I'll let you know once I get a flight."

"Okay. Call April and the others." She knew she didn't have to say not to call Em.

Peggy returned to Nevvie. "We need to call Thomas, honey. Do you want me to do it?"

Nevvie looked at her, her eyes red and glazed. "I'll do it," she whispered. She finally handed Adam—who was asleep, miracle of miracles—over to Peggy and used her own BlackBerry to call.

She dialed and Peggy held her breath, waiting for her son to answer.

Nevvie shook her head. Peggy knew that meant his voice mail picked up. "Tommy, it's Nev. I need you to call my cell as soon as you get this. Please. It's important." She hung up and looked at Peggy, then burst into tears again.

Peggy laid Adam in his carrier and put her arms around Nevvie. "Shh, honey. It's okay. He'll be okay."

Twenty minutes later, Pete and Eddie raced into the waiting room and rushed to Nevvie's side. Upon seeing them she broke down again and the friends clustered around her, holding her as she sobbed.

* * * *

Thomas felt his phone vibrate but with all the noise on the site he couldn't hear well enough to talk. Seeing Nevvie's number, he silenced it and returned to the conversation with the site manager, going over the project blueprints. He needed to focus on what he was doing so he didn't make a mistake. A half-hour later it rang again and he silenced it before glancing at the screen. Two voice mails.

A vague feeling of unease settled over him. If it was an emergency wouldn't Nevvie keep calling back until she got him? Or send him a text message?

When it rang again fifteen minutes later he looked at it. Nevvie. With the heavy equipment running he couldn't hear even if he did answer. He ignored it, then a few minutes later decided he'd better find out what was up.

"Glen, I need to make a call. I'll be right back." Thomas retreated to the air conditioned construction office trailer to call Nevvie.

* * * *

A nurse dressed in surgical scrubs walked in. "Mr. Paulson's family?"

Pete and Eddie stood up and the nurse walked over to them. Pete pointed to Nevvie. "She's his wife."

The nurse knelt in front of her. "Dr. Robertson will come out and talk to you in a few minutes, but we have to take Mr. Paulson into surgery."

Nevvie sobbed and leaned into Peggy, who hugged her. She looked at the nurse. "Tell me—I'm a nurse."

"We have to prep him for surgery. His vital signs are strong, he's doing very well." She looked up as a doctor walked in. "Here he is."

The doctor walked over and introduced himself. "Mrs. Paulson?"

Nevvie nodded against Peggy's shoulder. The nurse whispered in his ear and he addressed his comments more to Peggy than Nevvie. "I expect the surgery to take around four or five hours, possibly less, sometimes more. If it takes longer don't be alarmed, it doesn't mean anything's wrong. From looking at his chart and what I saw in the cath lab, I think he's going to do very well. I don't know if he'll need an implanted defibrillator or not but we'll cross that bridge when we come to it." He explained what he had to do while Peggy asked questions. Nevvie didn't understand any of it.

With tears streaming down her face, Nevvie cried against Peggy's shoulder. Peggy stroked her hair and looked at the doctor. "How much damage did you see?"

"The rapid response saved his life. There's some damage, of course. He's going to need a cardiac rehab program and medication, but once we get him through the first few days I think he'll do well. He's relatively young, in otherwise good health, he doesn't seem to have any pulmonary problems, so that's very encouraging. He'll probably be in the ICU for a few days. From there we'll move him to a telemetry unit until we're comfortable discharging him."

"What does that mean? What's a telemetry unit?" Nevvie asked.

"It's not as intense as the ICU, but he'll be hooked up to monitors and closely watched for any problems."

Nevvie looked at Peggy. "Mom, if you hadn't been there, he would have died."

"Shh. Don't even think about that. He's gonna be fine, sugar."

He glanced at the wall clock. "I need to get back there. I'll send out updates on his condition. It'll be at least an hour before the first update, so if you need to go eat—"

Nevvie shook her head. "I'm not leaving," she insisted. "I won't leave him. They didn't leave me when I was hurt. I won't leave him."

Peggy looked at the doctor. "Thank you, Dr. Robertson."

Nevvie's BlackBerry rang.

* * * *

Thomas borrowed the site manager's office, closed the door for privacy and played his voice mails. All from Nevvie, the first sounding very strange. By the third his heart pounded and he knew something was horribly wrong.

He called her back and tried not to crush his phone as he waited for her to answer.

"Nevvie, sugar, what's wrong?"

She didn't answer him at first. When she finally did her voice sounded flat and soft. "Tommy, you have to come home. Right now."

"Baby girl, you're scaring me. What's going on? What's wrong?"

Again she paused. "Tyler."

"What? Honey, tell me. What's going on?" He fought to control his voice and heard her choked sob, then a noise that sounded like the phone being dropped. His mother came on the line.

"Thomas, sugar, I need you to sit down."

He stood up. "Momma, dammit, what's wrong with Tyler?" He couldn't control his fear and his voice rose in agitation.

"Sugar, he's going to be okay but he's in surgery right now."

"*What?* Momma, what the hell happened? What's going on?"

"Baby, he had a heart attack this morning. They're doing surgery on him."

His legs failed him. Stunned, he collapsed into the chair. *Ty?*

"Oh my God."

"Now, you need to stay calm. He's gonna be in surgery for at least four hours the doctor said, maybe longer. Can you have someone drive you, or rent a car?"

He still couldn't feel his legs. "What happened?"

"Hold on." It sounded like she moved to a quieter location. Her voice also dropped. "He wasn't feeling good. He was standing in the kitchen with Nevvie when he collapsed. I started CPR and the ambulance took him to the hospital—"

"*CPR?* His heart stopped?"

"Sugar, you need to settle down. I'm having a hard enough time keeping Nevvie calm. She needs you, and she needs you back here in one piece. Don't you dare drive that bike back here. You get a car or you have someone drive you."

"Where is he?"

"Tampa Community."

Thomas closed his eyes. That's where Nevvie was taken after Alex stabbed her. It was also where Adam was born. "How is Nevvie? How's the baby?"

"The baby is fine, you leave him to me. I called Bob for you already, he's on his way. I have the folder of paperwork here for y'all. I also got Karen coming down, and Pete and Eddie are here. But I need you here for Nevvie. She's not doing good. She needs you."

"Let me speak to her."

"You need to keep it together on the phone with her or I won't. Promise me?"

"Yes, just let me speak to her." He felt too numb to be upset.

After a moment, Nevvie came back on the line.

He took a deep breath and tried for what he hoped sounded like a strong, steady tone. "Honey, you let Momma and Pete and Eddie and Bob take care of you. I'll be back in a few hours. Hang tight. Are you okay?"

There was a long pause. He almost thought the call had dropped. "No. I'm not."

Thomas closed his eyes, struggling with his tears, fighting to keep his voice steady. "You know as well as I do that he's strong, he's tough. Our boy will make it just fine. If Momma says he'll be fine, he'll be fine. Right?"

"Tommy, I love you."

"I love you too, sugar. If you get to see him before I get there, you tell the evil genius I love him, okay?"

"I will."

"Okay. Put Momma back on the phone for me."

There was yet another pause before Peggy spoke. "Tommy, take your time coming back, you hear me?"

"I'll be there in about five hours. I'll come straight to the hospital."

"You're not driving that bike."

"Don't worry. Please take care of Nevvie for me."

* * * *

Thomas waited a moment to try to stand but ended up crying with his head on his arms on the desk. Dammit, he couldn't lose Tyler. He should have been home, should have sent Kenny down here for this. He should be there for Nevvie and his guy.

It took him time to compose himself. When he finally did he walked to the outer office where Glen waited.

"I'm sorry Glen, I've got to go. I've got a family emergency."

"What's wrong?"

"Tyler had a heart attack. He's in surgery." He grabbed his bike gear from the chair he'd left it in and pushed out the door, Glen on his heels. "Call Kenny, please. Tell him what happened. He can come down tomorrow and work with you."

"Don't worry about this. You go take care of your family."

Tom's hands shook so badly he almost couldn't zip his jacket. He finally managed it, pulled on his helmet and gloves and mounted the Harley. Now he wished he'd taken the truck instead. No, he had to be a fucking stubborn asshole and not let his mom tell him what to do.

Thomas cranked the bike then waited a moment for his nerves to settle before pulling onto the highway.

Emotionally numb, he returned to the hotel he was staying at and quickly packed what little he'd brought. He checked out before making his way to the interstate and heading north on I-75. When he stopped for gas near Punta Gorda, he called to check on Tyler. Bob answered Nevvie's cell.

"What's going on? Where's Nev?"

"It's okay, Tom. Your mother and Eddie finally talked her into going to the cafeteria. She hasn't had anything to eat all day. I'm here with Pete and the baby in the waiting room."

"How is he?"

"They just gave us an update, everything's going fine, his vital signs are stable and strong, that's all we know right now. Where are you?"

"Punta Gorda."

Bob hesitated. "Are you on the bike?"

"Yeah, but don't tell Momma or Nevvie, okay? I didn't want to screw around waiting for a car. I need to be up there for them."

"Don't get yourself killed, Tom. Take it easy. I already paid a visit to administration and have been assured there will be no problems."

"Thanks."

Thomas pulled onto the highway. Yes, he remembered. Alex had stabbed Nevvie, putting her in the ICU. A nosy, self-righteous prig in administration was upset by their unconventional relationship and tried to convince Nevvie she was being mentally abused by them. Bob got the bitch fired.

If the hospital wanted to give them trouble about their relationship, they could. Bob did all he could legally with paperwork—powers of attorney and the like—to hopefully prevent any issues. But if someone wanted to really be an asshole it could cause them problems.

Tom tried to focus on the traffic, not worry about Tyler or stare at the phone clipped to his gear bag on the tank. He needed to focus. Nevvie needed him.

His guy needed him.

Mile marker signs flew past at increasing regularity. By the time he reached Brandon, he'd tied a knot in his last nerve and was barely hanging on. Resisting the urge to floor it, it kept the Harley at seventy and silently chanted, "He'll be okay. He'll be okay."

With no small measure of relief he turned off at the Fletcher Avenue exit and worked his way through traffic toward the hospital.

I'm almost there, buddy, he thought. *Hang on.*

* * * *

Antonio felt more than relief to finally clock out. He'd filled in for a buddy in housekeeping and hadn't slept in over twenty-four hours. Exhaustion didn't begin to describe how drained he felt.

He checked his cell as he slid behind the wheel. Shit, he'd forgotten to call his girlfriend and tell her he'd worked a double shift. She would have his balls. Maybe it was time to think about ditching her. She acted crazy jealous about every little friggin' thing. He didn't need that kind of stress in his life.

He dialed her cell as he started the car and put it in reverse with a careless glance behind him.

She answered after two rings. "Where the fuck you been? I been callin' you."

"I'm sorry. I worked a double." He jammed on the brakes and waved an elderly man across in front of him. Damn, he'd nearly hit the dude. "Dave's wife just had a baby, it arrived two weeks early. I worked his shift for him."

"Why the fuck you can't call me and tell me this?"

He weaved his way through the parking lot toward Fletcher Avenue. "Because it was last minute. I'm sorry, but I'm freaking exhausted. Look, I don't want to fight with you right now, okay?"

* * * *

Thomas spied the hospital and fought the urge to speed up. He was almost there. It would be okay. Everything would be okay. He'd spent plenty of time here, between Nevvie's hospital stay, and then when she had Adam, and he knew his way around. He decided to cut through the employee lot instead of swinging around to the main entrance.

* * * *

"What the fuck you mean you don't want to fight with me right now? Maybe we should just call it quits, is that what you sayin'?"

Antonio groaned. "Look, baby—"

"Don't you look baby me!"

He glanced to the left, didn't see anything, then looked to his right. He had to wait for an oncoming car so he could make a left hand turn across Fletcher.

* * * *

Thomas glanced down at his cell phone to check the time and popped his helmet strap off to scratch his chin. He'd be taking it off in less than a minute anyway. When he looked up, an old shit-brown

Ford had pulled out in front of him. Thomas had time to register the shock on the young driver's face, as well as the fact that the guy was talking on his cell phone, before the Harley plowed into the driver's door.

Thomas' world went black.

* * * *

John Dekins walked outside the ER entrance to take a smoke break and lit his cigarette. His sixth attempt to quit had failed and his wife would have his balls. Again. After taking a long drag he looked up to see the car pull out of the parking lot and the motorcycle T-bone it. In stunned disbelief he watched as the biker tumbled over the car and hit the pavement on the far side.

The biker didn't move. Cars going in both directions on Fletcher slammed on brakes.

Tossing his cigarette to the ground, Dekins ran into the ER and yelled at the nurse on duty at the desk. "Call a code, and get a gurney! We just had a motorcyclist get hit out front!"

He ran outside and raced across the parking lot, adrenaline pumping, jumping shrubs and bolting out into the street where he checked the biker's pulse. The biker had lost his helmet in the crash, but he was alive.

Dekins glanced at the car and expected to see the driver moving, considering it was a huge, old, piece of shit car. Then he realized the bike's front wheel was buried inside the driver door, through the window.

On top of the driver.

"Aw, damn." Three more nurses and a doctor ran over, as did an ambulance crew that had just dropped off a patient. They'd have to deal with the driver, if he wasn't DOA. He already had one patient to work on.

Well, if he had to get creamed, at least he picked a good place to do it. He waved the ambulance crew over to the biker and they slid a backboard under him and fitted him with a cervical collar to stabilize his spine before loading him onto the stretcher.

"Where do you want him, Dr. Dekins?"

He jogged along with the EMTs. "Straight into three, I think it's open, but he won't be there for long. His leg's fucked, looks like he might have head trauma..."

Chapter Seven

Nevvie paced. Eddie volunteered to take Adam back to their house.

"Do you have your key to our place?" she asked.

"Yeah. Want me to pick up more stuff?"

"Can you keep him late for me? Maybe all night?"

"Of course I can. Jesus, babe, you know you don't need to worry about that."

She broke down crying again. "I'm sorry, Eddie."

He held her, trying to soothe her, looking at Pete over her shoulder. While at first uncomfortable with Tyler and Thomas' choice to add her to their family, as they got to know Nevvie they understood why their friends loved her. She was sweet and perfect for them, obviously devoted to the two men beyond any boundaries of sense and reason. He and Pete had both come to love her like a little sister. Seeing her this torn up broke their hearts.

"Nev, you know he's gonna be fine," Eddie hoarsely assured her. "He's a tough bastard. He just has you and Tommy fooled into thinking he's a big softy."

She choked out a laugh and sat back, wiped her eyes. "Thanks, Eddie."

Pete handed him his keys. "You take our car. I'll get a ride back later."

Peggy stood. "I'll get the car seat base for you. Nevvie, you want to walk outside, stretch your legs?"

She shook her head. "I'll stay here."

Bob took Peggy's chair, next to Nevvie. "We'll sit with her." Pete flanked Nevvie on her other side, comfortingly patted her leg.

When it was just the three of them she leaned against Pete's shoulder and he draped a meaty arm around her. "Now you listen," he said. "You stay tough for him. You know how he is. He'll feel bad you're upset and that'll make him feel guilty."

She sniffled and nodded.

* * * *

Eddie carried the baby and the diaper bag while Peggy carried the empty carrier. They heard sirens blaring from somewhere close by, looked up, and saw several emergency vehicles in the street a half a block away.

"How do you think she is? Really?" Eddie asked.

Peggy set the carrier down next to Nevvie's car and shook her head. "If that boy doesn't pull through, Thomas is gonna need y'all. She's one step from going off the cliff, I think. They lose Ty, it'll kill them both."

Eddie sniffled. "He's such a sweetheart. Goddamn, I hope he makes it okay." Eddie stared at the baby, who was trying to fall asleep again. "This little guy looks just like him. They're both crazy about him, but it's like Tyler changed for the better when Adam came along, you know? Like he was finally complete. I never thought I'd ever see him happier than when they got together with Nevvie. Then they had Adam, and now it's like Ty smiles all the time."

"I know." Peggy had noticed that herself. All the years she'd known Tyler, she had to admit Adam's birth seemed to bring something else out in him, in a good way.

Eddie traded her the baby for the car seat and base and she followed him to his car. He looked at the road. "Dang, looks like an accident over there."

Peggy followed his gaze before handing Adam to him and climbing into the backseat of his Mercedes to set up the car seat.

"Yeah, sure does."

* * * *

Peggy hadn't returned. Nevvie had to go to the bathroom. Tucking her phone into her sweater pocket, she walked down the hall to the bathroom. On her way back she felt the phone vibrate and looked. She didn't recognize the number.

She'd reached the waiting room door when she answered. "Hello?"

"Is this Nevaeh Kinsey?" a woman asked.

A chilled, creeping feeling she couldn't identify rolled through her stomach. She veered away from the waiting room door and walked down the hall. Bob and Pete exchanged confused glances and moved to the doorway to watch her.

"This is Nevaeh Kinsey-Paulson. Who is this?"

"My name is Andrea. I'm calling from Tampa Community Hospital, from the Emergency department."

Nevvie breathed a sigh of relief. It had to be an administrator about Tyler's paperwork. "How can I help you?"

There was an uncomfortable pause. "I need to talk with you about Thomas Kinsey."

"What? You mean you need to talk to me about Tyler Paulson."

"I'm sorry? No ma'am, I need to talk to you about Thomas Kinsey. You're the emergency contact listed in the information in his wallet."

Pete started down the hallway toward her.

Nevvie froze. "What?" she gasped.

"He's been admitted to our Emergency department. I'm sorry, but he's been in an accident—"

"*What?*"

Pete broke into a run, trying to keep up with Nevvie. She still talked on the phone, looking up at the hallway signs, making turns, heading to the ER.

"Ma'am, please, calm down."

"Where is he? How is he? Where are you?"

"He's alive. I don't have an update on his condition. I'm in the ER."

Nevvie ran down a hallway and flew through a set of double doors into the ER. She scanned the area, homed in on the desk. "Who's Andrea?" she screamed.

A startled woman sitting behind a desk turned, a phone in her hand. "Mrs. Kinsey?"

"Where's my husband?"

Pete had caught up with Nevvie and now another nurse and a doctor surrounded her, trying to calm her down.

Past the point of hysterics, Nevvie sobbed, "Where's Tommy? Thomas Kinsey. Where is he? What have you done with him?"

A doctor tried to reassure her. "Ma'am, they've already taken him to surgery. He's got a broken leg and head injuries—"

"Oh my God!" She sank to the floor and stared at Pete. "This is a joke, right?" she sobbed. "This is a really horrible fucking bad joke, right?" She looked at one of the doctors, who grimly shook his head.

She cried.

Pete dropped to his knees and grabbed her hands. "Nevvie, honey, calm down."

She glared at the doctor. "You can't have them both! You can't take them both from me!" She stared at the ceiling and screamed. "You hear me? You can't take them both from me, goddammit, it's not fair! You can't have them—they're mine!" She collapsed, inconsolable, against Pete's shoulder.

* * * *

Bob grabbed the women's purses and paced by the waiting room door, anxious for Peggy's return. This couldn't be good. He swore he heard a woman screaming from the direction of the ER. As soon as he saw Peggy he ran to meet her and made her follow him.

"What's wrong? Is it Tyler?"

He shook his head, following signs. "I don't know. Nevvie took a phone call and Pete rushed off with her this way."

They didn't need signs to follow Nevvie's anguished screams. They pushed through the ER doors and saw a doctor and two nurses surrounding Nevvie as she thrashed on the floor in Pete's arms while he tried to restrain her.

"Nevvie, what the hell is going on?" Bob yelled.

The doctor looked up. "Do you know her?"

"I'm the family attorney." He dropped to his knees and shoved them out of his way, captured Nevvie's chin in his palms. He pulled her face close to his. "Nevvie, honey," he whispered. "Stop. Calm down. Now."

She focused on him, sobbing. "They can't have him, Bob! Tell them they can't have him! Fix it! They already have Tyler. Tell them they can't have him, too!"

"Can't have who, honey?" He glanced at Pete's face and spotted the large man's tears. This couldn't be good.

"Tell them they can't have Tommy. Please, Bob. Tell them. Make them give him back! Please fix this!"

He froze and looked up at Peggy, who wore a horrified expression. By this time two hospital security guards had arrived.

"Pete, give her to me." The other man released her. Bob scooped Nevvie into his arms and headed for the first empty room he saw. Nevvie clung to him, still sobbing, pleading with him to fix it.

Pete dragged his bulk from the floor and grabbed the women's purses. He wiped his eyes and gently pushed Peggy into the room, followed by the rest of the staff that had gathered.

Bob set Nevvie on a gurney and, keeping his arms securely around her, he looked at the doctor.

"What is going on?" he asked, forcing his voice to stay calm.

"Andrea was talking on the phone with her and she suddenly burst in here, then she was in hysterics," the doctor said.

Peggy recognized one of the nurses from that morning and zeroed in on her. "Will you please tell us what's going on?"

The nurse looked uncomfortable. Peggy lost her patience. "Look, the three of them live together. They're not legally married but they've got paperwork that just as good as makes them that way. Tyler and Thomas are both her husbands. They're polyamorous, get over it. Now what the hell is going on?"

Nevvie kept begging Bob over and over to fix it. He held her face against his shoulder, stroked her hair, trying to calm her.

The doctor finally spit it out. "Mr. Kinsey was seriously injured in an accident in front of the hospital. A car pulled out in front of his motorcycle."

Luckily, Pete caught Peggy and guided her to a chair. Nevvie's sobs renewed. Bob held her tightly against him as she cried.

"How bad is he?" Bob softly asked.

"He's critical. I don't know the full extent of his injuries—leg and head injuries, possible internal injuries."

Nevvie shook her head against Bob's shoulder. "It's not true. Bob, make them quit lying. Make them stop. Make them give him back!" She tried to thrash against him. He maintained his iron grip on her until she settled again, still sobbing.

The doctor looked at Peggy. "Ma'am, are you okay?"

She looked stunned. "Thomas is my son." She looked at Pete. "Oh God, one of us needs to be in the waiting room in case they come about Tyler."

The doctor looked confused. "Ma'am?"

Bob took a deep breath and assumed control. "Tyler Paulson. He's in surgery. He had a heart attack this morning. Thomas was driving up from Ft. Myers. He'd been out of town. And yes, the three of them are partners together. That's why they called me, in case there were any issues."

The doctor closed his eyes. "I'm so sorry. I didn't know."

Nevvie thrashed against Bob again. "No! It's a lie! You can't have him!" she screamed.

Peggy closed her eyes and put a hand to her mouth, quietly crying. Pete gently squeezed her shoulder.

Bob tightened his grip on Nevvie, restraining her. "Nevvie," he said sternly, "you have to calm down or I will make them sedate you. You can't help Tom and Ty if you're unconscious. I promise I won't leave you alone, but you can't help them like this. They wouldn't want you to be upset like this. You have to calm down for them."

Like a splash of ice water his words and tone cut through her grief and she relaxed against him. Her tears still flowed.

He tried again. "Sweetie," he said, softening his tone, "we'll all get through this, but the guys need you to be tough. Adam needs his mom to be tough. You can do this. I'll help you. We'll all help you. You can do this."

"I can't do this alone," she whispered. "I need them. I need my boys. What am I going to do without my boys?"

"You have them, honey. No one said they're dying now, did they?"

She shook her head and took a long, hitching breath.

Bob looked at Pete. "Take Peggy back to the waiting area. Someone needs to be there in case they have news about Tyler." He spoke to the nurse. "Will they send word to the same waiting area about Thomas?"

"Yes."

He noticed she carried a large plastic bag. Nevvie couldn't see because he still had his arms around her, holding her with her face pressed against him.

He motioned for the bag. The nurse handed it over. He set it on the floor by his feet, out of Nevvie's sight.

Thomas' personal effects.

Pete helped Peggy to her feet and led her from the room, his arm around her for support, followed by the doctor.

Bob finally released Nevvie and cupped her face in his palms again. He suspected she perched on the verge of an emotional, if not mental breakdown.

"Look at me, Nevvie." He waited until her eyes settled on his. "I promise you, I will be right here for you. I know Ty and Tom want that. Pete and Eddie are going to help you, too. Peggy's here, and Karen's on her way. You are *not* alone, but you have to stay calm and let us help you. That's *your* job. That's your *only* job right now until we hear word about them. Okay? You *have* to stay calm. We'll do the rest. Can you do that for me, for them?"

She nodded.

"Good girl." His foot kicked the bag, making it rustle. Nevvie noticed.

"What was that?"

He silently swore and bent over, looked through it, found a smaller bag with Tom's watch and wedding band. He handed the ring to Nevvie. "Put this on, keep it safe for him."

After trying a few fingers, Nevvie finally settled for her right thumb. He realized for the first time that she wore Tyler's band on the middle finger of her left hand. Nevvie stared at her hands, her fingers working the men's rings.

"Can we get a wheelchair for her?" he asked the nurse. "And any paperwork we need to sign for Tom?"

She went to get it.

Now alone, Bob turned to Nevvie. "You can do this. The boys have faith in you, and so do I."

Nevvie wouldn't meet his gaze, just continued staring at the rings. He helped her complete the paperwork. Then he guided her off the gurney and into the wheelchair, carried the bag and her purse as he pushed her back to the waiting room.

* * * *

Bob stepped to the waiting room doorway and called his partner, Terry. He answered on the second ring.

"Hey, you. Where'd you disappear to?"

"I won't make it home for dinner, buddy. I'm sorry."

"What's going on?"

Bob took a deep breath and went through the brief version, which met with stunned silence.

Terry finally spoke. "Holy shit. Both of them?"

"Yeah."

"Crap. Listen, I'll bring you an overnight bag. You plan on staying with her. She'll need you there if she's that bad."

Bob closed his eyes and pinched the bridge of his nose. "Tell the kids I'm sorry and I love them. I'll call them before they go to bed."

"It's okay. Don't worry about it. I'll run home and get you some stuff."

"Thanks, Ter." They said their good-byes as Bob watched Nevvie. Pete sat between the women and held Nevvie's hand on one side, Peggy's on the other. Nevvie's blank face terrified Bob in a way. The shock was too much for her. He had no doubts if it was just Tyler, once Tom arrived she would have looked to him for strength and been the strong, kick-ass woman he watched take on her asshole ex-boyfriend and his lawyer during the trial.

This woman looked broken, an empty shell. Those two men *were* her life.

Dr. Robertson walked down the hallway to the waiting room. Bob stopped him. "Are you here for Tyler Paulson's family?" he whispered.

The doctor nodded. Bob pulled him a few feet down the hall. "Please tell me he's alive."

The doctor eyed him. Bob quickly added, "I'm the family attorney."

"What?"

He told the short version and the doctor closed his eyes. "Holy crap."

"Yeah, it's been one of those kinds of days around here. Please, tell me he's okay. If you're not gonna tell me that, go back right now and get a sedative ready for Nevvie, because it'll be her last straw."

"He's in recovery, and he's doing fine."

Bob blew out a relieved breath. "Oh, thank God! One down. Let's go tell her."

Nevvie and Peggy looked up when Bob walked in with the doctor. Bob immediately flashed them a smile and a thumbs-up. Nevvie started crying again, this time with relief.

The doctor knelt before her. "Mr. Paulson is critical, but he's stable. That's normal for his situation. His vital signs are good, and I think he's going to be fine."

She nodded, silent tears falling in her lap.

He continued. "He's going to be on the ventilator for at least a day but I'll take you back there to see him, okay?"

She nodded again, still weeping.

"He can't speak to you, he's unconscious. That's to keep him comfortable and out of pain." He dropped his voice. "Your attorney just talked to me. When we get done, I will go back to the OR and check on your other husband for you, okay?"

She closed her eyes. "Thank you." Dr. Robertson patted her leg and she stood, swaying on her feet, a little woozy.

Bob steadied her. "Honey, why don't you let me push you?"

She shook her head and straightened. "No. I can do this. He needs me."

Thatta girl. "I'll go with you." He turned to Pete. "Stay here with Peggy, please?"

"Yeah."

Bob kept his arm around Nevvie's waist all the way to the ICU. Irony of ironies, Tyler occupied the bed next to where Nevvie had stayed nearly five years earlier after Alex's attack. The doctor slid a chair next to Tyler's bed. Bob gently guided Nevvie to it.

The doctor glanced at Bob. "Mrs. Paulson, do you have any questions?"

She reached through the bed rail and carefully stroked the back of Tyler's right hand, being careful not to disturb his IVs. "Is he going to make it? Really?"

"I think so. There's always some risk. Infection, bleeding, blood clots. In my experience, since he's not overweight, he's not a smoker, he's not a diabetic and he's otherwise healthy, I think it's safe to say he should recover."

She carefully gripped Tyler's hand. "I love him so much. Both of them. He's my brain, Tommy's my tough guy. They're my life. I can't lose them. They're my boys."

The doctor laid a gentle hand on her shoulder. "I don't think you're going to lose Tyler. I don't know anything about your other husband's condition right now. I'll go check for you."

"Thank you."

Dr. Robertson turned to the nurse and whispered something to her. She noted the chart. He turned back to Nevvie. "I'll talk to the nursing supervisor, see if they'll bend the visitation rules for you. You can't sleep in here, and during shift changes you'll need to leave, but that way you'd be able to spend more time with both of them."

Nevvie turned to him, shocked. "Oh no! Thomas will be in here?"

"Most likely."

She frantically shook her head. "No. Tyler can't know. Oh, God, this will kill him."

Bob prepared for another bout of hysterics but she actually seemed calmer, determined.

"Make sure they put orders in his chart not to tell him about Thomas," Nevvie demanded. "They can't tell him. I don't want him having another heart attack!"

The doctor tried to reassure her. "Mrs. Paulson, it'll be okay."

"No!" She sounded strong, resolute. Bob glimpsed Nevvie the

fighter, Nevvie the woman who called him from this very hospital when the administrator gave her a hassle, the woman who, even while in ICU, stood up to Tyler and gave him a run for his money.

"No. They cannot tell him. Absolutely not. I'll tell him, but not until he's out of here and in a room."

Dr. Robertson looked at the nurse, who noted it.

"Can I be alone with him for a minute?" Nevvie asked.

They left to give her privacy. Nevvie bent close to Tyler's ear so she could whisper to him. She didn't know if he could hear her.

"You're going to be fine, Ty," she said, then choked back a sob. She stroked his hair. "Your little slave is very happy with her sweet master. You're coming home to me, do you hear me? They said you'll be fine. You have to come home to me because I love you and I need you. Thomas needs you, and Adam needs you. You're not allowed to die on me." She touched her forehead to his and took a deep breath.

Bob was right, she had to be calm, strong, for her boys.

After five minutes with him, she kissed his cheek and rejoined the others outside.

"Okay. Let's go find out how Thomas is."

Bob looked at her. "Are you all right?"

She forced a grim smile. "I have to be. I'm sorry I lost it earlier."

He put an arm around her and hugged her. "It's okay, sweetie."

They followed the doctor back to the waiting area and he left them with a promise to return in a few minutes. Peggy and Pete looked at Nevvie. She forced another smile. "The doctor said Tyler should be okay."

They both sighed with relief. Peggy was going to say something when Karen, dragging a rolling suitcase behind her, ran into the waiting room. "Nevvie!" She enveloped her with a hug. "How's Tyler? Is he out of surgery?"

Bob raised an eyebrow. Nevvie shook her head. "Karen, we need to talk."

"Is he okay?"

"He's in the ICU. He's out of surgery."

"That's good, right?"

"Yes, but—"

Peggy spoke up. "Sit down, Karen."

Karen picked up on her mother's tone. "What? What's wrong?"

Nevvie sat next to her. "Thomas had an accident on his way up here from Ft. Myers. A car pulled out in front of him. He was on the bike."

"Oh no! Is he okay?"

Nevvie tried to retain her calm. "We don't know. He's in surgery."

Pete stood. "I need to call Eddie. I haven't told him yet. I'll check on the Ant for you, babe."

When he patted her shoulder she covered his hand with hers and squeezed. Before she met and "married" Tyler and Thomas, Nevvie was essentially alone in the world. Now she had an extended network of family and friends she could lean on. Bob was right—she could do this.

But it hurt so much.

While Pete was gone, Dr. Robertson returned and talked to them. "He may be in surgery another hour or more."

Bob moved to stand behind Nevvie and put his hands on her shoulders. She gripped them for comfort.

"How is he?" she asked.

"He's critical, but don't let that scare you because that's just a label. He's stable, which is more important to focus on. His left leg had been broken in several places and they surgically set it. That's already been done."

She took a deep breath. "Okay."

He continued. "They removed his spleen but except for some broken ribs, that looks like the extent of his internal injuries to his torso.

That's not so bad. She could deal with that but she suspected there was more.

"Apparently his helmet came off during the accident and he suffered head trauma. That's what they're working on now."

She'd been doing so well until that. Bob firmly gripped her shoulders and leaned down. "Stay strong for him, Nev. You know he'd want that."

She met the doctor's eyes. "Does he have brain damage?"

"I don't know the full extent of his head injuries. I got the short version. Someone will come out and talk to you in the next hour and update you. I talked to the surgeon's PA and told them about your family situation so they know what's going on."

"Thank you, Doctor."

Nevvie looked at Peggy and Karen, who held hands and stared at her, both in shock. Bob was right—she had to be strong for her boys and for the rest of her family.

"He'll be okay," Nevvie insisted. "I know he will."

Both women nodded. Karen fought her tears. "Oh, God, I've got to call the others."

"No," Peggy said, her firm tone surprising Nevvie. "I don't want them to know. I especially don't want Em to know. Not after she showed her ass."

"But Momma—"

"No! Do you hear me? Don't you *dare* call them. Once he's out of surgery and we know more, we'll call April and Cheryl and tell them. I don't want Katie knowing, because she'll tell Em sure as God made little green apples, you know she will. Your brother wouldn't want Em here after the stunt she pulled. I don't want a fight on my hands on top of everything else."

Peggy looked at Nevvie. "They love you, Nevvie, they love each other, and they love that baby. They'll be okay."

Nevvie hugged her and felt Karen wrap her arms around them from behind.

Chapter Eight

Pete volunteered to stay in the waiting room while Bob took the women to the cafeteria. Karen had taken a cab from the airport and they stowed her suitcase and the bag of Thomas' effects in Nevvie's car along the way.

Bob made the women eat and wouldn't let them return to the waiting room until they'd each had at least a bowl of soup. Nevvie's initial burst of determination after learning Tyler was okay had waned, although she wasn't as despondent as before.

They'd just settled in the waiting room when another doctor entered. "Mr. Kinsey's family?"

Nevvie stood. Bob moved to stand next to her.

"Follow me, please."

They all exchanged nervous looks and followed the doctor down the hall to a small conference room. "I'm sorry, I didn't want to talk in front of others out there. Dr. Robertson informed me of the special circumstances. Mrs. Kinsey?" he asked Nevvie.

"Yes." She introduced everyone else.

"I'm Dr. Gonzales, the neurosurgeon. Dr. Spivey—his other surgeon—will be in here in a few minutes."

"Is he going to be okay?"

The doctor took a moment to collect his thoughts. "During the accident his helmet came off. So the good news is it saved his life during the initial impact. The bad news is he sustained a severe blow to his head. We've relieved the pressure and we're giving him medication to take care of the swelling, but we're keeping him in a medically induced coma while we monitor the situation."

Nevvie tightly gripped Bob's hands.

"Once we take care of the swelling we can see if there is any lasting damage."

"Brain damage?" she gasped.

"I'm not saying there will be, I'm not saying there won't be. We have to wait and see."

Even Peggy seemed stunned, unable to ask questions.

Dr. Gonzales continued. "Now, his other injuries, he'll heal from those. There's no reason he won't. As long as there's no infection or complications, physically he should recover from this, too. The big question is lasting neurological effects. He might be fine. He might have memory loss. He might need occupational or physical therapy."

"Whatever he needs, I'll get it for him. Whatever he has to do to heal, I'll do it."

The doctor patted her hand. "And with an attitude like that it'll help him a lot." The door opened and another doctor walked in and looked at them. "This is Dr. Spivey, I'll let him tell you about the rest."

Dr. Spivey ran through a laundry list of what happened and what they did. Nevvie finally tuned out. She had her answer—Thomas wasn't dying. She didn't care what shape he was in, she would take care of him, both of them. They were her boys, and if they weren't dying, that's all that mattered. A third doctor, an orthopedic surgeon, took care of Tom's leg. He'd already taken on another case and was unavailable to talk.

"When can we see Tommy?" Nevvie asked.

"They're getting him settled in the ICU now. Give them about twenty minutes then go on back. I understand that they already have special instructions concerning your situation and will be flexible with you with visitation."

"Thank you."

"Go ahead and stay here for a few minutes if you need to."

The doctors left. Nevvie laid her head on her hands and cried, long and hard, with Pete and Bob patting her back. This wasn't hysterics—this was relief.

Peggy spoke up. Her voice sounded ragged. "He's tough, sugar. Our Tommy's a tough man. He'll be fine."

Pete stepped out to update Eddie. When Nevvie composed herself she looked at Bob.

"Will you please handle all the paperwork about the accident? Insurance, his bike, all that?"

"Of course I will."

"Oh, dammit. I need to call Elliot and Steve about Tyler before word gets out." Tyler's publicist and agent needed to know what was going on before the press caught wind of it.

Bob stopped her. "Write them down and give me Tyler's phone. I'll call them and anyone else who needs to know."

She closed her eyes. "Crap."

"What?"

"I've got to call Delores."

"Who?" Peggy asked.

Nevvie sighed. "Tyler's mother."

* * * *

Nevvie walked outside with Tyler's phone. She found a bench in the shade and looked up Delores' number in Tyler's contact list. With a deep breath she hit the send button and waited for an answer.

She didn't know or care what time it was in England. She needed this done and off her plate. She wasn't fond of the woman, had only met her once and spoken on the phone with her twice during her five years with the boys. Tyler rarely talked with her.

When Delores answered, Nevvie forced herself to speak. "Delores? I'm sorry I didn't check the time before I called. This is Nevvie."

"Nevvie?"

"Tyler's wife."

"I know who you are. Why are you calling me?"

"I'm calling you because I don't want you finding out from the press. Tyler's in the hospital. He had a heart attack this morning."

"Oh my God! Is he all right?"

"He had surgery. He'll be in the hospital for a few days at least."

There was a moment of stunned silence from the woman. "Is he going to die? Is his will in order?"

Nevvie bit back a sarcastic reply. Maybe she should have called Delores at the start. Her anger would have kept her from losing her mind over the news about Thomas. "No, he's going to be just fine."

"Did you two finally get married? Did he get rid of that guy?"

"What?"

"You called yourself his wife. Did he finally marry you so my grandson's not a bastard?"

Delores had never even seen Adam, never acknowledged him in any way despite Nevvie sending her quite a few cards and letters with pictures of him enclosed.

Nevvie tried counting backward. Nope, didn't work.

"If you're referring to Thomas, no. We are still a marriage of three, like it or not, you old harpy."

"*What* did you call me?"

Nevvie couldn't help herself. She needed a target to unleash on and had her sights locked and loaded. "I called you an old harpy. H-A-R-P-Y. He loves Thomas, you old bat, and Thomas loves him. How dare you insult their relationship just because you don't like it."

"This is all his father's fault, you know. That bloody bastard, filthy bugger. If he hadn't left the way he did, maybe Tyler never would have turned into a homosexual like—"

"All right lady, you know what? I'm *not* having this conversation. I only wanted to give you the common courtesy of calling you so you didn't find out about this in the papers."

Delores' tone immediately changed, whining. "Can I come see

him?"

Nevvie knew what Delores was implying because the woman was perpetually broke. "I don't want you anywhere near him. I'm damn sure not paying for a ticket to fly you over. I've got enough grief to deal with as it is, and it's not like he'll want to see you."

There was a moment of stunned silence from the older woman. "How dare you talk to me that way!"

"I'll bloody well talk to you how I want to," Nevvie screamed, unconsciously mimicking Tyler's speech habits in her anger. "He's *my* husband, and it's *my* job to take care of him!"

"We'll see about that, missy," Delores hissed, then hung up on her. Nevvie was too angry to ponder what the hell she meant by that.

Fueled by rage, Nevvie stormed into the hospital and flung open the conference room door. "I'm going to the ICU. Bob, you come with me."

Pete and Bob exchanged startled glances. Bob scrambled to follow, grabbed her arm to slow her strides. "What happened?"

Nevvie turned on him. "Tell hospital security that if that woman shows up, she's not allowed to see Tyler or get any information about him. I don't even want people to know he's in the hospital."

"What? She's coming all the way from London?"

"I don't know, but I wouldn't put anything past that greedy bitch." Nevvie filled him in.

"Okay. So we hook up Em and Delores and they can gay bash together."

Nevvie froze, then laughed, throwing her arms around Bob and laughing until she cried. It took her a few minutes to regain her composure.

"You feeling a little more stable now, hon?"

She wiped her eyes. "I think so. I needed that. Thanks."

"Don't worry. You know I love a good fight and hey, it's just billable hours."

Nevvie laughed again. If Bob could crack jokes it meant her boys would be okay.

She maintained that upbeat mood until she stepped into the ICU. The nurse at the desk waved her in. After scrubbing up they first stopped at Tyler's bed. "How is he?" she asked his nurse.

"He's okay. I'm taking care of Thomas, too."

"They told you not to tell Tyler, right?"

"Yes, don't worry."

Nevvie kissed Tyler's forehead and brushed the hair away from his face. "I'll be back later, honey. I promise." With trembling legs she stepped to the next alcove, where the curtain was pulled but the sliding glass doors stood open.

The nurse, Carol, laid a hand on her arm. "Remember, he's been in an accident. He looks pretty bad right now. Don't let that scare you."

"I'm sure I looked pretty damn bad my first few days, too." Nevvie remembered Carol from her prior stay.

Carol smiled. "That's right, you did. Just remember, stay calm."

Nevvie stepped through the curtain, Bob right behind her.

Thomas looked horrible. Two black eyes, face bruised and battered, his head bandaged, on a ventilator. His left leg was bared, an incision on his hip still surrounded with orange residue from the surgical soap, and his leg bore several large, angry, sutured wounds. He also had IV tubes in both arms.

Nevvie closed her eyes and took a deep breath. She couldn't fall apart anymore, that luxury was gone. She opened her eyes and walked to the head of his bed, kissed him on the forehead.

"Tommy, sweetheart, you're going to be okay. I'll bring Mom and Karen back in a few minutes to see you. Tyler's going to be okay. He's out of surgery and he'll be fine."

She carefully took his hand, holding it so she didn't disturb his IVs. Dropping her voice she said, "I need my tough guy, Tommy. I need you back. I don't care what shape you're in, I don't care how bad you're hurt or what we have to do to help you. I don't care. All I care about is that you're alive and you don't leave us. You're my husband and I love you."

She kissed him again. With her lips near his ear she whispered, "I need my sweet master to come back to me. Do you hear me, Thomas? Your little slave needs you because she loves you and misses you."

She spent a few more minutes with him before letting Bob lead her to the conference room. Nevvie took a deep breath and pasted a smile on her face. "Okay," she said to Peggy and Karen, "you come back with me. Guys, why don't you wait in the waiting room for us?"

Pete looked at Bob, who shook his head, staying the other man's questions.

With Peggy on her left and Karen on her right, Nevvie held the women's hands and led them to the ICU.

Nevvie introduced Peggy and Karen to the nurse. "You'll be seeing a lot of all of us."

"That's okay. I'll make sure my replacement tonight knows what's going on. I think it'll be Ben. You might remember him."

Nevvie did. He was a sweetheart totally sympathetic to their situation and never gave them grief when the boys visited her—except for playfully trying to flirt with Tyler. He also frequently closed the curtain and let them well overstay the visiting times.

"Please tell them I want it to be Ben. For both of them."

"I will."

Nevvie led the way through the curtain. Karen gasped. Peggy seemed prepared and nodded.

"He'll be okay, girls. I know he will."

Nevvie stood at the end of the bed and let them have time with him. She absently stroked his right foot through the sheet and started to run through things in her mind. She'd need to talk to Karen in private, ask her to stay for a few weeks. She'd give her money to pay her bills so she could take the time off from work. She had to get with Kenny and Cal and Maggie at the office—crap! Another call to make.

She'd need to get organized, buy a calendar book so she could track doctor appointments and prescriptions and everything else. So much to do. More anguished tears threatened and she forced them back.

After twenty minutes, the women were ready to go. They all stopped by Tyler's bed one more time before finding the men in the waiting room.

"Bob, I have to call Tommy's office," Nevvie said.

"I'll do it. I know Maggie."

"Thank you." She looked at Pete. "Do you want to see them?"

His eyes looked red. Apparently the large man with the rough façade wasn't as tough as he portrayed. "Yeah. Can I?"

Nevvie held out her hand. "Of course you can. You're family."

He did okay with Tyler. The sight of Thomas's battered face finished him and he openly wept. "Nevvie, I'm sorry. It's just...dammit, I've known them for years. I knew Tyler before he ever met Tommy, you know that. They're like my brothers."

Nevvie's turn to comfort him. "I know."

"We can't let Eddie in here. He'll be a blubbering mess."

"I hope Eddie doesn't mind playing nanny for a few weeks. I'm going to need him."

"He loves the Ant, you know that." Eddie had nicknamed Adam "Ant" after one of his favorite rock singers. "Thank God he doesn't have a uterus or we'd have twenty kids by now."

Nevvie laughed. Pete always cracked her up.

He squeezed Tom's hand. "Don't worry, buddy," he said to Thomas. "We're taking care of them. You get to feeling better."

* * * *

It was after six o'clock. Nevvie felt she'd cried gallons of tears since waking up that morning. She got her keys from Peggy and drove the three of them to the house while Bob ran Pete home. Bob would bunk on the pullout sofa in Tom's study while Peggy and Karen shared the bed in the guest room.

Nevvie didn't relish the thought of sleeping alone in their bed, but she didn't want anyone else sleeping there. Her boys would be home soon. Then it would be the three of them again. It was one small piece of normality she could cling to, something to keep her wanting to put one foot in front of the other.

Pete returned to the house in his car and brought Chinese food and reports of the Ant's activities for the day. "Eddie will bring him by in an hour or so to visit and get more supplies."

"Can you keep him overnight? I'm sorry to impose."

"Babe, what part of 'you don't have to ask' don't you understand? You know we'll do anything for you guys."

"Thanks, Pete." Pete had remembered Nevvie's fondness for lo mein. Not remembering which kind, he brought three different varieties as well as enough food to feed half the Chinese Army. They'd never eat it all, but she was grateful for the gesture.

Maggie stopped by, her face red from crying. She started sobbing again as she hugged Nevvie. "I'm so sorry, Nev. They'll be okay, won't they?"

Nevvie vocalized the mantra she suspected would keep her going over the next days and weeks. "They're strong, and they're tough. They'll come back to me. I'm going back to the hospital in a little while. Want to see them?"

"Can I?"

"Of course you can."

They would have a full house. April and Cheryl would drive down the day after tomorrow and hadn't told the two eldest sisters squat, as per their mother's orders. They could only stay a couple of days and would take over the pullout in Tom's office. Bob could either go home or sleep on the sofa in the living room.

Eddie arrived with Adam. Nevvie fought a new round of tears as she took her son from him. She closed her eyes and pressed her lips against Adam's smooth forehead. She held him for a few minutes then passed him to Karen, who hadn't seen him in over two months.

Staring into Adam's blue eyes—Tyler's blue eyes—was both a comfort and a stabbing pain in Nevvie's soul.

Nevvie gathered what Eddie would need for Adam and took a few minutes to wash her face in the bathroom. She barely recognized herself, between the red, puffy eyes and dark circles. She'd woken up happy and in heaven. In a few hours, she'd go to bed in the depths of hell.

Maggie followed her to the hospital. Nevvie led her to the ICU. She took a deep breath and said a silent prayer before stepping through the unit doors with Maggie.

Tyler could be sleeping except for the ventilator and IVs. It was easy to picture him coming home soon. Nevvie steeled herself for Maggie's choked sob when she led her to Tom's bedside.

They didn't stay long. Maggie hugged her out in the parking lot before driving away. Nevvie got into her car and sat for a moment without starting it. Then she rested her forehead on the steering wheel and screamed at the top of her lungs for several long, agonizing minutes until she couldn't scream anymore. Only when she felt she could hold it together in front of the others did she drive home.

Chapter Nine

Nevvie gave her keys to Karen. "Drive my car while you're here. I'll drive Tyler's." Saying the words nearly choked her up. She couldn't bear the thought of driving Tommy's Ridgeline. She tried to sleep and couldn't, even with the boys' pillows stacked around her.

Curled alone in their bed, her mind drifted back to that very first day when she moved in. She'd been cleaning for the boys for six months when they asked her to move in as their assistant, afraid to confess their feelings for her. She'd eagerly agreed, but then Alex beat her to a bloody pulp when he spotted a necklace the boys had given her for her birthday.

When she didn't show up as arranged, the boys came looking for her. She remembered the stormy anger in Tommy's sweet eyes as he pushed Alex off her. The worry in Tyler's face as he protectively scooped her into his arms and carried her out of the rat hole apartment.

Forever theirs from that moment on, although it took awhile for the boys to admit their feelings to her.

She vaguely remembered sobbing in this very bed as her boys held her, the pain in her bruised and battered body vying with the relief she felt to be safe with them.

Her boys.

She couldn't lose them. *Please God, don't take them from me.*

Nevvie couldn't sleep. She called the hospital every hour to check on them, tried to control the emotion in her voice. Ben was sweet and understood how upset she was.

Carol took over again for the day shift. Nevvie drifted through her day, shuttling between her boys and the waiting room, drinking what felt like gallons of coffee to stay awake, making calls, answering as many of Bob's questions as she could in regards to Tommy's business, fielding calls between Tyler's agent and publicist and all their friends. Pete and Eddie again brought dinner over. Finally, a little after nine and at everyone's urging, Nevvie went to bed and tried to sleep.

Around three a.m. she gave up and took a long, hot shower. Even that simple act invoked sad thoughts. She hadn't been alone like this in…well, since her hospital stay after the second attack when Alex stabbed her. Since being with her boys she always slept with one or both men at night, never alone.

She left a note for the others and quietly let herself out. With the roads empty, she made it to the hospital in less than ten minutes. She brought two paperbacks with her, the ones Tyler and Thomas were currently reading.

Ben was on duty again. "Couldn't sleep?"

"No. Not without my boys. I figured it'd be quiet here now, maybe I could visit longer."

"Sure." He glanced at the desk. "I'll run interference. Just pull the curtain."

She went to Thomas first and pulled a chair close to the head of his bed so she could lean in and be inches from his ear. She turned to the page he'd bookmarked. In a soft voice, she started reading to him.

An hour later she kissed him on the forehead. "I need to go visit our guy now. I'll be back later. Mom and Karen will be here to see you today, too."

Restraints had been placed on Tyler's hands. Startled, she looked for Ben. "It's okay," he reassured her. "They've backed off on his pain meds and sedation. They can't pull the breathing tube until they know for sure he's stable. It's standard procedure. Some patients claw at the tube. We don't want him ripping it out. Once he's awake and the doctors are happy, they'll remove the tube and the restraints will come off."

Nevvie took up her position by Tyler on his right side and read to him. A few minutes before six she prepared to leave as the shift change started. She squeezed Tyler's hand. "I need to go, sweetie. I'll be back in a couple of hours."

He squeezed back.

Startled, Nevvie froze. "Ty," she whispered, "do that again."

He squeezed.

"Ben!"

The nurse ran in, alarmed. "What's wrong?"

"Watch! Tyler, honey, squeeze my hand."

He did.

The nurse checked his vital signs. "That's good."

"His eyes aren't open."

"That's okay. He's responsive, that's a good sign. Mr. Paulson, can you squeeze your wife's hand again for me please?"

He did.

Nevvie choked back a relieved sob. "I love you, Tyler. I love you so much. You're going to be okay, baby. I'm going to take care of you, and you'll be okay."

He squeezed her hand.

Carol came on duty again. Between her and Ben they bent the rules and kept the curtains shut and let Nevvie stay with Tyler during the shift change. Tyler kept squeezing her hand on command. Nevvie sat staring at Tyler, whispering to him, begging him to open his eyes. A few minutes before seven, he finally did.

"Tyler! Oh, sweetie!" She cried with relief. He was back.

His eyes fluttered closed again and she felt him pull against the restraint. She held his hand. "Don't do that, honey. Once they take the breathing tube out, they'll take these off."

He opened his eyes again and looked around the room without moving his head, then back to her. His deep blue eyes were the best sight she'd ever seen.

She knew what he wanted to know.

"It's two days later. Tommy's...asleep." Okay, technically the truth. "It's around seven in the morning. I couldn't sleep. Bob and the doctors helped me get the rules bent so I could come in when I wanted."

Tyler's eyes narrowed as he fought his way through the drugs' foggy grip. *Nevvie*, that gaze said. *Tell me the truth.*

She forced a smile. "Everything's okay. You had a heart attack. Peggy gave you CPR and they had to do surgery, but you're going to be fine."

His eyes closed again. He squeezed her hand, hard and long, before relaxing.

"You're in Tampa Community." He looked at her. "You want to know what's funny? You're next to the bed I was in."

He couldn't laugh but his eyes crinkled slightly in amusement.

"I knew you'd like that," she said. She glanced to make sure they were alone and leaned in closer. "You scared your little slave, Master," she whispered. His eyes squeezed shut in what she recognized as an attempt not to laugh.

"I'm sorry, but I had to say that." She smiled. "See? If I can crack jokes, you know everything's all right." She met his eyes and couldn't hold back her tears. "You really scared me. I thought I'd lost you. The EMTs had to use the defibrillator to get your heart going again."

He squeezed her hand, then let go and shook his, as if trying to signal something.

"What?"

He mimed writing.

"You don't need to work, for Christ's sake! Let's get you home first."

He rolled his eyes, grabbed her hand and squeezed hard, then mimed writing again. It finally hit her.

"Oh! I'm sorry. Hold on." She found Carol, who brought her a clipboard, paper, and a pen. Nevvie held the clipboard for him while he wrote.

Where's T?

Nevvie forced her face and voice to remain steady. The spooky connection she had with Tyler wouldn't help her in this case, it would make things worse.

"I told you, he's sleeping."

His eyes narrowed. He wrote again.

Lie.

"I'm not lying."

He tapped the clipboard with the pen and glared at her.

"Tyler. You have to calm down. You're just waking up from the sedation. Karen flew down from Savannah. April and Cheryl will be down today, everyone's back at the house. Bob's even spending the night." She took a deep breath, needed to distract him. "They didn't want to leave me alone. I had a pretty bad meltdown before you got out of surgery."

He closed his eyes for a moment then wrote again.

Sorry.

"No, don't apologize. I just felt...overwhelmed. I didn't handle the stress very well."

Tyler knew she'd lied to him. He didn't understand why, but Nevvie couldn't lie to him any more than he could lie to her. Not successfully, at least.

If Thomas was around and all right, she wouldn't *be* left alone. She wouldn't be speaking as if Thomas wasn't around. Tyler knew she didn't realize what she'd said.

He gripped the pen tighter. *Love you.*

She kissed him. "I love you, too. Baby, you don't know how much I love you."

A?

"Uncles Eddie and Pete."

OK

Nevvie reached across the bed. "I want you to have this back."

She slipped his wedding band onto his finger and squeezed his hand. "You're not allowed to scare me like that ever again, got it?"

He nodded. That's when he noticed her right hand and felt a chill wash through him.

She wore Thomas' wedding band on her thumb. Thomas never took it off, except to work on the car. He wouldn't have it off now.

He'd be standing by Nevvie's side, with her, not letting her go through this alone.

Whatever had happened while he was unconscious, Tyler knew he wouldn't find out from her. He wrote again.

Go eat. Now.

"I don't want to leave you."

Their one-sided discussion was interrupted by rounds. The cardiologist sounded cheerful and positive.

"We'll get that breathing tube out of you soon, Mr. Paulson, then we can get you up and out of bed sometime today. I know it's uncomfortable, but as I told your wife, it's necessary."

Tyler nodded, trying not to stare at Thomas' ring on Nevvie's hand. There was only one reason Tyler could think of that she'd be wearing it, and he didn't want to contemplate it.

As the doctor left, Tyler noticed Nevvie glanced out of the room. He tapped the clipboard again. *Go eat. Now.*

She finally smiled. "Okay. I'll be back soon. Everyone wants to see you."

You take nap.

"We'll see." She kissed his forehead, stroked his cheek. "I love you. I thought I was going to lose you."

He tapped the paper. *Love you.*

He noticed she closed the curtain behind her as she left, so he couldn't see where she went.

* * * *

Nevvie slipped into Thomas' cubicle with the doctors, pulled the sliding doors shut behind her, and kept her voice low as she spoke with them about his condition. Thank God for the solid walls and doors between the bed areas. Still wait and see. Nothing that could be done short-term except monitor him and wait for the swelling to go down.

"Okay. Please, remember, I don't want Tyler knowing he's here."

Tyler still had the breathing tube in place when Nevvie visited an hour later. The restraints had been loosened enough he could easily write but still not reach the breathing tube. He'd taken the time to write a few things on the clipboard. He tapped it, showing her.

What's going on? Where's T? What aren't you telling me? Be honest.

She looked at him, tears in her eyes. "Everything's fine. Don't you trust me?"

He studied her. Of course he trusted her. He also knew she would withhold information, thinking it would help, probably worried the news would give him another heart attack. He wrote on the pad. *Tell me.*

Her eyes flicked to his, then away. More confirmation of his suspicions.

"There's nothing to tell. Peggy and everyone else will be here in a little while. I need to talk to your doctors, and I need to take care of some things. I'll be back in a few hours."

He nodded. Before she could leave again he tapped on the clipboard to get her attention. *Leave curtain open pls.*

"Okay." She kissed his forehead and quickly left.

Now he had a clear view of the duty board attached to the side of the nurse's station. He'd glimpsed it off and on all morning as people came and went from his bed area. Finally, he could read it. Unfortunately his earlier views proved correct.

He knew he occupied bed twelve, and there he was, listed on the board: *T. Paulson, Carol, HOCM/SM, Robertson.*

In bed thirteen, the line below his name: *T. Kinsey, Carol, TBI-m/c acc, Gonzales/Spivey.*

Tyler closed his eyes and cried.

* * * *

He'd composed himself a few minutes later when Carol returned with a doctor.

"Mr. Paulson? We're going to remove your breathing tube." It felt like they spent forever checking his breathing before finally pulling the tube. Carol removed his restraints and after some coughing and gagging they raised his bed so he could sit up and gasp for air.

"Are you okay?" the doctor asked.

"I wish to stand up," he croaked.

"Let's let you settle for a little while. Just relax. We'll let you get out of bed in a few hours but we need to pull your catheter first. Right now, sit up in bed, don't rush it."

Tyler croaked, "Water?"

The doctor nodded. "A few sips at first. Take it slow." He noted the chart and left.

Carol brought him a cup of water and a straw, holding it for him while he drank.

"Thanks."

"No problem, Mr. Paulson."

He grabbed her hand. "Where's Thomas?"

The nurse froze. "Mr. Paulson, I'm not sure who you mean."

She was lying, he sensed it. He released her. "My partner, Thomas Kinsey. He hasn't been in with Nevvie."

"Do you want me to call your wife for you?"

"You took care of Nevvie before, didn't you? I recognize you."

"Yes."

"Where is he?"

She wouldn't meet his gaze. "Mr. Paulson, I'm sorry, but I need to check on my other patient." She quickly left. It looked like she went into the cubicle next to his. If he remembered the layout correctly, it would be bed thirteen.

He laid back and tried to relax. He hurt like hell, almost felt like his chest had been cut open from breastbone to bollocks although he didn't have the nerve to look or touch the area yet. He dropped off to sleep for a while. Over an hour later, when Carol returned, he pushed the issue.

"I wish to stand up. I need to use the bathroom."

"I can get you a bedpan."

"No. I wish to get up."

She finally relented. "Let me check with your doctor first to make sure it's okay. If it is, I need to get some help." She returned a few minutes later with an aide. They removed Tyler's Foley catheter, unhooked his monitor leads and juggled his IV poles around so he could use the small recessed toilet in the corner. When he finished he stood and, holding on to the bed for balance, he slowly shuffled toward the front of the cubicle.

"Mr. Paulson, you have to get back in bed."

"I'm going to check on my neighbor next door. You don't mind, do you?"

The nurse's face fell and he knew he was correct. Steeling himself for their protests, he pushed on. "Either bring the IV poles or I'll rip the bloody things out," he softly said. "You aren't stopping me." He hurt like hell. He wasn't nearly as steady on his feet as he pretended to be, but he had to see for himself.

Finally giving in, the women followed him. Tyler paused at the drawn curtain. He thought he was prepared for anything, but the sight of Tom's handsome face battered and bruised nearly beyond recognition almost brought him to his knees. He grabbed the end of the bed and held on as his knees weakened.

"Oh, my poor, sweet Thomas," he whispered.

The nurse took his arm. "Let's get you back to bed."

"I wish to sit with him. Get me a chair, please."

"Mr. Paulson—"

He couldn't pull his gaze from Thomas. His tears flowed. "Please," he begged, "just let me sit with him for a while. We've been together seventeen years. Surely you can't deny me a few minutes with him?"

She finally relented, setting him in a recliner on Thomas' left side, with pillows and a blanket to make him comfortable. She brought in a portable cart with monitors and reconnected him, and hooked him up to an oxygen cannula. "Look, don't get me fired. Worse, you're gonna get your wife pissed at me."

He shook his head and held Thomas' hand. "I'll handle her," he said, his eyes never leaving Tom's face. "I need to talk to his doctors. Please."

* * * *

Tyler spoke to Tommy's doctors, his own doctor, and called Bob's cell. Fortunately Nevvie was on the phone with Eddie when Tyler called Bob.

"Don't tell her you're coming. I need to see you right now."

"Déjà vu all over again," Bob quipped.

"Don't make jokes. It hurts too much to laugh."

"Sorry. I'll be there in a few minutes."

Tyler still sat at Thomas' bedside when Bob arrived.

"Close the doors and curtains, please," he asked.

Bob did, giving them more privacy.

"How is she? Really?"

Bob shook his head. "Again with the déjà vu. Didn't I have this conversation with her a few years ago in this same ICU? Do you have an asshole administrator on your case, too?"

Tyler managed a wan smile. "Seriously, how is she holding up?"

He leaned against the wall, on the other side of Thomas' bed.

"She's been better. We had a close call when she found out about Tommy."

Tyler knew Bob wasn't telling the full truth but didn't press further. "My poor girl. What would we do without you, Bob?"

"Yeah, you say that now. Wait 'til you get my bill," he teased. "She seems a lot stronger today. I think the shock has worn off. With you awake she was like a new woman when she got back to the house. If one of you had died I think she'd be in a hospital bed, too."

"According to them, I did die."

"Yeah, but you damn paranormal authors are like vampires, just keep coming back."

"Ow! Bob, please. No jokes."

"Sorry." He looked at Thomas. "How is he today?"

"They can't tell us anything. It's wait and see."

"I hate to be the bringer of bad news, but we need to look to the future. That's what you pay me to do."

"If he can't go back to work?"

Bob nodded. "Who runs the business, should you sell it, all of that. He could be back at work in a month, he might be dependent upon the two of you for the rest of his life."

Tyler willed Thomas to open his eyes even though he knew medication kept him in a coma. How was their poor girl supposed to take care of both of them? Tyler knew he was her emotional support, but Thomas was every bit as much a grounding foundation for him as for Nevvie.

How did they manage without him?

"We don't need to decide all that today, do we?"

"No. I just need you to keep it in the back of your mind. Nevvie is in no condition to think about it. I haven't even mentioned it. I've already talked with Kenny and Maggie. For the duration, I'm supervising operations at Kinsey Consulting. Nevvie needs to focus on you guys and Adam."

* * * *

Nevvie drove Peggy and Karen to the hospital. She felt a lot stronger knowing Tyler was awake. How long could she stall him? Certainly once they removed the breathing tube he'd be asking questions and she couldn't keep lying to him.

They walked into the ICU. When they approached Tyler's bed, Nevvie panicked when she didn't see him. The door and curtain to Tommy's bed were pulled closed.

They found Carol. "Where's Tyler?"

"Calm down."

Peggy tapped Nevvie's shoulder and pointed as Bob emerged from Thomas' alcove. Nevvie glared at him and pushed past, freezing when she saw Tyler seated next to Tom's bed. He looked up at her.

She turned on Bob. "You told him? I trusted you!"

"Nevvie." Tyler's soft, firm voice stopped her in her tracks. "Come here, love." He held up his hand and, unable to resist him, she went. "He didn't tell me, sweet. I figured it out." He pointed to the duty board. "I saw it on there. And I saw this." He touched Thomas' ring on her hand.

She closed her eyes and cried, kneeling in front of him, her head in his lap.

"Shh," he soothed, stroking her hair. "It's okay. I'm all right."

"I didn't want you to worry. I was afraid it would…that you would…" She couldn't continue, sobbed against him.

"Love, didn't you know I'd figure it out sooner or later?"

"I didn't think that far ahead," she admitted. "I had you back. I didn't want to lose you again. I wanted to wait until I knew you were stronger."

"I'm all right, sweetheart." He looked at the others. "Can we have a few minutes alone, please?"

Bob walked outside to wait with Peggy and Karen.

"Love, stand up."

She did.

He held Thomas' hand. "Let's put that back where it belongs."

She cried and slipped the ring from her thumb onto Tom's finger. Tyler captured her hand. Together they held Tommy's.

"Love," he whispered, meeting her eyes, "he *will* come back to us. Please don't stress yourself. You need to stay calm for him and for Adam."

"He told me on the phone, before he left Ft. Myers, while you were in surgery…" She closed her eyes. "He told me to tell you he loves you. That if I saw you first, to tell you for him."

Tyler somehow managed to hold onto his composure. "All right, love. Thank you." Talk about irony. She'd told Thomas to relay the identical message to him after Alex stabbed her.

He kissed Tom's hand and gently placed it on the bed, stroked him with his fingers. "Help me up, please. And call the nurse. I think Peggy and Karen should be alone with him, if they choose. I'm ready to go back to bed."

As Nevvie and Bob helped the nurses settle Tyler, Peggy and Karen hovered around Thomas. Finally, thirty minutes later, they came to Tyler's bed.

"Hiya, Blue Eyes," Karen said, her voice much softer and more somber than normal. She leaned over and kissed him on the forehead. "You sure are a frickin' drama queen, you know that?"

He weakly smiled. "I'm sorry I scared everyone."

Nevvie had sat at his side, holding his left hand, ever since he'd returned to bed. "Quit apologizing, Tyler. Next time you don't feel good you're getting dragged to the doctor, like it or not."

"Yes, love." He looked at Peggy. "Thank you, Mom."

"For what, sugar?"

"For saving my life."

"You think I'm letting you get outta raising my grandson, you're off your nut." Her tone sounded ragged but she smiled. "You just get better so you can help Nevvie with Tommy."

"You'd better believe it." He squeezed Nevvie's hand. "Did you eat today?"

"Not yet."

"Go eat," he ordered. "I'll be here when you get back." He gently tugged on her hand. She stood and kissed him.

"You'd better be here."

"Not like I'm running a marathon this afternoon, pet."

Nevvie visited Thomas again before she left. She leaned over and placed a long, lingering kiss on his forehead and stroked his arm. "Come back to us, Tommy," she softly pleaded. "Please. You have to come back to us. We love you."

They rode to the house in silence. Nevvie called Eddie to bring the baby home.

Eddie arrived after Nevvie had finished eating. Bob had gone to his office but would return later, and Pete had errands to run. Karen and Peggy drove to the grocery store to get more food before April and Cheryl arrived.

Eddie's red eyes and puffy nose betrayed him. He handed Adam to her and smiled. "There's Momma, you big chub."

Adam babbled and grabbed Nevvie's hair. She closed her eyes and inhaled clean baby scent. Eddie was, not counting Peggy and Karen, the world's best babysitter. "Thank you, Eddie. I appreciate it. I don't know what I would do without you and Pete."

He touched her shoulder. "Hey, you don't ever have to worry, you know that. Whatever, whenever you need something, you say it and it's done."

"You want to go say hi to them?"

He looked at his feet. "Pete warned me maybe I shouldn't see Tommy yet."

"Well, he's out. It won't bother him if you cry."

He rubbed his nose. "I don't want to get Ty worked up."

"It's okay," she gently said. "The evil genius has assured me he won't go into shock if we get emotional around him."

He sniffled. "Okay. Yeah, I'd like to see them."

She installed the car seat in Tyler's Lexus and loaded the baby and his stuff. Eddie followed her to the hospital. The found Tyler sitting up in bed, dozing.

When he heard them he opened his eyes. "Hey."

Eddie leaned over and gave him a careful one-armed hug. "Man, don't you ever scare us like that again, you friggin' jackass."

"Thank you for taking care of them, Eddie. You and Pete are truly the best." He reached for the baby. Nevvie shook her head. "No, you can't lift him yet." She carefully laid him next to Tyler. The baby looked up at his father and smiled, softly babbled.

"Are you sure you should bring him in here, love?"

"I wanted him to see his daddies. I know I shouldn't bring him in the hospital, but today I had to."

"It's okay, sweet. I understand."

Tyler stroked the baby's hand. Adam grabbed his finger, squeezed it. Nevvie sat next to the bed and rested her chin on her arms on the bed rail.

Tyler looked at Eddie. "Did our little demon give you any grief?"

Eddie finally smiled. "The Ant tried to eat his way through house and home. I should have nicknamed him 'the Termite.' He's always fun to have around. My sister's kids are all obnoxious teenagers now. They won't make me an uncle again for a few years yet."

Carol came in to check Tyler's vital signs. "Sorry to run you guys out for a few minutes."

"That's okay," Nevvie said, scooping up the baby after Tyler gave him a kiss. "I appreciate you giving us the extra time. We'll go see Tommy."

The nursing staff kept the curtains drawn around his bed. Nevvie turned to Eddie. "He looks a lot worse than he is. Keep thinking that, okay?"

"Okay." His eyes already brimmed with tears. He wiped at them with a handkerchief.

The lights over Tom's bed were dimmed. It did nothing to soften his ugly black eyes and other injuries.

Nevvie looked at Eddie. He clapped a hand over his mouth, trying to choke back his sob. She slipped her free arm around his waist and hugged him.

"He'll be okay, Eddie. I know he will. Tyler said he will, so it has to be true, right?"

Eddie nodded a little too strenuously. He took a deep, gasping breath as he finally dropped his hand. She encouraged him to sit by the bed while she stood at the end, stroking Tom's right foot through the sheet while she balanced the baby on her hip. She'd need to find out about physical therapy for him, one of the doctors had mentioned it.

After ten minutes, Eddie was more than ready to go. Nevvie carefully held Adam close to Tommy, reaching out his hand so he could stroke his father's cheek.

"Poppa's going to be fine," she whispered. "I know he will."

They stopped by Tyler's bed one more time to say good-bye before they walked out to the parking lot. Eddie slumped against his car and cried. Adam reached for him, also crying, which set Nevvie off. The three of them cried together, Eddie's arms wrapped around her and the baby, for several minutes.

Eddie finally composed himself. "Let me know when you need me to take him again, okay?" He chucked the sniffling baby under his chin and blew a raspberry at him. Adam immediately smiled, babbled, and blew one back.

Nevvie laughed, trying to wipe her own tears. "Thanks. With Cheryl and April around they'll want to spend time with him, but they'll only be here a couple of days. That'll give you time to recharge," she joked.

He kissed her on the forehead. "Anytime, Nev. You know that."

He left. She buckled the baby into the car seat and headed for the house. She beat Peggy and Karen home by a few minutes. Nevvie handed Adam off to Karen and helped Peggy unload and put away the groceries. When Peggy went to change clothes, Nevvie pressed a check into Karen's hand.

"Nev, what's this?"

Nevvie held Karen's hand closed around the check and kept her voice low. "I'm going to need you here, and I know you can't afford to take time off work. This is between you and me. Don't you dare think about saying no. You let me know if it's enough to pay your bills. If it's not, I'll give you whatever you need. I don't want Mom running herself ragged."

Karen's eyes watered as she hugged Nevvie. "Thank you," she said. "This is one time I won't argue with you."

Nevvie and Karen had grown close since Nevvie joined Thomas and Tyler. Nevvie knew Karen didn't discuss her finances with her family. Karen did okay, but she was too proud to ask for help and, like most people, she couldn't afford to just take off for long periods of time.

"Will your boss give you the time off?"

Karen wiped her eyes with the back of her hand and slipped the check into her pocket. "Yeah. I've worked for them for years. They were going to let me use my two weeks vacation and then the rest as unpaid leave."

"Keep your vacation time. You'll need it for yourself once we're through this mess." Nevvie forced a smile. "Seriously, Kar, whatever you need, ask, it's yours."

Karen met Nevvie's gaze. "Do you really think Tommy's going to be okay?"

"Tyler said he will, that's good enough for me."

"Ole' Blue Eyes snaps his fingers, Tommy will jump through hoops," Karen joked. "He always has. All these years."

"Yeah, and with me and Tyler ganging up on him to get better, plus all of you, he has to be okay, right?"

Being Tommy's older sister, Karen was more than willing to play along and agree. "Right."

Chapter Ten

Nevvie tossed and turned and gave up trying to sleep a little after one in the morning. She changed clothes, grabbed a few things, and left a note for the others so they knew where she went. Peggy and Karen had already told her they would take care of Adam if he woke in the middle of the night.

Ben was on duty and nodded when he saw her. Tyler was asleep. Nevvie stepped into Tom's cubicle and waved Ben in. "Don't tell Tyler I'm here, please. He needs his sleep."

He noticed her tote bag. "You getting any sleep?"

"Not without my boys I'm not. Can I ask a favor?" She explained what she wanted to do.

"Give me a few minutes to get you some towels and soap and a basin. Need any help?"

She looked at Tommy and shook her head. "No. Just show me what not to do so I don't hurt him."

"No problem." Ben went in search of what she'd need while she removed a few items from her bag. Ben returned, explained what to do then stepped out. "I'll be out here working on his chart if you need me."

"Thanks." Ben pulled the curtain and door shut.

She'd brought her MP3 player and headphones. With the volume turned up and the headphones on the bed, it sounded just loud enough for the two of them to hear.

Well, she could hear it, at least.

She set it to Tommy's favorite Jimmy Buffett album, one they both loved.

Fighting her tears, she ran warm water in the plastic wash basin Ben had brought her, tucked a towel around Tom's neck, and used a wash cloth to sponge his cheeks. Then she applied shaving gel and carefully shaved him. Tommy usually used an electric razor and he was religious about shaving. Nevvie couldn't stand the increasing shade of stubble across his cheeks and didn't want the staff to do it. She was his wife, she would take care of him.

Working slowly around his mouth so she didn't disturb the ventilator tube, she took her time and then gently stroked his face with her fingers when she finished fifteen minutes later. Nevvie made sure she sponged off all remaining soap residue. She patted his face dry and kissed his smooth cheek.

"That's better, sweetie," she softly said.

She dumped the basin and refilled it with warm water. As she started to unsnap the shoulder of his gown there was a light tap on the door and she heard it slide open beyond the curtain. Ben stuck his head in. "He wants to come in. And no, I didn't tell him you were here. He woke up and asked how long you'd been here."

Nevvie tried to stifle her laugh. "He's freaky."

"I'm getting that."

She went to help Ben get Tyler out of bed. His hair looked disheveled but he sat up, his legs over the edge of the bed.

"You're sneaky, love," he mumbled.

"How did you know I was here?" Ben juggled the IVs and monitor leads, silencing the alarms when he disconnected Tyler. He'd bring the portable monitor cart into Thomas' room once they had him settled.

Tyler looked at her. "You look as bloody awful as I feel, and you never have been able to sleep alone. I wasn't quite asleep when you arrived. It just took me a while to get conscious enough to get up."

When she kissed him on the cheek he touched her face. "I'll be all right, love. Quit worrying about me. You need to take care of yourself, right?"

"I'm okay. I just need you both home so I have my boys back."

She hooked her arm through his, helping support him as they walked him to the recliner next to Thomas' bed. Once Ben had him hooked up again and situated, he closed the curtains and door and left them alone.

Tyler's eyes glistened. For a moment Nevvie thought he would cry. She hoped he didn't, because if he did, she would too. He didn't though. He reached through the bed rail and slipped his fingers through Tom's. He gently stroked the back of Tom's hand with his thumb.

"He looks much better, love. Thank you."

"You know how he is. If he comes to looking like Sasquatch, he'll kill us both."

Tyler started to laugh then groaned. "Ow, love, no snark. Not yet."

She smiled. "Sorry." Nevvie tested the water in the basin, it was still warm enough. Starting on her side, Tom's right, she carefully bathed him, making sure to rinse all the soap from him and thoroughly pat him dry. She worked her way from his shoulders down his abdomen, avoiding his surgical dressings.

Tyler's eyes followed her every movement. She knew he wanted to help and it had to be killing him that he couldn't.

She carefully massaged Tom's arms and hands, as much as she could with the IV lines taped to him. Tyler leaned back so she could slide between him and the bed and take care of Tom's left arm. That left his lower body.

The left leg was out of the question. Ben had assured her if she didn't move Tom, she could wash his foot. She'd leave that until last.

While she'd had a catheter during her stay in the hospital, and knew that Tom had one, it still startled her to see it in place. She carefully washed and dried him, not using soap around his groin, afraid of irritating his skin. Then she washed his right leg and foot, gently massaging them, carefully working them the way the physical therapist had showed her.

Ben checked on them every so often. After an hour she was seated on Tom's other side, his hand in hers, her head resting against the bed and dozing lightly as the MP3 player played.

Tyler watched her nap, his heart breaking for her, angry that he couldn't take care of her, of them, they way they needed him. When Ben next checked, Tyler lifted a finger to his lips. Ben quietly stepped into the room and edged around Tyler to check both men's vital signs and IVs and then leaned close.

"Have you considered talking to your attorney about admitting her? No offense, she looks horrible. She looks like she's near collapse."

"It wouldn't do any good. She'd simply run herself ragged here. At least she can try to rest at home, have a little normalcy."

"You're a couple of lucky guys to have someone like her watching over you."

Tyler nodded. "I thank God for my sweet angel every day."

Nevvie slept for over an hour. When she lifted her head with a start she looked disoriented, dazed.

"Are you all right, love?" Tyler asked.

Nevvie yawned, wincing when she sat up. "A little better. Are you okay?"

"I think I'm ready to go back to bed."

She jumped to her feet, fully awake and at his side to help. It both warmed and shamed Tyler that she was ready to help and him so helpless. She was his angel, he'd promised to take care of her. She shouldn't be saddled with this horrible burden.

Ben came in to help. Tyler held onto Nevvie's arm as they slowly made their way back to his bed and got him settled. He motioned her close and gently kissed her on the lips. His hand slid to the nape of her neck and he pulled her down so her ear was by his mouth.

"My sweet little slave," he breathed, "your master orders you to go home and rest."

Her body tensed before a smile crept across her weary face. She looked near tears as she stroked his cheek. "You're *really* going to be okay?"

"That's what I keep telling you, sweetheart. But we don't need you collapsing from exhaustion. I want you to go home, try to sleep. Rest, at least. Don't come back here before," he glanced at the clock, "ten this morning. Right?"

She nodded and kissed him one last time. "Okay. I need to get my stuff from Tom's room." She weaved her fingers through Tyler's. "I miss you guys so much."

He squeezed her hand. "I'll be in a regular room in another day or so, love. You can stay longer then, at least nap with me. That will be easier on you, I should think." He raised her hand to his lips and kissed it. "Seriously, I want you to lie down and try to rest, right?"

"Okay."

When she left he settled in and closed his eyes.

* * * *

Tyler's fifth day in the hospital brought good news. Nevvie had just arrived a little before ten, after spending several early morning hours at their bedsides before going home for breakfast and a shower. The doctor flipped through his chart and smiled.

"Well, Mr. Paulson, we're going to transfer you out of ICU this morning."

Nevvie brightened. "Really?"

"Yep. You'll be in a telemetry unit for a few days. We already discussed this. As long as everything continues to look as good as it does now, we'll be sending you home in a few days."

Nevvie squeezed Tyler's hand. One step closer. And a good thing too, because she felt like she was about ready to collapse. Despite her stress and exhaustion, she couldn't sleep. Add to that the gallons of coffee she drank to keep herself awake and it wasn't healthy. Not that she'd ever admit any of that to Tyler and worry him.

She was still there when the nurses moved him soon after. Nevvie carried Tyler's personal items and followed as the nurses pushed his bed to the elevator. Ten minutes later he was settled in a private room and just in time for lunch to be served.

He wrinkled his nose at the bland meal. Nevvie laughed and removed the cover from the bowl of chicken broth. "You're going to eat every last bite of this meal, buster," she groused.

"And you'll stand there and make sure I do, won't you?"

She grinned and grabbed a spoon. "If I have to force feed you myself."

He reached out and touched her hand. When their eyes met, Nevvie dissolved into tears. He carefully scooted over in the bed and she climbed in next to him. Ten minutes later she'd cried herself to sleep. When Peggy and Karen arrived to visit an hour later after handing Adam off to Eddie, Nevvie was still sound asleep. Tyler's lunch had gone cold, but Peggy talked with his nurse and got him a fresh one and helped him eat, all without waking Nevvie. Karen went downstairs to sit with Tommy.

"It's probably the first good sleep she's had since this happened," Peggy whispered.

"I suspected as much." He was afraid to move for fear of waking Nevvie. The deep, dark circles under her eyes broke his heart.

"I don't think she's slept more than an hour or two at a time," Peggy said. "We can't keep her home, you know that. She can't sleep, she comes to the hospital in the middle of the night."

"How bad was she when she found out about Thomas? Really?"

He could tell Peggy didn't want to answer. "I don't want to talk about that, Ty. We don't need to talk about it. It's done and over."

Peggy sat with Tyler. April and Cheryl stopped by then switched off with Karen for a while in ICU. The women went downstairs for an early supper, and still Nevvie slept. They all agreed with Tyler it was best to let Nevvie sleep as long as possible. Nine hours after crawling into bed with Tyler, she stirred, then startled.

"It's all right, love," he soothed, holding her hand.

She looked dazed and disoriented. "What time is it?"

"Nearly nine."

She started to sit up but he laid a hand on her arm. "Just lie here for a little longer. Please?"

She nodded and relaxed against him. "Where is everyone?"

He knew from the groggy sound of her voice she was still in no condition to get up yet. "They went home a couple of hours ago."

"I need to check on Tommy."

"He's fine, love. You will stay right here with me for a while longer."

"Okay." A half hour later she felt awake enough to get out of bed. She used the bathroom then helped Tyler get up and go. Peggy and Karen had helped him out of bed at one point when he couldn't hold it any longer. Surprisingly, Nevvie had slept through him getting up. Just more proof to him that she was beyond exhausted.

He took her hand when he was back in bed. "Listen to me. I want you go to home, take a shower, and relax. I understand you are having trouble sleeping, but you cannot exhaust yourself like this again. I won't allow it, do you hear me?"

She smiled. "I don't think it's that easy, but I'll try."

"Good enough. Give me a kiss and go home."

She gave him a kiss, but she stopped by the ICU to see Tommy on her way out. She felt guilty she hadn't been down most of the day, but Tyler was right, she had been on the point of collapse.

* * * *

Tyler loved the nighttime solitude of the private room but hated being far from Thomas. Far was a relative term. It was a three-minute walk for Nevvie and everyone else, and a five-minute ride in a wheelchair for him. He couldn't contemplate attempting to walk it alone just yet, not the entire distance anyways.

His room became a daytime staging area of sorts, where everyone came in to wait for their turn to go sit with Thomas instead of sitting down in the waiting room. He spent most of his time napping, sometimes with Nevvie curled by his side, the pain medicine keeping him pretty well zonked.

He glanced at the wall clock—two a.m., and Nevvie would be due any minute, if he knew his angel. She would spend time downstairs with Thomas, bathing him and reading to him, then come upstairs to him. Three minutes later, she walked in. He smiled and simply held out his hand in greeting. Without a word she dropped her tote bag next to his bed, carefully climbed in on his right side and almost immediately fell asleep.

He closed his eyes, his face buried in her hair, fully appreciating that the only reason the staff allowed such latitude was because of his celebrity status. When the nurse, Elise, showed up to take his vital signs twenty minutes later, Nevvie never awoke.

"Your wife's exhausted, isn't she?" Elise whispered.

Tyler nodded. "Poor love is wiped out. She can't sleep alone. She was attacked years ago, has nightmares."

"How's your partner doing?" This time around, the hospital staff had proved sympathetic to their family situation.

"No major change. He improves a little each day. They're not ready to bring him out of the coma yet."

She finished and peeked at Nevvie. "Do you need another blanket or pillow?"

"No, thank you. She's fine. Just pull the door shut, please."

She glanced at the clock. "You're due for meds at five. If you promise not to die on me, I'll hold off on taking your next vitals until then."

Tyler managed a smile. "Thank you."

He actually managed to doze a little, Nevvie's presence doing him as much good as it did her. When he felt a tug on his arm, he opened his eyes, surprised to see it was five o'clock already.

"Sorry," Elise whispered. "I was trying not to wake you."

He nodded and closed his eyes again as she did what she had to do, leaving them alone a few minutes later. Nevvie didn't stir. It was after six when she finally opened her eyes.

"Morning, love," he said, kissing her cheek.

She closed her eyes again. "I hate this."

"Just a few days, then I'll be home."

"I know." She shivered in his arms and he carefully pulled her closer.

"Try to grab a few more winks. You can't go see him right now, it's after six. Shift change."

She nodded and a few minutes later, she fell asleep again. This time she slept until after seven-thirty. She helped him to the bathroom, gave him a sponge bath then took a moment to freshen up before heading to the ICU. When she returned an hour later she had a carryout tray from the cafeteria. His breakfast had just arrived. Together they silently ate and watched the *Today Show*.

* * * *

The routine was a comfortable way to numb Nevvie's emotions. Between shuttling back and forth to the office to help Bob with Kinsey Consulting, relaying information to Tyler's publicist and agent, and dealing with the crush of their friends and media, she was usually emotionally and physically wiped out every evening.

Still, she couldn't sleep. Not at home, at least.

Not alone.

Despite Tyler's urging, she returned to the hospital every night, first to take care of Thomas, then to go upstairs to Tyler's room and curl up with him to catch a couple hours sleep.

Not usually one to wear make-up, at Karen's suggestion Nevvie started using a light concealer and powder to hide the deep, dark circles under her eyes from Tyler's scrutinizing gaze.

Chapter Eleven

Nine days into Tyler's stay, a timid-looking young woman in office clothes and a hospital name tag appeared in the doorway of Tyler's room. Karen was down in the ICU, Peggy sat in Tyler's room with Nevvie, Tyler and Bob. Eddie and Pete were watching Adam for the day since Cheryl and April had returned home to Georgia.

Bob, sensing something amiss, immediately took over. "Yes?"

"I need to speak to Mr. Paulson."

Bob pulled himself to his full height. "I'm his attorney."

"I'm from Administration. We have a woman downstairs demanding to see him. She claims she's his mother."

Nevvie glared. "Aw, fuck. I'll take care of her."

Tyler grabbed her arm before she could stand. "No, love." He looked at the girl. "Go ahead and send her up."

"Tyler, the last person I want to deal with is Delores! You don't need the stress—"

"Love." He turned the full force of his eyes on her. "Do I look like I'm stressed? I won't die, I promise. Sooner or later we need to deal with her. Especially if she's here."

Nevvie finally nodded. "Okay. Bob, you stay close."

The woman left. Ten minutes later, they heard Delores get off the elevator down the hall, her loud, brash voice muttering dangerously.

Nevvie tensed, but Tyler held her hand and squeezed.

Like flipping a switch, when Delores appeared in their doorway, her dark muttering stopped and she put on a false, cheery front.

"There's my baby!"

She tried to swoop across the room to hug him, but Nevvie stayed firmly planted next to his chair and refused to move.

Delores glared. "I'd like to hug my son."

"You've just rode in a small metal tube full of germs across the Atlantic Ocean with a couple hundred strangers. I'd rather you didn't get too close and risk getting him sick."

Tyler apparently knew even his considerable sway with Nevvie would be taxed, so he didn't press the issue.

Peggy stood and started to gather her things. "I'll go on down to the cafeteria for a while."

"No." Tyler's firm voice shocked Peggy. "Please don't, Mom."

Delores' face darkened as Peggy glanced at them then retook her seat.

Nevvie couldn't stand it. "I thought I told you to stay the hell home, Delores."

She stood maybe an inch taller than Nevvie in bare feet, but her shoes added a little height. Tyler didn't get his blue eyes from her, that's for sure. In fact, Nevvie realized Tyler looked nothing like his mother, whereas his younger brother and sister strongly resembled her. Her muddy hazel eyes looked washed out in stark contrast to her dyed bright red hair. She was maybe five years younger than Peggy, but with her face deeply lined with wrinkles she looked fifteen years older. She positively reeked of cigarette smoke.

"I didn't come here to see *you*," Delores said through gritted teeth. "I came to see my son."

Tyler squeezed Nevvie's hand but didn't make her move. "You should have called, Mother."

Delores frowned. "Aren't you happy to see me? I've come to help take care of you." She pasted a fake smile on her face. "I can stay as long as you need me."

"You aren't needed," Tyler said before Nevvie could. "We don't have room for you to stay."

"But you have that big house! And I wanted to see my grandson." She shot a nasty look at Peggy.

Nevvie sensed Peggy tense, but the other woman said nothing.

"Mother, we have a full house right now. Frankly, we don't have room. I'm not going to be able to spend any time with you because our focus is on taking care of Thomas."

She frowned. "What's wrong with…him? If he loves you as much as you claim he does, shouldn't he be here with you?"

Nevvie started to speak when Tyler clamped down on her hand and answered, the anger in his voice thinly disguised. "Thomas was in a motorcycle accident. He's in a coma in the ICU."

Nevvie watched Delores' face. Her eyes took on a cold, calculating look. "Well, I should think with his family here they could take care of him. You need your rest. I'll take care of you. You need your mother."

Nevvie couldn't hold it back any longer. "How would you know what he needs? You practically disowned him when he left home, until he became successful!"

"How would *you* know?" Delores shot back. "Do you think it was easy having two normal children, and then knowing that my eldest child decided to waste his life living like—"

"Don't say it," Nevvie growled. Tyler tightly gripped Nevvie's hand again, keeping her by his side. The murderous look in Nevvie's eyes drove Delores back a step. "Don't you fucking say it, you goddamned bitch. He loves Tommy, and Tommy loves him. That's none of your business."

"What do you really want, Mother?" Tyler asked. "Quit blowing smoke up my arse."

Delores tried for indignant. "I don't know what you're talking about! I come all this way to see you—"

"You haven't asked to see me in years. How many times have I been to London and rang you up to get together, but you were too busy to make time for me? How many times have you called me? The last time was when Nev was hurt and it made it into the news. I've always called you. I send you cards. Oh, wait, there were times you needed a thousand pounds here or there for miscellaneous items, then you didn't hesitate to call. Yet when I nearly die, you suddenly make a grand gesture. Certainly you can see where I'm skeptical."

Tyler's angry words stunned Delores into silence. Nevvie couldn't believe it. Delores finally blustered, "You are obviously not feeling well, son." Then Nevvie recognized the reptilian glint in her mother-in-law's eyes. "When the *Mirror* and *The Sun* called me up asking for quotes, I certainly never suspected I'd receive this kind of reception."

Ka-ching. "So which one paid for your ticket?" Nevvie snarked.

Tyler squeezed her hand again. "Of course," he said, "a logical, rational person would have called first, before coming all this way, if they didn't have ulterior motives."

That seemed to put Delores off her game for a moment. "Why do I need to call for permission to see my son?" She shot another withering glare at Nevvie.

Tyler nudged Nevvie to the side so he could stand. "You've seen me. Was there anything else?"

Obviously this wasn't going nearly as well as Delores thought it would. She opted for outright extortion. "Perhaps my big shot son could see his way to help his mum out. The papers invited me to give them a call upon my return to update them personally on your...condition." That was definitely an evil look in Nevvie's direction.

"Well that's certainly helpful of you," Tyler said.

"This is all your damn father's fault," Delores snapped. "If that filthy bugger hadn't left us, you never would have gotten involved with these people. It figures you're the spitting image of that bastard, and look how you turned out. Just like him."

"Mother, you can go to bloody hell for all I care."

Her jaw dropped. "What?"

"You heard me." He turned to Bob. "Call security. Get her out of here."

Desperate and realizing she'd fucked up, Delores switched tactics again. "You're obviously not well, son," she whined. "You need your mother."

"He has a wife," Nevvie said. "He told you to leave."

Delores glared at Nevvie. "You're just a little slut after him for his money, don't think I don't see what you are. You and that freeloading bastard—"

"Out." Tyler's threatening whisper caught their attention as if he'd screamed. "Get out, right now, or so help me I'll wring your bloody neck with my bare hands."

"But Tyler, I'm your mother!"

"Not anymore." He pointed at Peggy. "That woman has been more a mother to me than you ever have. I want you out of my life. Get out. Now."

Nevvie stood behind Tyler and put her arm around his waist, supporting him.

Delores looked at him, the color rising in her cheeks. "How can you say that to me?"

"Because you have never once considered anyone else's feelings but your own. You practically disowned me when I left for the States until I sold my first novel. Then suddenly you wanted to be a part of my life again when it suited your needs. You've never once acknowledged Thomas as my partner. You only want money from me, you disrespect my spouses, and you're irritating. So, Mother, I'm telling you now, get out of my life."

Bob had slipped out of the room and returned with hospital security.

Delores, realizing her ill-conceived plan had backfired, stared at Tyler. Her eyes coldly glittered. "You haven't heard the last of me, Tyler," she said.

The security officers escorted her out.

After Delores left, Nevvie breathed a sigh of relief. "What's next?"

"Call Elliot. We need a pre-emptive strike."

"What?"

"Love, she'll try to sell her sob story to the tabloids. We have to put out a story first."

"What story?"

He turned to her, his blue eyes playfully gleaming. "Isn't it a shame? I suspect my mother is suffering from early Alzheimer's, poor dear. She's obviously in early dementia. What a pity. She vehemently refuses all help despite her irrational behavior. I gave my siblings a trust account so they'll be able to properly care for her in her dotty state."

Nevvie didn't bother to try to contain her laughter. "You didn't?"

"I did, years ago. I set it up with my brother and sister. They're as sick of her as I am, they'll back me up. No one will pay her a dime for her version after our story comes out. Exploitation of the aged and infirm, you know."

She laughed. "You really are the evil genius. I hand the crown back to you."

Peggy smiled. "Dadgum, I'm glad I'm on the right side of the fence on this one."

He hugged her. "Don't worry, Mom, you absolutely are."

Chapter Twelve

Nevvie had already come and gone earlier that morning when the doctors made their rounds. Tyler's cardiologist looked at his chart and made a few notes.

"Well, Mr. Paulson, are you ready to go home?"

"Really?"

"Everything looks good. We'll set up follow-up appointments and get you started on a cardiac rehab program, but we've done all we can do for you here. You can go home and continue recovering there."

"Thank you." As soon as the doctor left, Tyler grabbed the phone and dialed Nevvie. It was only seven-thirty and she sounded worried when she answered.

"Tyler? What's wrong? Is Tommy okay?"

He laughed. "Love, at least one thing is right with the world. Make sure you bring me something when you return this morning."

"What?"

"A decent pair of trousers and a shirt. And some shoes."

"Why? What..." She hesitated. "You get to come home?" she whispered.

"I was just given the final okay."

He heard her sob.

"Love, please don't cry..."

But she still looked puffy-eyed when she raced into his room less than an hour later, an overnight bag slung over her shoulder with his things in it. She gently hugged him. "Really? You're not kidding?"

He smiled. "I'm not kidding love. You can take me home today. I'm just waiting on the paperwork now."

Tyler changed into the clothes Nevvie brought him. Seeing him in a pair of slacks and a button-up shirt comforted her in a way she didn't anticipate.

Normal.

He looked normal. No more IV tubes in his hands. The surgical incision hidden by his shirt. All that remained was the hospital ID bracelet on his wrist.

Nevvie anxiously paced until the nurse arrived with the paperwork. She explained everything to them, went over all the discharge instructions and forms, and Tyler signed. Nevvie made several trips to the car to stow his things. When she returned from the last one, the nurse followed her in with a wheelchair.

Nevvie pointed at it. "Get in, your ride's here."

"I can walk, love."

"Hospital rules, Ty. You know the drill. Just don't expect me to carry you across the threshold when we get home."

He laughed, groaning a little. He was healing.

Nevvie wanted to snatch the wheelchair out of the nurse's hands and run Tyler down to the car. Instead she leaned in and kissed him. "I'll meet you at the front entrance, okay?"

"All right, love."

Nevvie hurried ahead, nearly floating with joy. *One down. One down. One down.*

One to go.

The only thing that tempered her enthusiasm was knowing Tommy still lay unconscious in the ICU. Karen and Peggy would stay at the hospital with Tommy while Nevvie got Tyler settled.

Got him home.

* * * *

At home, Nevvie closed and locked their bedroom door behind them and helped Tyler to their bed, quickly pulling back the covers so he could lie down. Once he was settled he crooked his finger at her and she carefully curled next to him, his arms around her. Then she closed her eyes, buried her face against his chest and took a deep breath. Sobs wracked her body as he tightly held her.

"That's right, love," he whispered. "Let it out. I'm home to stay, and part of this nightmare is over."

She sobbed so long he wondered if he'd need to call a doctor for her. Eventually she cried herself to sleep and he tried to nap, glad she finally had a chance to get the worst of it out of her system. He knew there would be more tears—hers and his both—once Thomas was safely home. For now she'd vented a little pressure and hopefully could function again. She could release some of her burden to him. Emotionally, at least, even if he couldn't do much physically yet to help out.

After an hour she stirred and opened her eyes, carefully placing her palm against his chest.

He laid his hand over hers. "It's still beating, love."

A soft, sad smile caressed her face. "You guys aren't allowed to die before me. I can't stand it. I can't handle losing you."

He touched his forehead to hers. "You're not losing either of us, sweet. You still have us, and we love you. Thomas is simply away for a while. I have every faith in him and his love for us that he will pull through this."

She lay there with him for more long, quiet minutes. "I can't lose you."

He kissed her forehead. She looked aged since that morning, deep lines in her face, dark circles under her eyes.

"Listen to me, angel." He waited until she tipped her head back to meet his gaze. "You aren't losing me." He curled his fingers around hers and brought her hand to his lips. "I love you more than my very life, and you are not losing me."

He shifted position slightly, until she was nestled against his chest, her head tucked in the crook of one arm while his other hand lightly rested on her mid-drift. "You're *not* losing me," he firmly repeated and kissed her.

"Wait, Ty—"

"Shh." He kissed her gently, slowly, taking his time and savoring her. No, he wasn't in the mood, between his pain, exhaustion and the medication, but he desperately wanted to bring her some normalcy, a tangible sign of recovery she could hold on to. He slipped his free hand inside her waistband.

When her body stiffened and she reached to push him away, he softly said, "No, angel. Don't do that." He kissed her until she relaxed again. His fingers found their way between her legs and gently parted her. She sighed against him, one hand cupping the back of his head, her fingers tangling in his hair.

"Remember when you were hurt and we got you home? How you asked if I loved you?" he asked as his fingers slowly stroked her.

She nodded, her eyes focusing on his.

"Remember how you made me promise to do anything for you?"

"Yes."

"Remember what else you made me do for you?"

A smile curled her lips, lifting tons of worry from her face. "Yes."

"And remember how scared I was of hurting you?"

She nodded again and kissed him, understanding, some of her fear finally leaving and allowing her to enjoy his touch.

Nevvie relaxed against him. He nuzzled his lips against her forehead. "Let me love you, angel. I want to feel you come for me, my sweet, sweet love."

He moved his hand lower, enjoying her soft moan as he slipped two fingers inside her and slowly stroked. "You made me come for you, remember?"

"Mmm hmm."

"Now Master will ask his little slave to return the favor."

She gasped, shivering against him as her passion truly took over.

He dropped his voice even lower as he circled her clit with his fingers. "You are my sweet, beautiful slave. I want you to come for me."

Her soft mewing sound made him smile. He knew she was close. This many years together, he could read her body as well as he could Thomas'. "Come for me, love. Come for your husband—"

"Ah!" she pressed her face against his arm as she cried out, muffling the sound of her passion as her body stiffened, spasming against him, trembling.

He knew when to back off but didn't withdraw his hand. When she reached for him he stopped her.

"No, love," he said. "You stay right there, just like that. I'm not done with you yet."

She relaxed against him as he stroked his fingers into her ready entrance, adding a third and making her moan. "That's it," he said. "You don't get to leave this bed until you've given me another one." He lifted his head so he could meet her beautiful green eyes. "You're going to come for me again, aren't you?"

"Yes," she whispered.

"Because you're my good girl, aren't you?"

She nodded as her breath quickened at his words.

He kissed her, his tongue plunging between her lips, fucking her with it and mimicking the way his fingers explored her. When he lifted his head again so he could look at her, he stared into her eyes, entranced.

"I want my beautiful wife to come for me and show me how much she loves me."

She closed her eyes and pressed her face against him. It took longer but as he heard her muffled cries against his arm he drew her close and held her as she recovered.

"My poor, sweet girl, you've been so very brave for us. We are truly blessed that you're our wife." He pressed his lips against the top of her head, inhaling the scent of her shampoo, how she sounded trying to catch her breath. "See? I didn't keel over."

She laughed. While her cheeks were streaked with tears she also wore a brilliant smile. Laying a palm against his face she kissed him. "Okay, point made."

"No, love, point not made. I'm going to keep you rather busy and distracted now that I'm home. I owe you quite a bit for the grief I've caused you."

She grinned. "Ty, I get the—"

"Shh." He laid a finger against her lips and narrowed his gaze. "Little slave, don't talk back to your master."

He gave her credit for attempting to keep a straight face but she laughed again and kissed him. "I love you, Evil Genius."

He hugged her. "And I love you too, darling."

* * * *

Karen and Peggy had returned while Tyler and Nevvie were in the bedroom. Nevvie took a few minutes to freshen up and change clothes. Eddie brought Adam home a short time later. As much as Tyler wanted to go back to the hospital with her to visit Thomas, he knew he needed to spend the evening at home catching up on his own rest. Nevvie brought the baby into the bedroom and laid him on the bed where he grinned and babbled at Ty.

"There's my buddy."

"Mom's in the kitchen getting your dinner ready. She'll bring it in once it's ready. Don't you dare lift him, got it?"

"Yes, love."

She leaned over and kissed him, then the baby. "Can I bring you anything?"

"Just yourself, sweet. I'm looking forward to a long, uninterrupted night's sleep."

"That makes two of us."

Nevvie left. Tyler ignored the TV and lay on his side, holding his son's hand. They'd had so many plans, the three of them, with none of this on the radar. He would never admit to Nevvie that he was just as scared they'd lost Thomas. But she needed him to be strong or she might lose what courage she'd regained.

For years Tyler envisioned growing old with Thomas. Then Nevvie entered their lives and life had only got better. What if Thomas didn't get better? What if he had lost his love forever?

He blinked back tears and tried to force that thought out of his mind, choosing to cling to the hope that regardless of his physical state, Thomas would somehow return to them.

Peggy brought his dinner in a few minutes later. Adam was falling asleep. "You okay, sugar?"

"Yes, thank you, Mom. How are you doing?"

She forced a smile. "We'll get through it, Ty. Tommy loves y'all too much not to make it." She carefully scooped her grandson from the bed. "He's beautiful, Ty. He's a beautiful baby. You're a good daddy."

"You're his grandmother. You're biased."

She smiled but there were tears in her eyes when looked at him again. "I'll admit I was a little dubious when y'all first got together with Nevvie. I worried things wouldn't work out between y'all. I love her, and she's a damn good momma. Even though I was convinced long before now how much she loves the two of you, the past couple of weeks have proven it beyond any doubt. I'll snatch that stupid daughter of mine bald next time I see her for puttin' y'all through extra stress."

"Yes, but if you hadn't been here I might have died. So it worked out all right, didn't it?"

* * * *

Ben was back on duty. He smiled when Nevvie entered the ICU. "So how's my other patient?"

"He's home. Discharged this morning, thank God." She sat by

Tom's bed. "One down, one to go." Her new mental mantra.

The neurologist walked in with Tommy's chart. "Oh, Mrs. Kinsey, glad you're here."

Nevvie's breath caught. "Yes?"

"Good news, I promise. The latest scan showed significant improvement. I think we'll be able to bring him out of the coma soon."

She clapped a hand over her mouth, tears filling her eyes as she tried to stifle her sob.

The doctor patted her shoulder. "I can't promise you what's going to happen after that. We've talked about this. We won't know for sure what level of damage he'll have until after he's awake and we can fully evaluate him. From what we see so far, the results are encouraging."

She nodded, squeezing her eyes shut and crying into her hand. Ben brought her a box of tissues and she rested her head against the bed and gripped Tom's hand as she tried to get her emotions under control. When she looked up several minutes later, she realized Ben had brought everything she'd need to bathe Tommy and closed the curtain, leaving them alone.

Nevvie had a routine now. She shaved Tommy first, then worked her way down his body, massaging his arms and his good leg, checking him for pressure sores and carefully drying his skin. She talked to him in soft, low tones the entire time, telling him about Adam, updating him about Tyler. No one knew for sure if he could hear her, but everyone told her it certainly didn't hurt.

After she finished bathing Thomas, she put a clean gown on him and Ben came in to help change the bed and check his dressings. Then she sat and read to him for an hour. She'd marked the page he was on when she first started reading to him so he could go back to that point and start over when he recovered. It was something to do and feel connected to him.

She left two hours later, quietly entering the house so she didn't wake anyone. Adam slept in his crib. Tyler sat up in bed, reading.

"Hey, you should be asleep," she said.

He put his book down. "I napped, love. I promise."

Nevvie quickly undressed and slipped into bed with him, naked, sighing at the feel of his warm flesh against hers. She tried not to look at his surgical scar. He turned off the lamp and wrapped his arms around her.

"How is our sweet boy?"

"He's okay. The neurologist came in when I got there and said the latest scan looked good, that they'll hopefully bring him around in a couple of days."

"Wonderful," he whispered against the back of her neck. "I told you, he'll come back to us. We may have to do a lot of work to help him heal, but he will return to us, somehow."

She pulled his arms around her while fighting the urge to cry again. "I know."

"You smell so good."

She laughed. Leave it to Tyler to say something to break her out of her funk. "Smell good, huh?"

"Having you back in my arms is beyond description."

Nevvie looked at the empty side of the bed. Normally, she'd be nestled between her boys. She touched Tom's pillow and pulled it to her, holding it against her. It wasn't the same, not even close.

Sometime in the night she awoke and realized she was still firmly wedged in Tyler's arms. Nevvie held her breath, listening for the sound of Tyler's slow, steady breathing. Relieved, she closed her eyes and tried not to cry but couldn't hold back the hot, heavy tears and sobs that wracked her body.

He knew. Ingrained from their early days together when the men helped soothe her nightmares away, he awoke immediately when he felt her cry and pulled her tightly against him, murmuring to her, soothing her back to sleep.

The smell of coffee awoke her the next morning. Nevvie panicked briefly when she realized Tyler wasn't in bed with her. She pulled on her robe and ran out to the kitchen and saw him standing at the counter in his robe, reading the paper, his back to her.

He heard her and turned, opening his arms. When Peggy walked out with the baby a few minutes later, she found them, Nevvie still crying against Tyler as he tried to soothe her.

"Your face is gonna freeze like that, sugar, you keep crying," Peggy joked.

Tyler winced as he laughed. Nevvie reached for Adam. "I'm sorry."

"Don't apologize. I know it's good to have half of them home."

* * * *

They ate breakfast and Nevvie drove Tyler to the hospital to visit Thomas. Even though Delores was long gone, the incident with her still ran through Nevvie's head. Especially the woman's particular choice of words. Nevvie finally asked.

"Tell me about your father." It was a subject she normally never broached.

He froze. "Does it matter, love?" he stiffly replied.

"Please?"

He closed his eyes, rested his head on the seat back. "It's not something I wish to revisit."

"Did he treat you badly?"

Tyler shook his head but didn't open his eyes. "He grew quite stern in the year or so before he left, always pushing, always demanding more and better."

"From you?"

"All of us." He finally opened his eyes and looked at her. "But especially me. Why do you wish to know now, love?"

She shrugged. "I just wondered."

"Because of Delores?"

Nevvie nodded.

He sighed, closed his eyes again. "It hurt when he left. We came home from school and he'd left without even saying good-bye. Moth—Delores told us he'd packed and ran off with another woman."

"You haven't seen him since you were seventeen?"

"He left when I was thirteen. I haven't seen him since I was fifteen. I haven't spoken to him since I was seventeen."

"Do you have any brothers or sisters by his new marriage?"

"I don't know. I don't know if he ever married her."

Nevvie's intuition screamed. "Did you ever meet the woman?"

"No."

"Wait a minute." They'd stopped at a red light. Nevvie looked at Tyler. "Did he tell you what happened? Why he left?"

"No, I must say he didn't. He never talked about it. The few times I saw him after he left, he only asked about school, sports, how we were doing. We didn't ask him for details about the other woman, and he certainly didn't offer any."

"Did you visit his home?"

"No. He moved away from London. Near Oxford, I believe. Love, why is this important?"

"Because I've never asked and I'm curious." It technically wasn't a lie.

He studied her, eventually answered. "He always took the train, met us a few times. He never offered any details about his life except his job. He was a teacher."

"Did you have his phone number?"

"I called a few times."

"Did his wife ever answer?"

"Love—"

"Tyler."

He sighed again. "No, none of us ever had contact with her."

"Do your brother and sister talk to him?"

"I don't think so. If they do they haven't said so."

Nevvie couldn't confess her theory to Tyler. If she was wrong…

She didn't think she was.

"I want to go with you the next time you go to London."

He eyed her suspiciously. "Why?"

"Because I don't want you going alone. And I want to see your brother and sister again." She'd called them and told them about Tyler, then kept them updated with calls and emails. While she couldn't claim a close relationship with them, at least they were cordial, polite, and people she didn't mind being related to. Especially since they hated their mother almost as much as Nevvie did. Over the past few years, Tyler had formed a closer relationship with them.

"Again, love, why?"

"Because they're family. I don't have family except for you guys and yours. You said it yourself, they're nothing like your mother. This whole bullshit mess has put a few things into a different perspective for me."

Okay, so that was the truth. Apparently her response satisfied Tyler. "Very well, love."

She'd always sworn if she ever met Tyler's father that she'd deck the son of a bitch for the emotional scars left on Tyler's psyche when the man abandoned his wife and children.

Now…well, maybe her anger had been directed at the wrong parent all along.

Chapter Thirteen

At least Nevvie could sleep a couple of hours each night, although it felt weird and wrong not having Thomas in bed with them. Nevvie still awoke, praying, in the middle of the night that she'd look over and see him lying in bed with them.

She had grown to like the quiet night shift in the ICU. Nevvie greatly appreciated the staff bending the rules, allowing her to visit and take care of Thomas every night. The third night Tyler was home, she realized after waking at one a.m. that she wasn't going back to sleep.

As she tried to dress in the dark, Tyler's voice drifted to her.

"What are you doing, love?"

She sat on the bed next to him. "I need to go see him. I'm sorry, I can't sleep."

He felt for and found her hand, squeezed it. "It's okay, love. Kiss him for me, too. I'd go with you but I'm hurting right now."

"Want your medicine?"

"No, don't panic. Not that kind of pain. From the surgical site. I'm cutting back on the pain medication. I don't like how it makes me feel."

She leaned over and kissed his forehead. "Okay. I'll be back soon."

Ben was on duty again. "Are you a vampire?" she joked.

He'd brought her towels and other supplies as soon as he saw her arrive. "No, but I've been accused of biting too hard."

The comment briefly stunned her. Then she clapped a hand over her mouth to stifle her screams of laughter as Ben smiled. He hugged her. "How's your other half?"

"He's good. Healing. We miss Tommy. We need him back."

"Well, you'll be happy to hear they're backing off his meds."

"Really?"

He patted her shoulder. "Just take it one day at a time."

She set up the MP3 player and started her routine, shaving him, bathing him, his massage and range of motion exercises. Then she read to him for a while until she started yawning. It was after four o'clock. Ben returned from his break. "You'd better head home. You look beat."

"When should we come back?"

"Wait until after nine. Get some sleep, rest. He'll be here."

At home, Tyler stirred when she slid under the covers after undressing. "I'm glad you're home, sweet."

They were the best words she'd heard in weeks.

* * * *

Nevvie worried Tyler would wear himself out and end up back in the hospital. The fourth day after Tyler was discharged, the women agreed amongst themselves to let him stay by Tom's bed while they took turns rotating out so they wouldn't have too many people in the ICU at once. Tyler tried to protest but the women overruled him. They all ate lunch together in the hospital cafeteria. Later, Nevvie walked back to Tom's bedside with Tyler to sit for a while.

Tyler watched his lover's face, held his hand. For the first time, Nevvie saw how much the previous weeks had aged Tyler. He'd always looked younger than his years, and the lines now etched around his sweet blue eyes saddened her.

Sensing her gaze on him, he looked at her, mustered a smile for her benefit. "It's a waiting game, sweetheart." He noticed her shocked expression. "What?"

He followed her gaze to Thomas. His lover's eyes were open, but unfocused. He squeezed Tom's hand. "Welcome back, love," he said, his voice choked with emotion.

Thomas didn't acknowledge Tyler's voice. Nevvie waved at Carol and stepped back while the nurse checked his vital signs. "Mr. Kinsey, can you squeeze Tyler's hand for me?"

Tom's eyes finally drifted to Carol, then closed.

Nevvie fought the urge to shake him. Instead, she squeezed his other hand. "Tommy, please, honey, wake up," she desperately urged.

He didn't open his eyes again.

"That's okay," Carol assured her. "I'll get his doctor and let him know he opened his eyes." She left them alone. Nevvie looked across the bed at Tyler. His eyes were focused on Thomas.

* * * *

Thomas didn't open his eyes again that afternoon. Nevvie forced Tyler to go home with Karen because he was obviously in pain. Peggy sat with Nevvie, on the other side of the bed, holding Tommy's other hand. Eventually after midnight, Peggy returned home. Karen came back with Tyler a half-hour later.

"I thought you were supposed to be sleeping," Nevvie gently scolded him.

"I wish you'd go home and get some yourself."

She stared at Thomas and stroked his hand. "No. Not until he wakes up."

Tyler settled in his chair with a pained grunt. "Love, he would not want you to wear yourself out."

She shook her head and refused to meet Tyler's gaze, knowing if she did she couldn't resist him. "No, Ty. I'm not going home until he wakes up. I was here when you woke up. I'll be here for him, too."

He realized there was no sense arguing with her and settled in to wait. Karen only stayed a few minutes, then returned to the house.

Around two a.m., Nevvie dozed with her head resting on the bed when she felt Tom squeeze her hand. She sat up, immediately alert. Tyler was awake but lying in the recliner and staring at Tom's face.

"He's trying to come out of it, I think, love," he softly spoke. "He's moved his head a few times."

"Why didn't you wake me?"

Tyler's face hardened. "Sweetheart, if you collapse from exhaustion it does no one any good. You have to rest. I would not have let you slept if he awoke."

"I'm sorry."

"No apologies, love. Just please, take care of yourself and don't run yourself ragged over us, right?"

She stroked Tom's hand. He squeezed, but it felt more like a reflex than Tyler's deliberate motions when he'd emerged from sedation. She squeezed again, praying he'd respond. He didn't. The staff had put restraints on him once they discontinued the drugs that kept him in the coma, so he couldn't rip out his breathing tube. She hated the restraints even though she knew they were necessary.

Nevvie dozed again, her head snapping up at the sound of Tyler's voice.

"Nev."

She looked at Tom. His sweet brown eyes stared at her. Her vision tripled as she cried. "Hi there, handsome."

He squeezed her hand and she dropped her head to the bed again as she cried with relief.

Tyler changed position so he could lean closer to the bed. "You gave us a rather bad fright, love," he whispered.

Tom slowly swiveled his head toward Tyler.

"By the way," Tyler said, reaching out to stroke Tom's cheek, his eyes never leaving Tom's face, "I love you, too. More than you'll ever know." He kissed Tom's hand.

Tom's eyes slowly shifted back to Nevvie. She kissed his hand, nuzzled it against her cheek as best she could. "I love you, Tommy. You're not allowed to scare me like that again, got it?"

He weakly squeezed her hand.

* * * *

Nevvie and Tyler stepped out while Ben and the on-call doctor checked Thomas. Twenty minutes later, Ben called them back from the waiting room. "Are you two going to get some sleep now?"

Tyler nodded and slipped his arm around Nevvie's waist. "After we say good night to him, I promise."

Tom slowly opened his eyes when he heard them by his bed. Nevvie didn't tell Tyler that Tom's awakening felt drastically different than Tyler's. While Thomas had obviously returned, it seemed like there was still something missing. Tyler had been immediately awake and aware once he came to. She prayed it was only effects of the sedation and not brain damage.

Tyler carefully leaned over and kissed his lover's forehead. "I need to take our girl home so she can sleep. We've run her ragged between us. Mom and Karen are at home with the baby."

Thomas didn't respond, just stared at Tyler with a blank look on his face.

Nevvie leaned in and kissed him. "We'll be back in the morning, sweetie."

His eyes seemed to focus on her but he didn't make any acknowledgement he understood her words.

They reluctantly stepped out of his alcove. Ben talked with them by the nursing station. "Don't worry. He's been out for two weeks, it'll take him a while to feel like himself again."

Nevvie didn't want to ask but the words came out before she could stop them. "Brain damage?"

"I'm not a doctor. You need to talk to his neurologist about that. Now that he's awake they'll evaluate him, see what's going on. From my personal experience, anyone coming out of a two week coma isn't going to be fully with it as soon as they wake up. It's common to have disorientation, weakness. Talk to his doctors after they have a chance to evaluate him."

They walked to the car in silence, hand in hand. Tyler started to open the driver side door for Nevvie when she looked at him. They hugged, both sobbing, holding each other as their relief poured out of them.

Their tough guy came back. They'd take him any way they could get him.

* * * *

The next morning, Peggy and Karen cried when Nevvie told them Tommy had awoke. Nevvie and Tyler hurried to the hospital. Peggy and Karen would join them later and bring Adam.

As they walked into the ICU, Nevvie found Tyler's hand. Tom looked asleep, but when he heard them he opened his eyes.

He was still intubated and restrained. Perhaps marginally more aware than the night before, his eyes followed them as they stepped into the alcove. His nurse talked with Nevvie while Tyler settled next to him and leaned in close.

"I'm so sorry, Thomas," he whispered, gripping his lover's hand. "I feel like this is my fault. If you hadn't been rushing to be with me..." He choked up and couldn't continue.

Tom stared into his face but made no sign he'd comprehended Tyler's words.

Nevvie finished with the nurse and leaned over to kiss Tom's forehead. "She said they'll get that tube out pretty soon. It's going to be good to hear your voice again, mister."

His eyes slowly followed her as she settled into the chair on his other side. When she took his hand and squeezed, he didn't return it. Eventually his entire head moved, and he stared in her general direction. As she tried to look into his eyes it was as if he didn't focus on her.

Swallowing back her fear, Nevvie tried to hide it from Tyler.

"You need a haircut," she said, trying to joke with Thomas, wanting to provoke a smile or a wink or any expression at all she could hang her hat on as comprehensive acknowledgement of her words.

Nothing.

After twenty minutes, Tyler dozed off in his chair. Nevvie stood and walked to the end of the bed, watching Tom's face as she did. His eyes eventually followed her movements, then he moved his head. When she walked back to stand next to him, again he was slow to move his head even though his eyes moved to follow her.

Don't compare them. It's totally different. It means nothing.

That would have to be her new mantra. What Tyler went through and what Tommy went through were totally different. She'd done a little research and knew just the sedation alone could take a while to fully leave his system.

It means nothing.

She leaned in and kissed his forehead, gently squeezed his hand. "I'm going to see if Mom and Karen are out there yet. I'll send them in if they are. They'll want to see you." She straightened and watched him. As she was about to release his hand he gave hers a weak squeeze.

"Do that again. Please, Tommy."

After an agonizingly long moment, he did.

She choked back a sob. "One more?"

He squeezed.

Nevvie closed her eyes and took a deep breath. "Two?"

They were weak, but they were squeezes.

"Tyler."

His eyes opened and he carefully sat up. "What?"

She nodded to Tom's other hand. Tyler held it.

"Tommy," she said, "squeeze Tyler's hand now."

At first he didn't, but he slowly swiveled his head to look at Tyler.

Then he squeezed.

Tyler breathed a sigh of relief. "Oh, love, thank you."

Tom's eyes still didn't look right, dull and empty. Maybe that was an effect of the medication. She prayed that's all it was.

* * * *

Eddie and Pete sat in the waiting room with Karen and Peggy. After a quick update, Peggy and Karen handed Adam off to Nevvie and hurried to the ICU.

Nevvie leaned in to Eddie when he put his arm around her shoulders. "You know he's gonna be fine, Nev. He'll come out of it. He has to."

"Can you watch Adam today?"

"I'm all yours, babe."

Pete sat across the way. "Tom-Tom loves him. Hasn't quite figured out he's not a puppy." Tom-Tom was their yellow Labrador retriever, so named because of the sound his thick tail made beating against things when he was happy or excited.

Adam reached up and grabbed Eddie's chin. "Dee!"

Nevvie smiled. "This keeps up, he'll be saying 'Eddie' before he says 'dada' or 'poppa.'"

When the squealing baby strained to reach Eddie, Nevvie handed him over. It was a relief to have him to depend on.

* * * *

Nevvie returned to the ICU with Tyler after lunch. Tom's eyes were closed. As Nevvie and Tyler quietly talked with the nurse, Carol, Tom must have heard them. Nevvie watched Thomas follow them with his eyes as they walked around the bed and settled into their usual positions.

His head slowly turned toward Nevvie. She sensed something

more, perhaps awareness. "Tommy?"

He looked at her, but steadier than before, as if struggling to focus.

She held his hand. "Blink for me, Tommy."

He did, once, slowly. Deliberately.

"Blink two times."

He did.

Fighting back tears, she said, "Squeeze my hand two times."

He did.

Tyler sobbed from the other side of the bed. Thomas' head slowly swiveled to look at him.

"Are you really back, love?" Tyler asked.

Thomas blinked once, slowly, deliberately.

The doctors decided to remove his breathing tube later that afternoon as long as he continued making progress. Around four o'clock, Tyler and Nevvie gathered with Peggy and Karen in the waiting room while it was done. Tyler and Nevvie silently held hands, anxious.

Nevvie closed her eyes. They were both awake. Tyler was home, Tom would be too, soon. She could quit crying and get on with helping them heal. She'd already signed up for a CPR class, determined to know how to do it before Peggy left. She wouldn't take a chance like that again.

Carol called them back to the ICU an hour later. Thomas, his eyes closed, sat up in bed, free of the restraints and the breathing tube. He'd lost weight, at least twenty pounds, and his face looked gaunt.

Tyler tightly gripped Nevvie's hand, steadying her. He had to be as much of a wreck as she felt, and here he was trying to be strong for her. At their approach, Tom's eyes slowly slid open.

Carol touched them on the shoulders and leaned in between them. "He's very weak, and he'll have trouble talking for a while, so stay calm, keep him calm, and don't worry about how he sounds. Don't make him talk too much."

Nevvie and Tyler nodded and took up their usual positions. Thomas looked at Tyler and tried to raise his hand to Tyler's face. Nevvie held back her tears as Tyler laced his fingers through Tom's and nuzzled his hand against his cheek. "Hello there, handsome. It's good to see you back."

Tommy slowly licked his chapped lips. "Hey." His soft, whispery voice drew a sob from Nevvie. He sounded nothing like himself, but he was talking. He couldn't be horribly brain damaged if he was responding, could he?

Tommy slowly turned his head to her and tried to reach for her as well. She grabbed his hand and kissed it. "Hey, you," she said.

He gently squeezed her hand and whispered, "Hey. Love you. Both."

Tyler and Nevvie cried.

* * * *

Tyler needed a nap, so Peggy and Karen came in to sit with Tommy. After dinner, Nevvie and Tyler returned to the ICU with the baby.

Tom managed a weak smile. "Hey," he croaked.

Nevvie carefully laid Adam next to Tom. "Someone else wants to say hi. I haven't been bringing him in since you were first admitted, we didn't want him picking something up in here, but today's special."

Tom's eyes glistened. When he touched Adam's hand with his finger, his son tightly gripped it.

Nevvie swallowed back her tears yet again. Her boys were back. Thomas looked at her and weakly smiled. She leaned in and kissed him and that's when she finally lost it, sobbing against his shoulder.

"S'okay," he hoarsely whispered, kissing the top of her head. Beyond the obvious his voice sounded slurred and slow.

Tyler brushed away his own tears. "They'll probably move you to a regular room soon. Life will start to get back to normal, I should think."

Tom slowly nodded. Nevvie sat up and kissed him one more time before picking up the baby. She held him so Tom could kiss him. "I love you, Tommy."

"You too." He looked at Tyler. "Love you."

Tyler frantically nodded, kissing him. "As I love you."

Tom's eyes closed. "Go rest."

"All right, love. We will."

"Make Nev sleep."

Tyler and Nevvie exchanged a look and laughed.

* * * *

Nevvie gave up trying to sleep around midnight. Tyler caught her hand as she tried to get out of bed and pulled her back to him for a kiss. "And give him another for me," he said, kissing her again.

"I'm sorry."

"Why are you apologizing?"

"For waking you up."

"Don't feel guilty that you wish to go to him. I'm all right. He needs you."

Ben had her things ready when she arrived. Tommy's eyes were closed, but his soft, hoarse whisper startled her.

"Hey."

"Hey, you." She leaned in and kissed him. He opened his eyes. "Ready for your bath?" She gently brushed stray hair away from his forehead.

"Bath?"

It was hard for her to get used to his weak voice. She hoped that would be the first thing to return to normal. "Yeah. Do you think I'm going to let anyone else do this for you?" She forced a smile and set up her MP3 player. He watched as she prepped everything and pulled the curtain and door shut to his alcove.

She unsnapped the gown shoulders and tucked the towel around his face. "Have to shave you first. It's going to be easier now without that damn tube…"

He touched her hand.

The floodgate broke. She sat in the chair next to his bed and buried her face against his side and softly sobbed.

He couldn't do much more than rest his hand on the back of her head. "S'okay. Don't cry."

After a few minutes she composed herself and took a deep breath. "I'm sorry. I wasn't going to do that in front of you, but you don't know how glad I am to have you back." She blew her nose and continued her routine, only now his eyes followed her, his ears heard her, and he occasionally smiled or responded to her comments.

After he was shaved she patted his face dry. "Now for your sponge bath."

"How bad?"

"Your injuries?"

He slowly nodded.

"Bad enough. Could have been a lot worse, all things considered." He closed his eyes and didn't look while she bathed him, not wanting to see. He winced a little as she did his range of motion exercises.

"I'm sorry."

His eyes were closed, but his face looked pinched, tight with pain. "S'okay."

An hour later, she sat down and reached for the paperback in her bag, then laughed. "I guess I should back up and start from the point where you were."

"Go home. Sleep."

She shook her head. "I can't. Not without both my boys home. This is my routine. I need you back. Then we can all get a good night's sleep."

"Routine?"

"Every night." She stroked his hair. "I come in every night with you."

"What time is it?"

She looked at the clock. "Two."

"Go home at three. Deal?" His brown eyes struggled to focus on her.

She nodded. "Deal."

* * * *

Thomas spent most of the next two days sleeping, awaking a little to say hi before drifting back to the safety of darkness. It was fucking hard to talk, like the words didn't want to come. Everything hurt. And he couldn't eat, even though he suspected trying to satisfy the constant hungry growl in his belly would cause a flurry of new problems. He settled for the water, broth, sports drinks, and supplement shakes they let him have between his naps. Time blurred for the most part, night distinguished from day by Nevvie coming in to give him his bath.

The weakness more than anything scared him. He could barely lift his arms, had difficulty holding things. Perhaps it was best he was still on a liquid diet he could drink through a straw, because he didn't know if he even had the strength to lift a spoon to his lips, much less the dexterity to get the damn thing in his mouth.

It touched and shamed him that Nevvie came in each night to take care of him. She shouldn't have to do this, she should be able to focus on Tyler, not him. She talked nearly non-stop, and he usually closed his eyes while she worked, enjoying the feel of her hands on him and the sound of her voice.

He hadn't asked exactly what happened, knew there'd been an accident, but he wasn't ready to hear the details yet. He knew he was pretty fucked up, that much was obvious, but didn't even want to know all those facts either. He was content to sleep and sip his drinks and lie there and listen to Nevvie's chatter at night or feel Tyler holding his hand during the day.

None of those activities required the exhausting activity of stringing conscious, cohesive thoughts together.

* * * *

Thomas looked at his mom and Karen when they visited one morning. For once he felt coherent enough to talk. He'd heard the doctor and nurse talking about backing off on his pain medication, so maybe that was a side effect. "Hey."

Peggy smiled and kissed him. "You look more awake today."

"I feel more awake."

"You know how to put more grey in my hair, don't you?" Peggy teased.

"Sorry."

Karen leaned in to kiss him. "How you feeling, baby brother?"

"How are they?" He knew damn well Nevvie wasn't telling him everything. Tyler probably wouldn't either.

Peggy patted his hand. "A lot better the past few days, now that you're awake."

"What happened? The accident."

She froze. "How much do you remember?"

He slowly shook his head. "I sort of remember getting off the interstate in Tampa. Nothing else."

"That's probably a good thing. You were a mess."

He lifted his left arm and touched his head where a small dressing covered the surgical wound.

His right arm didn't want to work that well this morning.

He knew he'd need a haircut, but wasn't brave enough to ask for a mirror yet. "Still am a mess." It felt difficult to talk, like he had to hunt for the words and focus on them before he could push them out his mouth.

"Honey, you were in a coma for two weeks. That's to be expected. You won't be salsa dancing any time soon. You've got to heal."

"Tyler?"

"Do we really need to worry about that?"

"Mom."

She sighed, recognizing the stubborn set to his jaw, and retold the events. "What's important is he's alive, he's gonna be just fine, and so will you."

He rested against his pillows. "Poor Nev. You were right. I shouldn't have taken the bike."

Karen laughed. "Tommy, now I *know* you're brain damaged. You admitted Momma was right."

He managed a rough laugh. "Yeah."

Karen patted his shoulder. "You just focus on getting better. Those two need you. Tyler's been as worried about you as Nevvie. He needs you as much as she does, bro."

"Was it my fault? The accident?"

Peggy shook her head. "No, sugar. One of the ER doctors saw it happen. The guy pulled right out in front of you. Talking on his cell phone."

"Charges?"

He spotted the nervous look Peggy and Karen shared. She didn't answer.

"Mom."

"They buried him three days after the accident. He died on impact, sugar. I'm sorry."

He claimed he wanted to go to sleep a few minutes later, waiting until they'd left him alone to close his eyes and cry. Someone died because of him? It didn't matter the accident was the other guy's fault. If he'd taken the fucking truck in the first place, instead of being stubborn about it, none of this would have happened. The guy would have seen him. Or at the very least he wouldn't have been hurt and he'd be taking care of Tyler and Nevvie, without this additional fucking stress on them.

Fuck.

He'd set his mind about the bike when his mom started grousing about it. He had thought about taking the truck instead, but that old stubborn streak of his, when Momma asked him not to take the bike, that made his mind up for him.

By the time Nevvie and Tyler returned later that morning he'd pulled himself together. Tyler waited until Nevvie left Tom's bedside to consult with the physical therapist to lean in close.

"Talk to me, love."

Thomas struggled to focus his eyes on him. "What?"

"What's bothering you today? You look upset."

He should have known Tyler would pick up on his mood. "That guy died because of me."

Tyler shook his head. "No. That man died because he'd worked an extra shift and had very little sleep. He was on the phone, fighting with his girlfriend. It was not in any way your fault."

"Did he have kids?"

"Thomas—"

"Did he have kids?"

"One. With his ex-wife."

Thomas looked away and tried to hide his tears.

"Love, it wasn't your fault. Do not feel guilty about this."

"I killed a guy and you're telling me not to feel guilty?"

Tyler's tone hardened. "You didn't kill him. It was an accident. He pulled out in front of you."

"I should have taken the truck. I almost did."

"Stop." Thomas finally looked at him. "Love, you are going through a lot right now, emotionally and physically. You've only been awake and aware a few days. Your focus should be on getting better so we can bring you home where you belong. No one blames you for what happened. That's why they're called accidents."

Thomas didn't respond, but he couldn't quit thinking about the fact that there was now a child out there without a father because of a decision he'd made.

Because of his pride.

* * * *

A week after they brought him out of the coma, Thomas was transferred to a private room on the floor. The private room was a lot better than the ICU. Everyone could visit at the same time when they wanted, and they could close the door for privacy. He hated physical therapy and knew from the way Nevvie hung on the PT's every word that she would be as tough as any drill sergeant.

He loved her for it even if he hated the exercises.

He still felt weaker than hell and needed help eating most of the time. His coordination hadn't improved much from when he first awoke. When Tom tried to sign his name to a hospital form, he found he couldn't hold the pen.

Nevvie came in every night around midnight and napped in bed with him, the only bright spot of his day. He soon started sleeping much of his afternoons away so he could lie awake and stare at her, enjoy having her with him. During one of their few alone times together, Tyler assured Thomas she'd done the same thing with him.

The occupational therapist worked with Thomas on his dexterity. Handwriting was the worst, because he could barely grip a pen. Beyond frustrated, one afternoon he threw the pen across the room and had a mini temper tantrum while Nevvie quietly looked on. Their appointment was almost over anyway, so the therapist gave him a break and told him she'd return the next day.

He wouldn't meet Nevvie's gaze when she sat at the end of the bed. "It's okay, Tommy."

"No, it's not okay! I can't fucking get out of bed by myself. I can barely fucking walk with a goddamned walker." His anger simmered, bubbling over. "Just...leave me alone for a while, okay?"

The doctors had warned them Thomas might have outbursts of anger. Some of it genuine, some of it possibly due to his brain injury.

Nevvie nodded. She leaned over and kissed him. "I need to pick up Tyler downstairs from his cardiac rehab appointment. I'll go home and see how everyone is. We'll come back to visit later."

He snorted in disgust. "Yeah, come visit the gimp."

"Stop it." She squeezed his hand. "We love you. We're just grateful you're alive, you have no idea."

His anger dissolved. He slumped back in the bed and cried. "Nevvie, babe, I'm sorry."

She carefully curled up next to him and held him while he cried. "It's okay to be upset. We're here for you, every step of the way, Tommy. I swear we are."

"This fucking sucks for you."

She shrugged. "After what happened that day, believe me, having both of you awake again is a walk in the park. Trust me. We'll do whatever we've got to do to get you home. Don't rush it." She kissed him.

"How is he? Really, is he okay?"

She smiled and brushed the hair away from his forehead. "Evil Genius says he's fine, his doctors say he's recovering right on schedule. So you just chill out and enjoy being the center of attention, mister."

She kissed him again and carefully got out of bed. Alone in his room, he tried using one of the hand exercisers they'd brought him. When Nevvie learned about them from the physical therapist, she'd gone out and bought several different ones in various resistance levels. He could—barely—manage the lightest one after working up to it from a gelly squeeze ball. Now at least he could usually feed himself if the food didn't require cutting.

When his arms cooperated.

Two weeks after awaking from the coma, Thomas was finally free of IVs and on oral pain meds. He could walk to the end of the hall if he had a walker and someone to keep a steady arm around him. Nevvie usually hovered for this task, constantly sniping at Tyler to sit down and rest when he tried to do too much. Some more hand strength had returned, but not much in the way of dexterity. In fact, books Nevvie brought for him to read remained unread because he got too frustrated by not being able to easily turn the pages.

He didn't tell her.

Then there was the guilt. During one of his physical therapy walks, when Nevvie was with Tyler at a doctor appointment, Thomas had overheard two of the housekeeping staff talking about the man he'd killed, Antonio Juarez. The staff was holding a fundraiser for his young son.

"I need to go sit down," Thomas whispered through clenched teeth.

The therapist looked worried. "We're almost done—"

"Now."

"Okay." She helped him turn around and make his way back to his room. "Are you all right?"

"I just need to be alone for a while."

"Did you want me to call your wife?"

"No."

She left. Thomas didn't bother turning on the TV, just laid there staring at the ceiling. One fucking decision ruined so many lives. Again he remembered that morning, how he'd almost changed his mind and thought maybe he would take the truck until Momma chimed in about the bike.

Then his pride wouldn't let him *not* take the bike. Just like when he was a kid. Stupid fucking ego. And now...

He closed his eyes, hating himself.

Chapter Fourteen

Karen returned to Savannah three weeks after Tommy awoke. She had to take care of things at home. Nevvie gave her another large check and made her sister-in-law promise to tell her if she needed more. She would return in four days, then Peggy would go home. The other sisters, except for Emily, had come back to visit Thomas in the hospital. Eddie was now a regular fixture around the house, either helping by taking care of Adam, shuttling Tyler to doctor or cardiac rehab appointments, or just in general being there to help prevent Nevvie from collapsing out of sheer exhaustion.

One morning when Eddie arrived at the house for baby duty, Nevvie hugged him long and hard. "Do you know how much I love you?" she asked.

Eddie hugged her back. "Hey, kiddo, you're the closest thing I'm going to have to babies for a while. You're stuck with me."

She laughed and wiped her eyes. "I'd marry you if we weren't both taken. You make a fantastic wife."

He grinned. "Sorry, sweetie. I love you, but you're not my type." He kissed her cheek. "You don't have the right parts."

She roared with laughter. Now, with Thomas out of the woods and on the mend, Eddie had devoted himself to making her laugh as if his babysitting duties weren't enough of a blessing to her.

Tyler emerged from the bedroom. "What are you out here cackling about, love?"

Nevvie grinned. "I just propositioned Eddie and he turned me down."

Tyler laughed. "I would hope so. I'm rather territorial. I'm not about to share you or Thomas with anyone else." He winked at Eddie. "Not even you, mate. Sorry."

Eddie gently slapped him on the back. "Throw him in, Nev, maybe I could turn a blind eye to your shortcomings."

She'd started to take a sip of coffee. At Eddie's quip she choked and snorted it through her nose. Fortunately for her, it had cooled somewhat already. She laughed, long and hard until both men realized a moment later she was crying.

They crowded close, both hugging her as she cried. Tyler handed her a dishtowel. "Are you all right, love?"

"Other than losing my fucking mind, I'm fine."

Nevvie spent most of the day with Tyler, shuttling him to appointments and taking care of things at the office while Peggy stayed with Tommy at the hospital. Later that afternoon, Eddie brought Adam home and stayed with Tyler until Nevvie swapped off with Peggy.

Tommy looked at her. "Why don't you go home, babe?"

"Why? Are you sick of me?" she teased. "Don't want any more sponge baths?"

He lay back in bed and closed his eyes. "You should go home and get some rest."

Nevvie sat next to his bed. "Talk to me."

"Go home."

"Why?"

"Because Tyler needs you."

"You need me."

"I'm okay. Not like I'm going anywhere," he grumbled.

"You need your bath." Peggy had already told Nevvie he wouldn't let her shave him that morning. Stubble shadowed his cheeks.

"I'm fine."

Maybe the playful approach would work. "Are you going to let me play naughty nurse today? Give you a bath?" She gently goosed him. When he grabbed her wrist and pushed her away, it startled her.

"I'm not in the mood, Nevvie." He wouldn't look at her.

"I'm sorry. I was just playing—"

"You know what? Go home, get some sleep. You look like a fucking zombie."

Her stomach hardened, she felt blood race to her cheeks. "Tommy? What's wrong?"

"Nothing's wrong except the world fucking sucks right now, okay? So just go home and leave me alone. I want to be alone for a while. Don't come back tonight either." He closed his eyes and refused to look at or talk to her.

Her whole body trembling, she finally stood and quietly gathered her things. "I'm sorry, Tommy. I didn't mean..." She quickly walked out before he could hear her cry. She knew he had a lot of emotional shit going on, between his injuries and rehab. She didn't want to dump more on him.

When she got to the car she sat behind the wheel and cried for ten minutes before finally starting it and heading home.

* * * *

Thomas heard the tears in her voice, but wouldn't look at her. If he did that he'd feel even shittier than he already did. She shouldn't have to be his fucking nurse, she already had so much to take care of. The baby, Tyler, the business.

Why not act like an asshole? He already felt like a piece of shit. He felt guilty he'd hurt her feelings, and he knew she was just trying to be playful. Hell, he'd already screwed up their lives anyway, why not one more thing to feel guilty about while he was at it?

He used the hospital phone to call Tyler's cell.

"Well hello, handsome."

Thomas ignored the endearment. "Keep her home tonight, Ty," he said by way of greeting.

Tyler hesitated. "What's wrong?"

"Just keep her home. She looks like shit. Make her stay home and sleep."

"Love, what's going on?"

"Nothing's going on, goddammit. I'm not a fucking kid. I don't need a goddamned babysitter at night. Make her stay home with you." He slammed the phone down on the rolling tray.

Tyler looked at the phone. He'd noticed over the past few days that Tom's mood had darkened, but between the logistical issues of not being able to drive, his own doctor appointments, and juggling the schedule so someone stayed with him and the baby, he hadn't had time to sit down and talk to Tom about it.

Peggy was out in the kitchen. "What's wrong?"

Tyler shook his head. "I think our boy is in a foul mood."

She snorted. "Yeah. If he wasn't in pain I'd take a damn switch to his hide." She sighed. "He'll be okay when y'all get him home. He's tired of being in the hospital."

"I hope that's all."

Nevvie walked in and hurried past the kitchen without a look their way. He shared a glance with Peggy, then followed Nevvie to their bedroom.

She was already in the shower. "Are you all right, love?" It was odd for her to shower in the afternoon when she'd already had one that morning.

"I'm fine, Tyler." Her voice didn't sound right. When he stuck his head into the shower, Nevvie turned her back to him. "I'll be out in a little while."

She sounded anything but fine, her voice too tight and strained.

"What happened?"

"Nothing."

"Then why did he just call here a few minutes ago, asking me to keep you home tonight?"

Her shoulders slumped. She leaned against the wall and cried.

He quickly shed his own clothes and stepped in with her, holding her as she cried against him.

"It's okay, love."

"I just want to take care of him, get him home. I don't know what I did that upset him. What did I do?"

He kissed her temple. "You didn't do anything wrong, I'm sure. He's going through a stage, that's all."

The next morning, Nevvie arose before Tyler and quickly showered, dressed, and left for the hospital. Maybe if she got there early, when Thomas had pain meds and before his physical therapy, he might be in a better mood.

His untouched breakfast sat on the rolling tray. He stared at the TV with a grim look on his face.

Nevvie hesitated at the room door. The doctors had warned them to expect mood shifts, possibly even a different personality from him, because of the accident and his injuries.

This man felt like a total stranger to her, nothing like her sweet, playful Thomas.

She forced a cheerful smile. "Hi, sweetie."

He didn't look at her. "Hi."

Fighting back her tears, she walked in and sat next to him. "I'm sorry about yesterday."

"Don't fucking apologize. You didn't do anything wrong."

Her false cheer dissolved. "Then why are you mad at me?"

"I'm not mad at you."

After a few chilly minutes, she stood and reached for his breakfast tray.

"What are you doing?"

"I'm going to set this out for you."

"Don't bother. Leave it. I'm not hungry." He finally looked at her. "You know, maybe you should go today. Go to the office or something. You're here every day. You need to get back to normal."

"I can't do that until I get you home. I want you home."

"There's probably a shit load of stuff to do at the office. You'll be buried when you get back."

"No, that's okay, it's—"

"Go." He looked away, focused on the TV again. Conversation over.

She tried to beat back the fear in her gut before it consumed her. When it was obvious he wasn't speaking to her anymore, she slowly picked up her tote bag and leaned in to kiss him good-bye. He didn't turn away, but he didn't look at her either.

"I love you, Tommy."

"Love you, too." But his voice sounded chilly, hard.

She managed to hold back her tears until she reached the elevator.

When the nurse walked in ten minutes later, she noticed Thomas hadn't touched his breakfast. "Not hungry?"

"I don't have a lot of strength in my arms this morning. I need some help, please." He was tired of Nevvie and everyone having to wait on him hand and foot, tired of the pitying looks in their eyes every time they saw there was something he couldn't do.

At least the staff was paid to take care of people. He shouldn't have to put his family through it.

"I'll get an aide in here to help you."

"Thanks."

He'd tried to get the cover off himself minutes before Nevvie arrived and realized it was a bad morning, barely able to lift his arms off the bed. If he tried to eat while she was there, she'd see how fucking weak he was. Then she'd never leave, she'd stay, hovering over him all day, trying to help.

And he'd feel even more fucking guilty.

Despite his stomach growling from the smell of the food going cold, he refused to let Nevvie see him helpless.

He hated that he hurt her feelings, but he hated even more the helpless feeling. Hell, Adam could feed himself better on a good day than he could sometimes.

* * * *

Later that evening, with Tyler and Adam at home with Peggy, Nevvie told them she was going to the grocery store but instead she drove to the hospital. As she approached his room she heard voices inside, Tommy talking to someone.

She felt a little relieved. He almost sounded normal, like he was in a good mood.

Forcing a smile she didn't feel, she walked in. A nurse's aide was helping him eat. Mentally she stumbled over that, but hoped the smile held. "Hey, handsome." She leaned in and kissed him.

It was as if a mask dropped over his face. "Hi."

"Want me to help you with that?"

"No."

Nevvie stepped back as if he'd slapped her. "Tommy, I don't mind."

"I'm almost done. You should go home and rest. Don't bother coming back tonight. You need to stay home and get some sleep."

He wasn't almost done. In fact, it looked like he'd just started eating. "I'm okay. I want to spend time with you."

He finally looked at her. "Go home. Go take care of Tyler. He needs you. I'm fine."

Nevvie thought her heart would stop, pain flaring deep in her soul. She didn't want him to see her cry. "Okay. Have a good night." She was actually glad she had to go to the store. It would give her time to stop crying, to get herself cleaned up so Tyler didn't see.

* * * *

The nurse's aide watched Nevvie walk out. "Ouch."

Thomas set his jaw. "She's wasted too much time on me as it is."

"Doesn't seem like she thinks it's wasted time." The older woman, Marge, fed him another spoonful of mashed potatoes. The physical therapist had stopped by earlier, assured him that sometimes intermittent weakness this soon was normal, especially after two weeks in a coma and a traumatic brain injury.

He still could barely lift his arms that day, had needed help with lunch, too.

Needed help to even wipe his fucking ass. Nevvie already had one baby at home, she didn't need two to take care of.

"She doesn't need me dragging her down."

"Shouldn't that be her decision?"

"She doesn't think straight when it comes to me. Tyler needs her more right now. He's got his shit together. I'm just a fuckup. One fucking decision and I ruined a bunch of lives. I'm the last person she needs in her life."

"Sounds like you've got yourself a raging pity party going there." Marge shoved another spoonful of potatoes into his mouth before he could answer.

* * * *

Five days later, the doctors discharged him. Nevvie didn't spend another night at the hospital with him, and Tyler's attempts to talk to her about it only seemed to upset her. For once, he let the subject drop. Since he wasn't cleared to drive yet, he couldn't go visit alone and try to pry the truth out of Thomas.

Or pound some sense into him.

Peggy stayed at home with Tyler and Adam while Eddie went with Nevvie to the hospital to bring Thomas home. Eddie stayed in the room with him while she made several trips to the car to load all his things.

"What's going on with you?" Eddie asked.

Thomas sat in a wheelchair, his new crutches propped between his legs. He also had a walker that he had to use on the really bad days, but much of the time now he could get by with the crutches. At least one thing he could manage. "I'm in pain."

"What did you say to Nevvie?" Eddie quietly asked.

"What are you talking about?"

"She's been upset the past few days. It happened after she came to visit you. She won't talk about it. Tyler can't even get it out of her. I'm your friend. Talk to me if you can't talk to them, but talk, dammit."

Thomas inwardly swore. Just call him King Caca, because everything he touched turned to shit. "I'm fine. I'm just in a lot of fucking pain. I'm sorry I'm not Mr. Congeniality right now."

Eddie shut up. When Nevvie reappeared it looked like she'd pasted a smile on her face. "Okay! We're all set, all we need is the paperwork and we can spring you."

Thomas watched TV. "Yay. Yippee."

Her forced cheerfulness didn't help his mood, either. "Can I get you anything while we're—"

"No. I'm fine."

He noticed Eddie and Nevvie exchanged a look. Eddie stood. "I'm gonna run to the bathroom. I'll be back in about fifteen minutes." He left.

Thomas closed his eyes. "Well that was fucking subtle."

She sat on the bed. "What did I do? I'm sorry, I was just trying to be playful the other day." Her eyes welled up. "Please, tell me what I did to make you mad at me."

Fuck. "I'm *not* mad at you." He finally looked at her. He wanted to kill himself over how miserable she looked. She'd busted her ass for his worthless hide, and here he was treating her like shit. He took a deep breath. "Seriously. You didn't do anything wrong."

She walked into the bathroom and he heard her blow her nose. A moment later she returned. "Please let me take care of you."

He reached out and she took his hand. He softened his voice. "I love you. I don't deserve someone as good as you."

She stroked his cheek. He needed a shave and he was overdue for a haircut. "I love you, and you guys stood by me. Why wouldn't I stand by you?"

* * * *

Tyler and Peggy walked outside when Nevvie drove up. Eddie rode in the backseat and pried himself out to help Thomas get out of the front seat. Nevvie unloaded the folding wheelchair and brought it around for him.

Thomas struggled for a moment with his crutches, then finally allowed them to help him sit in the wheelchair. "Thank you," he said.

Inside, his mood and attitude softened. They'd prepared a welcome home party, including cake. It'd been over a month since he'd been home, and yet it weirdly felt like he'd just left the other day, a strange disorientation.

He forced a smile he didn't feel, said the words he knew they wanted to hear, but later that evening when he realized he was nearing collapse he laid down on the couch and asked Nevvie to bring him some pillows. Peggy had already gone to bed after putting Adam down.

"Don't you want to come to bed, Tommy?" Nevvie asked. Tyler stood behind her, looking hopeful.

Great, more guilt.

"I can get up and down better from the couch for now." At least it was partially the truth.

Nevvie walked back to the bedroom to get the pillows. Thomas tried to ignore Tyler's sad expression when he sat on the couch next to him.

"I was so worried about you, love," Tyler whispered.

Thomas wouldn't look at him. "I'm okay. I'm sorry I've fucked everything up."

"Thomas, it was an accident! You didn't do anything wrong."

"I should have been here for you, for her." He didn't react when

Tyler slipped his arm around him.

"We love you."

Thomas shrugged Tyler's arm off. "You need to go to bed, get some rest." He didn't watch as Tyler finally stood and left.

Nevvie returned a moment later with his pillows and a light blanket. From her red eyes, he knew she'd been crying. She helped him lie down and stood there for a moment, watching him.

"What?"

"I'm just so glad to have you home, Tommy. You have no idea." She leaned in and kissed him before going to bed.

Thomas channel surfed. His mind wouldn't shut down. He was home, should be happy to be here, and yet he felt even worse. Now Nevvie would have to spend even more time taking care of him, and Tyler would be worried, too.

He must have drifted at some point. When he awoke later, he felt something warm resting against his upper arm and realized it was Nevvie's head. She was asleep, sitting on the floor next to the couch.

Choking back a sob, he carefully reached over and touched her hair, stroked it. He didn't deserve her. When he finally composed himself he gently prodded her shoulder. She sat up with a start, rubbing her eyes.

"Go back to bed, sugar," he whispered.

"I keep waking up. I was worried about you."

He stroked her cheek. "I'm okay. I'll yell if I need you."

She finally broke down crying, buried her head against him. "I missed you so much."

He nuzzled his face against the top of her head. "I missed you too, babe. But you need to go to bed. You need to sleep."

"I want to sleep with you."

"Once my leg's a little better I'll move back to bed. You go sleep."

She finally did after kissing him. He wondered what was wrong with him that he felt not just emotionally, but physically dead.

Normally a long, sweet kiss from her or Tyler would give him a hard-on and have him panting after them.

His cock felt as dead as his heart.

He watched her walk toward the bedroom as the realization struck him. *Dead.*

That's exactly how he felt.

He rolled onto his back to watch TV for a while.

* * * *

This wasn't how it was supposed to be. Nevvie knew getting Thomas home wouldn't be the final end of their journey, but she thought things would take a seismic shift back toward normalcy.

How wrong could she be?

At least Thomas was under the same roof with them again, even if after two weeks he constantly rebuffed their attempts to get him back into their bed or even allow them to show him anything other than the most basic affection.

Peggy and Karen finally returned home to Savannah at Nevvie's insistence. She hoped maybe having the house to themselves might allow Tommy to loosen up a little.

Nothing.

They finally got him approved for home physical therapy visits, but until they started, Eddie helped her shuttle Thomas to his appointments. Thomas was always grumpy and foul-tempered after. Nevvie struggled to maintain her forced good mood, but admitted there were days she wanted to smack him.

She knew he hurt, knew he was in pain and frustrated that his progress wasn't as fast as he wanted. Tyler's recovery went perfectly, with his mood even sweeter than normal, if that was possible. While she felt guilty for her selfishness, she longed to have her sweet Tommy back, her playful husband, even if just for a day.

The new version acted like a stranger in nearly every way, and

Nevvie felt like he was slipping away from them.

* * * *

One afternoon a week later, Nevvie curled against Tyler in their bed, stroking his chest, her fingers lightly tracing his scars. That morning, his doctor had cleared him to return to sexual activities.

"I want you to make love to me. I want you inside me."

He rolled on top of her. "It's what I want too, love. We shouldn't do that today."

"Why not?"

"For one, because we only have a short time right now until Eddie brings Adam home. Two, because you're not back on the Pill yet and it's not a safe time of the month for you, and frankly, I don't think I have enough self-control to stop in time. And three, because Thomas is asleep. If he wakes up and needs us I'd rather not explain what we were doing and risk hurting his feelings. He's in a foul enough mood as it is. The three of us need to talk about all of this."

She studied his eyes. "I want another baby," she said.

He kissed her. "Is it time for you and I to have this discussion?"

She nodded.

He stroked her cheek. "You and I both know Adam is most likely my son. I want our next child to be Thomas' and I think you do, too."

She closed her eyes. "I don't want to go months without you making love to me." And at the rate they were going, she wouldn't be making love to Thomas either, if they couldn't get him back into bed with them.

"We can use condoms, sweetheart. Arrange it so he doesn't know what we're doing. You know as well as I do how he would get if he thinks we're planning behind his back. He's a 'let things happen as they will' kind of chap. He would be happy regardless of who is the father, but you and I are on the same page, as it were."

"Don't you have any condoms?"

He snorted. "Why on earth would I? Sweetheart, I bought a box years ago, before that first night in case you wanted them. I tossed them once I realized we didn't need them. They'd be over five years old now."

"Oh, right." She sighed. "Can you get some?"

"I promise. Until then…" He kissed his way between her breasts, taking time to tease first one, then the other nipple into hard peaks. She tangled her fingers in his hair as he crept lower, taking his time, teasing her. Then his breath, hot and soft on her mound and she spread her legs wider.

"Please," she whispered. "Please do it, sweetie."

"Absolutely." He teased her with the lightest of flicks of his tongue on her clit. Gently circling and tasting, making her gasp and moan for more.

He resisted her pleas to deeply plunge into her, and spent his time bringing her to the edge before pulling away and gently blowing on her mound.

"No, don't stop!"

He laughed. "Darling, I'm going to make good use of my time. It won't take you long to get me off, and I'm damn sure not looking for a quickie. You're going to have to be a good girl and lay there, or I'll tie you up."

She moaned, shivering, then lifted her head to meet his eyes. "What if I want you to tie me up?"

"You cheeky little thing." He swiped his tongue across her clit, making her jump. "You'd like that, wouldn't you? If your master tied you up and kept you begging for it."

"Mmm hmm."

He used his lips to lightly tug on her swollen nub and she ground her hips against him. "You'd love for me to keep you like this all day, I bet. Wet and open for me to plunder."

She gasped. "Yes!"

He teased her with one finger at her wet entrance. "I bet my little slave would do anything I asked of her if I kept her busy all day like that."

She bucked her hips against him, trying to goad him into making her come.

He finally rewarded her with first one, then two fingers slowly stroking inside her. "Maybe we'll have to try that one day once Master Thomas is feeling better. We'll have Eddie and Pete watch the baby, and then Thomas and I will spend the day with our little slave tied up in bed, satisfying her masters' every need—"

"Ah!"

He grabbed her clit with his lips as she started coming, licking and sucking it, feeling her muscles grip his fingers as he stroked her, prolonging her orgasm.

When she eventually finished, trembling and shuddering on the bed, he curled next to her and drew her into his arms. "How was that, sweetheart?"

A fine sheen of sweat covered her flesh. "Mmm hmm," she mumbled against his chest.

He laughed, holding her tightly. "Will that tide you through until later, love?"

"Mmm hmm."

Her hand found his stiff member and he rolled onto his back as she went down on him, taking her time.

He gently stroked the back of her head. "Oh, sweetheart, that's fantastic." He closed his eyes and thrust his hips in time with her mouth and lips, not bothering to hold back, knowing he would explode shortly. When she lightly stroked his sac his climax surged through him. "Get ready—" She went deeper, rolling her tongue along his shaft, and swallowing every drop he pumped out.

She knew when to stop and curled up in his arms as he kissed her. "Exquisite, my sweet. Wonderful."

Chapter Fifteen

Two days later, Nevvie swore when she checked her calendar.

"What's wrong, pet?" Tyler asked.

"Tommy's got PT this morning. Home visit."

Tom snorted in disgust. "Great. Physical Torture follows me to my own home. Fan-fucking-tastic."

"Shut up, you. You're getting it and you'll like it," she ordered. He glared. She realized what she'd said. "Well, you won't like it, but you're getting it, like it or not."

Tyler stepped in. He knew Tom's ire wasn't at Nevvie. "Love, I can go to cardiac rehab by myself. I've been cleared to drive, you know."

"But—"

"No buts. I'll drive myself."

Nevvie sighed. "All right. Are you sure?"

"Of course I am."

Thomas watched them from the living room as they went through their morning routine. They checked on him one more time before heading to the bathroom. The brief surge of jealousy he felt both startled and shamed him. He loved them.

On the heels of that, rage that he was stuck in a body that no longer worked the way it had. Yes, he was damned lucky he wasn't dead or more severely disabled, but they had to treat him like a fucking baby and he hated that shit with an ever-lovin' passion. Fuck, he couldn't even button his own goddamn shirts, could barely write his name.

Yes the doctors warned him about this, said it most likely would get better with time and rehab, but it still sucked.

And how was it going to be between them now? They'd asked him to sleep in bed but neither of them had tried to be intimate with him, afraid of hurting him, treating him like some fragile doll. Could he even have the kind of relationship with either of them that they'd had before?

Had they been doing it at night without him? Not that his body seemed interested in that anyway.

Jesus, what's wrong with me?

He tried to watch TV and not think about why their shower was taking so long when Nevvie appeared wearing her robe, her hair wrapped in a towel.

Coming to check on him.

"Do you need anything?"

Guilt flashed over to irritation. "No, I'm fine, dammit."

She blinked. Before he could apologize for the bite in his tone she nodded. "Okay, Tommy," she softly said, then quickly returned to their bedroom and shut the door behind her.

Dammit. He'd done it again. He saw the pain in her face, caused by his words. She deserved better than that from him. She'd been through so much trying to hold it together for them when they'd promised to take care of her.

He heard a car outside and a moment later, the doorbell rang.

"Come on in," he hollered. "It's open."

A young woman—jeez, couldn't be any older than her early twenties—stuck her head in. "Hi, I'm with the home health care team. Mr. Kinsey?"

He pointed to his leg. "I sure as hell ain't Pegleg Pete," he quipped. "Come on in, honey."

She blushed a little but walked in, a large tote slung over her shoulder. She crossed into the living room, sticking her hand out in greeting. "Hi, I'm Jennifer," she said with a nervous smile.

She must be new at this. "Hi, Jennifer. Are you here for my daily dose of torture?"

She laughed. "I've heard it called worse but yes, I am."

The bedroom door opened and Nevvie raced out. She was now dressed in shorts and a blouse. "Tommy? Are you okay?" She pulled up when she saw Jennifer. "Hi."

"Nev, this is Jennifer from the home health care place," Tommy explained. "The physical torturer."

"Oh, good."

Tyler walked out of the bedroom and kissed Nevvie. "I need to fly or I'll be late. I'll check the mail for you, love," he said. He glanced at Thomas. "Have fun," he said with a wink.

"Fuck you, Ty," he groused.

"Later, if you're good," he joked as he left.

Jennifer apparently didn't know what to think of that comment, so she acted like she didn't hear it.

Nevvie shook her head at Tyler's departure. "Did you need my help?" she asked the girl.

"Oh, no. I'm going to do a preliminary evaluation and then start some range of motion exercises with him today."

Nevvie started to say something when the baby cried. "Okay, call me if you need me." Nevvie disappeared down the hall, leaving them alone.

The girl sat next to Thomas on the couch, asking questions, making notes on a form. Fifteen minutes later, she put her clipboard down. "Okay, let's see what we've got." She looked at his leg and started carefully checking his range of motion.

"How long you been torturing people, sugar?" he quipped. "You don't look like you've been out of school long."

She smiled. "I'm three months out of my internship."

"So how does a girl get into this kind of gig? Are you a closet sadist or dominatrix?"

She blushed again, reminding Thomas of how Nevvie used to blush when she first came to work for them years earlier, flushing at their compliments and endearments. "I couldn't have made it in nursing school. A friend of my mom's was doing this, it seemed interesting."

He chatted with her while she worked. She wasn't nearly as cute as Nevvie but…

The way she paid attention to him, it wasn't like the nurses in the hospital with cool efficiency and practiced rapport.

They neared the end of the hour. Nevvie had been in and out, taking care of Adam and working in his office on stuff for the business. The session had been painful, but not nearly as bad as he'd expected. Jennifer tried to be as gentle as she could and still do the exercises.

"Well," she said. "I'll be coming in three times a week at first, then we'll see how you do and progress from there."

"So you'll be back the day after tomorrow?" He didn't understand the uncomfortably expectant thump in his chest at that thought.

"Yep." She started packing her things, then finally asked the question he'd expected. "Was that really Tyler Paulson? The man here earlier?"

"Yep, that's Ty. The evil genius himself."

"Wow. I've read all his books. I thought I'd heard that he was… Um, well that's really neat. Are you friends or related?"

Thomas blinked, not understanding her question at first.

He certainly didn't understand his response. "We've known each other for a long time."

"His wife's pretty. Seems very nice."

Dangerous territory here, Tommy boy. What the fuck *are you doing?* "Yes, she is. That's Nevvie." *Say it. Say it, stupid!*

Jennifer smiled. "Well, I need to get to my next appointment. I'll see you Wednesday, day after tomorrow. Same time."

He nodded, stunned. "Okay. Looking forward to it."

She stood to go while his heart hammered in his chest. *What the fuck?* What the *fuck* was wrong with him? He wasn't even attracted to her.

As Jennifer prepared to leave, Nevvie appeared, Adam on her hip. "All done?"

"Yes, Mrs. Paulson. I told Thomas I'd be back the day after tomorrow, same time. Three times a week at first." She looked at the baby. "He's adorable. Wow, he's got Mr. Paulson's blue eyes, doesn't he?"

Nevvie smiled while Thomas cringed inside. What had he done? What was he thinking of doing?

"Yes, he does," Nevvie said. "Ty's spooky blue eyes. Right, Tommy?"

He swallowed hard. "Yeah, he sure does."

* * * *

Thomas hated himself, withdrew into an angry shell. They wouldn't want him anymore anyway, would they? Ty could have the girl, he already had the baby. He knew damn well Adam was Ty's biological son. No Kinsey baby ever had eyes looking like that. And he was the spitting image of Ty without a doubt. It didn't matter how much he loved Adam, he technically wasn't that baby's father.

Nevvie and Tyler tried to talk to him that afternoon and evening and he blew them off, focused on the TV. When Nevvie brought Adam out to him for dinner, he shook his head.

"No, just leave me alone, please. I'm...I'm in pain from this morning." Thomas tried to ignore her hurt look.

"Are you sure? He wants to spend time with his daddy."

Then go take him to Tyler, he thought, but bit it back before he could say it. "Not tonight."

She sicced Tyler on him a little later. The evil genius sat on the coffee table and stared at him until Thomas finally looked at him.

"What do you want?"

"What's wrong?" Tyler quietly asked.

"I want to be left alone, that's what's fucking wrong. I want to be able to walk to the goddamn bathroom to take a piss without needing a fucking crane to get off the couch. I want my life back."

"Please talk to us. We're worried about you."

"I just told you what I want. Leave. Me. Alone."

He mentally swore at Ty's hurt look but refused to apologize. He wanted to be left alone. They asked what he wanted, he told them, and they didn't give it to him.

Before Nevvie went to bed she came out to check on Tommy one last time. "Can I get you anything?"

"No."

He didn't miss the hurt in her eyes, the way they suddenly looked too bright, like unshed tears were building up, struggling for release.

"Okay, Tommy," she softly said. "I'll leave the door open. If you need me, call me. Are you sure you don't want to be in bed with—"

"I'm fine."

She nodded, then with her head bowed, she turned and left. He'd hurt her feelings he knew, but wouldn't take the words back.

He settled in for a long, restless night channel surfing.

* * * *

It turned out Tyler had cardiac rehab on Wednesday morning. He'd stayed mostly clear of Thomas all day Tuesday, but sat on the couch next to him before Jennifer arrived.

"Are you all right, love?"

"I'm fine. I just want life to get back to normal. That's all." That wasn't all but he damn sure wasn't going to admit that he looked forward to Jennifer's visit.

He didn't even want to admit it to himself.

"Can I get you anything? Something to drink?"

"No. Just go to your appointment."

With wounded eyes, Tyler leaned over and kissed him. Thomas

guiltily kissed him back.

Nevvie walked into the kitchen with the baby. Tyler was about to kiss her good-bye when the doorbell rang.

She walked with Tyler to the front door and they let Jennifer in.

"Back to torture the patient some more, are we?" Tyler joked. Thomas knew from the forced joviality in Tyler's voice that he still stung from their earlier exchange.

She smiled. "That's me. I wanted to tell you, Mr. Paulson, I love your books. I've read all of them."

"Why, thank you! That's very sweet of you to say." He leaned over and kissed Nevvie and Adam. "Do I need to stop at the store, sweetheart?"

"No, I've got everything I need for dinner tonight."

"Right. Then I'll see you later." He left.

Jennifer looked at Nevvie. "It must be neat having a famous author for a husband."

She shrugged. "He's a normal guy, just like Tommy, just like everyone else. It's his job."

Thomas cringed, worried Nevvie would say too much, then he mentally kicked himself for thinking that.

What the fuck is wrong with me?

Nevvie walked into the kitchen and plopped Adam into his high chair. "I'll leave you alone with Mr. Grump in there."

Jennifer laughed. "I'm not usually a welcomed visitor, that's for sure."

Thomas nervously chatted with Jennifer during their session, not sure how much Nevvie could hear. She had the small under-counter TV turned on and talked to Adam while she fed him, making silly baby voices and faces at him. She was a great mom, a wonderful wife. She deserved better than him.

She deserved Tyler, not the stress of taking care of someone like him who could barely walk.

By the end of the session he knew he was overtly flirting with

Jennifer, pushing the envelope. He enjoyed making her blush, enjoyed the way his heart raced, wondered why he was going this far and if he'd crossed the line yet. Nevvie had taken Adam back into his office after she fed him and couldn't hear them in the living room.

He'd sussed out Jennifer didn't have a boyfriend. So what if he flirted with her? It was just words.

She was almost finished with his exercises. They were alone in the living room when he blurted it out after another of his double-entendres made her blush.

"You don't mind that I'm a flirt, do you, baby girl?" He'd never called anyone but Nevvie that.

She smiled, finally met his eyes. "No, I don't mind, Thomas."

He knew he held her gaze a little too long. "Call me Tommy, sugar. No need to be so formal. Hell, the way you get to handle my body, we might as well get to know each other." Okay, he hadn't overtly lied to her, but he certainly led her to believe that Nevvie was Tyler's wife, cementing that over this visit with a few well-placed comments. Not his fault she misunderstood, was it? She couldn't get involved with him anyway, he was her patient. A little friendly flirting, right? No harm, no foul. Nothing could—would—ever come of it.

Then why the fuck had he slipped his wedding band off and put it in his pocket?

She smiled again. "Okay, Tommy. Thanks."

* * * *

Thomas lived for the appointments. Somehow his luck held. Three weeks later, Jennifer still didn't realize the truth of their home life. The few times Tyler didn't have cardiac rehab during Jennifer's visits, he would stay out of their way during therapy. Sometimes Nevvie would leave Adam home with Tyler and go to the office, relieving Thomas that she wasn't there to catch on.

He lived to flirt with Jennifer. She loosened up, flirting back openly now, filling him with a new kind of excitement he hadn't felt in a while.

And guilt.

But he shouldn't feel guilty, right? No touch, no harm, no foul.

He'd started sleeping in the guest room instead of on the couch with the excuse that he didn't want his leg to get jostled. He ignored Nevvie and Tyler's hurt looks when he refused to sleep in the bedroom with them despite their repeated requests. He didn't know if Nevvie and Tyler were having sex or not. Then again, he hadn't given them much reason to want to have sex with him, had he? And he refused to be their pity fuck.

* * * *

Nevvie knocked on the guest room doorway one Monday night. Thomas sat propped up in bed, reading. She'd noticed he'd been in a good mood all day, which was odd. She thought he'd be in a horrible mood after his PT appointments, but every time seemed to be almost...cheerful afterwards.

"What is it, Nev?"

"Can I talk to you?"

He put his book down. She shouldn't feel like this, feel like she had to climb a wall to get back to her husband.

She carefully sat on the bed next to him and reached for his hand. She felt as much tenderness in him as a store dummy. "What's going on, Tommy?" she quietly asked.

"What?"

"This," she said, indicating the guest bed. "Do we ever get to sleep with you again?"

"Do you want to?"

She felt shocked, hurt. "Of course we do! Why the hell do you think we keep asking you to sleep where you belong? What is going on with you?"

He jerked his hand free. "I don't want my leg to get hurt."

"This is more than your leg. You're pushing us away. You've barely said more than five words to Tyler in the past couple of days, you don't spend time with Adam, and you practically ignore me. Talk to us. Please? You're not just sleeping in a different room. It's like you're living on another planet."

"I'm fine. I'm just trying to adjust."

"How long do you keep pushing us away? We're waiting for you to let us back in. We aren't going anywhere."

Thomas wanted to put his arm around her and pull her to him, love the hurt from her face. And yet he also hated himself for thinking ahead to Wednesday.

To Jennifer.

"I'm not pushing you away," he lied.

She stared at him for several minutes, then finally leaned in and kissed him. "Just know that when you're ready to have us back, we're waiting for you, Tommy. We love you, and we miss our tough guy. We want him back."

He couldn't stop the words. "Well, you don't get a tough guy back, do you? You get a guy with a fucking leg that's got more metal than bone in it," he spat.

She flinched, hurt, startled by his angry tone.

"Wait, Nev, honey—"

Before he could reach out and grab her hand and apologize, she sobbed and ran from the room.

He closed his eyes and swore. She deserved better than him. She deserved someone who had his shit together.

She deserved Tyler.

Chapter Sixteen

Thomas wanted space, he got it. Nevvie left for the office early the next morning, leaving Tyler at home with him and not returning until nearly dark. Tyler's quiet, hurt looks all day tore at his heart, but what could he say to him?

Wednesday morning, Nevvie was already gone when Thomas got up. Tyler heard him and came in to help.

"Where's Nev?" Thomas asked.

"Does it matter? Do you really care?" Tyler quietly asked, carefully helping him limp to the bathroom. "It's not like you've taken a great interest in her in the past several weeks. There's only so much she can take, love. She needs a break until you're ready to let her back in. Getting rejected by you hurts her. She's about ready to stop trying, I think."

Thomas bit back a reply. Nothing he said to Tyler would be right or even fair and he damn well knew it.

Later, he sat at the kitchen table and watched Tyler feed Adam. He loved the little guy. Adam kept reaching for him, stretching and kicking and fussing until Tyler slid the high chair closer to Thomas.

He smiled, trying not to cry. This little guy loved him, would see him as his daddy as much as Tyler, no matter what the birth certificate said.

"He's missed you, too," Tyler said. "We all have."

Thomas glared at Ty. "I'm right here. I'm not going anywhere, if you haven't noticed. I can't with my leg fucked up anyway."

"You don't have to be gone to be absent," he replied. Tyler glanced at the clock. "Can you sit with him while I go shower? Help him with his breakfast?"

Thomas nodded. Tyler left the room.

Adam gazed at him with those big blue eyes. Tyler's big blue eyes, the same eyes he fell in love with so many years ago.

He knew it wasn't fair to treat them like this. He hated himself for it. He also didn't know how to find his way back to them. Tyler wasn't stupid. Tyler had to know Adam was his biological child. The baby looked just like him, for chrissake. Yet he'd never staked a claim. When Tyler talked, he always referred to Adam as "our" son, not his.

Just like he called Nevvie "our" wife.

Another bolt of white-hot guilt shot through him. Nevvie and Tyler loved him. How long would they wait for him to get his fucking head on straight?

When the doorbell rang, Tom's heart took off at a runaway pace.

Shit. "Come in!"

Jennifer walked in. "Oh, you're babysitting today?"

His heart pounded, but now he wasn't sure if it was eagerness or self-loathing.

The bedroom door opened down the hall, Ty's voice calling to them. "Are you all right, Thomas?"

"We're fine. It's just Jennifer."

"All right. I'll be finished in a moment." The door shut again. Tom's stomach knotted as he realized what he'd been doing.

No, that wasn't right. He knew damn well what he'd been doing, just not *why* he'd been doing it. And he needed to rectify it. Today.

He would set the record straight today, apologize for flirting.

He had to.

Jennifer reached out and tickled the baby's chin. "He's such a cutie pie. I cannot get over those eyes. Just like his father."

Her words burned inside him. "Yeah," he agreed. "Just like his old man."

"Do you need help getting out to the living room? I can sit here with him."

He handed her a damp towel. "If you could just wipe him off and bring him, he'll be okay crawling around on the floor for a minute until Ty's done."

"Okay."

He watched her with his son, knowing in his heart Nevvie would kill him if she knew what he was thinking, what he'd been doing. When Jennifer picked Adam up, part of him wanted to tell her to put his son down.

But he wasn't his son. Not really. He was Tyler's.

He turned and carefully limped out to the living room on his crutches.

Tyler appeared a few moments later. "Ah, I see you've got our little chub taken care of. Did he give you any trouble?"

Thomas knew Tyler's comments were directed at Jennifer, but he quickly answered.

"None at all, Tyler."

Jennifer scooped the baby up and handed him to Tyler. "He's a cutie, Mr. Paulson."

Tyler cast a loving look at Thomas. "We think so. We've been very blessed, haven't we, Thomas?"

Thomas silently groaned as he nodded his agreement, hating himself. Tyler still wasn't laying sole claim to Adam, but Jennifer wouldn't understand his comment.

"Well, I shall leave the two of you alone. Call me if you need me." To Tommy's immense relief, Tyler took Adam into his study and closed the door behind him.

Jennifer smiled. "Happy to see me?"

"Yeah." He hated himself. "Real happy."

* * * *

Near the end of their appointment, his leg cramped up. She

stopped the exercises and started massaging it for him. About that time, Nevvie walked in the front door, carrying take-out sacks from a fast food restaurant.

"I brought lunch, Tommy," she announced in a neutral tone as she put them on the kitchen counter, then disappeared into Tyler's study and closed the door behind her.

"Thank you, Nevvie," he called after her. His heart quickened, then he turned back to Jennifer.

He should tell her, tell her right now.

She smiled. "Better? Or…" She paused, her hand hesitating on his inner thigh. "Is there anywhere else you need massaged?" Her eyes bored into his. He'd picked up the pace of his flirting over the past few appointments, the adrenaline rush he got from each visit carrying him through to the next.

He stared at her, trying to force out a declaration of the truth but instead said, "What did you have in mind?"

"I could get into a lot of trouble," she whispered. "I'm not supposed to get involved with clients."

Thomas thought his heart would race out of his chest. "Who said I'm telling, sugar?" *Fuck!* It was like someone else controlled his goddamn mind. Maybe he could claim brain damage?

She leaned in closer as her hand traveled north up his thigh. "I really look forward to our sessions."

"Me too."

He froze when Nevvie opened the study door. She carried Adam on her hip and walked to the kitchen without a look his way. He couldn't blame her, but now part of him prayed she would turn around. If she looked through the counter, she would see what was going on.

She would stop it. Stop him. Apparently he didn't have the power to stop himself.

Nevvie turned away from the living room and settled Adam in his high chair.

His eyes returned to Jennifer. She didn't think anything of it. Why the hell would she? He had led her to believe Nevvie was Tyler's wife, not his.

Not theirs.

And that Tyler, the man he considered his soul mate—the man he'd been lovers with for most of Jennifer's life—was just his friend. And that he was only staying there while he healed.

He felt helpless to stop her when she leaned in to kiss him. As her lips brushed his, he heard Tyler's shocked voice.

"Bloody hell!"

Jennifer jumped. Tyler, his jaw gaping, stood in the living room doorway.

Startled, Nevvie turned and looked at Tyler, then followed his line of sight to the living room.

Thomas reddened.

Nevvie recovered her voice first although the calm, even tone of it scared the crap out of Thomas. "What the hell is going on?"

Jennifer sat back, embarrassed and jumping to the wrong conclusion. "I'm sorry. I didn't mean to offend you."

Tyler finally spoke. "You're kissing our husband and you don't think that's going to offend us?"

Jennifer blinked in total confusion. "*Your* husband?" She looked at Thomas, to Tyler, then to Nevvie. "But you're married to Mr. Paulson."

"My name's Nevaeh Kinsey-Paulson for a reason." She pointed at Thomas. "He's my husband, too. We're polyamorous. He and Tyler were together for over ten years when they met me. They're bisexual, honey."

Jennifer stared, shocked. Tyler stood silent in the doorway. Jennifer looked at Thomas and backed away. "I thought you said they were married."

"I know. I'm sorry, baby girl."

Nevvie gasped. Her jaw dropped, like she was going to say

something, then snapped closed again.

Jennifer jumped up, muttered apologies, and quickly gathered her things.

Tyler turned, silently stalked down the hall to their bedroom and slammed the door behind him.

Tyler never slammed doors. In their eighteen years together, Thomas could never remember Tyler slamming a door. He could count on one hand the times he'd heard Tyler raise his voice in anger, one of those times being just now.

Jennifer hurried from the house. They heard her car pull out of the driveway.

Thomas forced himself to look at Nevvie. He knew that look well—Nevvie was too upset to speak. She clamped her lips together and turned from him, her back stiff. She picked up the baby. When Thomas called out to her, she raised her hand without even looking at him.

He heard their bedroom door open and close. She didn't slam it with the baby in her arms.

She was the door slammer. The fact that Tyler had slammed the door and Nevvie didn't, even with the baby in her arms, told him more than any words ever could.

Ten minutes later the bedroom door opened again. He heard Tyler's desperate, low pleas, then heard Nevvie walk to the nursery. She appeared a few minutes later with Adam and breezed past him without a glance his way, the diaper bag and—was that an overnight bag?—on her shoulder. He tried to call out to her and she completely ignored him as she rushed out the front door.

Tyler didn't appear.

Thomas hated himself. *Now I've done it. The two people who really love me and give a damn and that's what I do to them. I don't fucking deserve them.*

He carefully made his way onto the couch and took a moment to catch his breath. It hurt, but it wasn't as bad as a few weeks ago. He was healing.

He grabbed his crutches. While he'd intended to go all the way to the bedroom to talk to Ty, he only made it as far as the kitchen and sat at the table. The food, now cold, still sat on the counter in the bags.

She'd come home to talk, probably, because she wouldn't have driven all the way home just to bring lunch. And he'd acted like an ass.

Dammit, would she ever forgive him? Would either of them forgive him? Tyler had looked as hurt as Nevvie.

He'd started to get up when he heard the bedroom door open again. Tyler had changed clothes and carried his keys. When he walked by the kitchen, he didn't look at Thomas.

"Ty!"

Tyler stopped, frozen, but didn't turn. "Yes?" he quietly asked.

"I'm sorry."

After a long moment, Tyler finally nodded, still not turning. "I'll tell her you said that, if I find her." Still the same soft, hurt tone. "She wouldn't tell me where she was going."

* * * *

Nevvie cried. Fuck, it's not like she caught him with his dick in the girl's mouth, but now she felt like a fucking moron. All these weeks, looking back, the pattern was crystal clear. Tommy pushing her—them—away, then all happy and shit after an appointment that should make him hurt like hell.

Fuck.

Not sleeping in bed with them despite their repeated requests, opting for the guest room. Why would he want to sleep with them when his mind was on Jennifer? She hadn't seen the kiss—Tyler told her what she'd missed—but she'd *heard*.

Nevvie drove to the office, knowing she had maybe a twenty minute head start. Tyler would look for her there first. She ignored his calls, sending them straight to voice mail. She unbuckled the baby and raced inside to get her laptop and some files. She'd go to a hotel for the day, calm down, and then go home tomorrow to talk. She knew she couldn't talk to Thomas like this. She was too angry, would say something she'd regret.

Would want to kick his bad leg or smack him upside the skull. Maybe rip his tongue out of his head and shove it up his ass so he could lick his balls from the inside out.

When she was this mad, she knew she needed to calm down. It wouldn't do anyone any good for her to confront him feeling like this. She had to get her emotions under control first, get rational again.

Maggie tried to waylay her but Nevvie had her follow and carry Adam while she gathered her things.

"What's up, Nevvie?"

She couldn't face her friend. "Long story, I'll tell you later. But if Tyler or Thomas—especially Thomas—calls looking for me, you didn't see me."

"What?"

Nevvie shook her head, fighting her tears. If she started crying she wouldn't stop. "Please," she pleaded. "It'll take too long to explain."

Confused, Maggie nodded. "Okay."

"Thank you. I'll call you tomorrow to check in and see if there's anything I need to take care of." Maggie followed her to the car. Nevvie loaded the stuff in the trunk, then took Adam. "Thank you."

Nevvie quickly buckled him in and drove off.

Her phone rang fifteen minutes later, Tyler's cell, and she let it go to voice mail. By that time she was already on the interstate heading…she didn't know where. West, for now, toward downtown Tampa. From there, who knew? She played the voice mail. Tyler's soft, hurt tone crushed her heat.

"Nevvie, darling, please. Call me. Maggie wouldn't tell me you'd been here, but from the looks of things I'm assuming you were. Please, talk to me. I love you."

How long since Tommy had said that to either of them? Felt like forever, that's for sure. He used to say it to them every day, all the time. Especially making a point to say it to Tyler every night before bed, a routine they'd had since the very start of their relationship. The past few weeks he'd been like a stone wall, nothing in, nothing out.

How stupid was it that she wasn't even pissed off so much about the kiss? That she could have taken, because she didn't actually see it, Tyler did and filled in the blank she'd missed.

But he called Jennifer "baby girl."

She was his baby girl.

Or, that's what she's always thought.

Maybe Tommy didn't think she was so special after all. Maybe he called lots of women that. Maybe another thing she'd been too stupid to notice.

She cried so hard she had to take the Dale Mabry exit and sat crying in the Wal-Mart parking lot and tried to collect herself. Her phone rang three more times and she put it on silent.

All Tyler, not Tommy.

How would the boys play it? Would Tommy sweet talk Tyler and try to have him do the dirty work for him? Or maybe he didn't really give a fuck about them anymore and wanted them to really leave him alone for good. It's what he'd been asking for, right?

Baby girl. From the early days, even before she ever moved in with them when she was still just their cleaning girl, she'd been Tyler's angel and Tommy's baby girl. Those were their pet names for her.

They'd made her feel special—truly loved—for the first time ever in her life.

When she calmed down she drove south a couple of blocks to the large Borders bookstore. Fortunately she had Adam's stroller in the trunk and she spent hours browsing, finally buying a few things. She left her phone in the car.

She didn't feel like eating. It was now after six. Tyler had called five more times since she went in the store.

It wasn't fair to punish him like that. He'd done nothing wrong. She opted to send him a text message.

I'm fine. I'll call you later.

It was a lie because she wasn't fine, but she had to calm down. Tyler would try to get her to come home and she had to control her anger before she faced Tommy. Twenty seconds later, her phone rang. *Tyler*. She sent it straight to voice mail. Another fifteen seconds after that, a text message arrived.

Whr r u?

She knew he had to be upset to be using abbreviations. He was nearly as adept at typing with his BlackBerry as he was on a computer, and he abhorred text shorthand with a passion.

Later Tyler, she replied.

She made her way back to the office. How ironic, that she ended up at Tommy's office? She'd changed her mind about going to a hotel. She knew if she did, Tyler would be monitoring credit cards online and find out where she went. She had to come back to work the next morning anyway. Not to mention while they had the money, her old thrifty habits died hard and she couldn't bring herself to spend the money when staying at the office was free.

She let herself in, glad to note there were no other cars in the lot. She brought Adam and her things into Tommy's office and settled in for the night. He had a TV and cable, a couch comfortable enough to sleep on, there was a bathroom with a shower, and she already had extra supplies for the baby right there. She'd have a damn short commute in the morning. She retrieved Adam's portable crib from her office and locked herself in. Eventually, around eight o'clock, she sent Tyler a text message.

Go outside. I'll call in 3.

She did. He answered immediately. "Sweetheart, where are you? Are you all right?"

Now she felt guilty. "I'm fine, Ty. I just can't come home right now. I'll kill him if I do."

"Where are you? Please tell me."

"No, because you'll show up."

"Are you mad at me?"

"No! You didn't do anything wrong. I'm not mad at you, baby, I swear."

"Let me come be with you then."

"Someone's got to stay with the asshole."

He was quiet for a long moment. "What makes you think I wish to be here with him any more than you do?"

Yikes. She hadn't thought about that. He had to be as pissed off as she was. Maybe more. If she'd actually seen the kiss, she might feel even more pissed off than she already did.

"I'm at the office. I got here a little while ago. I'm going to spend the night here. Adam and I spent the afternoon doing some retail therapy at Borders."

He faked a hurt tone, trying to cheer her up. "Ah, my favorite store. And you didn't take me, love."

She fought the urge to cry. "Did you hear what he called her?" she whispered in a choked voice. "Did you hear him?"

"Yes, love." She knew from his tone of voice that he hurt as much as she did. "I heard him. I'm so sorry."

She cried, the one thing she didn't want to do because she knew he would come for sure. "I can't be around him right now. I have to calm down before I come home or I'll say something I can't take back. I'm sorry. I love you."

"I love you too, sweetheart."

Sobbing, she hung up and curled up on the couch.

* * * *

Thomas watched as Tyler looked at his phone and then walked outside, closing the back door behind him. Tyler stared at his phone like he was waiting for a call.

Ty had said nothing to him all afternoon despite his repeated apologies and trying to get him to talk. Tyler had anxiously paced through the house after he returned from trying to find Nevvie. She wouldn't answer his calls. That Tyler—the peacemaker, the soother, the fixer, the talker—that he wouldn't talk, much less look at him told Thomas how much he hurt.

Guilt ravaged Thomas. God he was a stupid asshole. What the hell had come over him anyway?

Then Tyler put the phone to his ear, talking. She must have called him back. Thomas waited. Tyler finally returned, hurrying straight for the bedroom, talking on the phone again, this time to someone else apparently. When Tyler reappeared a few minutes later, he also had a bag packed.

Well, he deserved for them to leave him. Between acting like an asshole and then what happened, he'd finally succeeded in pushing them away.

Tyler brought Thomas his cell phone. "There's your phone. Pete will be here shortly. Keep it with you. If you fall or have a problem before he gets here you can call him or 911. Frankly, I don't care which. I'll leave the front door unlocked." Tyler turned to go.

"Where are you going?" Thomas asked, fear creeping into his heart. He'd really fucked up this time.

Tyler didn't turn. "I'm going to her and will try to talk her into coming home. If I can't get her to come home, I'll stay with her tonight. I don't want her alone as upset as she is." His voice sounded quiet. "You know damn well she doesn't sleep well when she's alone. Or have you forgotten that also?"

"Where is she?"

"If I tell you, she'll have my bollocks. And I'm rather fond of them. At least one of us needs to keep her best interests in mind since apparently you aren't capable of it anymore." He wouldn't turn.

"It didn't mean anything. It...I was just flirting with her and it got out of hand. I never thought anything would happen."

Tyler snorted with disgust. "Yes, kissing someone who doesn't mean anything to you after we've been together for nearly two decades. That makes me feel sooo much better, Thomas. Be sure to tell that one to Nevvie. She's liable to neuter you with her bare hands."

Tyler let out a long, deep breath. "When we started this, with her, we agreed no one else. Just the three of us. If you wish to change that, you're on your own. I do not want anyone but you and Nevvie. If you want someone new…well, then you'll have to pursue that without the two of us."

"I'm sorry, Ty."

Tyler finally turned, his eyes bright with tears. "I'm sure you are. But try telling her that. Anything else. Couldn't you have said *anything* else, you stupid sod?"

"What?"

Tyler shook his head, stared at the ceiling. "She's mad about the kiss, yes. What has Nevvie distraught is what you said to that girl. I don't know if Nevvie will ever forgive you that. I can't say as I blame her if she doesn't, either."

Now Thomas was confused. "What did I say?"

Tyler glared at him. "Think about it. Was it really worth breaking Nevvie's heart over that girl? Especially over someone who 'didn't matter' to you? Replay that little vignette in your brain damaged head and think about it long and hard. The kiss she can forgive. Perhaps I can, too. What you said to that girl ripped a piece of Nevvie's soul right out of her, and for that I don't know if *I* can forgive you. You bloody well know what her life was like before us. We were the two people she trusted to never hurt her, to always love her, and then you went and did that to her." Tyler headed for the door.

Thomas panicked, afraid if Tyler left he might not see him—or Nevvie—again. "I love you."

Tyler stopped, his hand on the doorknob. "Yes, I love you, too. I fancy you should have been saying that to Nevvie and myself over the past few weeks. Or were you too busy saying it to Jennifer?" He walked out. Thomas flinched when Tyler slammed the door behind him.

He sat, confused, replaying it in his mind.

It hit him immediately. Nevvie's stunned look.

Aw, *Christ*, could he have fucked his life up any worse if he'd tried?

It'd just been words. Just words. No touch, no foul? But man had he fouled up.

Pete arrived twenty minutes later, looking confused, an overnight bag slung over his shoulder. He left his bag in the hall, dropped his large frame into a living room chair and stared at Thomas.

"So," Pete said. He stared at Thomas.

Thomas looked down, unable to meet the weight of Pete's gaze.

Pete sighed. "You gonna tell me what the fuck you did to piss them off, or I gotta call Ty back and ask him myself?"

Thomas shook his head, still studying the floor. "I fucked up bad. Real bad."

"I get that. I don't get a call at night to come babysit your ass so Tyler can go find Nevvie and possibly stay with her because you left the toilet seat up and a floater in the bowl. What the fuck did you do?"

Thomas told him.

Pete sat back and groaned. "Jesus, you stupid fucking asshole." He shook his head. "Those two were *dying* over you, man. You go do something fucking stupid like that?"

"I know."

"No, you *don't* know!" Pete roared, hauling his frame out of the chair, pacing in front of the couch. "Did they tell you what happened when she got the call about your accident?"

"Bob told me she got upset."

He snorted, shaking his head. "Upset? Fuck that. Bob didn't tell you everything, asshole. Ask your mom, she saw some of it, not the worst. You weren't the one holding her down in the ER when she collapsed—I was. I held her while she was fucking screaming for you, sobbing at the top of her goddamn lungs, begging the doctors to give you back to her, about to lose her fucking mind over you, asshole. You don't know *shit*! I will never in my life ever forget how she sounded, how she looked, how much she was hurting for the two of you. That will haunt me till my dying fucking day, man."

He turned and jabbed a meaty finger at Thomas. "You didn't see her losing fucking weight, spending all day every day, and then every goddamned night in the ICU with the two of you, worried about every fucking blip on your monitors. How she bathed and shaved you every night, talking to you, reading to you. And even after Tyler was home she was usually still over there with you every night after being there all day with you."

He ran his hand through his hair. "Jesus Christ, Tommy. Jesus Christ." He turned on his friend. "Bob didn't fucking tell you and Tyler everything, man. We nearly had to drug Nevvie that day, okay? I'm not exaggerating when I say she lost her fucking mind. I could barely hang on to her, to keep her there, keep her from ripping that goddamn place apart looking for you. If Bob hadn't been there to calm her down, I don't know what I would have done. Fuck, man, she was this fucking close to losing her mind with Tyler in surgery. Then the ER calls about you, she panicked."

Pete couldn't stop his tears as he relived the events. "We were all fucking trying to hold it together for her, because if any of us lost it, we knew she was one Thorazine drip away from being admitted. What the *fuck* got into you, man?"

"I don't know. I didn't mean anything by it. I was being friendly and flirted a little and I got carried away and couldn't stop."

"I'm gay, asshole, and even I know the last fucking thing you do is call any woman by the same fucking pet name you call your wife. How could you even let it happen? Why flirt? You've got Tyler, who, frankly, is out of your league in the looks department. But he loves you crazy. I've never seen him so much as look at another man or woman, just the two of you. He still makes puppy dog eyes over both of you. And Nevvie? Hell, I thought she looked hot that night at the party when you guys had her dressed up, and I haven't lusted over a woman in about three decades, okay? What the fuck?"

"It was stupid."

"No, asshole. Stupid is leaving your doors unlocked and the goddamn keys in the ignition of a brand new Porsche, and a 'steal me' sign on the dash. This puts stupid right out the fucking window."

"I don't know!" Thomas collapsed against the back of the sofa. "I don't know. It just got out of hand. I felt good, I started looking forward to her coming over here, it made me feel good."

"Did you ever think about asking your husband and wife to pay attention to you?"

Thomas studied his hands. "Why the fuck they gonna want me anymore, Pete?"

"You stupid asshole. They love you, that's why. So you push away the two people who would have gladly switched places to be in that hospital bed instead of you, to flirt with some fucking cunt you don't even want?"

Pete shook his head in disbelief. "You know, I wasn't real sure about this whole thing when it started, frankly. You two and her. I liked her—I love her now like a baby sister—but I thought man, this is trouble. I honestly thought it'd be her wanting to leave or you wanting her all to yourself and not share her with Ty. I never in my wildest dreams would have imagined you'd do something so fucking goddamned *stupid* as to throw away not only what you have with her, but with Ty!"

"If I lose her, he'll leave with her."

Pete heavily sat, nodding. "Yep. I don't doubt it. He loves you, but he won't lose her, I can tell you that right now. Not after what she went through with Alex, and especially because of Adam. And you've stomped Ty's heart to pieces in the process."

"He's mad about Nevvie being upset."

"Fuck, yes. But worse, you cheated on him, dude. It doesn't matter it was 'just' a kiss. To him, that was like telling him he wasn't good enough for you anymore. He loves you. I've known him longer than you have. He's never even looked at another guy since you came along. Or a woman, until you both hooked up with Nevvie. That's what everyone was always amazed at, seeing you at parties before Nevvie, they'd say, 'Look at how much he adores Tommy.' That's what people said. You could see it in his face."

"How do I make it right?" he quietly asked.

Pete held up his hands. "Don't ask me. You'd just better hope you get a chance to make it right, then spend the next few years on your fucking knees groveling like a son of a bitch. If you can do that, they're letting you off easy."

* * * *

Tyler still had keys and an alarm code to get into the building. He locked the outer door behind him and knocked on Thomas' office door. "Nevvie, sweetheart?"

After a moment, she opened the door, her tear-streaked face breaking his heart. She broke down, sobbing, at the sight of him. He pushed in and locked the office door behind him, then led her to the sofa. She curled up with him and cried as he held her, his own tears flowing freely.

When she calmed down, she lay with her head in his lap and stared at their sleeping son. "What do we do? He keeps pushing us away. Doesn't he want us anymore?"

"He did say he was sorry. I told him I'd pass along the message."

She bitterly snorted. "I suppose he wants you to do his apologizing for him."

"No, love," he softly said. "I've barely spoken to him." Dare he burden her with his pain?

As if reading his thoughts she rolled onto her back to meet his gaze. "Is it stupid for me to be more upset about what he said than the kiss?"

He shook his head. "No, love, it's not. I understand why that hurt you so deeply."

"It hurt you that he kissed her."

He glanced away. "Perhaps he wants a newer model. Maybe he's tired of me."

She snuggled tighter. "I'll never get tired of you. I love you. Promise me you'll never be a jerk."

"My love, I only have eyes for you. No one else could ever tempt me away." He caressed her cheek. "I only have one angel, and it's you. Always and only you."

She cried again. "I'm such a moron. How many other people does he call that? Now I'm wondering, am I too stupid to have seen it? Does he call the check-out girl at Publix that? How about a waitress at the restaurant we have lunch at sometimes, you know? I've never heard you call anyone else angel but me."

"That's because I never have, and I never will. Only you. If it's any comfort, I've never heard him call anyone else 'baby girl' but you."

"Until today."

He sadly nodded. "Until today."

"So how much longer would it have gone on? I look back and I see it all clear as day. Every week he pushed us further away, he was practically eager to see her. Does he even love us anymore?"

"He claims he does. To be honest, I was too upset to talk with him." He gently stroked her arm. "It's late. Are you sure I can't talk you into a hotel?"

"I don't want to wake the baby."

"Do you still have pillows and blankets here?"

"Yeah." When she was pregnant she used to curl up on the couch to take naps in the afternoon while Tommy worked. "Now I sit and think back and wonder how long he's been like this. Did he really love us? Ever?"

"Of course he did. Sweetheart, I don't know what's gotten into him—and believe me, I'm not making excuses for him—but it's been since the accident."

"He doesn't even want to spend time with Adam anymore. How could he lie and tell her he wasn't our husband? Is he ashamed of us?"

"Let's try to sleep and we can sort it out in the morning, all right?" He couldn't answer her because he had no answers. Her questions were the very ones running through his brain, and he knew he had to be strong for her. She'd shouldered so much over the past few months. He felt loathe to add to that burden.

They settled in on the sofa. It was a comfortably snug fit but considering they both needed the comfort from each other, they tightly spooned together. They eventually drifted to sleep with the TV sound turned low.

Chapter Seventeen

Thomas wanted to pace and couldn't because of his fucked up leg. As the clock ticked closer to midnight, he knew damn well Tyler wasn't coming home. Ty wouldn't let Nevvie be alone no matter what. Especially when she was that upset.

Pete eventually walked to the guest room without another word and left the door open. Thomas knew he should go to bed but the thought—the guilt—of sleeping in their bed when he'd driven the two people he loved out of it was too much to bear.

I'm a stupid fucking asshole.

Where did she go? Was she still crying? Would she call Bob and ask him to dissolve their unusual union, to legally separate her from him, from them?

Would Tyler?

Hell, the two of them could go get married and make it official. Nevvie always swore no one would make her choose between them, but maybe he'd made her choice for her, and for Tyler.

He couldn't sleep, his guilt gnawing at him. *Stupid fucking asshole.* It became a silent chant in his brain. *Stupid fucking asshole.* If he'd died in the accident, at least the two of them would be moving on, healing.

They'd be better off without him.

* * * *

Pete arose a little before seven and walked out to the kitchen to make coffee. "You awake?" he asked, his voice even huskier than normal from sleep.

"Yeah," Thomas said from the couch.

"Did you sleep?"

"No."

"Good."

Not only had he hurt the two people he loved, he'd pissed off his best friend in the process.

"You don't have to stay all day, Pete."

"I don't plan on it. Eddie's coming over around eight. I've got shit to do."

Aw, fuck. "Does he know?"

Pete snorted. "You'll be lucky if he doesn't castrate you himself. You think you're getting away with pulling shit like this and no one finding out, you're fucking nuts. Just wait'll your mother finds out. She'll nail your balls to the wall if Karen doesn't do it first."

Thomas closed his eyes and silently groaned. Of course Momma would find out. She and Nevvie talked several times a week, as did Nevvie and Karen. There's no way it wouldn't come out.

"What do you want in your coffee?" Pete grumbled.

"Black, please."

Pete brought a mug out and set it on the coffee table. "Need help getting to the bathroom or anything?"

"No. I'm okay."

"Feeling fucking guilty?"

"Yes."

"Good." Pete turned on his heel and walked down the hall. A few minutes later, Thomas heard the shower in the guest bathroom.

He didn't blame Pete. If their positions were reversed, he'd be just as pissed. *Poor Nevvie.* She'd been through so much, even before all this shit. Nearly getting killed by Alex twice, and now this. She'd run herself ragged taking care of them, and then he went and did something stupid like this to repay her.

He tried calling Tyler's cell, hoping he would answer, knowing

Nevvie probably wouldn't talk to him.

* * * *

Tyler looked over Nevvie's shoulder and saw his phone light up from where he'd left it on the end table, set to silent mode. She was still asleep. He didn't dare move and wake her. She hadn't slept much better than he had last night, restless until well after two a.m. before finally drifting off.

He could read the screen. Thomas.

Well, if he fell he can damn well call 911 or have Pete help him. If Thomas didn't want or need their help, he wouldn't get it. He wanted to be left alone? He'd get that, too. In spades, if he so desired.

He dropped his head to the pillow again and closed his eyes. He'd heard a few people enter the building already, knew Nevvie would awaken soon. Adam awoke and rolled over in his crib. He stared at him, a huge, gummy grin creasing his chubby face.

Tyler smiled back and waved. Adam flailed his arm, then jammed his fist in his mouth and greedily sucked on it. He would be okay for a few more minutes, hopefully.

Adam. Even if nothing else, how could Thomas do this to their son? Turn his back on him like that? Just when Tyler thought their life could get back to some semblance of normal, albeit healing and still fragile, to do something so utterly selfish and stupid like that boggled his mind.

To hurt their poor Nevvie like that.

To hurt him.

It didn't even matter so much for him, he could put it past him if he had to. But Nevvie? Thomas couldn't be that blind to see how much something like that would hurt her, could he? Not after all she'd gone through for them.

She stirred, rolled over to look at him.

"Hey," she whispered. "Did you sleep?"

"A little."

She winced as she stretched. "Maybe I should have let you take me to a hotel last night."

"I doubt we would have slept any better there, love." He kissed her. "How are you feeling?"

"I still want to kill him, but I think I can keep from acting on the urge now."

Tyler forced a wan smile. "When do you wish to return home?"

"We could run off together."

Although he knew she was joking, a tiny part of him wanted to call and make the arrangements right then and do it. Take Nevvie and Adam and fly away, have Bob send him paperwork to void their arrangement, and put it behind them. He would never do something like this to Nevvie, betray her trust like this, even if it meant losing Thomas in the process. He would never hurt her. He'd almost lost her once and that memory terrified him like none other. How could Thomas, having gone through that very same thing, not remember those emotions?

"Fly away into the sunset, love?"

"Vegas wedding?"

He carefully guarded his reaction. She was looking for an answer, guidance, from him. He could easily say yes and they would be legally married by nightfall. "Is that what you really want?" he whispered.

Her eyes filled with tears. "I want us back. I want everything like it was. I want my boys. I want my brain and my tough guy. I want Tommy to quit pushing us away. I want to feel like he still loves us."

Tyler nodded, then tenderly kissed her. "That's what I want, too. Before we give up on him perhaps we should allow him a chance to explain and apologize and see if he still wants us."

"What if he doesn't?"

He tightly hugged her, trying and failing to hold back his tears. "Then we still have each other, love. You and I. Always."

He helped her change and feed Adam, then they took a shower together. A little after eight, Nevvie took Adam out to Maggie to watch while the two of them left for the house in Tyler's car. Maggie was surprised to learn they'd spent the night there but didn't ask questions.

* * * *

Thomas carefully made his way to their bedroom. The bed looked huge and empty, mocking him. He could be curled up there with the two people he loved. Why had he pushed them away?

God I've lost my mind. Totally fucking lost it.

He sat on the edge, catching his breath before finding a clean pair of shorts in his drawer and going into the bathroom.

He took a quick sponge bath and shaved. Thank God for the electric razor, it was the only way he could shave by himself. He carefully made his way back to the kitchen. Pete stood at the counter, reading the paper while eating a bagel.

He threw a quick glance at Thomas. "Glad you didn't bust your ass."

"They're going to hate me, Pete."

"Yep. If you're looking for sympathy, sorry, I'm fresh out right now."

Thomas sat at the table to rest before fixing his breakfast. "I'm not looking for sympathy. I'm hoping for a miracle."

"I don't understand you. I thought you loved them."

"I do love them." Thomas studied his hands. "I'm a stupid fuck, just like you said."

"No argument here."

Pete looked up as Eddie walked in. "Guess what, Tommy?" Pete said. "Your life just went to total shit."

Eddie looked pissed. He walked into the kitchen and leaned in, gave Pete a kiss.

"Hi," Pete greeted him.

"Hey." Eddie glared at Thomas, but didn't speak to him. Instead he poured himself a cup of coffee and turned to Pete. "What time are you getting home?"

"Should be finished by four, so probably around five. I'll call if I'm running late."

"Okay. I'll have dinner ready for you."

Pete left, taking his bag with him. Eddie sat at the table across from Thomas, conspicuously ignoring him, reading the paper.

"Hi, Eddie."

Eddie glared at him, but didn't say anything until after he'd turned back to the paper. "Good morning."

Thomas carefully stood, made his way to the counter, and then toasted himself a bagel. He knew Eddie was totally pissed. Eddie was even more of a caretaker than Tyler, would have normally jumped up to help, insisting Thomas not get up. The fact that Eddie only spoke two words to him, apparently under duress, cemented how pissed he felt.

"How much do you know?" Thomas asked.

Another long, chilly pause. Eddie didn't even look up from the paper. "Pete called me last night before he went to bed."

Nothing more. Not even a good reaming out for doing it.

Christ.

"You don't have to stay, Eddie," Thomas quietly said.

"Yes, I do. We promised Ty we'd help him out. I'm not here for *you.*" The way he emphasized "you" made it sound like he'd tasted something nasty.

"Thank you."

"I'd rather not speak to you, if you don't mind."

Thomas cringed and took his bagel to the living room. He thought about trying to call Tyler again, but knew if he hadn't called him back by now, he wouldn't.

He wondered if they'd at least come by to say good-bye, or if they'd let him see Adam one last time.

* * * *

Tyler pulled over before they reached the house. He took Nevvie's hand. "How do you wish to handle this?"

She shrugged. "I honestly don't know. I don't want to lose him but…" She shrugged again. "Can I trust him? Can *we* trust him? How do we know he won't do something like this or worse? The only reason he stopped was because you caught him in the act. Otherwise, he'd still be carrying on. I stood right fucking there in the kitchen while he kissed her. Our *son* was there." She met his eyes. "What do you want to do?"

He caressed her cheek. "I follow you, love. You are my world. You and Adam. I would rather have Thomas in it as well, and while I love him and don't wish to lose him, if you decide to move on then so do I, with you. You do as your heart tells you. Don't worry about me because I will be there."

"But what do you want me to do? Tell me."

He shook his head. "No. If you find you cannot stay, then I go with you. You do not have to choose between us, I will never make you do that. If you choose to stay, then so do I. If you leave, we leave together."

Nevvie closed her eyes and cried. "I don't want to lose him, Ty. I love him."

"So do I. Perhaps this is something that needed to happen, to show him he's not dealing well with this. Maybe we can use this to force him to talk to a professional or at the very least open up to us." He gently squeezed her hand. "Can you forgive him?"

"I want to. I mean, it's not like he fucked her. It's just…" She stared out the windshield. "It hurts. It really hurts. Maybe I'm making too big a deal out of this, but it still hurts."

He released her hand with a final squeeze and shifted the car into gear. "I know, love. I know."

* * * *

Thomas froze when he heard the car pull into the drive. Tyler's Lexus, he knew from the sound.

Not Nevvie's Acura.

He held his breath, waiting. The front door opened and Nevvie and Tyler walked in, holding hands. Without the baby.

His heart sank. They were coming back to say good-bye. He knew it.

Eddie looked up from his paper. Tyler released Nevvie's hand and left her standing in the hall. He walked into the kitchen and leaned in and said something too softly for Thomas to hear. Eddie nodded and left, kissing Nevvie on the cheek before he went.

Thomas willed her to look at him, but she wouldn't. She kept her gaze on the floor or on Tyler, not him.

His fault. No one to blame but himself. He had the best family in the world and he'd fucked it up.

Tyler walked back to Nevvie and took her hand, led her to the living room. She sat in one of the chairs and Tyler stood protectively behind her with his hands on her shoulder.

When she finally lifted her gaze to his, he saw how red and puffy her eyes looked, making him hate himself even more. He'd done that to her. How he'd reamed Tyler out years earlier, when a stupid mistake, a misunderstanding made her think they'd played her. Now the shoe was on the other foot but unlike Tyler's unintentional fuck-up, this was solely his own damn fault.

They didn't speak, waited for him.

"I'm sorry, babe," he finally choked out. "Both of you. I'm so sorry. I don't know why I did it. I love both of you so much." He didn't want to cry, but he did anyway. "Will you at least let Momma see Adam?"

Nevvie reached up for Tyler's hand, gripped it tightly. "We came to talk, Tommy," she said. "Not to leave. To see what the hell's going on and if we can fix this."

He didn't dare hope. "You're not leaving me?"

Tyler shook his head. "We don't want to," he said quietly. "We love you. But you've spent the past months pushing us away. Do you still want us? That's the question. Are you tired of us?"

"Of course I want you! I don't want to lose you. Either of you."

"Then tell us what's going on," Nevvie said. "Why don't you want us anymore? We beg you to sleep in bed with us, and you move into the guest room. You won't talk to us. You're flirting with some bimbo. You're not acting like someone who gives a shit. If you want out, do us the decency of telling us. If you want us to stay, you're going to have to start giving back a little. We'll walk to hell and back by your side, Tommy, but you need to let us in."

"How can you still want me? I can barely get around."

"I don't give a shit what shape you're in. If you'd been stuck in a bed for the rest of your life, I'd still be sitting right there by your side. Don't you get it?" She sobbed. "I can't lose you guys. I don't give a shit if you're fucking vegetables. I can't lose you. I need to be able to hold your hand and tell you I love you and I don't care if you're on two good legs or flat on your ass as long as you're alive!"

Tyler held her, but didn't say anything.

It bubbled out of her, the pain and anguish. Tears rolled down her face. "I was so scared I'd lose Tyler, I felt like a fucking zombie, I couldn't even think. Thank God Mom was there. Not just for the CPR but for everything. Then they called me about you and I thought my world ended. I don't want to be alive if I don't have my boys."

She took a deep, hitching breath. "I thought I was special, Tommy. You made me feel special. Then to hear you…" She couldn't continue. She sobbed, leapt to her feet and raced for the bedroom.

Tyler watched her but didn't follow. He stared at Thomas, who was also crying. "Go to her," Tyler said.

Thomas pulled his gaze away from Tyler and shook his head. "I can't. She hates me."

Tyler's strained, hissing tone startled him. "You stupid fucking arsehole! Did you *not* hear a bloody word she just said?" He stormed across the living room and forced Thomas to his feet, shoved his crutches at him. "Get your fucking arse in there and talk to her!"

"Can you forgive me?" Thomas whispered.

"This isn't about my feelings," he said, struggling to keep his voice low. "This is about trying to heal her broken heart. If you give a damn about her, then go in there and tell her. You and I shall settle things later. I could give a bloody shit about you at this moment, to be honest, because if she's not happy, I'm not happy."

Thomas had never seen that level of rage in Tyler's eyes. Tyler never became enraged. Tyler was as capable of getting upset as the next person, but the cold, glittering edge in his lover's blue eyes scared him.

He limped down the hall on his crutches. The bedroom door stood open. Nevvie sobbed face down on their bed. Taking a deep breath, he carefully made his way over to the bed and sat on the side closest to her so he could reach her.

Thomas carefully rolled to his side and gently placed his hand in the small of her back. "I'm sorry," he softly said. "I'm so sorry. I'm an asshole, and whatever it takes to make this up to you, I'll do it, bab—" He bit the words back.

"How do you unsay it, Tommy?" She wouldn't look at him. "How many times did you say it to her? How many other people did you say it to over the years when I thought it was something you only said to me?"

"Nevvie, you're my baby girl, I swear. No one else, sugar. Just you, only you. I love you."

"Then why did you shut us out? Why don't you want us anymore?"

More guilt. "I do want you guys, honey. I swear. I didn't think you'd want me anymore. You've got Tyler. Why would you want me?"

She rolled over, stunned. "I've begged you to let me in. I've pleaded with you. We both have. I don't know what more we can do to make you understand how much we love and want you."

"Have you two been having sex?"

She sat up. "Are you shitting me? Is that what this is about? Why the hell do you think we want you back in bed? It's kind of hard to make love to you when you tell us to leave you alone! You've been turning us down!"

She was right, and he knew it. "You aren't getting your 'tough guy' back, you know. I might not be able to ride a bike or even do half the shit I used to do." He picked at his fingernails and flinched, startled, when she touched his shoulder.

"Tommy, we love you. We want you. All of you, the way you are. You're always my tough guy." She tapped his chest, over his heart. "My tough guy is in here, not in your legs, asshole." She attempted a smile, giving him hope. "You'll always be my tough guy, just like Tyler's my brain. That's who you two are. You're alive. You came back to me. You didn't die. That's all I care about."

"But it's my fault this all happened. It's..." He closed his eyes. "It's my fault that guy died."

She shook her head. "No. It was an accident. It wasn't your fault."

"Yeah, it was. If I'd taken the truck instead of the bike—"

"He still might have pulled out in front of you. Only then at least you wouldn't have been hurt as badly, and he still might have died." She laid her hand on his cheek and made him look at her. "We have never blamed you for that. The guy's family doesn't even blame you. Is that what this is about, you hate yourself?"

"I don't know." And that was the truth. He didn't. He remained silent for a moment, trying to sort out his thoughts. "I feel guilty. All this extra shit I've heaped on you because I made a stupid fucking choice to take the bike. You both needed me, and the one time you really need me, not only am I not there for both of you, but I'm making things worse."

He wiped his hand across his eyes. "I'm sorry I said it to her. I'm sorry I flirted with her. I'm stupid. I wanted to stop. I didn't mean to lead her on, it just happened. It doesn't excuse what I did. I never told her I wasn't married to the two of you. I just helped her jump to a few conclusions."

Nevvie's face grew sad again. "You never told her Adam was your son. Why?"

Now was not the time to delve into the legalities of the situation, not when it seemed he might have a chance of not losing them. "I'm sorry. There is no excuse for what I did except that I'm a brain damaged asshole."

He looked up at her shocked laugh. She smiled. Weak and sad but still a smile.

He'd take whatever he could get.

"Maybe that's your new nickname for a while," she joked. "The BDA."

"Can you stay around long enough for me to earn something better?"

She nodded. "I'm pissed. I won't lie to you. I'm really, really pissed. Not just because of me, but because of how you hurt Tyler."

"I know. You have every right to be pissed at me. I deserve it."

She studied his face for long, silent minutes. "How do we learn to trust you again?" she finally asked. "How do I get that back? I never would have thought we couldn't trust you. How do I know you really want me and Tyler?"

He grabbed her hand and pulled it to his cheek, nuzzled it. "Sweetheart, I love you. And him. I do."

"I won't share you guys with anyone else and you guys promised you'd never share me. We agreed it would only be the three of us."

"I don't want anyone but you two, I swear."

Nevvie stared at him. "She can't come back here. You get to call the agency and request someone else. You led her on, you do the dirty work."

"That's fair."

"Today. When we get done with this. I don't care what excuse you use. Feel free to say your wife is a bitch if you want, I don't care. She doesn't set foot in this house again. Not that she'll probably want to."

"Done."

Nevvie didn't pull her hand away, a fact he didn't miss.

A fact that kept his hope alive.

"You've got to quit pushing us away. You sleep in bed with us."

He nodded.

"You talk to us. Even if you think it's stupid, you tell us what you're thinking when we ask what's going on. You quit shutting us out."

He nodded again, not daring to speak.

She stared at him. "Yes, Tyler and I have made love. Does that really bother you considering you wouldn't come to bed with us?"

"It's..." He regrouped, trying not to fuck this up. "It doesn't bother me. Not like that. I just thought you guys wouldn't want me. I know I pushed you two away"

"You didn't really want us to leave you alone, did you?"

He didn't answer.

"I am not a mind reader, no matter how spooky that freaky little connection is between me and Tyler. Tyler's good, but he's not a mind reader either. You tell us enough times you want to be left alone, we're going to leave you alone. If you don't want to be left alone, you need to tell us what the hell is swirling around in your brain."

"You didn't do anything wrong. Neither of you. It was just me being stupid."

She lay down again, a little closer than before, facing him.

"You have to make it up to Tyler," she softly said. "You really hurt him. I can forgive the kiss. What hurt him was seeing you kiss someone else, someone younger—much younger—a younger woman. Look at it from his point of view. I think it would have been easier on him if it'd been a guy, because he wouldn't be worried you're giving up on him altogether."

Thomas cringed inside. He never thought about it like that. "I love him. He's my guy. You know that."

"No, we don't know that. It feels like we don't know anything about you anymore. Tell him. Show him. We're his world. You haven't been telling him or showing him lately."

Thomas cried again, hating himself. How could he have done that to Tyler?

"Jesus, I really fucked up."

"Yeah. We're not giving you a pass, Tommy. As much as we love you, we need to know we can trust you. And frankly, right now, we don't trust you."

"I know."

Nevvie was quiet for a long time. "You'll go talk to someone, a psychologist, about all of this. Alone and the three of us. You've got to get this out of your system. You need to start healing."

"Yes."

"You make the calls on that, too. By Monday morning, I want you to have found someone and made an appointment for as soon as they can see you."

"Okay."

"And you have to make it up to Tyler. If you can't do that…If that doesn't happen, none of the rest matters because I won't stay and have him be hurt. I'll leave with him."

Desperate pain flared in his heart. "I'll do anything. I promise."

"You need to start going to the office with me. Even if you hurt. You can't stay cooped up here all the time."

"Plus you want to keep an eye on me."

"Fucking A I do."

"I'm sorry."

She grimaced. "No, wait, you can't go to the office with me."

"Why not?"

"I need someone here with Tyler." Her eyes welled up again.

He looked at her, confused. "Why? He's..." He watched her face. She finally met his gaze. "You're scared."

She nodded, her voice dropping to a tortured whisper. "If Mom and I hadn't been here..." She started sobbing again and he awkwardly hooked an arm around her, pulling her against him as she cried.

More guilt. While he'd been moping around, pitying himself, he'd totally ignored Nevvie's pain and fear. "He's okay, sugar."

She shook her head. "I didn't think about it before, with everything else going on. Once I got you home it hit me. I can't leave him alone. Not for a whole day. I won't. I hate letting him out of my sight. I was standing there in the kitchen and turned to talk to him and he just collapsed. Like that. He was gone! If I hadn't been there...If I'd been in the shower or back in your office even, in five minutes he would have..." She sobbed again.

As best he could, Thomas held her, trying to soothe her, despising himself. He'd been blind thinking she was doing so well when she wasn't.

Not at all.

"He *died*, Tommy!" she cried. "He died right there and the EMTs had to shock him. And then they called me and told me about you..."

He buried his face in her hair, not bothering to hold back his own tears. "I'm so sorry I wasn't here for you when you needed me. I'm here now, I swear."

She balled up her fist and beat on his chest. "He *died*," she sobbed. "He *died* in my arms. He died, Tommy! You don't get to bitch about your leg or your head, because you didn't fucking die on me! He *died*! Someone's got to stay with him in case it happens again!"

He wrapped his arms tightly around her and held her while she cried it out. He'd never looked at it like that. Now he understood. The worst wasn't over for her, even if he and Tyler thought it was. The worst had just begun. She was terrified of Tyler having another heart attack and no one being there to help him.

When she finally settled down he kissed her temple. "I can work from home. They don't need me there every day. I can stay here and work and go in once a week or something. Or I can sell out and stay home. We'd be okay. More than okay. Whatever you want to do, honey, I swear, that's what we'll do. Tyler has to write, that's who he is, it's not just a job for him. I'll never ask him to give that up, but if you want, I'll sell and stay home for you."

She tipped her head to look at him. "You would?"

He brushed the hair from her eyes. "Say the word. I'll ask Bob to start the ball rolling."

"But you love what you do."

"I love you two—three—more. If it's what you need to feel secure, another set of eyes on Tyler all the time, I'll do it."

"I don't know. Maybe in a few months I won't feel like this. Right now I'm scared to leave him alone. I mean, I know he wants to be alone so he can work, but it scares me." She went quiet for a moment. "Don't be surprised if it gets thrown in your face."

"I deserve it."

"If you ever decide you want out, you need to tell us, be up front about it."

"I don't want out. I want to be here with you. After all this crap you two still want me. I'm not about to do something else stupid and throw that away."

She lay quietly in his arms while he stroked her back. "You have to make it up to him, Tommy," she softly said. "You need to talk to him right now and make it up to him."

He kissed her. "I will. Send him in."

She looked at him, touched his face, the new scar across his cheek. "I love you. Please don't push us away anymore. Please make this right. I don't want to lose you."

"I don't want to lose you two either."

She carefully climbed out of bed so she didn't jostle him. A few minutes later Tyler, his eyes red, stood in the doorway. "Nevvie said you wish to talk," he softly said.

The knife twisted deeper in Tom's gut, turned by his own hand. He'd done this to his guy. Even when Nevvie was in the hospital after Alex's attack, Tyler hadn't looked quite this bad.

His fault. All his fault.

Thomas held out his hand to Tyler. "Please?"

Tyler slowly walked across the bedroom and sat on the edge of the bed, out of reach, his back to Thomas.

"I'm sorry," Thomas said, trying to get it all out before he lost it again. "I'm so sorry. Like I told Nevvie, you two didn't do a damn thing wrong, it was all me, my fault. I love you guys, and I don't want to lose you."

Tyler studied his hands, didn't say anything.

"Please, Ty," he whispered. "I'm sorry. I swear to God, it won't ever happen again. Never. It had nothing to do with you and Nevvie."

Tyler snorted but said nothing.

"I love you. You're my guy. You'll always be my guy. We've been together too long to lose what we've got."

Tyler's soft, agonized voice broke Thomas' heart. "How do I really know? How do I know for sure you're not tired of me altogether? Then again, I never expected you to kiss someone not even a fraction as beautiful as our wife. I can understand flirting, I suppose. A lot has happened to you. But to kiss someone else? And then to say what you said to her?"

He finally turned, crying. "She's our girl, Thomas. *Our* Nevvie. I would never dream of calling someone else my angel. How could you do that to her?"

"Nevvie agrees my new nickname is 'Brain Damaged Asshole.'"

Tyler closed his eyes at that, but the slightest of smiles curled his lips.

Thomas tried again. "Whatever you want, I'll do it. She won't stay unless I can make this right with you. You say it, I'll do it. I can't lose you. I can't lose the three of you. Pete said I should pray for a miracle and then spend the next few years on my knees groveling. That sounds like a good fucking idea, honestly."

"How could you *not* brag about our son? We have the most beautiful wife and son in the world. How can you not be proud enough of them to brag to everyone that we're the two luckiest bastards on the face of the planet?"

Thomas pointed at himself. "Brain Damaged Asshole."

Another almost amused snort. "Right."

Thomas reached out to him again and Tyler looked at his hand for a long moment before lying down on the bed. Not as close as Thomas hoped, but at least he was on his side facing him, within touching distance.

"I love you, Ty. I've loved you from the moment I met you, I think. I never could understand what you saw in me. Even Pete said you're out of my league in the looks department." He prayed for a smile and a ghost of one crossed Tyler's lips. "You've always stood beside me no matter what. I'm ashamed of myself. I'll grovel, I'll do whatever you need me to do to prove to you how much I love you, to give me a chance to earn your trust back."

Tyler reached out and stroked Thomas' cheek. "I've always thought you were quite handsome, love."

Thomas' breath caught in his throat. He grabbed Tyler's hand and kissed it. "Can I have another chance? Please? I swear to God I won't fuck it up. Never again."

Tyler's blue eyes searched his face. "What did you promise Nevvie?"

He ran through the list, ending with making things right with Tyler.

Tyler lay silent for many long minutes before taking a deep breath and letting out a long sigh. "Brain Damaged Arsehole?"

Thomas nodded, smiling. "Yeah. Want me to get it tattooed on my forehead?"

A real smile. Ty shook his head. "No, love. Your forehead is just fine the way it is."

"Can you ever forgive me? Please?" He still clutched Tyler's hand.

After what felt like forever, Tyler closed his eyes and nodded. "She's right that I might not be able to resist throwing it in your face. I'll try not to, but I can't promise."

"I don't care. You can remind me every day if you want." He knew he was begging. He didn't care how he sounded. All he knew was he had to do whatever it took to get their forgiveness.

"I love you, Thomas. I want the three of us to spend our lives together, raising our son, any other children we might have. I don't want to waste life worrying whether or not you're making eyes at anyone else. I don't want to live like that. I lived like that once. I won't do it again."

Thomas cringed. He'd forgotten about Tyler's first ex wife cheating on him. "Can I have another chance?"

"I don't know how many I can give you. If it ever happens again—"

Thomas vigorously shook his head. "Never again. I swear."

Tyler's eyes crawled over his face for what felt like forever but Thomas knew he had to wait him out. Eventually, Tyler closed his eyes and nodded. "All right, love. We'll pick up and carry on."

He opened his eyes again, fixing him with the full, hard force of the earlier chilly glare. His voice turned harsh and cold. "If you *ever* do anything like this again, or if you hurt her again, that's it. No more. I will not put her through that."

"Thank you." Tyler let him pull him closer, hugging him. "I swear, I'll never do it again. Ever." He closed his eyes, inhaled Ty's comforting scent. He loved how Ty smelled, always had. His natural scent, even without shampoo or cologne, always smelled right, like it was where Tom belonged.

Tyler carefully ran his hand through Thomas' shaggy hair. "You are in dire need of a haircut."

"Feel free to shave me bald if you want."

Tyler smiled. "How about you go with us, we run Nevvie back to the office to pick up Adam, and then I'll take you to get a haircut."

"I'd like that." He never paid attention to that. Tyler and Nevvie were always the ones who scheduled it for him. Otherwise it'd be down to his ass before he remembered to get it cut.

They took care of him. They always had.

Jesus, how could I have been so stupid?

"I love you, Ty. I swear I'll make you proud of me."

"You've always made me proud. I've always been proud to be by your side."

"I told Nevvie I'd sell the business if she wants, so I can stay home."

Tyler frowned. "I think that's a little harsh, to keep you..." He stopped, realizing the truth. "Oh. Because of me."

Thomas nodded.

Tyler sighed. "Our poor, sweet girl. She's still worried about me, isn't she?"

"Yeah." He rested his forehead against Tyler's. "I agree. I don't want to lose you. I don't want to risk something happening."

"I won't be the one setting off metal detectors in airports."

"She's got a point." Thomas thought back to Pete's words. "Pete told me they almost had to drug her when she found out about me."

Tyler tensed. "Yes, that's what Bob said. I didn't want to worry you. He said she was nearly out of her mind."

"It's just billable hours."

"Quite."

Both men froze, then laughed.

Tyler looked at him. "Never again, Thomas," he whispered. "I can't go through this again. I can't stand seeing her in agony. My own pain is inconsequential. I will not see her suffer like that *ever* again, do you understand?"

Thomas nodded. "Never again."

Tyler kissed him and Thomas wanted to cry with relief. His guy forgave him.

"I love you, sweet. And I love her. However, as you yourself once said, she might not ever want to choose, but I can and will if forced. My life would be empty without you, but it would be worthless without her. Understand?"

Thomas nodded.

Tyler kissed him again, long and sweet. Thomas closed his eyes, savoring it, almost moaning at the sensation of Tyler's tongue gently tracing the seam of his lips.

Why had he flirted when he had not only Nevvie, but Tyler, a man who could make him hard just by winking at him?

Right.

Brain Damaged Asshole.

Thomas felt his cock stir for the first time since the accident—not even Jennifer's visits had performed that little magic trick. Thomas pulled his lover tightly to him, trying to rub against him despite his bad leg getting in the way.

Tyler broke their kiss and chuckled. "Now, wasn't that a lot better than anything you could get elsewhere?"

"Yeah," he breathlessly agreed, pulling Tyler to him again. Tyler was probably the world's best kisser, with Nevvie a close second.

Carefully sliding a hand between them, Tyler gently squeezed Thomas' hard bulge, keeping his hand in place, making Thomas moan.

"I know what you love, sweet. Just remember, if you're ever even slightly tempted to stray again—" he rubbed Thomas' cock, drawing another low, deep moan from him, "—you come to me and I'll fuck your brains out and remind you that you have no reason to stray."

Thomas dropped his head to Tyler's shoulder, his eyes closed, trying to work his hips against Tyler's hand. Now that his libido was back it had returned with a screaming vengeance.

Tyler chuckled and pulled his hand away, making Thomas groan. "Love, if you want more you're going to have to work for it. I believe you said our girl gave you some assignments."

Thomas nodded, still trying to wiggle closer to Tyler.

"Then I suggest you get on that. Because if she's not happy…"

"You're not happy," Thomas completed.

Tyler stroked his cheek and kissed him again. "Right." He rolled away from Thomas and stood, then walked around the bed to help him stand. He handed Thomas his crutches and kissed him one more time, raking his fingers along the front of his lover's shorts, feeling his hard bulge.

"No release for you yet. Maybe if you're focused on that it will help keep your mind on business. Then we'll take Nevvie back to the office and get you looking proper again. We'll have lunch together. Then—" he squeezed again, making Thomas moan, "—maybe, perhaps I'll consider giving you what you want. Can you live with that?"

Thomas nodded, beyond speech.

Tyler smiled. "I love you, Thomas. I love you so much, and I wish to spend the rest of my life with you. And her."

"I love you too, Ty. Christ, I love you."

"Get dressed. We'll be waiting." Tyler found Nevvie in the living room, curled on the couch. She looked up. When he smiled she burst into relieved tears.

He settled on the couch beside her and held her. "It's going to be all right. He's getting dressed, he'll take care of a few things and then we'll go get Adam. I'll take him for a haircut and we'll have lunch, right?"

Her relieved sigh soothed his heart. "It's going to be okay? *He's* going to be okay?"

"I think so. We all have a lot of healing to do." He stroked her cheek. "I'm not going to collapse again, love."

"He told you that?"

"I think you should have told me."

"Don't change the subject."

"I don't think he needs to give up his job. What can we do to make you feel better? If you wish to stay home, you can. You don't have to work. I know you enjoy it, but we're more than happy to keep you in the manner to which you've grown accustomed."

She'd die for his smile. "Let's have a few months to settle into a routine. The BDA can stay here for the most part. He can't drive yet anyway. Once he's driving, I can switch out working from home. Okay?"

"I daresay I do like that nickname."

"He's our BDA."

Tyler nodded. "And I do so love him."

Thomas emerged from the bedroom twenty minutes later, dressed in loose, khaki slacks and a shirt he hadn't buttoned yet, his surgical scars still angry pink welts across his torso. Nevvie had noticed some of his fine-motor skills were still a little slow or sloppy, sometimes both, which she suspected was why he hadn't buttoned the shirt yet.

But if he wanted help, he'd have to ask. She was done trying to guess what he wanted or needed.

He carefully limped into the kitchen on his crutches, then leaned against the counter. He looked through at them. "Nev, where's the number for the home health care place?"

She'd asked him to do this, but the fact that he was meant he really wanted to try. "It's in the front of my planner, there on the counter."

"Thanks, I see it." He grabbed the phone and leafed through the pages while Tyler gripped her hand. Thomas dialed the number. Nevvie realized she'd been holding her breath.

"Hi, yes, this is Thomas Kinsey. I'm supposed to have an appointment tomorrow with Jennifer…Right…Look, the bottom line is, I need to request a new therapist…No, she didn't do anything wrong. The fact is I'm an asshole." Nevvie tried to ignore Tyler's amused snort next to her.

"I made an ass out of myself…No, she was very professional. I have no complaints about her, seriously. I don't want to get her in trouble…Honestly? I'd better tell you now, so you know up front. I'm in hot enough water here at home as it is. I'm polyamorous. I have a wife and a husband…That's right…Well, I neglected to mention that to her up front and she drew a few wrong conclusions that I let her keep assuming…Yes, and she got a little freaked out, but it wasn't her fault. And now my wife and my husband are pissed at me…Right. It's not her fault I was a jerk, I'm just a brain damaged asshole right now."

Thomas laughed at something the person on the other end said. "Exactly. So if you could assign someone else to me, I can understand if they can't make the Friday appointment and…Okay, great. Thank you. Same time on Monday? Wonderful."

He hung up and looked at Nevvie and Tyler, who still sat on the couch. "Okay?"

Nevvie looked at Tyler, who nodded. She got up, walked into the kitchen and hugged him. "Very okay. Thank you."

He looked over her shoulder at Tyler, who agreed. "Very okay, love."

Thomas patted Nevvie on the back. "Okay, so the new era of glasnost is upon us." He pointed at his shirt. "Can you please help me? I tried three fucking times to line up the buttons right and it's not happening this morning. I'm tired of T-shirts. It's why I've been stuck wearing the goddamn things. I've been too embarrassed to tell you guys I've had trouble."

She smiled, trying to fight her tears—good ones this time. "Of course I don't mind." She buttoned his shirt for him as he stared into her face.

"I mean it, Nev. Whatever you want me to do, I'll do it. I swear."

"Just keep doing what you're doing."

Tyler joined them in the kitchen. For the first time in months, they formed their group hug.

"Welcome back, love," Tyler whispered. "It's nice to finally have you home."

* * * *

Nevvie insisted Thomas take the front seat. All the way to the office she rested her hand on his shoulder. There was still a lot of healing ahead for all of them, but Nevvie finally saw a marked change in Tommy's demeanor from the past weeks. At the office they were swarmed by well-wishers, some who hadn't seen their boss since his accident.

Nevvie went to Maggie's office to get Adam. She handed him over with a smile. "Thanks for the dose of reality. Two poopy diapers. Now I remember why I wanted my husband to get snipped after the twins."

She laughed. "Well, it's not so bad in the grand scheme of things."

Maggie closed her office door. "Spill it. What happened?"

Nevvie hesitated. Maggie was a good friend. She'd known Tommy since college and Nevvie didn't want to say anything to make Maggie hate him—and Maggie *would* hate him for acting like he did, regardless of his reason.

"Tommy and I had a fight, that's all. We've kissed and made up. He's going through a lot, and he sort of forgot he's not in it alone. His new nickname is the Brain Damaged Asshole, if that means anything."

Maggie grinned. "Hell, I've been calling him that for years. Seriously, I'm glad y'all worked it out."

"Just a lot of stress."

"I don't know how you've held it together, Nevvie. I really don't. I'd be a basket case by now."

"I was."

Nevvie took Adam back to Tommy's office and let him hold their son while she checked her messages and email. She took care of a few quick items then returned to Tommy's office. "Do you two want to take him with you? Boys morning out?"

Thomas smiled. "Can we?" He stared into his son's eyes, then at Tyler. How could he have been so stupid? Adam was his son as much as he was Tyler's.

Brain Damaged Asshole.

"Of course." She transferred the car seat and they made arrangements to meet for lunch. Once the men were in the car with Adam securely fastened, Thomas patted Tyler's thigh.

"Thank you," Thomas said.

Tyler laced his fingers through Tom's as he drove. "We've been blessed. Don't ever forget that, love." He squeezed Tom's hand. "We *are* blessed."

Tyler had called ahead and made an appointment for Thomas with the stylist before they left the house. By the time they pulled into the restaurant parking lot, Nevvie was waiting for them. She smiled as she ran her hands through Tommy's hair. The surgical scar on his scalp was barely noticeable. The stylist had done an excellent job of concealing it.

"Much better." You look like you again.

"I'm starting to feel like me."

She kissed Tyler and unbuckled the baby. They ate a long, relaxed lunch. Later that afternoon, once they returned home, Thomas went to their bedroom to lie down and Tyler joined him. Nevvie called Eddie with an update.

"Is everything okay?"

"Yeah. But would you mind babysitting tonight?"

"I thought you guys made up?"

"Not Thomas. Adam."

She could almost hear Eddie's smile. "Hell yes, we'll babysit the Ant!"

"I'll bring him over around seven. Can you keep him until tomorrow evening around the same time? I think the three of us need some alone time."

"Sure thing."

She hung up, her plan already half-cemented in her mind. She hadn't had time or opportunity to discuss it with Tyler, but knew he'd agree.

Chapter Eighteen

As promised, after his nap Thomas started making phone calls. An hour later he had an appointment set up with a counselor, but it wasn't until the end of the next week. Nevvie didn't care. Just the fact that he stuck to his word went a long way toward soothing her wounded heart.

With the emotional events of the past twenty-four hours, by the time they ate dinner and cleaned up the kitchen they were too exhausted to do anything but sleep. The next morning, Thomas lay in bed and moped. He hated himself, felt guilty, and the fact that they so readily forgave him in some ways made him feel worse. He felt he deserved to suffer for what he'd put them through.

After going out to the kitchen with Tyler to fix her coffee and tell him her plan, she returned to the bedroom. "How much longer do you act like this today, Tommy?" Nevvie asked.

"How can you even stand to look at me?"

His words stung, but she knew they weren't meant for her. It was anger at his frustration over his physical condition and his own actions.

"Because I love you, you big dumb guy. If you think we're going to quit loving you just because of this, you're mistaken. Pissed? Yes. But we still love you."

Tyler walked in with the paper and two mugs of coffee. "I brought your coffee, Thomas." He noted Nevvie's expression and realized Thomas had awoken moody. "Ah, I see the grump is still in residence."

"Fuck you, Ty," he muttered.

Tyler smiled. "Well now, *that* sounds promising. Especially considering it's been months since you've taken care of me properly."

Thomas closed his eyes, tried to ignore them.

Nevvie pulled the covers down and off him. "Listen, buster, if you think we're going to let you keep up the pity act, you've got another think coming."

Thomas reached for the covers. Nevvie grabbed his hand, pinned it to the bed. Unable to fight her he tried to pull free and then Tyler caught his other arm, pinning him spread-eagled to the mattress.

"No you don't, love," Tyler whispered, running his tongue from his lover's ear to the base of his throat.

"Ty, don't—" His protest was cut off by Nevvie's lips on his, her tongue plunging and searching, refusing to let him pull away.

After a long moment he quit fighting and responded. Only then did she sit up. "I think I have his attention, Master Tyler," she said.

Thomas moaned. His boxers instantly tented in response to her words.

"You've still got the magic touch, love." Tyler smiled and kissed Thomas. This time he eagerly responded, kissing Tyler back while Nevvie watched.

"I love watching my masters kiss," she murmured.

Tyler kissed her. "Then look closely, love. You'll see a lot more of it." He kissed Thomas again and she pressed close, leaning in, kissing them both.

Nevvie released Tom's arm and crawled down the bed, where she carefully worked his boxers off, freeing his stiff cock. She knelt to the side, careful not to jostle his bad leg. "Master Tyler, may I suck Master Thomas' cock?"

Tyler winked. "Absolutely, my sweet little slave. I'm sure he needs some relief. It's been many months."

She used just the tip of her tongue to tease him, slowly circling the head and around the ridge. She closed her eyes and stroked his sac and shaft with her hands as she wrapped her lips around him, using firm strokes of her tongue to draw long, low moans from deep within Tom.

Tyler propped himself on one arm next to him. "How does our little slave feel, Thomas?"

His eyes closed. "Damn, that's good."

Tyler nibbled his ear, licking and kissing the sensitive spot on the side of his neck that always made him moan. "Do you want our little slave to make you come? She's missed you very much. She's been wanting to taste her master."

"Yeah."

Nevvie moaned around his cock, using firmer strokes and taking him deep into her mouth. It didn't take long. He reached down, tangling his fingers in her hair as he thrust into her mouth while his climax took him. She waited until he finally softened before lifting her head with a smile.

"Did my master enjoy that?" she whispered.

He nodded. "Hell yes."

She met Tyler's gaze and winked. "Will my master please make me come now?"

Thomas opened his eyes and looked at her. "I'd love to watch him make you come, baby girl."

"Not Master Tyler," she purred in her best slave girl voice. "You, Master."

He shook his head. "Sugar, I can't."

Tyler kissed him again, then lifted Tom's head and pulled the pillows out from under him. "Oh, yes you can. Get up here, Nevvie. Let's see if Thomas still remembers how to use that sweet tongue of his."

She scrambled up the bed, turning so she could straddle Tommy's face while she kissed his cock. Tyler switched position and kissed Nevvie, enjoyed watching her face as she closed her eyes and moaned when Thomas stroked her clit with his tongue.

"Is he licking you, sweetheart?"

"Oh, yeah," she whispered, then went down on Thomas, trying to get him hard again.

Tyler pushed in close, running his tongue along Tom's sac, drawing aimless circles with his tongue across Tom's inner thighs, making him moan.

"Do you like that, Thomas?" he asked.

His reply was muffled by Nevvie's clit in his lips, but sounded affirmative.

"Lick him well, angel," Tyler whispered in her ear, holding her hair away from her face. Her eyes flicked toward him. He smiled. "That's it, sweetheart. Suck our sweet Thomas," he murmured, kissing her neck.

She moaned, shifting her hips against Tom's face.

Tyler pressed his lips to her ear and breathed, "Don't let him come, my sweet little slave. Let him make you come, then we're going to get down to the business of making you a mommy again, aren't we?"

She moaned again. The sensation around his cock made Thomas moan. Which in turn made her squirm harder against him and she cried out, his erection popping free from her lips as she came.

Tyler held her, murmuring in her ear, "That's it, sweetheart, come for me, come for him, my beautiful angel."

When she crested the final wave she kissed him deeply then carefully rolled off Thomas. Tyler took Tom's stiff shaft in his hand, keeping him hard. "Do you want to come again, lover?" Tyler asked.

Thomas' eyes were closed. He nodded. "Yeah. God, yeah."

"Well then, it's about time you stop loafing around and work for it, isn't it?"

"What?"

"Thomas, sit up."

Nevvie met Tyler's gaze and winked. Tyler helped his lover sit up and changed position, sitting behind him, supporting him, his knees bent. Thomas closed his eyes and leaned back against Tyler's chest as

Nevvie carefully straddled his lap and faced him. She used Tyler's knees for balance and support and kissed Thomas.

"I'm going to fuck you, Master. I've missed my master's cock." With that she slowly sank his full length inside her, pausing to subtly adjust position and shift her weight.

Then Thomas realized something. "Wait, Nev, are you back on the Pill?"

"Shh," the other two said at the same time. Nevvie kissed him while Tyler trailed gentle love bites across Tom's shoulder. He relaxed in their arms.

"We promised our angel anything she wants," Tyler murmured in his ear. "She wants another baby."

He shivered in their arms, his hands coming to rest on her hips. "Okay," he said.

Using slow, careful strokes, Nevvie made sure to keep her weight off him and his bad leg. As he drew closer to climaxing she reached behind her, between his legs, found his sac and stroked it.

Tyler ran his tongue along his lover's neck. "Fuck her, fuck our beautiful wife," he murmured in his ear.

As Tom's fingers tightened on her hips she sped up her strokes, recognizing how close he was. She leaned in and nipped his lower lip. "Fuck me, Tommy," she said. "Come for me."

He cried out, his hands on her hips forcing her hard against him as he came. Tyler wrapped his arms around them, holding them, meeting Nevvie's gaze.

Thomas rested his head on Tyler's shoulder, his eyes closed. A tear squeezed out from under his eyelid and ran down his cheek as he nuzzled Tyler's cheek. "I'm sorry. I'm so sorry."

Tyler held him tightly while Nevvie wrapped her arms around them and he cried in their arms.

After Thomas finally composed himself, Nevvie sat back.

"Did you enjoy that, love?" Tyler asked, kissing him.

"Yes."

Nevvie kissed the base of his throat, tracing the hollow with her tongue. "Are you done fighting us?"

He lifted his head. "You're sure you want this, sugar?"

"Absolutely. Don't you?"

"A little late to ask me now, don't you think?" But he smiled.

Tyler carefully extricated himself from behind his lover. "Do you mind if I take our girl into the shower with me? I need to get ready for my cardiac rehab."

Thomas laughed. "I think you could have a good cardiac rehab right now, if you want."

Tyler grinned. He caressed Tom's jaw, his fingers lingering on his chin. "I do want it, but I also don't want to shake the bed and hurt you. It's all right if you want to say no."

Thomas kissed him. "Of course it's okay." He crooked his finger at Nevvie, who leaned in for her own kiss. "Go give the evil genius a good lathering, sugar. I expect a hot sponge bath of my own later."

"I think I like this naughty nurse gig. Might be as fun as being a little slave girl."

Both men groaned.

Tyler carefully got out of bed and headed for the bathroom. Nevvie joined him a few minutes later, closing the door behind her before grabbing him and kissing him, hard and deep.

"What's that for?"

She whispered, her mouth by his ear. "Master Thomas made sure I was warmed up for you."

Tyler chuckled. "Oh, did he now?"

"Mmm hmm."

He started the shower and turned, held up a foil pouch. "Think you can remember how to put one of these on me, love?" He kept his voice low.

She smiled and took it from him, then knelt in front of him. "I think so." She went down on him but he was already hard.

He tangled his fingers in her hair. "If you don't stop, we won't need that."

Nevvie ripped the pouch open and carefully rolled the condom on him, then sat back on the bathroom rug and spread her legs. "Let's not waste it."

He slowly slid into her. Once inside her he held still, savoring the feeling. "Let's hope our sweet boy doesn't take his time." He kissed her. "This is lovely, but I prefer my little slave totally au naturale."

Nevvie wrapped her arms and legs around him, nibbled on his ear, and whispered, "Then you need to help me keep him horny so he uses me well, don't you, Master?"

He thrust, hard, making her gasp. "Yes, I suppose I do." He thrust again and held still. "Jesus, you're so perfect I just want to explode."

"Then why don't you?"

"Because I want more than a quick run with you. I've missed this so much." He took possession of her mouth and slowly fucked his tongue against hers in time with his strokes. As he built up to his climax he slowed, trying to hold it off, touching his forehead to hers. "I love you, Nevvie. I love you so much."

"Maybe we can have one more after this one."

He froze. "I don't want you to be a baby machine, love."

"We'll see how this one goes. But for number three it's back to the pot-luck method."

Tyler laughed and took a long, slow stroke. "Makes life simpler, doesn't it?"

She pulled his head down to her shoulder, his ear near her lips, her fingers tangled in his hair. "Fuck me good, Tyler. You know you own my heart and soul."

He closed his eyes and moaned, his strokes coming faster and harder at her words.

Nevvie was relentless. "We need to figure out how both my masters can take me without hurting Tom's leg. It's been so long since I've felt both your sweet cocks inside me at the same time—"

"Ah!" Tyler gently bit down on her shoulder to stifle his cry as she tightened her grip on him.

"That's it, baby," she whispered. "Come for me."

He finally relaxed and carefully withdrew. "Yet another thing I hate about these. I have to rush away," he joked.

They flushed the evidence. By that time the bathroom had filled with steam from the shower. Tyler playfully swatted Nevvie on the bum. "Get in there and get wet, love."

"What about me?" She faked a pout.

He smiled. "Master Thomas will be more than happy to take care of you today, pet." He climbed into the shower next to her and held her. "Besides, I'll have plenty of time alone with you. He needs you right now. I'd rather he gets that time with you. It will help heal his soul."

She searched his deep, blue eyes. "Do you think he's going to be okay?"

Tyler nodded. "Once his physical wounds are healed we'll get him back into shape, never fear." He kissed her before stepping away. "Oh, one last thing."

She was already shampooing her hair. "What?"

The tone and timbre of his voice changed. "You're not allowed to wear *any* clothes today, my sweet slave."

Her entire body flushed with erotic heat. She recognized they'd slipped from the casual play into the full-on slave game, something they hadn't done since before "that day."

He continued. "The only item you're allowed to wear today is your pretty pink collar. Do you have a problem with that, darling?" he asked in the same, serious tone.

She rinsed her hair and shook her head, finally opening her eyes. "No, Master. I don't have a problem with that at all."

"Good. When I get home today I will ask Master Thomas for a full report of your activities."

Her heart raced. God she loved this!

"Yes, Master."

He stepped close again, his eyes burning into hers. "On second thought, I think I'll have a chat with Master Thomas about not letting you come while I'm gone. If you are a very good little slave we will reward you later. But only if Master Thomas says you deserve it."

She gulped.

He gently inserted a finger into her, slowly stroking, lightly caressing her clit, just enough to make her moan a little before pulling it out. "That's just a small sample of what you'll get—later."

Then he kissed her, back to sweet Tyler. "You do wish to play, don't you, love?"

Nevvie had lost her ability to speak under Tyler's piercing gaze. She eagerly nodded again.

His broad smile was well worth the hours of sexual frustration she knew lay ahead of her. The boys would tease and taunt her all day long until finally giving her the release she'd desperately crave. "Master Thomas needs a day of play to remind him we still find him sexy, I think. I trust you'll well-earn your reward, won't you?"

"Yes, Master," she gasped.

"That's my sweet, beautiful angel." When he hugged her she rested her head against his chest and thanked the universe for bringing him—both of them—back to her.

Tyler left the shower first. When Nevvie finished she dried off and walked into the bedroom. Thomas still lay in bed, smiling. Tyler wasn't there.

She noted Thomas held something in his lap. When he crooked his finger at her she walked over to him and saw what it was.

"Master Tyler said you're in a playful mood today, sugar. Is that right?"

She nodded and knelt beside the bed, next to him. "Yes, Master."

"Goddamn, girl, you know what that does to me." He'd pulled the sheet up to his waist. His erection lifted it like a small pup tent.

"Would you like me to take care of that for you, Master?"

He grinned. "Not right now, sugar. I want to pace myself. Lean forward."

She did, holding her hair up for him and bending her head so he could buckle the collar into place. They rarely used it in their play. Whenever they did it was always a hotter than normal experience. It was part of the little slave girl outfit they'd dressed her in the night of the Halloween party at Pete and Eddie's house, the night they made love to her for the first time.

The night they finally confessed their feelings for her.

"That's not too tight, is it, sugar?"

"No, Master. It's perfect."

"Goddamn!" he growled. "Come here and kiss me."

She did. He caressed her nipples with his fingers, turning them into hard pebbles. Then he stroked her cheek. "You do want this, right?"

"I love to play, Master."

"No sugar. That's not what I meant."

Nevvie carefully curled up in bed next to him. "I want to add to our family." She lightly trailed her fingers over his abdomen, gently traced his scars. "I don't want years between the kids. I want them close in age. I don't know if I'll want anymore after this, but I do want another one."

"So what have you and the evil genius got planned, hmm?"

Startled, she looked up at him. He laughed. "Girl, I know him, and I know you. You want a brown-eyed baby so we've got a miniature matching set for the daddios."

She sat up, her jaw agape. "What?"

He smiled. For the first time since he'd regained consciousness she saw her sweet, playful Tommy was back. "Baby girl, you two are gonna do your damnedest to make sure there's more Kinsey than Paulson in the next one. I know it."

She simply stared, still in shock. He'd never said anything about it before, not since their first conversations when they were trying to get pregnant with Adam.

"I don't care that Tyler was first, baby girl. Don't you two get it? Why do you think I told Bob to put Tyler's name on the birth certificate? I mean, really, sugar. Duh. He's got Tyler's eyes, he damn sure didn't get them from me. Adam is still my son—our son. If y'all are that bound and determined to be like this, I'll go along with you. You don't have to sneak around behind my back to make me a daddy."

"You're not mad?"

"Honey, life's too short for me to get upset about something like this. I'm flattered you two love me that much to worry about my feelings, especially after the way I acted. Yes, I would have been annoyed to find out about y'all's plan…before. I see things differently now." He kissed her. "I love you two, and if this is how you want to do it, I'll do it. I told you, I'll do whatever you want me to do."

"Tyler!" Her eyes never left Tom's face.

He raced into the bedroom. "What?"

She laughed at his expression. "No, everything's okay. But we're busted."

"What?"

Thomas crooked his finger at Ty. If Nevvie couldn't resist Tyler, Tyler couldn't resist Thomas. "I figured out your baby plan, Evil Genius. It didn't take much. I'm not *that* brain damaged."

Tyler laughed. "I'm sorry, love. We didn't want to upset you."

"Like I told Miss Evil Genius Junior, here, if it's what you want, that's okay."

"Really?"

He nodded. "Really. You're gonna get awfully tired of screwing on the bathroom carpet."

Startled, Tyler looked at Nevvie and she shook her head. "Don't ask me. Maybe he got psychic powers or something from that conk on the head."

Thomas laughed. "Dude, your knees were still red when you came out of the bathroom, and you've got a rug burn on one."

Tyler looked down at his legs and swore.

* * * *

Tyler returned to the kitchen to eat. Happy to finally have her tough guy on the mend emotionally, Nevvie curled up next to Thomas in bed, content to lay with her ear pressed against his chest, listening to his heartbeat, his arm around her.

He was really back for good, she felt it. His previous tension and emotional frigidity had disappeared.

Thomas kissed the top of her head. "Thank you, baby girl," he whispered.

She looked up and met his large, brown eyes. "For what?"

"For forgiving me. For not giving up on me. I owe the two of you."

"We love you. You're not getting rid of us that easily." She gently poked him in the chest. "But let me tell you something, I catch you flirting again with anyone but our evil genius, I'll neuter you."

He reddened but smiled. "I'm not getting off the hook for that one any time soon, am I?" Thomas looked away, unable to take the force of her gaze.

"You were jealous, and angry, face it."

He couldn't deny it. "You're as spooky as he is, sugar."

"It took me a few hours to not want to rip your nuts off. That's why I had to get out of the house until I calmed down. Considering I almost lost both of you, smacking you down for a little flirting is the least of my concerns. But Tyler…you're his rock, as much as you are mine. Maybe you don't see it the way I do, because you see him as a guy. He needs you every bit as much as I need you. Just because he's strong with me doesn't mean he doesn't need you the way I need you. And it worried him because he thought maybe you'd changed your views, that there wasn't room in your heart for him anymore."

She reached up and gently tipped his chin so she could kiss him.

"Show him how much you love him, Tommy. Please."

He nodded. "I will. I promise." He tightly hugged her. "What would us two losers do without you?"

* * * *

Once Tyler had left for his appointment, Nevvie helped Thomas into the shower and took her time soaping him up. He didn't mind that she kept him perpetually hard during the entire bath, and when she helped him back to the bed he waggled his finger at her to come hither.

"Yes, Master?" she coyly said.

Thomas grinned. He loved this game as much as she did. Hopefully she and Tyler wouldn't mind him changing it up a bit that afternoon.

"Why don't you come here and have a little fun?"

She carefully straddled him, reality breaking through for just a moment. "Tell me if I hurt you."

"Sugar, you're not hurting me," he assured her, his hands gripping her hips. He could do this with her all day.

In the back of his mind his guilty conscience still chanted "brain damaged asshole."

Thank God he hadn't done anything more than flirt or that one kiss. He'd be ready to kill himself now. The guilt wasn't worth it, not when he had two perfect people who loved him.

"You sure you want another one, Nev?"

She nodded. "Yeah." She stopped. "You do, don't you?"

"It's your body. We told you in the beginning that it's all up to you. Whatever you want, that's what you get."

She resumed the slow, gentle roll of her hips. "One more. Matched set," she teased.

"We'll get snipped if you want."

"Too soon to talk about that." She'd closed her eyes and he

enjoyed the slow, sensuous rhythm of her body, relentlessly pulling him closer to release.

His eyes settled on the collar again and he thought back to that night a few years ago, the Halloween party, watching her and Tyler dance on Pete and Eddie's lanai, the sexiest thing he'd ever seen in his life.

How right they'd looked together, and how lucky—and proud—he felt to know they were his. Well, Tyler was his and they'd prayed Nevvie soon would be theirs.

His climax rolled through him, taking him by surprise. When she knew he'd finished, Nevvie leaned forward and kissed him, slow and deep.

"Lay here with me, sugar," he whispered, keeping his eyes closed. She nestled in the crook of his arm. As best he could, he cuddled around her as they'd used to, the entire length of her body pressed against his.

Thomas didn't realize he'd dozed off until Tyler kissed him. He opened his eyes to find Tyler smiling down at him. Nevvie was still asleep, tucked against his side.

"How was your morning, love?" Tyler asked.

"Not as wild as you'd imagine. I fell asleep."

"Preparing for round two?"

"Sort of." He met Tyler's eyes. "I think I want to change things up a little."

Tyler frowned. "What do you mean?"

He glanced at Nevvie. "I think I want to try the slave gig for a little while." He reached out and brushed his hand against the front of Tyler's slacks, which were now full. "I think I owe the two of you. So how about it? Would you like to have a little slave boy for a while?"

Tyler's sharp intake of breath told Thomas more than any words could. He leaned over and kissed Thomas, hard. "Do you mean it? That would be…" He kissed him again.

"I can't hang off the ceiling fan or anything, but I'll do my best."

He gently squeezed the front of Tyler's slacks, his own cock stiffening again. "I'll do anything to please my master and mistress."

Nevvie caught the last part as she awoke. "What? What's going on?"

Tyler's broad grin lit his whole face. "Love, there's been a slight change of plans. I don't think you'll mind."

She sat up. "What?"

Thomas carefully rolled over. "I just told Master Tyler that I think I want to change the game...Mistress."

Her face went blank for a moment before she giggled. "Mistress?"

He caught her hand and brought it to his lips, kissing it. "Isn't that what good slaves should say?"

She looked at Tyler and he nodded, then back to Thomas. "Well...um...okay. That's new, but sure."

He winked at her. "Admit it. You'd love to have a little slave boy to service you."

Nevvie couldn't hold back her laughter. "Yes, it's sexy." Then to Tyler, "Did you put him up to this?"

"No, love. He came up with this all on his own. He's not as brain damaged as he claims, obviously." Tyler was already unbuttoning his shirt, his steamy gaze on Thomas. "Frankly, I don't know why we didn't think of it sooner." He stroked Thomas' cheek and kissed him again. "Maybe that's what we needed to keep our wayward one in line."

Nevvie quickly warmed to the game and pressed her body against Thomas. "Maybe I should go shopping for a collar for you."

He glanced at her. "No pink."

She grinned. "No, it wouldn't match your beautiful brown eyes."

Tyler laughed and shed his pants, sliding into bed on Thomas' other side. "So what should we have our little slave do first, Mistress Nevvie?"

She propped herself up on one arm. "I don't know. He was very naughty this morning. I didn't get to come while you were gone."

"Hey, don't blame me for that—"

"Shh," Nevvie and Tyler said together. Nevvie placed a finger over Thomas' mouth. "Little slave doesn't get to speak unless spoken to."

He laughed, then sucked her finger into his mouth, swirling his tongue around the digit.

"Very good," she whispered, nibbling on his neck. "That pleases me."

Tyler laughed. "Oh boy, you're in trouble," he said with a playful grin. "She's got, what, five years of lines stored up in that magnificent brain of hers to use against you now."

Thomas grinned at them around her finger, sucking harder.

"I wish that was my cock in his mouth," Tyler said.

Nevvie sat up and pulled her finger from Thomas' lips. He released it with an audible pop. "Well, Master Ty," she said, "I think you should put our boy to good use then, don't you?"

"Bloody hell," he growled, getting to his knees. "I don't know who's sexier, him or you."

"Let's call it a tie." She helped Thomas roll over and he sucked Tyler's stiff cock into his mouth. Both men eagerly moaned.

"How is he?" Nevvie asked.

Tyler's eyes closed. "Oh, love," he gasped. "Divine. Simply divine."

The encouragement made Thomas suck harder. Nevvie saw he'd grown hard too. She reached around him and stroked his cock while he sucked Tyler. "You know what I'd love to see," she said, dropping into the sexy slave girl voice. "I'd love to see you fucking our little slave, Master Tyler," she cooed.

Both men groaned. Tyler somehow gasped out, "Logistically, that might be an issue, love. I'm not sure how we'd do that without hurting him right now."

She grinned, wicked and cunning. "On his side."

Tyler's eyes popped open. "Brilliant!" He tapped Thomas on the head. "Over you go, love."

Nevvie grabbed a towel and the bottle of lube while Tyler helped Thomas sit up. Nevvie spread out the towel and then took her position in front of Thomas. She was more than happy to help him prepare. "Okay, little slave," Nevvie said with a grin, "roll over."

Laughing, he did, with her help. He moaned and tried to buck his hips against her hand as she lubed his dark hole.

"Okay, now on your side."

All three laughing, Nevvie held Thomas' cheeks open for Tyler's waiting shaft, his own cock throbbing and eager. A different, low, growl escaped them both as Tyler nudged into position and slowly sank his cock inside Thomas.

"How's that, boys?" she asked.

Two eager nods.

She could get used to this.

Nevvie let the men find a rhythm and movement that worked for them. They were soon lost in their passion. Nevvie knelt in front of Thomas, her hand gripping his shaft.

"How's it feel to have him back there?"

"Goddamn, it feels good, sugar. Real good."

Tyler held Tom's hips, carefully thrusting, his eyes squeezed shut. "Amazing, love," he murmured. "It's been far too long."

She slowly stroked Thomas, reading his body, not letting him climax. It didn't take Tyler long to come, pulling Thomas against his chest, his hands reaching around to stroke his arms, kissing his shoulders.

"I do so love you," Tyler said. "I've missed this so much."

When Nevvie cleared her throat, the men laughed. "Hey, what about your mistress?" she playfully griped.

Tyler carefully slipped out from behind Thomas and went to clean up. Thomas rolled onto his back while Nevvie straddled his lap and impaled herself on his rigid cock.

"That's better," she said as she closed her eyes.

Tyler returned from washing up and knelt behind her, holding her. "How is he, love?"

"Wonderful," she sighed.

She relaxed against Tyler as he played with her nipples. Thomas stroked her clit, and Nevvie realized some of the changes in Tommy had effected more than his handwriting and ability to button his shirts. He acted unsure, tentative, as if afraid or having trouble.

Nevvie leaned forward again and Thomas had to slide his hands to her hips. Trying not to be obvious, she nudged Tyler's hands lower and urged Tommy's north to her breasts.

Fortunately, Thomas was too engrossed in what was going on to pick up on the situation, but Tyler had clued in. After a few minutes it didn't matter, because between the sweet fullness inside her and Tyler's skilled fingers she quickly climbed to release. As he felt her come, Thomas grabbed her hips and thrust, groaning as he climaxed.

Trying to keep her weight off his leg she rested against him, his arms around her. "I love you so much, baby girl," he said, stroking her back. He looked up at Tyler. "I love you too, mister."

Tyler leaned in and kissed him. "As I love you, sweet."

Nevvie kissed Tom. "I love you too, tough guy."

She carefully climbed off Thomas and noticed him wince. "You okay?"

He nodded. "A little pain. I think I'm going to need a pain pill today."

Tyler and Nevvie helped him into the bathroom and they took a shower, then back to bed. Tyler fetched him his medicine. Then Tyler and Nevvie curled up next to Tomas in bed, one carefully tucked on each side of him. Together, they dozed.

* * * *

After their nap Nevvie fixed them a late lunch. They ate in bed together, watching TV, Thomas' past tension and distant attitude completely gone.

When she carefully extricated herself from them later that afternoon, the men questioningly looked at her.

"Where are you off to, love?" Tyler asked. If Tyler suspected she had ulterior motives, he didn't let on.

"I need to go shopping before I pick Adam up from Eddie and Pete. Did you guys need anything?"

They shook their heads and she kissed them both before leaving. It took her a few minutes to find the store, one of those cases where she'd driven past it countless times without really seeing it but knew it was around there somewhere. Fighting her deep blush, she walked inside.

The girl behind the counter looked younger than her and like she could be working at a coffee shop instead of at an adult sex store. Nevvie told her what she had in mind. The girl was more than happy to help her find what she needed, including making suggestions and referring her to another store not too far away for one of the items.

Now excited as well as embarrassed, Nevvie paid for the items, put them in the trunk to hide them, and made her way to the second store. This wasn't a bright, cheery place, definitely darker in tone and décor. The man behind the counter was just as friendly as the other girl, albeit a little scary-looking. Sensing her discomfort he took great cares to put her at ease. Thirty minutes later, Nevvie left with exactly what she'd had in mind.

Also hidden in the trunk.

She couldn't wait to tell Tyler.

Pete and Eddie greeted her with hugs when she arrived to pick up Adam. "How's things going?" Pete cautiously asked.

"I think he's going to be okay. I really do."

Eddie blew out a relieved sigh. "Good. Stupid asshole anyway."

"No, that's 'brain damaged asshole,'" she joked.

Tyler walked outside when she returned home. He leveled his gaze at her. "All right, love. Fess up."

She grinned. She should have known she wouldn't get away with it. Before she unfastened the baby from his car seat, she took Tyler around to the trunk and showed him her purchases.

His eyes widened, then he laughed and swept her into his arms, spun her around. She pressed her face against his chest.

"You are sweetly diabolical, love. Absolutely, incredibly, totally."

"You've worn off on me."

He looked at the items again. "I wondered what you were up do. I didn't want to say anything in front of Thomas and spoil your fun."

"He's still okay?"

"Quite. I dare say he's finally on the mend." He left his arm around her waist. "Well, when did you plan on springing this?"

"Tomorrow. Let's let him get a good night's sleep."

Tyler kissed her on the temple again. "Brilliant, love. You are absolutely brilliant."

"I did good...Master Tyler?"

"You did wonderfully... Mistress Nevvie."

She pouted. "Do I ever get to play little slave again?"

He dropped his voice to the seductive growl that always made her instantly wet. "How about you'll always be my little slave, even when you're playing his sweet mistress?"

Nevvie wanted to rip his clothes off there in the driveway. "Okay."

Tyler laughed and closed the trunk. "Ah, love, I've corrupted you."

Chapter Nineteen

At least one thing hadn't changed. Thomas was, as always, a little clueless. Totally unaware of the shared playful grins between Ty and Nevvie, he spent over an hour playing with Adam and watching TV in their bedroom. They ate leftovers for dinner and settled in to sleep.

Nevvie snuck the items inside before bed. The next morning, she got up before the men and made coffee. Adam was still sound asleep. Nevvie counted on at least another hour before he would awaken. She returned to the bedroom and Tyler lifted a sleepy eyelid at her, then winked.

Thomas was still asleep.

She put the items in the bedside table drawer and snuggled beside Thomas. He finally stirred and looked at her.

"Good morning."

She grinned.

Thomas glanced at Tyler and spotted his pleased smile. "Okay, what's going on?"

"Not for you to worry about, little slave," Tyler said. "Go take care of your morning business and get your arse back in bed."

Thomas smiled but didn't question them further. When Thomas returned, Nevvie told him to sit on the edge of the bed and close his eyes. Tyler helped Nevvie figure out the lock, and together they put the sterling silver link chain collar on Thomas. Anyone else would think it was a necklace. When they finished, they stepped back.

"Open your eyes," Nevvie said.

He did, trying to see it then reaching up to feel. "Do I want to ask?" But he grinned.

Tyler crossed his arms. "Mistress Nevvie went shopping for you yesterday, love. She decided it would be best to give our little slave a tangible reminder of who his owners are."

"And how long am I wearing this?"

Tyler looked to Nevvie, deferring to her.

She took a deep breath and held up the tiny key. "Until we say so. No one will know what it signifies but us."

"Are you all right with that, love?" Tyler asked Thomas.

"If that's what my mistress and master want, it's what I'll do." He felt the lock and his fingers came upon the tiny tag. "What does it say?"

"OWL. It stands for, 'Owned and Well-Loved.'"

He laughed. "Not taking any chances, are you?"

"Bloody hell, we just got you back, Thomas," Tyler said. "We're not about to lose you again."

"Now for the second part of your surprise," Nevvie said. "Stand up and turn around, put your hands on the bed."

With a curious look, he obeyed.

"And close your eyes," Tyler ordered.

He did.

This was new territory for Nevvie. She deferred to Tyler, handing him the butt plug. Then she sidled close to Thomas and rested her hand on his back.

"Hold him open, love," Tyler said with a grin. Nevvie slipped her hands down Tommy's hips to his ass, gently spreading his cheeks while Tyler lubed the plug.

Tommy laughed. "Uh oh. I'm in trouble."

"You sure are," Nevvie agreed.

His lower lip caught under his teeth as he felt the plug make contact with his rim. His cock instantly hardened.

"Relax, love," Tyler said. "This will only take a moment."

"Jesus," he gasped. "How big is that?"

Nevvie giggled. "Not even as big as Tyler. Quit complaining."

"Who said I was complaining?" He groaned as Tyler carefully slid it home.

Tyler nodded to Nevvie, who released Thomas after a pat on the ass. "All set."

Thomas carefully lowered himself to the bed and rolled over, his cock standing at attention. "How long you gonna torture me?"

Nevvie trailed a finger from the base of his member to the throbbing tip. "Doesn't look like you're in any agony."

"I'm not. But this is just plain mean."

Tyler put the lube away and cast a glance over his shoulder as he headed to the bathroom to wash his hands. "What's even meaner is you'll be wearing that for a few hours without relief, love. We want you to remember who your master and mistress are."

Thomas laughed. Nevvie lay down beside him. "You're going to remember this for a long time."

"Uh, yeah, kind of got that." He wiggled his hips, groaning. "I can't go anywhere like this. I'll look like I've got a friggin' pup tent in my pants."

"You should have thought about that before you misbehaved."

"Come on, sugar. Give me a little help here." But he smiled.

Nevvie knew she wore an evil grin and didn't care. "Nope. You'll take care of Master Tyler and myself. When we're happy with your performance, maybe we'll let you have a little relief."

Thomas wiggled his hips again, his cock bobbing in the air. "Aw, babe, I promise I'll be a good boy."

She carefully straddled him. "Oh, we know you'll be a good boy. We're going to make sure you don't forget this lesson." She teased him, rocking her hips so his cock rubbed along her clit.

His hands rested on her hips, trying to nudge her over his member. "Gonna make me beg for it?"

Tyler returned and slid into bed next to them. "You'd better believe it, love." His smile looked as wicked as Nevvie's.

Thomas made a big deal about sighing. "Well, I deserve it." He gave them the sad puppy dog look. "Will my master and mistress take pity on me?"

Nevvie burst out laughing. "Oh no you don't. No puppy dog eyes. Stop it."

"He is rather lethal with those, isn't he?" Tyler said. "Maybe we need to blindfold him, take away one of his weapons of persuasion."

"More like weapons of mass seduction."

Both men laughed. Thomas looked at Nevvie. "I thought you wanted to use me as your personal stud muffin. How am I supposed to do that if you keep me suffering?"

Tyler laughed again. "He's got a point there. I hadn't thought about it quite like that."

Nevvie frowned and crossed her arms over her chest, thinking. "Do you have any suggestions, Master Tyler?"

He shook his head. "Not off the top of my head, love." He ran his fingers through Tom's hair. "Perhaps his torture should be riding him to exhaustion."

Thomas eagerly nodded.

Nevvie laughed. "Doesn't sound much like punishment to me." It was so good to have her playful Thomas back. With him acting like this, she found it easy to forgive him. They had finally broken through his wall.

He pressed against her hips, trying to guide her onto his stiff shaft. "Oh, believe me, sugar. It's torture. Total punishment."

She studied his brown eyes and slipped out of their game for a moment. "I know I sort of overreacted the other day—"

"No, you didn't overreact. I deserved it." He looked at Tyler. "I promise I won't let you guys down again. And I promise I won't keep it bottled up anymore."

Tyler leaned in and kissed him. "We love you no matter what shape you're in. And she's right that, no matter what, you'll always be our tough guy."

Nevvie slowly, sensuously impaled herself on his stiff cock. A content sigh escaped her. "I guess I should focus more on using our little slave than I should on punishing him, shouldn't I, Master Tyler?"

Thomas groaned into Tyler's mouth. Tyler broke their kiss. "Use him well, love. Because when you're finished with him, I shall have my turn."

Nevvie was careful not to put her weight on Thomas' hips. She leaned forward, bracing herself with her arms while Thomas closed his eyes and held onto her.

Tyler stretched out next to Thomas. He reached between Nevvie's legs and stroked her clit. "How is our little slave boy, love?"

"Wonderful," she sighed. She took long, slow strokes, prolonging her pleasure, enjoying the feel of Tyler's hand skillfully playing with her sensitive nub.

She could easily do this all day but knew Tom's body couldn't take it yet even if his spirit was now willing. Nevvie deeply impaled herself and sat up. Both men moaned at the sight of her body. Tyler leaned in, taking one of her nipples in his mouth while playing with the other with his free hand.

Tommy stroked her hips. "Come on, baby. Moan for us."

Nevvie rocked her hips in a slow, gentle bump and grind as Tyler teased her closer to release. Her slick muscles clamped down on Tom's cock, drawing another deep, hungry growl from his lips. With the anal plug inside him, he was having a hard time holding back against the sensation.

"Come on, sweetie," he encouraged. "Give it to us."

As always, Tyler expertly read her body, knowing how to prolong her climb to release. It was only when he knew Tom was nearly too far gone to hold on that Tyler brought her over, making her cry out as her climax hit.

Tom's eyes closed as he moaned. He tightly gripped her as he bucked his hips. "Jesus!" he gasped.

Nevvie slumped into Tyler's arms. He kissed her, and as he leaned back they shared a smile. He stroked her cheek and kissed her forehead.

"You look so beautiful like that," he murmured. "Breathtaking."

Nevvie carefully moved, trying not to jostle Tom any more than she already had. His eyes stayed closed, a playful smile teasing his lips.

"Why do you look so happy, little slave?" Nevvie prodded.

He laughed. "I don't think I'm going to give up the slave role any time soon, babe." One eye slowly opened. "This is way too much fun."

She tried to fake a frown and failed. "It's supposed to be punishment."

"Yeah, you can keep punishing me as long as you want. I've been a baaad boy."

Tyler leaned in and kissed him. "Well, you've still got me to take care of. I suggest you get busy." He knelt close to Tom's face. Tom opened his mouth, swiped the end of Tyler's cock with his tongue, and stroked his lover's sac with his hand.

"You know I love this," Tom said, his voice a deep, hungry growl.

Nevvie's heart thumped in a pleasant way. That always happened when she watched the two of them together. Something else that had been missing from their relationship for too long.

She loved watching, being able to see both of their reactions. Tom slowly stiffened again as Tyler's eyes closed at the feel of his lover's lips around his shaft.

Nevvie stretched out on Tom's other side and wrapped her fingers around his cock. From this vantage, she was only inches from the action. "Suck him deep, Tommy," she whispered in his ear.

Thomas moaned in response, doing it.

Tyler groaned. "Exquisite," he gasped.

"Squeeze his balls, baby," she ordered, and he did. Her fingers slowly stroked Tom's shaft, still slick from their combined juices.

She kissed his temple. "Work your tongue around the tip some.

Don't make him blast off too soon."

Thomas followed her orders as Tyler gripped the headboard. She slowly stroked Tom's shaft, knowing she could easily make him come again if she wanted. He'd gone several months without release to the best of her knowledge, unless he'd been jerking off alone at night. Somehow, she didn't think he had.

She'd have to ask him later.

Tyler flexed his hips, slowly fucking Tom's mouth. The silver chain lay at the base of Tom's throat and sight of it stirred something deep inside Nevvie.

Theirs.

He was all theirs, back to them, hopefully for good.

She nuzzled Tom's neck, firmly gripped his throbbing cock. She stilled her hand but kept him hard. "You're going to swallow every drop, aren't you, Tommy? You're going to be a good little slave and take every bit your master gives you, aren't you?"

Tommy's mouth worked at Tyler's cock. She knew he had to be deep-throating him.

Tyler gasped. "I'm almost there, loves."

Nevvie nipped Tom's earlobe. "Do it, baby. Make him moan for me."

Thomas eagerly worked at his task. Tyler's other hand dropped to the back of Tom's head and he cried out as he fucked his cock deep into his lover's mouth.

Thomas didn't release him until he was sure Tyler had finished. Then he placed a kiss on the softened tip and looked up at him.

"Did I please my master?"

Tyler's eyes rolled open and he laughed. Nevvie snickered against his shoulder.

Tyler stretched out next to him. "You pleased me very much, little slave." His wicked grin told Nevvie more than any words ever could.

Thomas looked at her. "Did I please my mistress?"

"Very much." She kissed him, gently squeezing his shaft. "Looks like you're ready for round two."

"Whatever my mistress wants."

Nevvie was about to reply when they heard Adam on the baby monitor.

Tyler sat up. "I'll take care of him," he said, pointing at the baby monitor. Then he pointed at Thomas. "You take care of him." He stood, pulled on a pair of boxers, and left, closing the door behind him.

Nevvie carefully swung back into position and settled over his shaft, hovering. "Look at me Tommy."

He did.

"You want it, baby?"

He nodded, his hands resting on her thighs. She suspected without Tyler's assistance she wouldn't come this time but that was okay.

"How bad you want it?"

"Real bad, baby. Fuck me good, please."

She slowly lined his shaft up with her ready entrance and took her time settling into position. Then she leaned forward and kissed him. "You fuck me good and come for me again and I'll let you take that toy out of your ass."

He smiled. "Maybe I like having this toy in my ass."

Nevvie laughed. "Don't tempt me. I might make you wear it to work."

"I would if you told me to."

She paused. "I was kidding."

"I wasn't. I'm your toy. I'll do whatever it takes to make things right and keep them that way."

Nevvie took another slow stroke. "Love us. Don't shut us out again. That's all we want." She kissed him, gently fucking him. She longed for the days when he'd pound her into the mattress but getting back to that point would be a long time coming.

No pun intended.

Mindful of his leg, she maintained a steady rhythm she knew

would do the trick. Then she laid her head against his shoulder, enjoying the feel of his large hands on her back. "Come for me," she whispered. "Show me how much you love me."

His body tensed as he climaxed. Nevvie carefully kept her weight on her knees as she lay in his arms, not moving, enjoying the moment.

"You won't hurt me, sugar," he said. "You can relax."

"I'm okay."

She shivered as his fingers brushed down her spine in the familiar way. At least one thing was the same about him. "You're afraid of breaking me. I'm okay. If I hurt I'll say so."

"I thought my psychic connection was with Tyler."

"You're treating me the same way Tyler treated you when you were pregnant."

Nevvie propped herself up on one arm and trailed her fingers down his chest. "Now we've sort of got matching scars."

He captured her fingers and brought them to his lips, kissing each one, gently laving them with his tongue. "I swear to God I'm back for good, Nev. I won't screw up again." His deep, sweet brown eyes bored into hers.

"I'm not saying I think this is easy for you. I know this sucks. Just remember we love you no matter what shape you're in, and we'll help you no matter what, but you have to let us help you. I can't lose you." Her tears welled up again despite her best efforts to hold them back. "I love you so much, Tommy. I was so afraid we'd lost you. When you woke up and finally started talking, it was the best feeling in the world."

"What if I hadn't woke up?"

She shrugged. "Then I guess I'd be learning a lot about nursing, wouldn't I?"

He studied her. "You mean it, don't you?"

"Fuck, Tommy, what do you think we've been trying to say? Tyler will agree with me. You're our guy. You'll always be our guy and we don't give a shit what condition you're in."

He kissed her, his tongue gently tracing her lips. "I love you."

* * * *

Nevvie let Thomas take the butt plug out but ordered him to keep it in the bedside table at the ready. By the time Nevvie put Adam down for his afternoon nap, Nevvie was more than ready for another go at her slave boy. She gently pulled the nursery door shut and found Thomas in the kitchen, cleaning up the remains of his lunch. She slipped her arms around his waist.

"Go get in bed and wait for me."

His beaming smile reached his eyes. She felt his cock stiffen against her. "Yes, Mistress."

Nevvie reached up and flicked the tag on his silver chain. "What are you going to tell people if they ask what this is?"

He shrugged. "The truth." He leaned in and kissed her, his tongue gently exploring her mouth. "That my husband and my wife wanted me to have a tangible reminder of who I belong to."

Heat flared in her lower belly, sending a flood of moisture to her already throbbing sex. "Go get your ass in bed and prepared to be fucked."

"Whatever you say, Mistress." He grabbed his crutches and, as fast as he was capable, hurried down the hall.

Fuck! He sounded so sexy when he talked like that!

Tyler emerged from his study, coffee mug in hand. He glanced down the hall. "Did I hear something about a certain slave getting a good fucking?"

"You heard correctly."

He placed his mug on the counter and wrapped his arms around her, cupping her ass with his hands. With his mouth by her ear he growled, "I would love to slide my cock up your sweet arse while you're fucking him."

Nevvie's knees nearly failed her. "Do you think we can do that without hurting him?"

"Considering how you rode him yesterday and this morning, I daresay he'll be fine."

Her mouth went dry. She swallowed to form spit. "Okay," she squeaked.

She could play sexy mistress with Tommy, but there was no way she could ever pretend to be Tyler's Domme. No way in hell. Just his spooky blue eyes turned her knees to jelly, not to mention his voice.

His lips blazed a moist, hot trail down her neck to the base of her throat then he lifted his head. "You'll always be my sweet, beautiful little slave girl, won't you, angel?"

She nodded. Again their mental connection had come through.

He gently nuzzled her nose. "I'll always be your Master, love."

"Let's go, Master," she said. "We've got a slave to fuck."

Thomas was waiting, naked except for his collar, in bed. His stiff cock stood at rigid attention and his playful smile devastated her.

"Does this please you, Mistress?"

"Damn straight it does." She fought the urge to jump in the bed. Instead she quickly stripped and carefully mounted him with a satisfied sigh.

Tyler laughed. "Ah, loves, what a beautiful sight." He stripped and joined them, kneeling behind Nevvie with the bottle of lube. "Lean forward, sweetheart."

She did, keeping her weight on her elbows and knees. Thomas reached behind her and gently spread her cheeks for Tyler.

Desire coursed through her, running deep, demanding release. It had been a long time since they'd both taken her like this

Too long.

She buried her head against Thomas' neck, enjoying the feel of Tyler's fingers lubing her dark hole. "Yesss," she quietly hissed, trying to hold still and wanting to wiggle against his hand and take him deeper.

"Does that feel good?" Tyler asked her.

"Oh, yesss."

"Oh, God, baby," Thomas moaned. "It won't take much to make me come like this."

Tyler lined his lubed shaft with her rosette and gripped her hips. "You're not allowed to come before we do, little slave boy," he growled.

"Ah, fuck!" Thomas groaned, breathless with desire. "You keep talking like and that I'm gonna fucking blow."

"Don't you dare. You'll be wearing that butt plug during your next therapy session if you do."

Tyler's stern tone nearly finished Nevvie. She squirmed on Thomas' shaft, trying to impale herself on Tyler. "Fuck me, boys."

"Hold still then, love, and let me."

She forced herself to hold still while he slowly slid balls-deep inside her ass. The incredibly erotic feeling of them stretching her nearly pushed her over the edge. She just needed one more thing…

Tyler held still, his hands on her ass. "Don't move, darling. I want to feel you."

Thomas' eyes were firmly clamped shut. "Jesus, that's great!"

Tyler's lips brushed the nape of her neck, making her shiver. He carefully snaked one hand between her and Thomas and found her swollen, aching nub.

With his mouth near her ear, Tyler said, "You're going to come for me, love. I want my sweet little slave girl to squeeze my cock. I want to feel you come."

As if he'd waved a magic wand over her, something inside her broke free like an avalanche racing down a mountain. She threw her head back against his shoulder. He rolled her clit between his finger and thumb and she let out a primal scream—pleasure, passion, and relief.

Life was as it should be, finally.

She was still sobbing when he lowered her onto Thomas' chest and started thrusting. She tried to work her hips with him but the sensual explosion still rocketing through her had robbed her muscles of strength.

Thomas groaned, his hands on her waist.

"I can't hold it," he gasped.

"You'd better," Tyler growled.

Nevvie moaned, squirming between them, impaled on their large cocks.

Tyler took his time, holding back, enjoying her tight muscles squeezing him. After several minutes he quickened his pace. "All right, Thomas, get ready. You may come…now."

Tyler slammed home with one final, deep stroke as Thomas grunted beneath her. When all three had recovered, Tyler carefully untangled himself so he could let Nevvie hold her weight off Thomas.

Tyler kissed her shoulder. "Are you all right?"

She nodded, her hair hanging in her face and hiding her tears.

Happy tears.

"Thomas?"

His eyes were closed. "I'm good, man. Real good."

Tyler went to the bathroom, cleaned up, and returned with a warm, damp washcloth for Nevvie. After he cleaned her up she carefully moved to lie on Tom's other side. He winced a little, which didn't escape Nevvie's notice.

"Do you want a pain pill?"

He groped for their hands without opening his eyes. "Not right now." He brought their hands to his lips and kissed them, holding them on his chest. "Maybe later. Right now, I just want to lay here with you two."

"Did you enjoy that?" Tyler asked.

Thomas looked at him. "Fuck, that was…" He searched for the right words. "I nearly came when you ordered me not to. That was fucking hot, man. Jesus Christ."

"You're the one who volunteered to play our little slave boy." Tyler's playful grin melted the others.

"I hope you don't ever want a turn as slave, Ty," Nevvie said. "You've got two willing slaves."

Thomas squeezed her hand. "And I've got two fantastic masters. Mistresses. Wait…" He grinned. "I'm gonna like this a lot."

Chapter Twenty

Nevvie nervously exchanged glances with Tyler all morning. When their doorbell rang, Tyler answered it.

Thomas caught Nevvie's eye from the living room and tipped his head at her, motioning her over. He pulled her down to the couch as Tyler led an older man into the living room.

"Loves, this is John. Thomas' new physical therapist."

He looked at least ten years older than Tyler. Short-cropped hair, almost a military cut, liberally peppered with grey. Probably well-muscled at one time but some of that had softened into middle-aged flab. John nodded to them as Tyler made the introductions.

Thomas took a deep breath and grabbed Nevvie's hand. "Did the company tell you why I requested a new therapist?"

He shook his head. "No, but when I talked with Jennifer to get the case file, she didn't seem to want to talk about it."

"She's not in any trouble, is she?"

"Not that I'm aware of."

Thomas looked at Tyler, then Nevvie. "Well, I wasn't exactly honest and open with her when she first started and didn't do anything to correct her erroneous impression. It sort of shocked her when it came out, and it pissed off these two. Understandably," he added. "We're polyamorous. I told the company that when I called the other day. Will that be a problem?"

John dropped his bag to the carpet and shrugged. "Should it? I'm not doin' any of you, no offense. I'm happily married, and it's not any of my business."

That out of the way, he spent a few minutes talking with Thomas to make sure he had all his notes correct before starting on a similar set of exercises Jennifer had used.

Tyler and Nevvie watched from the kitchen. Thomas noticed John wasn't nearly as gentle as Jennifer, and thought perhaps this wasn't a bad change after all if it helped speed his healing.

Maybe she'd been too easy on him.

By the end of the appointment Tom was sweating from pain and exertion. John took a moment to update his notes. "I'll be back Wednesday, same time." He gathered his things and said a quick, friendly but professional good-bye to them before leaving.

Nevvie raced into the living room and hugged Thomas. "Thank you!"

He waved Tyler over. "Yeah, well, I deserve the torture, that's for sure. And I need help getting back to the bedroom. I want to take a warm shower and lay down for a while. I'm in real fucking pain."

Nevvie helped him while Tyler kept an ear out for Adam waking up. When she got Thomas into bed she gave him a long massage, trying to work the pain from his muscles. He looked so sexy with just his silver collar on. As his pain pill took effect he drifted, held out his arm to her. She cuddled close, snuggling with him until she knew from the slow, deep sound of his breathing that he'd fallen asleep.

Tyler stuck his head in the door and smiled. "Is he asleep?"

Nevvie nodded and carefully extricated herself. She pulled on her clothes and joined Tyler in the kitchen.

He enveloped her in his arms. "He's really back, sweetheart. He's not leaving us again. I know it."

"I still wonder if I didn't overreact."

He shook his head. "No, love. I think it was exactly the shock our sweet boy needed to get his head on properly."

* * * *

Three weeks after Tommy's change in attitude, Nevvie awoke

curled with him pressed into her back. From the slow, soft sound of his breathing she knew he was still asleep. Tyler wasn't in bed. Her heart sped with anxiety until she heard him in the kitchen making coffee and softly talking to Adam.

She relaxed. How long would it take her to quit feeling anxious about him when he was out of her sight?

Falling back to sleep looked like a tempting option. As she started to change position her stomach took a dangerous roll. She bolted from the bed straight for the bathroom.

The action elicited a startled yelp from Tommy as she jostled him but she didn't have time to apologize. She made the toilet in time to heave up what little was left of her dinner from the night before.

From the bedroom, Thomas yelled, "Tyler! Get in here, now!"

"What?"

Nevvie closed her eyes and fought another round of nausea. For a moment she worried she was sick. Then another realization struck.

Tyler appeared at her side a moment later, one arm around her, the other holding her hair away from her face. "Are you all right, love?" he murmured.

She shook her head and spit, tightly gripped the bowl.

He kissed her temple. "I've got a test kit in the cabinet. Let's get your tummy settled and see what's up."

Their psychic connection strikes again. She nodded as she dry heaved. Oh yes, how could she have forgotten *this* part of being pregnant?

Thomas' voice came from the doorway. "You all right, sugar?"

Tyler looked at him, his voice hopeful. "I think you might get a little respite from your stud services, dear."

He laughed. "Damn! I was really enjoying being a sex toy."

Nevvie laughed until another round of nausea cut her off. Ten minutes later she shakily climbed to her feet. Tyler brought her a wet washcloth and glass of water so she could rinse her mouth. Both men looked on as she took the pregnancy test.

She couldn't bear the wait. Five minutes later, Tyler turned from the test with his face a mask.

Tommy leaned against the bathroom wall and held Adam in his arms.

"Well?" she whispered.

Tyler's face broke into a beaming grin and he swept her into his arms, kissing her, then leaned in and kissed Thomas. "Looks like we're adding another to our family."

Nevvie sobbed with joy. This time, unlike with Adam, they were all together to receive the news. A tear rolled down Thomas' cheek as he kissed the top of Adam's head. "You hear that, buddy? You're gonna be a big brother." Nevvie wrapped her arms around him, burying her head against his shoulder. There was no doubt in her mind that he was the father this time. They'd been very careful.

Tyler completed their group hug. "Will you please consider taking it a little easier this time around? I thought you were going to work yourself to death the last time."

She nodded, wiping her tears. "Only if you promise not to treat me like I'm going to break."

"I promise, love."

* * * *

With Thomas now fully participating in their lives again, Nevvie settled in and relaxed as her pregnancy progressed. She let Tyler and Thomas coddle her and take over in many ways. As Thomas' physical rehab continued and doctors cleared him to drive again, he started taking over most of the daily operations at Kinsey Consulting. Although there were plenty of days Nevvie or Tyler had to drive him to work because of his pain.

Although these days were fewer in number, he made a point of asking when he needed extra help.

Now that Tom's secret about his fine motor skills was out in the open, Nevvie consulted with occupational therapists and started working with him several times a day on exercises designed to help him. His handwriting still sucked compared to what it had been, but Nevvie recognized his steady progress as he took less time getting ready in the mornings.

She gently teased him about it one morning while she watched him shave with his electric razor. She was sitting in the bathroom, waiting for her stomach to settle enough so she could stray more than twenty feet from the toilet. "I could have been helping you out with that all along, stubborn."

He smiled into the mirror. "Yeah, I know." He still wore the collar, never asked to take it off. He didn't hesitate to wear open-collared shirts to work that didn't hide the collar, either.

His cane was propped by the sink. He'd progressed from needing crutches to mostly using the cane. Sometimes he could limp from the bedroom to the bathroom or kitchen without it, but for now he kept it close. He drove her Acura, she drove his Ridgeline, because it was easier for him to get into and out of for now.

Nevvie stood and walked over to him, wrapped her arms around his waist. First he'd lost a few pounds from his hospital stay. Then regained it and a few extra once back home. Now he was back to his pre-accident weight. "Do you have to go in today?"

He patted her hands. "Kenny and I have meetings this afternoon with clients. Can't get out of them, sugar. Sorry." He looked over his shoulder at her. "Want to ride in with me?"

She started to say yes when another wave of nausea hit and she bolted for the toilet.

"I want to," she finally managed. "I don't know if I can."

He smiled. "I understand."

* * * *

Nevvie was relieved when the morning sickness finally

disappeared. As much as she enjoyed working, she enjoyed staying home with Tyler even more. This pregnancy, he wasn't afraid to make love to her like he had been with Adam. It also meant she didn't have to sneak around with Tommy this time either.

She walked into Tyler's study one morning to refill his coffee and found him sitting back in his chair and staring at his laptop, his hands templed, index fingers on his lips.

"What's up?"

He arched an eyebrow. "Darling, this many years later, and you still lead in with that?"

She perched on the corner of his desk and stuck her tongue out at him.

Tyler snagged her hand and gently pulled her into his lap. "I was thinking about our sweet little slave boy." Between her pregnancy and Tommy's pain, they didn't often play either version of the slave game. It'd been a couple of months since the last instance.

"What brought this on?"

He shrugged, but she recognized the playful glint in his blue eyes. "He certainly loves his collar, doesn't he? I have to admit I had a delicious thought while we were showering this morning."

Nevvie had slept in and missed that one. "What?"

"Well," he purred, "you are a very good girl and keep yourself shaved for us. Perhaps our little slave boy should keep himself shaved, too."

She had to think for a moment, then grinned. "No way! You want to make him shave his balls?" The very thought of running her hand over his bare sac drenched her sex.

"You and I have been rather neglectful owners for the past several weeks. I was thinking along the lines of his first time should be a more memorable sort of occasion." He placed his hand over her tummy. She was showing, but not uncomfortably huge yet. "You won't feel like playing very much at all in the not-so-distant future, so why not a little in-home slave spa treatment?"

Nevvie kissed him. "I'll call Eddie and see if he can babysit tonight."

He could. Tyler dropped Adam off and stopped by the store to pick up a few things they'd need, as well as the fixings for a nice dinner. When Tommy made his usual call home as he left the office, Nevvie talked to him.

"By the way, we have a surprise for you."

Tyler silently watched, grinning.

"What kind of surprise, sugar?"

She met Tyler's gaze and winked. Then she switched to the sultry Mistress voice, a variation of her little slave girl voice that she knew would instantly harden Thomas' cock. "Master and Mistress order you to come straight home."

There was a momentary pause then Tommy's hoarse, "Goddamn!"

"When you come home, you will immediately walk inside and stand inside the front door. You will strip all your clothes off there. Then you will walk into the bedroom."

She heard him gasp. "Fuckin' A!"

"When you get to the bedroom, you will lie down on the bed, on your back, and be ready for us. Do you understand?"

"Yeah!"

She smiled. "Yes, what?"

He gasped again, "Yes, Mistress!"

They were waiting for him. Nevvie and Tyler grinned at each other when they heard the front door open and shut. A moment later, Thomas walked into the bedroom using his cane and wearing nothing but his collar and a broad, beaming smile.

"Very good," Nevvie said.

His stiff cock led the way as Thomas walked over to the bed and laid down on top of the towels they'd put out. "Like this?"

Tyler nodded. "Exactly. Now spread those legs."

He did, without question.

Nevvie, who'd stripped, perched on the bed next to Thomas. "Do you know what we're going to do to you?"

"Don't care. I'm sure I'll enjoy it."

Tyler laughed as he brought a folding chair over and placed it in front of Thomas. "My, you are a trusting thing, aren't you?"

"Do I really have a choice?"

Nevvie shook her head. "Nope!" She'd spent most of the day wet and eager. Tyler, displaying a little of his evil genius streak, refused to give her any relief.

Tyler settled in the chair, the scissors in his hand. "First, I suggest you hold very, very still, love. Otherwise this will not be fun."

Thomas met Nevvie's gaze, his brown eyes twinkling. She leaned in and kissed him as Tyler started trimming. After a few minutes Tyler seemed satisfied and disappeared into the bathroom for a moment. When he returned he carried a bowl of warm water, a wash cloth, shaving cream, and a razor.

"Now as you've already no doubt guessed, we decided our little slave boy should be appropriately groomed. Once you're suitably bare, you shall keep yourself this way for us. Understand?"

Thomas broke his kiss with Nevvie. "Yes, Master!" he gasped.

Tyler chuckled. "Good. I didn't think you'd object."

Nevvie wanted to keep kissing him, but even more she wanted to watch Tyler shave him. She turned around on the bed and Tommy nuzzled her leg while she enjoyed the show.

Tyler took his time, making sure to tease and torment Thomas' stiff cock with his hand as he worked. When he finished ten minutes later, he wiped away all the soap and examined his handiwork.

"Well, Mistress Nevvie, what do you think?"

She reached over and cupped his bare balls. "I like it," she said. "Why the hell didn't you think of this earlier?"

Tyler shrugged and tidied things up. "I don't know. But he shall stay this way for us from now on." He lay down next to Thomas, who rolled over and kissed him deep and hard.

Nevvie pressed her body against Tom's back and slipped her arm around his waist, her hand cupping his sac again. "That's for damn sure. This is nice."

Beyond speech, Thomas moaned.

Tyler rolled Thomas over to face Nevvie and reached for the bedside table. Thomas kissed her, his tongue exploring her mouth as he ground his hips against her.

"Nev, love, hold him open for me."

She reached around Tom's hips and spread his ass cheeks for Tyler. Then Thomas groaned when Tyler lubed him. He rubbed his stiff cock against Nevvie's leg.

"You ready to get royally fucked?" Nevvie asked him.

"Oh, hell yes!"

She nudged Thomas on top of her, sighing as he slid inside her. He dropped his head to her shoulder as Tyler knelt behind him.

He gently swatted Tom's ass. "Get ready, love."

Tom wiggled his hips, which drew a moan from Nevvie. She reached down and spread his cheeks for Tyler, giving him unfettered access. Thomas fell still, his lips pressed against Nevvie's neck as Tyler breeched his rim.

Before the accident, Tyler or Nevvie usually ended up in the middle. Not because Thomas didn't enjoy it, but because it just naturally seemed to happen that way.

Thomas wiggled his hips again, encouraging Tyler. Nevvie stroked his back. "You're going to be a good boy and come hard for us, aren't you?"

"Uh huh!"

"Uh huh what?"

He snorted with laughter and lifted his head. "Uh huh, Mistress."

"That's better."

He lowered his head again, working his hips in time with Tyler's thrusts. Nevvie was afraid to move too much for fear of hurting him.

Thomas sensed it.

"It's okay, Nev. Have fun," he hoarsely whispered against her neck.

She gently rolled her hips, drawing another moan from him. She felt Tyler find a long, slow rhythm that would keep both men on the edge for a while.

Thomas closed his eyes and touched his forehead to Nevvie's. "Jesus, that's good," he softly said.

"Look at me, Tommy."

He did. Nevvie lost herself in his sweet, brown gaze. She tangled her fingers in his hair. "We love you, baby," she said. "You're never going to want anyone but us, are you?"

"No."

"You know we can keep you well fucked, don't you."

"Yes." He struggled to keep his eyes open and focused on her. She could tell Tyler had him close to the edge from the way Tommy was fucking her.

Nevvie pulled him down so his face was nestled against her neck, her lips by his ear. She knew from the look on Tyler's face that he was close. With her fingers cupping the back of Tommy's head, she whispered into his ear, "I want you to fuck me hard when you come, baby. I want you to let Master Tyler feel how you're coming for us."

That's all it took. With a loud cry he thrust hard into her before going limp in her arms.

Tyler grabbed his hips and thrust deep, his own release quickly following. He caught himself before falling on top of them, not wanting to hurt Thomas or squish Nevvie. "Are you all right, loves?"

Nevvie stroked Tommy's back, cradling him to her. "Fine and dandy, sweetie."

Tommy mumbled something affirmative.

Tyler chuckled and carefully withdrew, went to the bathroom to clean up. He returned with a warm, damp washcloth for Thomas and took care of him, then slid into bed beside them.

"Well, he can't be too bad off," Tyler snarked, "because he's smiling."

Thomas laughed and lifted his head. He kissed Nevvie, then Tyler. "I told you, I like this slave boy gig. It's fun."

"Well, you don't get dinner until you finish what we started," Nevvie teased. "Master Tyler's tortured me all day long."

"Oh, he has, has he?" Thomas propped himself up on his elbows. "Did he keep my poor baby girl horny all day?"

Nevvie loved the fluid way they could change the game around. She nodded, throwing in a little pouty lip for good measure.

Thomas roared with laughter. "Oh, stop. You're too much." He rolled off her and onto his back. "Come here and let me take care of you."

She eagerly scrambled onto her hands and knees and turned around, settling over his face. He grabbed her hips and pulled her down, laving her throbbing clit with his tongue.

"Ooooh! Yeah!" She rested her cheek against his abs and closed her eyes. She felt the bed move, then Tyler cuddled close next to her and gently teased her nipples.

"Use our boy well, love," he murmured.

She moaned. Thomas knew how to tease and taunt her just as well as Tyler did. He brought her close to the edge several times, backing off before she could come, until she finally begged him to do it.

He slowly fucked her with his tongue, taking his time. Finally, he focused on her clit again, alternated between flicking it and long, slow swipes from his tongue. Then he brought her over and she loudly moaned, her entire body trembling from the force. Tyler wrapped his arms around her and helped her roll off Thomas, cradled her to his chest as she caught her breath and recovered.

Thomas stretched and laced his hands together behind his head. "You okay, sugar?"

Tyler laughed. "I think she's just fine. I think she's a very happy girl, aren't you?"

"Mmm hmm."

Thomas sat up. "Anything else Master and Mistress want me to do?" He waggled his eyebrows at Nevvie, cracking her up.

"You did just fine, sweetie. Just fine."

* * * *

Tyler and Nevvie made their little slave boy stay naked—or nekkid, as Thomas said it—for the rest of the evening. After dinner they stretched out in bed and Thomas massaged her feet and legs, making her moan in a different kind of way than before.

She drifted to sleep in their arms. Thomas snuggled close to her, one hand resting on the gentle swell of her belly. The week before, the three of them had sat in the doctor's office while Nevvie received her ultrasound. They were having a son.

His son.

Their son.

He looked over at Tyler and caught his knowing smile.

"What?" Thomas softly asked, not wanting to wake Nevvie.

Tyler shifted position and laced his fingers through Thomas'. "You know what."

Thomas finally smiled. "Yeah." He gently brushed his thumb across Tyler's fingers.

"I hope he has your eyes," Tyler said. "Your beautiful brown eyes."

Tom's heart swelled, the intensity nearly painful. "You sweet talkin' thing you."

"You've always had me under your spell. You know that. From the moment I first saw you."

Thomas gently squeezed his hand. "We're freaking lucky, aren't we?"

"Truly blessed. Life is perfect."

Chapter Twenty-One

Adam called out, announcing he was awake and waiting for someone to come get him. Thomas sat up. "I'll take care of him, sugar. It'll take you an hour just to roll over to get out of bed."

"Fuck you, Tommy," Nevvie groused. She felt as big as a cow and only a fraction as agile.

He kissed her. "You did, darlin'. That's why you look the way you do."

Tyler snickered. "That was good, sweet."

"You're ganging up on me."

The men looked at each other and laughed. "And again she opens the door, right?" Tyler said, winking at Thomas.

"Who's team are you on?" she snarked. As her belly and ankles swelled, her mood deteriorated. Less than a month until her due date and she was more than ready to have her body back.

"You know we love you, sweetheart."

Thomas pulled on a pair of boxers and left the bedroom. Limping, but she noticed he didn't take his cane.

Must be a good day.

Tyler climbed out of bed and offered Nevvie a hand. "Here, love. Let me help."

With his assistance, Nevvie was able to sit up on the edge of the bed. She rubbed her back and looked at him. "Did I say I wanted another one after this?"

"You said you'd think about it. I take it you're rethinking it?"

"Yeah. I'm thinking not so much at this point. Maybe two is plenty."

Tyler leaned over and kissed her belly, gently caressed her. "It's always up to you. You know we're wrapped around your finger." He paused, feeling. "My, our little one is quite active this morning."

"And that's before I've even had coffee." She grunted as she lumbered to her feet with Tyler's help. "Feels like gymnastics."

She made it to the bathroom then stood under the shower, letting the warm spray hit her aching back. That's when she felt a gush of water between her legs.

"Tyler!" she gasped. Either he wasn't in the bedroom any longer, or he didn't hear her. She took a deep breath. "Tyler!" she screamed.

He bolted into the bathroom. "What? What's wrong?" He stuck his head in the shower.

The first contraction hit, not hard but strong enough. "My water just broke."

"But you're not due for three weeks!"

"Tell him that!"

"Oh, Christ! Right. Rinse off, love, let's get you to hospital—"

"THE hospital."

"Christ. Thomas!" He disappeared and she quickly finished, fear taking over. Adam had come two days before her delivery date. Was three weeks okay?

* * * *

Tyler sat in the bed behind her, supporting her, rubbing her back and coaching her through her breathing while Thomas held her hand and tried to help her focus. Over twenty hours and she hadn't progressed. Both men were worried. Another three hours later, the doctor walked in, looking concerned.

"We need to talk about doing a C-section. The baby is starting to get weak, and so is she."

Nevvie closed her eyes and cried while both men grabbed her hands.

"Love," Tyler soothed, "if it's what has to happen, let's do it and get it over with."

"I don't want a C-section."

"Nev," Thomas said, "we'll be right there."

She looked at the doctor. "They can both be there," he assured her.

"Okay," she said.

The men had to step out while they prepped her. They were given gowns to wear and had to scrub in. They rejoined her in the delivery room and each man took a side and focused on her face.

"You're okay, love," Tyler said. "We're here."

Thomas squeezed her hand. "Sweetie, we're right here, you'll be okay."

Ten minutes later, all three cried at the sound of their son crying.

"Who wants to cut the cord?" the doctor asked.

Tyler looked at Thomas. "You do the honors, love."

Thomas blinked away tears as he did.

A shrill alarm startled the men. The tone of medical staff's voices changed immediately.

"What's wrong?" Tyler asked.

He watched the doctor glance at his nurse and shake his head. She stepped toward the men. "Why don't you two come with your son while we take care of him and get him cleaned up?"

Nevvie looked at Tyler, then her eyes rolled back in her head and she lost consciousness.

In a blur of activity the men were hustled out the door as the doctor barked orders.

"What's going on?" Thomas asked.

The nurse herded them along. "She's hemorrhaging, going into shock. He needs to stop the bleeding."

Stunned, the men followed the nurse and watched as the staff checked their son. They brought a chair for Thomas, and the men cried when a nurse placed the baby in Thomas' arms. Tyler rested his head on Tom's shoulder, tried to stay calm. Thomas nuzzled his head against Tyler's.

"She'll be okay, sugar," Thomas reassured him. "Look how tough she is. She'll be fine." He stroked the baby's cheek. When their son opened his eyes, Thomas sobbed when he saw the baby did indeed have his brown eyes to match the shock of dark brown hair on his head.

Tyler's arm tightened around his shoulder. He pressed his lips to Tom's cheek. "He's beautiful. Just like you."

An hour later, Nevvie was still in surgery and the men barely spoke. United in their worry and grief, they cradled their son and drew strength and support from each other. When the doctor walked in two hours later, they froze.

He smiled. "She'll be okay. I'll admit she scared me there for a few minutes. One of her old scars opened up from her prior surgery. We'll need to keep her in the hospital longer, but I think she'll be fine. She shouldn't try having a vaginal birth again if you have more kids. Plan on a C-section. There's no reason to risk her ripping open another old scar putting her through labor."

The men hugged each other, crying. "When can we see her?" Tyler asked.

"They'll come get you shortly."

* * * *

Nevvie looked groggy from the anesthesia, her skin pale. Still, she smiled when the men appeared in the doorway with their son.

Tyler carefully stayed beside Thomas in case he needed extra support, nervously hovering until he'd gently placed the baby on her chest.

"He's beautiful," she said, stroking his hand.

"Our handsome little brown eyed boy," Tyler said.

A tired smile teased her lips. "Yeah?"

Thomas stroked her forehead. "Yeah. I'm sorry they made us leave."

"Shh." She cradled the baby to her. "It's okay." Nevvie stared into the baby's face. "Did you name him?"

Tyler looked shocked. "Of course not! Not without you."

"I thought we discussed this already."

"Love, we waited."

Nevvie was quiet for a few minutes. "Michael." When she next spoke, her voice sounded choked with emotion. "For my dad." He was her adopted father, but he died before she knew that fact. He would always be her daddy in her mind and heart.

Thomas reached over and stroked the baby's hand. "I was thinking Michael Tyler." He looked at his lover.

Nevvie blinked. "What?"

Tyler looked as surprised as Nevvie. "What?"

Thomas shrugged. "I think Michael Tyler would be a good name."

Nevvie let out an amused snort. "Great, they'll be calling him 'Mi-Ty' in school."

Thomas laughed. "I didn't think of that." He fell quiet for a moment, staring at their son. "I'd still like to name him that," he softly said. "I mean, Adam's name is Adam Ryan. Ryan's my middle name. It's only right."

Nevvie looked at Tyler, who now had tears in his eyes. He nodded.

She stroked the baby's cheek. "Welcome to the world, Michael Tyler Kinsey-Paulson."

* * * *

Tyler left to pick up Adam from Eddie and Pete's, to bring him to the hospital to visit. Thomas stayed with Nevvie. Remembering her agony with Adam, she elected to go straight to bottle feeding. Thomas took the first round as her pain meds kicked in and she drifted. She

292   *Tymber Dalton*

watched him take care of their son, feeling content and satisfied.

"You're a good dad, Tommy," she said.

He wistfully smiled. "You want to know what's stupid?" he softly asked. "I feel exactly like I felt with Adam. After all the bullshit I put the two of you through, I wasn't sure if I'd feel different this time knowing..." He regrouped. "I worried maybe I'd feel differently about this little guy than I did about Adam. But I don't. They're both my sons."

He met her eyes. "I feel like Tyler's his dad as much as I am. Now I understand why he could be like that. A few times I thought it was bullshit, like maybe he just humored me, you know?"

"Don't go back there, Tommy. We're a family. You were dealing with a lot and not in the best possible way. I don't want to think about the Dark Ages. That's all done and gone and over with. We've got a perfect life."

"I know, babe."

The nurse came in to check on them. When she left, Thomas carefully burped the baby and tucked him into Nevvie's arms. After a few minutes she dozed and he took the baby back, putting him into his basinet and pulling it close to his chair. Tyler walked in a few minutes later, carrying Adam.

The little boy pointed to Thomas and stretched toward him, trying to reach him. "Poppa!"

Thomas grinned and blinked back his tears.

Their sons.

* * * *

Because of Nevvie's complications, her doctor wanted her to take it easier longer than a normal C-section recovery. She chafed to return to her normal routine.

Normal.

Whatever that meant in their house.

Sometimes Thomas still walked with a cane, on days when his leg felt weak or he was in a lot of pain. As Nevvie healed and was cleared to return to her normal activities, it marked a return to their new slave game as well.

The evening after Nevvie had her final OB/Gyn visit, Tyler gently closed the door to the nursery and walked out to the kitchen where she was wiping down the counters after cleaning up from dinner. He slipped his arms around her waist and nuzzled the back of her neck.

"How do you feel tonight?"

She relaxed against him. "What's the context of the question?"

He chuckled and gently nipped her earlobe. "Feel like putting our little slave boy through his paces?"

She shivered. "I hope you're prepared."

"Oh, I certainly am, love. I made sure to stock up on condoms this time."

Nevvie turned to face him and draped her arms around his neck. "Then let's find our little slave boy and put him to good use."

They found Thomas in his study, hunched over his computer and working on a set of plans. He looked up as they walked in. "What's up?"

Nevvie snickered and exchanged a glance with Tyler. "He makes it too easy, doesn't he?"

Tyler grinned. "He certainly does."

Thomas looked puzzled for a moment, then sat back and smiled. He reached over, saved his project and shut down his computer. "I'm guessing I'm done working for the evening."

"You guessed right, love," Tyler agreed. He walked over to Thomas and ran his hand through his hair. "You're all ours for the rest of the night."

Thomas caught Tyler's hand and brought it to his lips, then sucked his thumb into his mouth.

Tyler softly gasped. "You know what I love, don't you?"

He sat forward in his chair and pulled Tyler to him, resting his face against Tyler's stomach. "You'd better believe it."

Watching the two of them together did what it always did to Nevvie, left her breathless and aching between her legs.

"Come on, boys. You don't get to play alone tonight. Let's go." The men laughed and followed her to the bedroom. They sandwiched her between them, Tyler standing in front. She felt their hard bulges through their clothes.

Tyler kissed her, melting her the way he always did. Tommy slipped one hand inside her shorts, found her clit, and started rubbing it. This was yet another thing she'd desperately missed after his accident. While his handwriting was still iffy sometimes, his fingers had regained their skillful touch when it came to her flesh.

She moaned. "That's so good!"

His lips brushed against her neck, behind her ear. "I would hope so."

They undressed and moved to the bed. Nevvie pushed Tommy back and knelt between his legs. She lightly trailed a finger across his bare sac. "I love this look on you."

He crossed his arms behind his head and smiled. "Anything to make Mistress happy."

Tyler arched an eyebrow at him. "Ahem."

Tommy grinned. "And Master. Duh."

"That's more like it, love."

She dipped her mouth to the juncture between his legs while Tyler kissed him. She reached out and stroked Tyler's leg, drawing a soft moan from him. He looked down Tom's body at her.

"What do you think we should do to our boy tonight?" he asked with a wicked grin.

She raised her head, releasing Tom's cock from her mouth with a pop. "I'm sort of playing it by ear, Master Tyler."

Both men sucked in a sharp breath. Tom's cock throbbed in her hand.

"Goddamn!" he muttered. "I don't care how many times I hear

you say it, that never gets old, sugar."

She smiled.

Tyler handed her a foil pouch. "Why don't you have some fun with him first? I'll keep myself busy."

She quickly rolled the condom on Thomas and impaled herself, sighing with pleasure at the sensation of him filling her. She sat there and enjoyed it for a while.

Thomas turned to Tyler and wrapped his lips around his cock. Tyler stroked Tom's head, fisting his fingers in his hair. "That's it, love," he encouraged. "Take your time."

Nevvie watched them together, her movements stilled by the sight. *Damn* they were sexy! When Tommy's thumb found and stroked her clit, Nevvie remembered she had another reason for sitting there and slowly started fucking him again.

Tyler's eyes dropped shut. "Don't make me come, Thomas. I want to finish inside our angel."

Nevvie ground her hips against Thomas. She could sit there fucking him all night, especially after the last couple of months of not feeling like doing much because of her pregnancy. Then he played dirty and gently pinched her clit, rolling it between his fingers and making her cry out as she climaxed. He released Tyler's cock and grabbed her hips, plunging into her from underneath, pounding into her until he finally came.

She collapsed on top of him and was enjoying the post-orgasmic bliss when Tyler nudged her. "Off, love. Condom."

"Shit." She rolled off Thomas, nestled in the crook of his arm while Tyler took care of things before settling in bed on Tom's other side.

Thomas feathered his lips across her forehead, gentle, tender kisses that always melted her. "You okay, baby girl?"

"Mmm hmm. You?"

He nodded. "Yeah. Little achy. I'll live."

Tyler propped himself up on one elbow. "I'll fetch your medicine as soon as I've had my turn."

She crooked her finger at Tyler. "Get yourself over here."

He grinned and grabbed another foil pouch. When he lifted her legs to his shoulders, Nevvie stroked his arms. "Bet Tommy's ass will be glad to get a rest." Tyler had been unusually frisky the past couple of weeks, even for him.

Thomas rolled to his side and kissed Nevvie. "Couldn't even bend over in front of him, he was jumping me."

"You loved it, and you know it," Tyler said.

"I never said I didn't love it. Loved the hell out of it." He kissed Nevvie again. "Damn, that means I've got to share him again," he teased.

"Yeah, but you've got me back, so it works out." Nevvie laced her fingers through his hand, stroked Tyler's arm with her other.

"True. It's good to have you back."

Tyler's eyes closed as his strokes increased in speed and force. "Very good," he whispered. "Too good for words."

Thomas caressed Tyler's other arm with his free hand. "Show us how good, buddy."

Tyler gasped, shuddered, then cried out as he came. He lowered her legs and started to cuddle with Nevvie when he swore and pulled out. "I hate these blasted things." He went to the bathroom to clean up.

Nevvie snuggled against Thomas. "We won't need them in a few weeks."

"Don't rush things on our account. We'll survive."

"Yeah, but he's right. I hate them." She ran her fingers across his chest, tracing his scars. "I want it all back the way it was. Life back to normal."

He captured her hand and brought it to his lips, kissed it. "Sugar, it is what it is."

She looked into his sweet brown eyes. Over the years she'd seen him passionate, enraged on her behalf, angry, loving, and now...

He was still sad in some ways.

"We can get another bike," she suggested.

Hesitation crossed his face. He was about to reply when Tyler walked out of the bathroom. "I'll go get your medicine for you since I'm up."

"Thanks," Thomas said. When Tyler was gone, Thomas looked at Nevvie. "I'm not saying I don't miss it. Between my leg still being fucked up, and it would damn near kill Tyler if we did, maybe it's not a good idea."

"Please? I want another bike."

He traced her jaw with his fingers. "I couldn't stand it if you got hurt."

"It was an accident. I want another bike, like what we had. I want to ride again. With you."

"We don't need to talk about this now."

"Please?"

He sighed. "Later, baby girl. Yes, one day we will. Let's let life settle down a little first, okay? Not to mention we'd probably have to dope Tyler to get him to agree to let us do it. It'll scare him to death."

Chapter Twenty-Two

Nevvie had other ideas. She didn't want to wait, and her eyes betrayed her intentions to Tyler as surely as if she'd told him whatever it was she had up her sleeve. No sooner had they pulled out of the driveway when he confronted her.

"What are you up to, love?"

"What?"

"Don't you give me that wide-eyed innocence," he playfully scolded. "I know you far too well for that. You can pull things over on Thomas, but not with me."

"We have plans today."

"I figured as much, leaving our little slave boy alone at home with the kids. What's on your mind?"

"You'll see."

He was surprised when they pulled into the parking lot of the Harley dealership. "Love—"

"Master promised me anything I wanted."

A cold thread of anxiety ran through Tyler's gut. "Nevvie, darling, please tell me you aren't contemplating what I think you're contemplating."

She was already out of the car. "Come on. I don't want to keep them waiting."

He reluctantly unbuckled his seat belt. Now he understood her insistence on wearing jeans and sneakers.

Apparently she'd already made a scouting run or two. She led the way inside and shook hands with one of the salesmen before introducing Tyler to him as her husband.

The man didn't bat an eye, but Tyler recognized him from when Thomas had bought the first bike. "We've met, I think," Tyler said.

Nevvie's plan soon became clear. Tyler fought his rising panic. He would do anything for her, even die or kill for her. The last thing he wanted to do, even before Tom's accident, was climb on a motorcycle.

No, correction, the *second* to last thing he wanted to do. The absolute last thing he wanted to do was drive one. And apparently, that was Nevvie's plan.

"I had to wait until after I had the baby to do this. I don't think I can carry Tommy as my passenger. So I need you to learn how to do this."

Cold sweat bathed his body. He dropped his voice and pulled her a few steps from the salesman. "Darling, please, let's discuss this."

Her green eyes grew wide and moist. "You won't do this for me? For Thomas?"

Damn her, she knew exactly what effect that sad look had on him. "I'm terrified of the things. Especially now. You know that."

Nevvie remained silent, just stared at him.

After a long moment he sighed and closed his eyes. "All right. For you."

She squealed and kissed him. "Thank you!"

"I'm guessing you want this to be a surprise for our boy?"

"Please?"

"I'll be honest, I don't like the idea of the two of you on a bike. Not after what happened."

"Yeah, well, I don't like the idea of leaving you alone or out of my sight for two minutes."

"Touché."

Tyler didn't even try to offer his opinion on the purchase. He stood by and docilely followed Nevvie and the salesman around the dealership. Her plan? To get two bikes. He didn't like it or understand her rationale, but after all she'd been through and everything she did for them, he couldn't deny her this.

Even though the thought scared the crap out of him.

She picked out gear for him. He tried not to think about a similar situation years ago, when it was just him and Thomas, as his sweet boy helped him with a helmet for the first time. Even then he didn't like riding, but he'd felt safe riding with his lover even if scared witless at the same time.

There were perks to being a rich and famous writer. Being able to afford private riding lessons was one of them. They spent the afternoon in a back parking lot learning how to ride. At the end of the first four-hour session, Tyler had to admit it wasn't nearly as terrifying as he feared it would be.

He still didn't enjoy it.

Nevvie, however, looked alive, rejuvenated. There was no way in hell he could deny his sweet angel this joy, not after she'd pulled them back from the brink of hell.

She'd brought her bike gear. He added his new gear to hers in the trunk. Once inside the car he looked at her. "And when do we spring this surprise on our boy?"

"After we get our motorcycle licenses."

* * * *

They used dance classes as an excuse to get out of the house without Thomas. Despite his fear, Tyler passed the class, as did Nevvie, and easily got their licenses. Riding the bikes to Pete and Eddie's house to hide them was the scariest twenty minutes of Tyler's life. He breathed a huge sigh of relief when they shut them off in the driveway. He pulled his helmet off with trembling fingers.

"Love, please don't expect me to do this a lot. I seriously doubt I could ride on the interstate.

She shook her hair out and smiled. The smile he'd die and kill for. The smile he'd lop off his own arm for. The same smile that twisted his heart around her finger. "Just until he's steady on the bike again. And he might not be able to ride with me as a passenger, but maybe he can ride alone, so I can still ride with him on the second bike.

Pete walked outside, shaking his head. "You guys are crazy."

"This will help him, Pete. You know it will," Nevvie insisted.

Pete and Eddie had a huge house with a triple garage. The door to the smaller garage bay where a golf cart could be parked slid up and Eddie walked out.

He frowned. "Jesus, I thought you were kidding. I hoped you were kidding."

"Guys, please. I want to do this for Tommy."

Eddie helped her walk hers into the garage while Pete helped Tyler with his. "I hope you two know what you're doing," Pete grumped.

"I don't," Tyler groused. "She's talked me into this insanity."

"Why the fuck you let her do this to you, asshole?"

Tyler pointed at Nevvie. She smiled.

Pete shook his head. "Fuckin' pussy whipped. That's what you are."

Eddie drove them to the dealership to pick up Nevvie's car. Tyler knew from the tense set of his friend's shoulders that he was far from happy about this. Tyler sympathized.

Neither was he.

When Mikey turned six months old, they'd been licensed for two months and practiced at least once a week. Thomas had regained most of the strength in his bad leg and his fine motor skills had nearly returned to normal. Normal enough Nevvie would trust him on a bike. She didn't like lying to Tommy about what they were doing but she wanted this to be a surprise for him, hopefully capping off their nightmare for good, the last piece to complete his recovery.

* * * *

Thomas didn't know what was going on. He knew Nevvie was up to something, but between his normal denseness and his new BDA status, he wasn't sure exactly what. He gladly watched the boys while Nevvie and Tyler went out dance class, but he wouldn't deny the slight ache he felt seeing them leave together each time. The weirdest thing, they always wore jeans and sneakers, something Thomas didn't comment on but thought very strange.

On yet another early Saturday afternoon, Nevvie and Tyler kissed him good-bye and headed off to class. Adam sat in the middle of the living room floor with a pile of blocks in front of him. Mikey was asleep on a blanket next to him but would be awake in a little while.

"Hey, buddy. You want to go out for lunch?"

"McD's, Poppa?" The precocious two year-old already had quite a vocabulary.

"Yeah, hit the playground for a while."

Adam threw his arms in the air and grinned. "Pwaygwound!"

"Can you go get your clothes ready?"

"Gotta go pee pee."

He laughed. "Okay, go do that first." Thomas remembered his mom's good-natured ribbing that she thought Thomas would be ten before she got him potty trained. Fortunately, Adam took after Tyler, smart as a whip, and wasn't too far from being in big-boy underwear all the time.

Adam clambered to his feet and toddled down the hall. Thomas winced as his son wobbled going around the corner, but then he heard him in the bathroom a moment later and went to supervise.

Actually, there were days Adam walked a damn sight better than he did, come to think of it. Not too many bad pain days anymore, but sometimes they were enough to put him on his ass. At least the strength had fully returned in his hands and arms. Thank God for the CAD software at work, because hand-drawing blueprints was still iffy on some days.

Twenty minutes later he had the boys loaded in the Ridgeline and they headed to the restaurant. When they finished there an hour later, Adam pointed down the road. "Unca Pete and Unca Eddie! Pwease, Poppa?"

Adam spent enough time there he knew the way by heart. "You want to drop by and see Pete and Eddie?"

Adam nodded, his big blue eyes sweeping away any possibility of Thomas refusing his son.

Just like Tyler.

Thomas smiled. "All right, buddy. We'll drop by and see if they're home."

"Yay! Wanna pway wif Tom-Tom!"

Thomas didn't know who would be happier—his son or the yellow Labrador retriever.

* * * *

Nevvie followed Tyler into a parking lot and pulled alongside him. "What's wrong?"

He pulled his helmet off. "Love, I'm completely shattered. Can we call it a day?" The traffic had been unusually heavy and his nerves were shot.

"All right. Let's go get the car."

* * * *

Thomas blinked when he drove up Pete and Eddie's street. The small garage bay door stood open and there were two cars parked in the driveway. One was Eddie's Mercedes.

The other...

Something cold welled up inside him as he pulled in behind Eddie's Mercedes and stared at the Lexus. There was no mistake. He knew Tyler's license plate.

Thomas wondered why Nev and Ty would visit their friends and not mention it. They were supposed to be at dance class all the way over in Town and Country, not up here just minutes from home.

Their class wasn't supposed to end for another hour.

By the time Thomas climbed out of the truck, Eddie had raced out of the house and looked shocked.

No, not shocked.

Panicked.

Eddie had the world's worst poker face.

Thomas struggled to keep his voice even. "Hey, Eddie. Where's my evil geniuses?"

"Hi, Tommy. What are you doing here?" The large man's voice sounded far too high and stressed to be anything but one second from freaking out.

"I decided to take the boys out for lunch. The question is, what are Nev and Ty doing here? They're supposed to be at dance class."

"Well, I, uh—"

Pete stepped out of the front door. "Tommy. Hey, man."

"Hey yourself. Where's my other halves?"

"Look, Tommy—"

The sound of motorcycles stood out in stark contrast in the quiet neighborhood. As the two bikes rolled down the street toward the house, Thomas felt something inside him curl up into a tight, hard ball.

They pulled into the driveway. The sudden silence as both bikes shut off nearly deafened him. Two Harleys, like the one he'd wrecked.

With Tyler on one. Tyler was terrified of bikes, rarely rode with him…before. The bike was something Tommy had in common with Nevvie. Something special they did together.

He turned from them and started for his open truck door. Adam squealed with delight when he recognized Nevvie and Tyler as they removed their helmets. "Momma! Daddy!"

"Tommy, please wait!" Nevvie ran up and stood in the doorway so he couldn't close his door.

He wouldn't look at her. "What do you want me to say?" He tugged at his shirt, where the silver collar lay against his throat.

"Please?"

He knew he had no right to be angry. But this was *their* special thing to do together, even if he couldn't do it anymore. How long had they lied to him?

Thomas let her take his arm and lead him from the truck to the bikes. Tyler kept his mouth shut and Thomas shot a glare his way. Tyler looked sheepish and uncomfortable.

Good.

"Tommy," Nevvie said, "please hear me out. I did this for you."

He snorted with disgust. "For me? If you haven't noticed—"

"Shut up."

Pete and Eddie got the boys out of the truck and looked on from a safe distance.

Nevvie continued. "You're a lot better than you were. I want us to be able to ride again. I know sometimes you have bad days. I needed to get licensed and I made Tyler go with me."

Now Thomas was confused. "Tyler hates bikes. He's always hated them."

"Still do, love," he snarked.

"Hush, Tyler," Nevvie said. She returned her attention to Thomas. "I made him take classes and get his license. Because I knew if you had a bad day, I might not be able to carry you. I needed him to be able to ride a bike in case he had to come get us with the car, so you could switch. Or he could ride the other bike with us, with me as your passenger, and if we needed help, he could carry you."

Thomas glared but felt the nasty, tight knot in his gut start to loosen.

Nevvie seemed to sense his hesitation and quickly continued. "I want us to ride again. You said you'd want another bike. I miss that, I want it back." Then she played dirty, turning her beautiful green eyes on him. "I want it back, for us, Master," she whispered, low enough Pete and Eddie couldn't hear, but Tyler did.

"Bloody hell," he muttered. "She's blasted lethal."

What little anger remained in Thomas dissolved. He looked up at the sky, trying to blink away tears before she could see them. He enveloped her in a long, strong hug, buried his face in her hair. Then he reached out to Tyler, pulled him in and kissed him.

"I love you guys, I really do. Can I ask one simple question?"

Nevvie nodded.

"Why the heck didn't you just get a trike? That would have been easy. Poor Ty wouldn't have had to go through, what, a few months of terror?"

Nevvie's jaw dropped in shock. Tyler swore. "Bloody hell!"

Thomas smiled. He finally had one up on them. "You didn't think of that, did you?"

"No," she finally admitted. "I didn't. I just wanted to get bikes like what we had. It's what we talked about."

He pulled Tyler in and kissed him, long and deep. "Skid mark in your drawers?"

"You have no idea, love. Please tell me I don't have to drive one of those things again."

Tommy chuckled. "No, buddy. I won't make you do that."

"You're not mad?" Nevvie asked.

Tommy shook his head and kissed her. "No, sugar. Not now that I know what y'all are doin'. How about we go to the dealership tomorrow and see about trading one of those in on a trike?"

Tyler sighed with relief. "Thank the gods!"

Pete and Eddie sensed the positive turn in their conversation. Eddie piped up, "Want to stay and watch the game and then have dinner with us? I was going to grill chicken. I've got plenty."

Thomas draped his arms around Nevvie and Tyler's shoulders. "That sounds really good."

* * * *

Three days later, Tyler happily stayed home with the boys while Nevvie and Thomas took off on the new trike. It wasn't exactly the same, but Nevvie didn't bother trying to hold back her happy tears as she wrapped her arms around Thomas. They rode over to St. Pete for lunch at a beachside restaurant. As they sat on the shaded patio, he reached across the table and grabbed her hand.

"You okay?"

She eagerly nodded, another unbidden round of tears falling. She laughed, trying to dry her face with her napkin. "I swear, Tommy, I'm okay. Really." She looked at him. "Are you okay?"

His broad, beaming grin almost set her off on another crying jag. Normal. It really felt like they were back to normal.

"I'm real good, baby girl." He leaned in close and dropped his voice. "Can I assume Mistress has some plans for me later?" He waggled his eyebrows at her, sending her into a laughing jag punctuated by another round of happy tears.

"You bet your sweet ass I do."

Later that night, after the kids were in bed, Nevvie wrapped her arms around Tom as he stood in the kitchen.

"Go get your ass in bed and prepare to be fucked." She felt his cock immediately harden against her through his shorts. Thank God she was back on the Pill and they didn't need condoms anymore.

He kissed her. "You know what that does to me when you talk like that."

She gently swatted his ass. "Then go do what I tell you and wait for us."

He grinned and walked to the bedroom.

Tyler emerged from his study. "I believe I heard the magic words."

"What?"

"Prepare to be fucked."

She ground her hips against him, realized he was also hard. "You sure did."

"Then let's not keep our sweet boy waiting."

When they reached the bedroom, Thomas was already in bed, naked, his stiff cock at attention. The sight of him laying there sent a flood of moisture to her sex.

"Is this what you had in mind?" he asked.

She grinned and quickly undressed. "You'd better believe it." She resisted the urge to throw herself at the bed, not wanting to hurt him. Instead, she knelt over him and teased him, sliding her slick cleft along his cock and drawing a moan from him.

Tyler cupped one of her breasts and drew her nipple between his lips. He flicked it with his tongue, refusing to relinquish his captured prize until he'd teased it to a hard peak. He released it with an audible pop. "I want to fuck your brains out, love." He looked at Thomas. "And perhaps your brains, too."

Thomas grinned. "How much energy you got saved up, buddy?"

Tyler arched an eyebrow. "Who said I needed energy?"

Nevvie laughed. "Oooh, someone's getting a toy up their ass." She swung off Thomas while Tyler reached for the bedside table, retrieved the butt plug from the drawer and a bottle of lube.

Thomas rolled over, laughing, and wiggled his hips at them. "I know, I know. Assume the position."

Tyler growled and swatted Tom's ass. "Damn straight. Now hold still."

Nevvie reached under Thomas and stroked his cock. Tyler slid the butt plug home, then swatted Tom's ass again. Thomas didn't want to move, continued to flex his hips in time with Nevvie's hand stroking his shaft.

"Don't get him off yet. Let him suffer for a while. He got to hog your attention this afternoon. He has to pay the price."

When Nevvie released Thomas, he groaned. "Oh, man! Don't

stop!"

"On your back, and turn around," Tyler ordered. "You need to earn your reward, little slave boy."

Nevvie read the writing on the wall. Once Thomas had repositioned himself, she straddled him, his face between her legs, while Tyler knelt behind her.

Tyler stroked her back before grabbing her hips. "Don't make our boy come, sweetheart. Keep him on the edge." He sank his cock balls deep inside her as she felt Tom's lips and tongue swipe at her swollen clit.

She dropped her head to Tom's hip. She wrapped her fingers around his cock and closed her eyes. "How about I just lie here and enjoy it?"

Tyler chuckled. He leaned over and trailed kissed down her spine. "That's fine with me, love. Ah! Thomas, did I say you could play with my balls?"

Below her, Nevvie felt Thomas laughing. He mumbled something that sounded like, "Sorry, Master."

"Sneaky thing, trying to make me come faster. Not that it didn't feel good, but I want to take my time and enjoy this."

Nevvie closed her eyes and sighed. "That makes two of us." Tom's skilled tongue gently traced her clit, alternating between long, sweet strokes and gentle flicks. Her fingers tightened around his cock, which felt even more rigid than before. She hoped that meant he would be giving her a good hard fucking when Tyler finished.

"How is our sweet boy treating you, love?"

She teased Tom with a swipe of her tongue along his shaft. "He's being a very good boy."

Tommy moaned.

Tyler took his time, alternating long, slow thrusts with quick, deeper ones. Combined with the tongue between her legs, Nevvie hovered on the edge, the men working in tandem, prolonging her pleasure.

"Do you wish to come, love?" Tyler gasped.

"Please!"

"Hurry, Thomas. I'm very close."

She moaned as Tom's lips wrapped around her clit and he gently sucked. The familiar explosion ripped through her. She ground against his face, crying out as Tyler grabbed her hips and deeply fucked her.

Tyler's climax wasn't far behind. He slammed home one final time as his fingers dug into her hips, clinging to her. When he caught his breath he carefully rolled to his side and pulled her with him, his arm hooked around her waist. She didn't let go of Tom's cock.

Tyler's breath against her neck sent a pleasant wave of gooseflesh across her shoulders. "How was that, darling?" he asked.

She tipped her head back. "Fantastic."

Thomas reached over and stroked her thigh. "Did I do good…Mistress?"

Nevvie laughed. "You did great."

Thomas flexed his hips, trying to get a little traction from her hand on his cock. "Does your good boy get a reward?"

Tyler reached over and stroked Tom's bare sac. "Patience, dear one. Let me savor the moment a while longer." Thomas made a little noise. Tyler chuckled. "Don't whine, it's unbecoming."

Nevvie snickered. "He was a very good boy, Master Tyler."

Tyler's fingers idly stroked Tom's sac. "In a moment. I'm enjoying this." As ordered, Thomas now kept himself thoroughly shaved between his legs. Nevvie and Tyler loved playing with their slave boy's bare nether regions.

The extra attention didn't help Tom's condition. He wiggled his hips even more. "This is torture. You said I was a good boy."

Tyler prompted Nevvie to sit up. He leaned over and wrapped his lips around the tip of his lover's cock and slowly circled it with his tongue. "You were absolutely a good boy, Thomas. That's why we're going to make this last for you."

"Torturin' me."

"I should think you'd be thanking us. We could always tie you up in bed and make you spend the night with your toy up your arse and no relief in sight."

Nevvie snickered. "That would be mean."

Tyler shrugged. "We don't usually punish our boy. Maybe he needs a reminder of who's in charge. What do you think, darling?"

"He *was* a good boy."

Tyler made a big show of considering it, played with Tom's sac as he did, and gently pushed the butt plug a little deeper in Tom's ass. "What kind of reward did he earn, love?"

"I think he earned a fucking."

"Did he now? Was he that good?"

She nodded, then leaned over and kissed Thomas. "He was." When she stroked Tom's cheek he caught her fingers and sucked them into his mouth.

Tyler laughed and released his lover after a final kiss on the tip of his cock. "Very well, then."

Nevvie scrambled to change position, lying on her back as Thomas rolled on top of her. When he slid his thick cock inside her he paused, enjoying the feel of her slick muscles around him. Tyler knelt behind him and rested his hand on Tom's ass.

"How's she feel, love?"

Thomas dropped his head to Nevvie's shoulder, his lips against her neck. "Wonderful."

She wrapped her arms around him and kissed his forehead. "Take your time and enjoy it. You earned it."

He slowly worked his hips, his cock filling and fucking her. She knew she wouldn't come again, not like this, but simply enjoyed the feeling.

Tyler slid his hand between his lover's legs and cupped his sac. "You may take your time—if you can hold back."

Thomas groaned.

With his other hand, Tyler pressed on the butt plug, holding it firmly in place and triggering another moan from Thomas.

"Good luck holding back," Tyler teased.

He knew how to torment Thomas.

Nevvie wrapped her legs tightly around Tom's waist. "Fuck me, baby," she said. She trailed her fingers down his back. "Fuck me real good."

She rolled her hips in time with his, her fingers tangled in his hair. Then Tyler played dirty and leaned down, ran his tongue along the underside of Tom's sac.

"Fuck!" He took a final, hard thrust and fell still. "That was mean," he mumbled against her neck.

Tyler sat up and patted him on the ass. "No, mean would have been not letting you come at all. Hmm, now there's an idea. Maybe I should look into buying you one of those chastity devices."

Nevvie snickered. "That *would* be mean."

Thomas finally rolled off her and carefully got out of bed, walking a little oddly with the butt plug in him, and went to clean up. Tyler took his place next to Nevvie.

"That would be pretty mean," she said with a snicker.

"I know," Tyler agreed. "I don't think I have the heart to do that to our boy anyway. He's been so good."

She nodded. He had. Not only had she completely forgiven him for his indiscretion, neither she nor Tyler had an urge to throw it in his face. If anything, it had been exactly the mental slap Thomas needed to get his head on straight and jump-start his emotional healing. She wouldn't complain about that. When she'd asked Thomas a few months earlier if he wanted to end his new slave game, he'd smiled, shrugged, and pulled her into his arms.

"It's whatever Master and Mistress want to do," he'd said. "I'm having fun."

In other words, no. As long as Nevvie got to have her turn when she wanted, she didn't mind.

Thomas returned a few minutes later and she tightly snuggled between them, falling into a sweet, sated sleep.

Chapter Twenty-Three

Nevvie smiled as she packed for their trip. Remembering the first time she accompanied her boys—the men—to Peggy's Savannah home brought a smile to Nevvie's face. Terrified didn't begin to describe how she'd felt.

Emily's less than warm reception didn't help matters either.

Now she looked forward to their drives. Mikey was eight months old and it would be his first Christmas. They'd arrive in Savannah four days before Christmas and stay through New Year's, allowing Tommy plenty of time to spend with his family as well as give the little boys time with their grandma and aunts.

Well, except for Emily.

Because of the baby gear and gifts, Nevvie opted to take the Ridgeline. Tyler volunteered to ride in the back seat with the kids, letting Thomas stretch his leg in the front seat. Nevvie did most of the driving, only letting Tommy take over when they were two hours south of Peggy's large home.

Her grandmother radar finely-tuned, Peggy waited on the large wrap-around porch when they emerged from the long, rutted driveway that wound through the woods and into the huge yard.

Adam happily screamed from his car seat. "Gwamma!"

A surprise, Emily's twin son and daughter would also be staying at the house. Peggy told Nevvie this after they'd finished unpacking into the two bedrooms they'd use and had settled at the kitchen table. Tommy and Tyler were in the living room with everyone else, leaving Peggy and Nevvie alone.

"Why aren't they staying at Em's house?"

Peggy looked at her glass of iced tea. "Apparently they aren't very happy with their mother either, even after all this time."

Nevvie nodded. "Who told them?"

"Karen, of course."

"Ah." Nevvie trailed her fingers through the condensation on the outside of her glass. "They don't have a problem with us?"

"Hell no. They've always liked Tyler. They love their uncle Tommy. They like you even though they don't know you that well. I think Elle's words were, 'I wish I could get that deal.'"

Nevvie blushed, unsure how to respond. "She wouldn't want what we've been through." They hadn't told Peggy or the rest of the family about Tommy's lapse in judgment. Tyler and Nevvie agreed their boy did a good enough job beating himself up that they didn't need to involve anyone else.

They also hadn't told Tom's family about the trike.

Peggy reached out and laid her hand over Nevvie's. Nevvie met her gaze. Peggy's brown eyes looked full of sadness. "You've done good. They are where they are because of you."

Nevvie shook her head. "Damn good doctors put my boys back together."

"Don't you dare discount the role you played in their recovery. You worked your ass off, rode them, made sure they had the care and physical therapy they needed. You fought for them, Nevvie. And they fought to stay with you, because they love you." She patted Nevvie's hand before letting go and sitting back in her seat. "Enjoy life, sugar. God knows you've earned it."

"Why the hell did Emily name them Daniel and Danielle?"

Peggy snorted. "Because she thought it was cute at the time, even though we all told her it was a damn stupid idea. No one's ever called that girl Danielle except for her hard-headed mother."

They talked for a few more minutes. Speak of the devil, Elle walked into the kitchen and made a beeline for her grandmother. "We're here," she announced, hugging Peggy. With a hesitant smile she hugged Nevvie. "Hi, Nevvie." Nevvie hadn't seen the twins since the Christmas before "the incident."

Nevvie smiled in return, reassuring the girl. "Hi, Elle. It's good to see you. Your brother's here too?"

Elle seemed to relax. "Yeah, he's out there with Uncle Tommy and Tyler." She slid into a chair across from Nevvie. "I want to say something now, and this is from me and Danny." She looked at her hands and took a deep breath. "I know it's not our fault what Mom did, but we were really pissed when Aunt Karen told us, okay? I mean, what business is it of hers what you guys do? I hope you don't hold it against us."

Nevvie shook her head. "No, I don't blame anyone but your mom, Elle. It's okay. It's done, it's over. Let's just enjoy the holidays, okay?"

Elle relaxed. "Okay. Thanks."

* * * *

When Adam Kinsey built the house, he kept in mind the needs of his five older daughters and one lone baby son. Three of the girls had their own bedrooms, as did Thomas. Thomas got the added benefit of his own private bathroom that he didn't have to share with his sisters.

After Nevvie's first nerve-wracking Thanksgiving weekend at the Kinsey house, Peggy had gone out and bought a large king-sized bed for Tom's old room. Instead of one of them falling out of a full-sized bed, as happened to Tommy that first weekend, they could comfortably sleep together. They settled the babies in the bedroom across the hall with a baby monitor to keep an ear out.

As exhausted as she felt, Nevvie curled between her two men and almost immediately drifted to sleep. The next morning she started to get up when she heard Mikey fussing, but Tyler placed a hand on her shoulder.

"I'll take care of him, love. You sleep in."

She mumbled her thanks and cuddled closer to Thomas.

The door opened, closed, then she heard Tyler's voice on the baby monitor.

Tommy's soft laugh in her ear warmed her heart. "He's a good daddy."

She rolled over so she could look into his eyes. "You both are."

"I'm sick and tired of the rat race, sugar. I want to be home. I don't want to work my ass off and miss them growing up." He took a deep breath. "I'm thinking about taking Kenny up on his offer. I'd still own the building, it'd give us some good income for a lot of years, and I'll have a provision that I can always take it over again if he backs out."

"Will you be happy doing that?"

"I can still do design work when the mood strikes me. I can be choosy." He stroked her cheek. "Life's too short to waste it working all the time. This is what I busted my ass for all those years, to get to a place where I can say dammit, I want to sleep in and stay home, and afford to do it."

"What about me?"

"If you want to work there, you can. Kenny would kill to keep you."

This was exactly why she'd busted her ass, to make a better life for herself, to improve herself, get to the point where she could be self-sufficient if she wanted to be.

But she wanted to be a mom. A wife. She wanted to enjoy the love of these two men, and she'd fought damn hard to bring them back to her.

"Maybe Tyler would benefit from me being around more, so all he has to do is write."

Thomas' smile lit his entire face. "Nakey naptime."

She laughed, burying her face in his shoulder. "Only for another year or so. Then Adam will be in pre-K."

He waggled his eyebrows at her. "Even better. Nakey school

time."

She fingered the silver collar around his neck. He'd never asked to take it off, and frankly, she wasn't sure where the key was. "Maybe you'll be the one getting nakey."

"You won't hear me complaining." He rolled on top of her, his stiff erection poking her thigh.

She put her arms around him. "Everyone's going to be up soon."

"I'm up right now, baby girl." He kissed her. "Is Mistress ordering me to stop?" He nuzzled her throat, running his tongue around the hollow at the base of her neck.

Nevvie tangled her fingers in his hair. "No. Don't stop."

He disappeared under the covers, lifting the oversized T-shirt she'd slept in above her breasts. He gently sucked one, then the other, drawing soft moans from her. In her belly a dull, needy ache settled deep between her legs.

He froze at the soft knock on their bedroom door.

Peggy's voice drifted through to them. "I'm gonna start the coffee."

"Busted," Tommy whispered from under the quilt, setting Nevvie off on a giggling jag.

She smacked his shoulder. "Thanks, Mom. We'll be out in a little while."

"Okay."

When Nevvie knew the coast was clear, she lifted the quilt. "You're *so* going to get us in trouble."

He used the wide-eyed innocent puppy dog look on her, which set her off on another giggle fit. "Who, me?"

"Yes, you. Dammit, now you've got me in the mood, too."

He crawled up the bed and kissed her. "How about we grab our shower?" He slid his hand between her legs. She hadn't worn any panties to bed. Two fingers skillfully slipped inside her. "You're already wet, baby girl."

Nevvie closed her eyes and squirmed on his hand. Seven years, and he could still make her instantly wet. Both men could.

"Okay."

He sat up and the quilt slid down his back, pooling on the bed behind him. She'd kill for his broad, beaming smile. If Adam's birth had healed Tyler's old emotional scars, it seemed Mikey's birth had erased most vestiges of Tom's trauma. He was almost completely back to his old, playful self.

They slipped into the shower. He carefully dropped to his knees and smiled up at her. "Is this what you wanted, Mistress?" he asked with a playful grin.

She nodded and ran her fingers through his hair. The tile wall felt cool against her back. "Take care of me, baby."

His skilled tongue set to work. As his large hands gripped the back of her thighs she braced her arms on his shoulders, tightly clamping her lips together to hold back her loud moans. His tongue firmly laved her clit, from the top of her steamy folds down to the deepest recesses of her sex, burrowing deep within her.

When he slid two thick fingers inside her she exploded, his lips sucking her swollen nub as she dug her nails into his shoulder. After the final wave crashed through her she leaned back on shaky knees and took a deep breath. Tom climbed to his feet and kissed her, his stiff shaft throbbing.

"How was that, Mistress?" he asked with a playful smile.

"Very good. I think you've earned a reward." She turned and braced herself against the wall, wiggled her ass at him.

Needing no further encouragement, he carefully lined up his cock with her ready sex and slid in with a soft moan. He gripped her hips and the two of them found an easy, familiar rhythm.

"Jesus, I love you, babe," he whispered into her ear.

Nevvie rolled her hips against him. "Show me."

His low, hungry growl told her how close he was. She met each thrust, enjoying the feel of his wet flesh against and inside her. With two more hard thrusts he came. He wrapped his arms tightly around her and moaned into her shoulder. After a minute he kissed her and stepped back.

Nevvie turned and moved to stand under the spray with him. "Better?"

Thomas smiled his handsome, playful grin. She'd never take it for granted again, that's for damn sure.

"Absolutely…Mistress."

* * * *

Thomas finished his shower. Nevvie was drying her hair when Tyler squeezed his way into the bathroom.

"I'm guessing the two of you have had a little fun."

Nevvie and Thomas exchanged playful smiles. "Hey, Mistress ordered me," Thomas said in a low voice.

Tyler grinned. "Likely story."

"No, it's true. I did use our little slave this morning," she said. She knew from the front of Tyler's pajama bottoms that he was more than ready to have some fun.

"Well, perhaps I want a little fun, too," he said. "Love, go lock the bedroom door. Peggy's watching the little ones."

She eagerly raced to do it.

Tyler rummaged through their bags and found a bottle of lube. He crooked his finger at Thomas and pointed to the end of the bed.

Wearing a face-splitting grin, Thomas dropped his towel to the floor and bent over, hands on the bed.

Tyler's low, hungry moan set Nevvie's insides stirring. Tom began to stiffen again.

Tyler removed his pajama pants and slicked his rigid cock. "Get him ready for me, love."

Nevvie sat next to Tom and held his cheeks apart. Tyler carefully nudged into place, waiting to thrust until Thomas flexed his hips and drove himself back onto Tyler's shaft.

"Oh, yeah!" Tommy grunted. Nevvie watched his face. His eyes dropped closed, his bottom lip caught under his teeth. His cock had completely hardened again.

Tyler's eyes also fluttered closed. As Nevvie moved her hands out of the way she turned around and slid under Thomas, sucking his shaft into her mouth. He needed no encouragement to drop his lips to her mound, where he eagerly laved her clit with his skilled tongue.

Nevvie closed her eyes and enjoyed the sensations, reaching between Tom's legs to stroke both men's sacs. Their low, responding moans sent deep waves of need through her. This many years later and they still responded to her slightest touch.

God she loved them.

It didn't take Tom long to make her come. When she did she sucked his cock deep into her mouth, muffling her moans with his man-meat.

"That's it, love," Tyler whispered. He picked up the pace of his thrusts, knowing Tom wouldn't be far behind Nevvie. Tom buried his face in the quilt and moaned, his hips jerking spasmodically against Tyler. Tyler took two last thrusts and came deep inside his lover.

They didn't move for a moment, catching their breath. Nevvie was the first to untangle herself from the bottom of the pile.

"Great," she joked. "Now I need another shower."

Tyler laughed and carefully withdrew. "I'd be more than happy to shower with you, love."

* * * *

Nevvie left all her boys at the house and went shopping in Savannah with Peggy and Karen. It was fun having a day out with "the girls," something she had rarely experienced in her life before Tyler and Thomas. While they ate lunch in a small sandwich shop, Nevvie looked out on the quaint street with a little melancholy.

"What's the matter, sugar?" Peggy asked.

"I wish we lived closer. I love Florida, but it'd be nice being closer to you guys."

Karen grinned. "What, now that I'm taken you think it's safe to let Tyler be closer to me?" She'd introduced her new boyfriend to the family and they all adored him.

Nevvie laughed. "You know what I mean. I want the boys to know their aunts and their grandma, not just see everyone at the holidays."

"Well," snarked Karen, "most of their aunts." She took a sip of her coffee to hide her evil glare.

Peggy let out an exasperated sigh. "Come on, girls. Let's not ruin our afternoon talking about Emily, all right? That's in the past. She's not gonna be at dinner, so why let her mess up things when she's not even here?"

Nevvie nodded. "Agreed." Emily was the last person she wanted to give thought to.

Unless that thought was of giving her a good, hard slap across her face.

When they returned later that afternoon, everyone had gathered out back to play touch football. Tyler sat on the sidelines, watching Adam, Mikey, and two of the younger kids.

Nevvie winced as Tommy went down while leaping for a pass. She breathed a sigh of relief when he stood and walked without more than his normal limp.

"Takes some getting used to, doesn't it love?" Tyler murmured, slipping his arm around her waist.

"You did it again, Evil Genius."

His spooky blue eyes turned on her. "We'll always have that as our special thing, I should think."

Nevvie nodded and let him pull her tightly against his side. "I hope to hell so."

They watched for a few more minutes, then Tyler helped her get the boys inside and put down for a nap. Adam didn't go willingly, kicking and complaining that he wanted to watch a little longer. When Nevvie pointed out he could sit in the window seat in his room and watch, he sullenly agreed.

Twenty minutes later, when she went to check on him, he was sound asleep.

Nevvie was closing the kids' room door behind her when Tyler walked up, a grim look on his face.

"What's wrong?" she whispered.

He shook his head and motioned her to follow him onto the front porch. Emily's husband, Clay, stepped out of his truck. He looked damned uncomfortable and hesitated before walking up to the porch steps.

"Hi Tyler. Nevvie."

Nevvie forced her voice to stay calm. She didn't have anything personal against her brother-in-law, he was just another of Emily's casualties.

But he slept with the enemy, so to speak.

"Hello, Clay."

Tyler didn't speak.

Their chilly silence forced Clay to forge ahead. "Look, Emily doesn't know I'm here. I'd like to spend Christmas with my kids, not with my bitchy, hard-headed wife."

Tyler snorted and tightened his grip around Nevvie's waist, but said nothing.

Nevvie paused before responding, drawing out Clay's wait. "Why don't you talk to your kids, then? Why are you talking to us?"

"Because they won't come home for Christmas. They've refused to speak to their mom since she pulled that stupid stunt of hers. I'd like to know if I could spend the day here. With all of y'all."

Nevvie exchanged a brief glance with Tyler, who shrugged. She turned back to Clay. "You'll have to talk to Tommy and Peggy. Frankly, I don't want to see your wife's face anywhere around here. I especially don't want her around my children."

"I understand that. I couldn't believe it when she told me what she did. Look, I'm really sorry—"

"Don't you dare apologize for her." The hard edge in Nevvie's voice surprised even her.

"I'm not, Nevvie. I'm apologizing…well, for being her husband, I guess."

Nevvie walked down the steps and motioned Clay to follow her around back where the others still played. When Thomas saw him, he immediately left the game and angrily strode over.

"What the fuck is he doing here?"

Tyler stepped in front of him, his hands raised to ward him off. "Hear him out, love."

"Why should I?"

Nevvie met his angry eyes. "Because you should."

Thomas set his jaw but stepped back.

Clay repeated his apology. The twins weren't there, they'd gone into town with two other cousins, but they were due back at any moment.

Thomas turned and took a few steps away from them. Nevvie knew from the set of his shoulders that he needed a few minutes alone. Then he finally turned back. "Okay. If it's all right with Momma."

Peggy and most of the others had gathered around by this time. Peggy also nodded. "I don't want Emily here."

Clay shook his head. "I have a feeling I might be getting a divorce for Christmas, but I want to see my kids."

* * * *

On Christmas morning, Nevvie left her men in bed and arose early to help Peggy with preparations. Predictably, Tyler joined them in the kitchen a few minutes later. He wrapped his arms around her waist from behind and kissed the back of her neck.

"You're sneaky, love."

She patted his hands. "Thought you needed a little rest."

He gave Peggy a peck on the cheek and poured himself coffee. "Do we make wagers on whether or not Emily tries to make an appearance?"

Peggy shook her head. "Doesn't matter. She's not setting foot in my house." She was about to say something else when Danielle walked in, looking like she just woke up.

For the first time since her first visit to Peggy's home, Nevvie felt nervous. The twins knew their dad was coming for dinner, but the unknown factor was Emily.

Thomas and the boys awoke a little later. Adam ran into the living room and screamed, "Santa came! Mommy, Daddy, Poppa, Gwamma!"

Peggy laughed. "Let the games begin."

Thomas changed and dressed Mikey. The three of them, with Adam's assistance, helped Mikey with his presents while the twins and Peggy took turns with the video and digital cameras.

Nevvie had walked into the kitchen to refill her coffee when she looked out the window and saw Clay's truck pull into the yard. She intercepted him at the front porch. He carried a few shopping bags full of presents.

"Thank you, Nevvie. I really appreciate this."

"She's not showing up here, is she?"

"She doesn't know I'm here. She went to church this morning. I left her a note that I'd be back later today, that I went fishing."

Nevvie stepped aside and let him pass. Thomas frowned, but after a few minutes he relaxed. They had a good morning. Clay had even brought presents for Adam and Mikey, boy toys she suspected he'd shopped for and wrapped in secret judging by his handwriting on the gift tags.

Once presents were opened, Nevvie and Peggy returned to the kitchen. Nevvie noticed the older woman wiping her eyes.

"You know," Peggy softly said, "Adam—my Adam, Tommy's dad—probably wouldn't have agreed with Tommy's choice in Tyler." She shook her head. "But he would have supported him and loved him, and he would have welcomed Tyler into our home. He would have loved you, and he would have adored those two babies."

Peggy sniffled and turned to the kitchen window, removed her glasses to wipe her eyes again. "And he would have snatched Emily bald for what she tried. It would have broke his heart that one of the girls turned on Tommy like that.

"I thought my world ended when Adam died. There's days I wanted to walk down to the road and step out in front of a truck myself just to be with him. It took me a long time to want to live again." She turned back to Nevvie. "Not once," she whispered, "not one single pea-pickin' time in all these years since he died have I *ever* even thought the phrase, 'Thank God your father wasn't alive to see this,' because the first thing I do every morning is wake up talking to him, and the last thing I do every night before I go to bed is say good night to him. Even this many years later.

"Until she did that to y'all. Until all of that happened. I never thought I'd live to see the day one of my children would do something like that. Thank God Adam wasn't alive to see it. It would have just plumb broke his heart."

Nevvie hugged her. "This is going to be a good day today, Mom."

Peggy patted Nevvie's hands. "I know, sugar." She sighed.

* * * *

The other sisters all nervously queried Nevvie and Peggy in the kitchen when they arrived and saw Clay in the living room with the others. They had all cut Emily out of their lives after she'd turned on Tommy. Nevvie assured them they were okay with Clay being there as long as Emily wasn't.

They had a good meal together as a family. After, they spent time looking through photo albums, showing Adam pictures of his Grandpa Adam and his father and aunts, and even a few of Tyler in earlier years before Nevvie was a part of their lives.

Adam sat in Nevvie's lap, paging through an album, pointing at people and asking who they were. Tyler had walked into the kitchen to fix Mikey a bottle.

"Momma?"

"What, baby?"

"Where's Daddy's daddy?"

She immediately glanced at Thomas, who shook his head. Her mind raced. "Well, honey, Daddy isn't close to his father."

"Why?"

She glanced at Thomas again. He shrugged. *Great, no help there.* "I don't know, baby. It makes Daddy sad to talk about it, so we don't."

He sat quietly for a moment, then turned to look at her, his big blue eyes piercing through her. "Did he do somefing like Aunt Emiwy?"

Thomas snorted in amusement. Adam didn't know all the details, but in typical precocious toddler fashion, Adam had picked up enough bits and pieces to know the whole family was mad at her.

"No, baby," Nevvie said. "I don't know why Daddy's upset at his father. Please don't ask him about it, okay? We don't want Daddy to feel sad today."

"Izit a secret?"

"No, but sometimes people don't like to talk about things that make them sad. Today's a happy day."

He looked at Thomas. "Does talkin' bout Gwampa Adam make you sad, Poppa?"

Thomas smiled. "The kind of sad you feel when someone dies is a different kind of sad. I like talking about Grandpa Adam. It makes me feel happy remembering him."

Adam chewed that one over for a moment. Then he dropped his

voice to what he thought was a whisper. "I don want Daddy sad. We should keep dis a secret today."

Nevvie and Thomas looked at his serious expression, then at each other, and burst into laughter.

* * * *

Later, once the guests had left and Nevvie had a few moments to herself, she stared out at the backyard and thought about the discussion with Adam. Between Tommy's rocky start on his recovery and then getting pregnant with Mikey, she'd put a few things on the back burner.

Her theory about Delores' version of events was one of those things.

She knew Tyler's publicist was scheduling a series of interviews in London for Tyler's latest book. He had called the week before and asked about open blocks of time so he could make the arrangements. He would most likely be getting back to her in a week or two, after New Year's.

Nevvie pulled her BlackBerry from its holster, looked up Elliot's private email address, the one she and a few other privileged people had access to, and sent him her request.

Chapter Twenty-Four

Nevvie welcomed Elliot's call the second week of January. "Tyler's booked for four days in London, and I padded an extra couple of days in for R&R like you asked," he said.

She glanced toward Tyler's closed study door. "Fantastic. I'm going with him, but Tommy's staying home. We'll need tickets and hotel for me and Tyler."

"Done, kiddo. You guys leave in three weeks."

"Oh, can you arrange me a rental car?"

"Well, sure. Why?"

"Because I want to do a little exploring while I'm there."

After her call she nervously killed an hour of time then grabbed her purse. She stuck her head in Tyler's office. Tommy was napping, the babies asleep. "I'm running out to the store, Ty. Do you need anything?"

He sat back from his computer and studied her face. "What's going on?"

"What do you mean?"

He crossed his arms. "Love—"

"Elliot's got you a week in London. I need to go shopping."

He smiled. "Why didn't you simply say so?"

"Because sometimes a girl's got to have a few secrets."

He laughed as she closed his study door and walked out to her car.

When she turned out of their subdivision, she pulled into a parking lot and called Bob's private number. Fortunately, he answered.

"What's wrong?"

"Nothing. We've got the London trip booked."

"Good. I've got your info."

She breathed a sigh of relief. "Don't tell the boys."

"I told you I won't."

"Will you be in the office for a while?"

"Yeah. Are you coming right now?"

"I'll be there in a half-hour." She made it to his office in twenty-five minutes and studied the papers Bob handed her. "And this is it? You're sure?"

He nodded. "Yep."

She tucked the papers into her purse. "I really appreciate this."

He laughed. "Hey, it's just billable hours."

* * * *

Tyler protested her going off on her own. "Love, you're not used to driving here. And it's winter."

"Neither are you. We don't get snow in Florida."

"I was raised here. It's a little different."

"You've got a full day of interviews. I want to explore." She prayed he didn't pull out his secret weapon blue-eyed stare or she'd never be able to stand up to him. "Please, Ty? It's not like it's a third-world country. It's London." And an invisible clock ticked in her head. She was losing driving time.

He finally sighed. "All right. You have your phone?"

She nodded. They'd bought two cell phones upon arrival in London. Their U.S. phones didn't work here.

"Be safe, love," he said.

"Thank you!" She grabbed the tourist books and maps she'd randomly purchased and had yet to open before bolting out the hotel room door.

In the car she tried to calm herself. She took a folded piece of paper from her purse, hidden in the inside zipper pocket where she normally stashed her tampons, and looked at the highlighted route. Before they'd left home she'd used the Internet to find her destination.

It felt weird driving with the steering wheel in what was, to her, the passenger side, but she quickly adapted and took her time.

An hour later she pulled up in front of a line of older two-story row houses. Not too crappy, but certainly not the richest neighborhood.

She took a deep breath. The thought of calling ahead had crossed her mind, but might have caused problems.

She could do this.

Nevvie stepped out of the car and locked it, then walked up to the front door and knocked.

She held her breath. Inside, finally, she heard a man's voice. "All right. Just a moment."

The small window in the front door didn't allow a good view, but Nevvie saw someone coming. When the front door opened, Nevvie felt the breath sucked out of her lungs.

A brilliant blue pair of eyes, Tyler's blue eyes—Adam's blue eyes—stared at her.

"Can I help you, miss?" Here was her preview of Tyler in about twenty years, except she suspected the deep worry lines etched in this man's face wouldn't plague her husband. He was approximately Tyler's height and build, his hair grey but not thinning.

"Andrew Paulson?" she whispered, because it was all she could do to speak.

He frowned. "Yes? Are you all right, miss? You look a little ill, quite frankly."

"May I please come in? I need to speak with you."

He cautiously studied her. "I'm sorry, I don't mean to sound rude, but what is this about?"

Nevvie reached into her purse, took out her wallet, and opened it. With trembling fingers, she removed a picture, of her, Tyler, Thomas, and the boys. She handed it to him.

She heard his shocked gasp as he stared at the picture. After a long moment he looked at her. His eyes brimmed with tears.

"Please, come in," he softly said, stepping out of her way.

The small home looked neat and tidy, but not overly decorated and definitely not richly furnished. No sign of a woman anywhere. She noted he didn't wear any rings.

There was a small sitting room at the back of the house with a couch and chair, two full walls of bookshelves. Something familiar caught her eye and when she stepped over for a closer look, she was the one crying.

Every book. On one dedicated shelf, he had every one of Tyler's books, various English editions—hard cover, trade paperback, mass-market paperback, even different covers depending on whether it was a U.K. or U.S. release.

He had them all.

"Is…is he all right?" Andrew asked. "Is he happy?"

She turned, nodded. "He has interviews this morning. I wanted to meet you."

He still stared at the picture. As she looked around, she realized there were other things, framed newspaper and magazine articles about Tyler, the good ones. Copies of his book reviews, interviews. A framed movie poster from one of the film adaptations.

The man collapsed into the chair and finally looked up at her. "Does he know you're here?"

"No. I didn't tell him I tracked you down."

Tears ran down his face. "I'm so proud of him. Please tell him that for me. I've always wished I could tell him." Then he laughed, a sad, choked sound. "I'm sorry, miss. What is your name?"

She sat on the couch, leaned over and gently touched his knee. "My name's Nevvie. I'm your daughter-in-law."

It took Andrew a few minutes to compose himself. She refused when he tried to hand the picture back. "I want you to have it."

He sniffled. "Thank you. They're cute little devils, aren't they?"

"I can't wait for you to meet them. We'll fly you over—"

He vigorously shook his head. "No."

"Why not?"

"He won't want to see me."

"He will. I know Thomas will want to meet you."

At his questioning look, Nevvie knew she had some explaining of her own before she coaxed the truth out of him. "How much do you know about Tyler? About our private life?"

"Not much, I'm afraid. I remember reading a few years ago about an incident, a woman was attacked and stabbed." He looked at her. "You?"

She nodded. "Guilty."

He sniffled, looked at the picture again. "Then about his heart attack."

"I need you to please hear me out and keep an open mind. I'm going to tell you what I know before Tyler and I met, and you can correct my version after I'm done. I suspect Tyler doesn't know the full story."

Nevvie spent nearly thirty minutes relating what she knew, Tyler's two failed marriages and how he met Thomas, their happy life together, her life from when she met them. Then the recent events, including Delores' trip to Florida. They had managed to keep Tommy's accident out of the news, miracle of miracles.

When she finished, Andrew's face had softened, relaxed. He sadly smiled. "I was so scared when I heard about his heart attack, but I didn't know how to contact any of the children. I didn't want to track down Delores."

Nevvie's intuition buzzed again. "So our relationship doesn't shock you?"

He shrugged. "It's certainly different. I'm not one to judge."

Nevvie played her ace. "Tell me the truth about why you left."

His blue eyes nailed her, nearly paralyzing her. He proceeded to tell her the story of how when he'd asked Delores for a divorce, finally admitting he was attracted to a man, she ran him out that very afternoon. If he hadn't left, she threatened to tell everyone the truth about him, including the children. Back then it was far from readily accepted.

"I could have lost my job," he softly said. "It would have blackballed me from teaching. I hated leaving the children but the cards were stacked against me, right? A homosexual and a single father. There's no way the courts would have given me custody had I fought for it. Probably not even visitation. I didn't want them to feel ashamed."

Nevvie felt relief mixed with sadness. "She told them you ran off with another woman."

"More for her ego than mine. I suspect you've seen enough of that woman to know why she would rather claim another woman took me than the fact that her husband had 'turned gay,' in her words."

"Or bisexual?"

He harshly laughed. "No-sexual, is more like it, love." He reddened. "I'm sorry. That was rude of me. I shouldn't have said that. No, it's been a long time since I've had any sort of relationship, man or woman."

"Do you still teach?"

"I retired a few years ago. I get by on pension."

She spent an hour talking with him. He was sweet, gentle, reminded her so much of her husband. As much as Andrew had been able, he'd followed Tyler's public career. He'd amassed quite a scrapbook of clippings, even of magazine advertisements for Tyler's books and movies made from his books.

Delores probably couldn't even name Tyler's books. Andrew had practically memorized them.

Nevvie found out he didn't have a computer, couldn't afford one. When she offered to buy him one he waved her off. "No, love. That's all right. Please don't spend money on me. I get by." He shook his head and stared at her. "I'm still in shock, I suppose. I cannot begin to tell you how much this means to me, that you looked me up."

"I can't wait for Tyler to see you."

"No!" His face paled. "No, you can't bring him here!"

Nevvie frowned. "Why not?"

"He won't want to see me. Not after how I left them with her."

Nevvie wasn't about to have her plans spoiled. "Yes, he will. He needs to know the truth. I want my sons to know their grandfather. You are the only living grandfather they have. Dammit, you're going to let me do this!"

Perhaps sensing her fortitude, he finally nodded. "I'd be willing to bet you're wrong though. About him wanting to see me." He studied his hands. "I wasn't the best father. I worried I pushed them, especially Tyler, too hard. When Tyler was about seven or eight, I realized I couldn't stay married to that woman. I did my best to try to get them to stand up for themselves. I knew they'd need it against her. Tyler was so much like me. I worried she would walk all over him and make his life a misery."

Another question answered.

He started crying. "As a mother, how can you even stand to look at me? I abandoned my children."

"You did the best you could."

She had to get going, to meet Tyler, and she had a few other stops to make first. "Look, what are you doing tomorrow night?"

"A night in front of the telly. Why?"

"I'll come by tomorrow morning after Tyler leaves and take you to the store. My treat. How about you cook dinner, and I'll bring Tyler over?"

"He won't want to come, I'm telling you."

"Yes, he will." She smiled. "He always enjoys meeting dedicated fans."

* * * *

On her way back to the hotel, Nevvie made a few stops and several purchases, arranged a few things. She hadn't told Thomas what she'd done. Keeping this secret from both men had been hard on her. Once Tyler learned the truth she hoped he wouldn't be upset.

Getting him through the initial shock might be tricky.

She left some of the items in the trunk because they were for Andrew, whether he wanted them or not. When Tyler walked into the restaurant and spotted her, he immediately scowled.

"What's wrong?" she asked.

He leaned in to kiss her before taking his seat. "I should ask you that, love."

Her heart hammered in her chest. "What?"

"You look like you've been up to something."

Nevvie fought the urge to gulp. "I went shopping."

He raised an eyebrow, but his lips curled in a smile. "You're not much of a shopper, pet."

"I was today."

He laughed. "Is that it? You're concerned about how much you spent?"

She nodded, latching onto the deception. "I went a little overboard." Technically it was the truth.

"Well, no matter. I want you to enjoy yourself. Not like we can't afford it, darling."

Nevvie edged closer to the facts now that his suspicions had been allayed. "I do have something else to admit."

He looked at her over the top of his menu. "What's that?"

"We're going to have dinner tomorrow night with someone. Really big fan. I didn't want to tell you ahead of time because I wanted it to be a surprise."

He cocked his head, studying her. Finally, he asked, "Anything else you wish to admit?"

She smiled. "I looked them up today, they're really big fans, very sweet, and have all your books."

"You're sneaky."

Her voice dropped to a whisper. "I also bought something else today, Master." She knew how to derail his train of thought.

His eyes playfully narrowed. "And what's that?"

Whew! He'd apparently fallen for it. "You can see me in it when we get to the room."

His eyes traveled her body. "Are you wearing it now, my little slave?" he murmured.

Okay, now she was on the receiving end. A deep, comfortable throbbing started between her legs. "Yes, I am." She'd stumbled across the lingerie shop and figured it'd be a great way to distract Tyler after breaking the other news to him.

Thank God.

* * * *

After dinner, he walked with her to the elevator and they waited in silence. Alone inside after the doors slid shut, he hit the button for their floor and pulled Nevvie to him.

"Little slave, your master expects to see your purchase when we get to our room."

She ground her hips against him. "Whatever Master wants, Master gets."

He growled against her neck as he pulled her to him, his lips scorching her throat. "Damn right."

In their room, Tyler closed and locked the door behind them then started unbuttoning his shirt. "Get Master Thomas on the phone."

Nevvie called him. It would be early afternoon in Florida, hopefully the boys were taking a nap or Thomas wouldn't be able to play. They might not be able to have a full phone sex session.

She sat on the end of the bed.

"Long distance love line," Thomas teasingly answered. "Florida phone fucking at your service."

She grinned. That most likely meant the boys were asleep. "Master Thomas, Master Tyler asked me to call you."

There was only a moment of hesitation. "Goddamn, girl!" he hoarsely muttered. "We're playing that today?"

"Yes, Master." She winked at Tyler, who now had his shirt off and draped over a chair. She activated speakerphone mode and set the phone on the bed. "Are you able to play?"

"The boys are safely sleeping, probably for another hour or so." He let out a soft grunt she suspected was from him lying down. He must be in pain. "Don't want me in slave boy mode, huh?"

Nevvie shimmied out of her slacks, giving Tyler a preview. The lacy thong panty was uncomfortably chafing her but his pleased smile when he saw it made her wedgie well worth it. "Master Tyler is going to punish me for shopping today," she said, nudging the conversation the way she wanted it to go.

"Oh, really? And what did you buy, little slave?"

Tyler worked on his belt. "So far, it looks like she's added to her delicates."

"Huh?"

Tyler rolled his eyes. "She bought some lacy undergarments."

"Oh. Well why the hell didn't you say so? Just say underwear."

Buzz kill. Time to get her boys back on track. Nevvie started unbuttoning her shirt, giving Tyler a view of the matching lace camisole. "Master Thomas, I didn't ask permission to spend the money," she coaxed. Which all three knew was bullshit, because she didn't need their permission. But it added a little spice to the game.

Thomas finally followed her well-laid path. "Master Tyler, I think our slave needs a lesson, don't you? She needs to work off what she spent." From the way his voice deepened, she suspected he'd started stroking his cock.

"Absolutely, love." Tyler's passionately smoldering blue eyes fixed on her. "I think she needs to be taught a lesson. What would you suggest?" He slipped his pants and underwear off. His cock stood at rigid attention.

"What's she got on?"

Tyler knelt on the bed as she lay back. "A very pretty off-white ensemble. Lace and satin. Thong panties."

"Goddamn!" Thomas grunted again. He wouldn't take long to come.

"Yes, quite." Tyler leaned in and kissed Nevvie, traced her lips with his tongue. His cock brushed against her thigh. "She looks exquisite."

"Why don't you suck Master Tyler's sweet cock, baby girl?"

Her turn to moan. Her boys knew what she loved. "Anything my masters want." Tyler knelt over her and she swirled her tongue around his cockhead.

"Oh, Christ, that's beautiful," Tyler gasped.

"She doing it?"

"Damn right she is." He leaned forward on his arms while she swallowed his cock.

Tommy's soft grunts told Nevvie he was really close. After a few minutes, he hoarsely said, "Why don't you fuck her, Ty?"

Tyler gently tapped the top of her head and she let him go. In a fluid motion, he yanked down her thong and pushed her legs wide. "How should I fuck her, love?"

"Fuck her hard."

Nevvie moaned, her own need sending waves of aching pulsations through her sex. Thomas was usually her fast and furious fuck, when he felt up to it. Since his accident it was sometimes difficult for him to be as vigorous as he once was, settling for a gentler, calmer way.

Tyler firmly grabbed her hips and thrust, hard, deeply burying his cock inside her.

"Oh, Jesus she's wet," Tyler moaned.

"She damn well better be. Give her a good, hard fucking."

Tyler met her eyes. "Is that what you deserve, little slave? A good hard fucking?"

She eagerly nodded. "Yes, Master!"

Both men moaned. "Fuck her hard, Ty," Thomas said. "You know I haven't been able to do that for her lately."

Tyler studied her face as she wrapped her legs around his hips. "Hard, Master. Please." Tyler was always passionately sensuous, in a different way than Thomas.

He slammed his hips against Nevvie, drawing a deep, needy moan from her.

She tried not to dig her fingers as hard into his back as she usually did with Thomas, not wanting to hurt him. "Yessss!"

"Like that, love?" He did it again.

"Oh, yes, Master!"

He thrust, hard, repeatedly pistoning his cock inside her.

"Is he fucking you good, sugar?" Thomas gasped.

"Yes, Master!" She closed her eyes and hung on for the ride. She wouldn't come like this, but still enjoyed the hell out of it.

"Oh, baby, you sound so good—ah!" And there went Thomas.

She opened her eyes and looked at Tyler. "Come for me, Master. Please come for me."

With a final thrust and cry he did, trembling as he dropped his head to her shoulder. She held him, her arms tightly wrapped around him.

"You guys okay?" Thomas asked.

Nevvie laughed. "We're okay."

"When slowpoke gets his act together, we'll take care of you next, sugar."

Tyler lifted his head and laughed. "Oh, right. Nice. I could bloody well outrun you, I should think." He kissed Nevvie and slipped his hand under her camisole. Her nipples were tightly peaked already from the friction of his body and the filmy garment rubbing against her.

He pushed her legs apart and settled between them. "Talk to her,

Master Thomas," he said. "I'll do the hard work while you lie there and loaf," he teased.

Thomas laughed. "Hey, babe?"

She closed her eyes. "Yes, Master?"

"When you get home, I'm going to have a little surprise for you."

Tyler bent his mouth to her mound, laving her clit with his tongue while Thomas continued.

"I'm going to take you into the bedroom and I think I'm going to spend a little time playing Master again. Would you like that?"

"Oh…yes, Master!"

Tyler pushed two fingers inside her, stroking in time with his tongue.

"I'm going to put your pink collar on you and bend you over the bed and fuck your sweet brains out. You know I love having my hands on your gorgeous ass while I fuck you."

Nevvie shivered from what Tyler did to her, and from the mental image of what Thomas had in store.

"And if you're a good girl, maybe Master Tyler will do to you what's he's doing now, while I'm fucking you. Would you like that?"

"Please, yes, Master!"

His voice dropped to a hungry growl. She suspected he might have grown hard again. "Then I want you to show me how much you want it. You'd better come for me, baby girl. Come hard for me."

She cried out as Tyler brought her over, playing her body, stretching her climax out for what felt like hours. With his hands firmly gripping her thighs he kept working at her sensitive nub, refusing to stop or let go while she twisted beneath his skilled mouth on the bed.

"That's it, baby," Thomas whispered. "Come for us."

Only when Tyler knew he'd almost pushed her from pleasure to pain did he relent. He kissed her inner thigh. "How was that, my pet?"

Unable to speak, she simply nodded.

"Did you fry her brain, Ty?"

"I think so." He moved to lie next to her, cuddling her to him. She automatically rolled into his embrace, one leg hooked around his. "I think our girl is suitably well-fucked."

"Yeah, well, now I've got a problem."

Tyler chuckled. "Then why don't you stroke that sweet cock of yours and let me hear you come, love. You are still my little slave boy, you know."

"Goddamn!"

Enjoying her bliss, Nevvie didn't open her eyes. "Yes," she said. "Our little slave boy needs to show his Master and Mistress how much he misses them."

"Holy fuck!" he gasped.

Tyler gently squeezed her. "Imagine how good it'll feel when I get to slide my cock up your arse. Maybe instead of me taking care of Nevvie, perhaps while you have your cock buried in her, maybe I'll be fucking your sweet arse."

"Aw—oh!"

Nevvie quietly giggled. "That didn't take long."

They heard him gasping for breath. "Fuck, that was hot."

"We know what our little slave boy loves," Nevvie purred.

Thomas laughed. "I'm so screwed."

"You will be once we get home, love," Tyler assured him. "As for now, go clean up and we'll talk to you tomorrow."

"Love you guys. Be careful."

Nevvie reached for the phone. "Love you, too. Kiss the babies for us."

After she hung up and put the phone on the bedside table, she returned to Tyler's arms.

"Ready to go to sleep?" he asked.

She nodded. "Exhausted."

It was only after she knew Tyler was sound asleep next to her that she allowed herself to think about tomorrow.

How would he react? He'd never refused her anything before, but this was different. This intruded into his past, his personal pain. Could she get him to listen long enough to mend the rift?

Chapter Twenty-Five

Nevvie and Tyler went their separate ways after breakfast. Tyler had four interviews and lunch with the head editor of his publisher's London branch. Tyler had tried coaxing Nevvie into coming, but she gently refused.

"I want to sightsee and wander around. You enjoy yourself. Remember, dinner tonight." She kissed him and quickly left before he could question her too much.

She would pick him up after his last interview. By her best guesstimate, it would take a half-hour to make it to Andrew's house from there.

When she knocked on Andrew's door around ten that morning, Nevvie's arms were full of boxes. His eyes widened.

"What's all this?" He reached for one, but she gently shouldered him aside and carried them inside to his small kitchen table.

"These are for you." She turned and hugged him. "And you're not saying no, either."

He looked at the boxes for the laptop and printer. "Love, I don't want you to waste your money on me."

She grabbed his hands. "Andrew. Listen to me. I don't have a dad. I haven't had a dad in a lot of years. My sons haven't had a grandfather." She struggled and failed to contain her tears. "Tyler will understand and you two will get back together. And you're damn well going to let me spoil you, whether you like it or not. I don't know if I can ever get Henry and Wanda to see the truth, and that's not my business. But you are part of *my* family. I want you with us."

His own eyes brimmed as he tightly hugged her. "Thank you,

Nevvie. Thank you so much."

Once they composed themselves she set up the computer for him. "Do you know how to use the internet?"

"Not well. I've used it at the library a little, for research."

She'd already done research of her own and had the internet service activated for him. "I've paid for the first year already," she said. "You can email us any time, and I can send you pictures." She set him up an email account and then pulled up a private page on Tyler's website, one accessible only by password. "Here's some for you." She moved out of the way so he could look at the online scrapbook, his eyes brimming again as she went through the pictures with him.

"They're gorgeous. Adam looks just like Tyler."

She smiled. "He does. And Mikey looks just like Tommy." She patted his shoulder. "I can't wait for you to meet them."

Once she knew he understood the basics of the computer, she drove him to the grocery store and made him shop for whatever he needed. Apparently he was as good a cook as his son.

"We used to cook together, me and Ty," he softly said as he pushed a cart down the aisle. "He used to help me cook dinner all the time." He sighed. "I worried Delores might be harder on him after I left because he did look and act so much like me. I worried about him so much. All of them, but especially him. Her side of the family, they were a vicious bunch of barracudas, every last one of them." He looked at Nevvie. "What about Henry and Wanda? How are they?"

She shrugged. "They're all right. No children, but they're both married." Nevvie couldn't get over how much Tyler resembled his father. Even his voice sounded similar despite Tyler living in America for over twenty years.

She refused to let him pay and helped him unload the groceries at his house. By late afternoon, she knew everything was ready and had planned how she wanted Tyler to meet his father.

Before she left she hugged Andrew. "Remember, let me get him

inside first and talk to him for a minute. I'll call you out of the kitchen
when I'm ready for you."

"Nevvie, how can I ever repay you?"

"By being the world's best grandpa to my sons." *And by being my
dad,* she thought.

* * * *

Tyler looked tired when she pulled up outside the television studio
where his last interview took place. He got in.

"Want me to drive, love?" he asked.

She shook her head. While she sometimes had to think for a
minute when making a turn, for the most part she'd adapted rather
easily to driving on the left. "I've got it. We need to get moving, don't
want to be late."

He settled back in his seat. "How long are we staying?"

"They're preparing us a nice dinner. We'll stay and chat for as
long as they'll have us." She tightly gripped the steering wheel.

She sensed his eyes on her. "What aren't you telling me, Nevvie?"

She didn't dare take her eyes off the road. "I stopped by and
talked to them again earlier today. Very sweet."

"Ah." Apparently he was more tired than she thought, because he
didn't ask any other questions.

When they neared Andrew's house, Nevvie fought to control her
nerves. Adrenaline coursed through her, her hands trembled. She
locked the car after Tyler got out and led him up the front walk. She
smelled something delicious cooking inside.

So did Tyler. He closed his eyes and deeply inhaled. "My, that
smells quite lovely. Brings back memories."

Nevvie mentally jumped for joy. Andrew said he would cook
some old favorites. Perhaps that would help soothe Tyler's soul.

"They told me to come right in when we got here." She knocked
and opened the door, stuck her head in. "We're here."

Andrew called from the kitchen. "Come in. Be out in a minute." That was their pre-arranged cue.

Nevvie opened the door all the way and firmly gripped Tyler's hand. She led him down the hall—he couldn't see into the kitchen from there—and directly to the small sitting room.

Tyler looked around as they walked. "What did you say their names were?" he softly asked.

"Look here," she said, trying to distract him. She led him to the bookshelf and leaned in close, pointing to the shelf dedicated to Tyler's books. "They've got every one of your books printed in English." She barely let him take that in when she yanked his arm and dragged him to look at some of the framed reviews. "And look at this—"

"Love," he murmured, glancing around nervously, "that's flattering, certainly, but isn't it a tad...obsessive?"

"Why would it be?" Nevvie silently swore at the nervous edge in her voice. "You're their favorite author!"

Tyler frowned. "Nevvie," he firmly said, "what is going on?"

She pushed him into the chair. "Sit there. I'll be right back."

"Nev—"

"Tyler, please." She kissed the top of his head and raced to the kitchen.

The smell there was even more wonderful, thickly filling the air. Andrew had his sleeves rolled up and the entire table filled with food, way more than the three of them would be able to eat. He looked as nervous as she felt. The sight of him there...whether it was because he resembled her husband or because of her desperation to make her plan work, she didn't know, but she felt her heart thump in a pleasant way. One way or the other she would make sure this man stayed in their lives.

Her sons could have a grandfather.

She could have a dad again.

"Everything ready?" she asked.

He nodded. "I'm so bloody nervous," he muttered, wiping his hands on a dishtowel.

She firmly gripped his hand and led him out to the sitting room. Tyler's back was turned to them and she knew from the angle of his head he was taking in the shelf of books.

Her heart pounded and she had to take a deep breath to steady her voice before she spoke. "Ty, I want to introduce our host."

Tyler stood and turned. Then the color washed out of his face. For a moment Nevvie worried he might faint. "Bloody hell," he whispered.

Nevvie held up her other hand. "Don't say another word. Hear me out. I had Bob find him for me. He had no idea I was coming to visit him yesterday."

"Yesterday?"

"Hush." Tyler did. Nevvie continued, speaking quickly, hoping to get the story out as fast as she could before he could object. "He had no idea, it was just as much a shock to him as it is to you right now. After what you told me about Delores, I decided I wanted to do a little digging of my own. My suspicions were correct."

She gently squeezed Andrew's hand. "I'm going to give you the short version, and then you can hear him out." Nevvie took another deep breath. "Delores lied to you about why he left. She kicked him out. He didn't want to lose contact with you, but she was a real bitch and had him by the nuts. Now I know that doesn't make up for all the years you guys have lost, but goddammit, I want my sons to have a grandfather."

She set her chin in a defiant glare. "You've got two choices, Tyler. One is to make me happy, hear him out, and keep an open mind. Two is you keep your mouth shut, because whether you like it or not, I will make sure my sons and I have a close relationship with Andrew."

Tyler's mouth opened, then shut. He stared at them for a long, stunned moment. Finally, in a weak voice he asked, "All these books?"

Nevvie let out a breath she didn't realize she'd been holding. While Tyler was still in emotional shock, his question indicated to her he would keep an open mind. She squeezed Andrew's hand, wanting him to stay silent.

"All those books, Tyler. All these years. He's your biggest fan, always has been." Tyler's mother only had three of his books, ones he'd personally autographed for her and given her as presents.

Tyler looked at the walls again, walked over to read the clippings. After a few silent moments he turned to face them.

She finally stepped behind Andrew and gently nudged him across the room toward his son.

Tyler stared.

"I'm proud of you, son," Andrew managed in a choked voice. "I'm so very, very proud of you. All these years I've wished I could tell you."

Tyler's paralysis broke. He sobbed and embraced Andrew.

"I love you, Tyler," Andrew said, tightly hugging him. "I've missed you all so very much. I'm sorry I had to leave you with her. I couldn't tell you the truth. I'm so sorry."

Nevvie cried, unable to help it. It wouldn't be an overnight thing, but she knew Tyler would rebuild his relationship with Andrew. Then her eyes fell on something else, a new picture, pinned to the wall. Using regular paper, Andrew had apparently figured out how to print an image from the internet. It was of the five of them, from the scrapbook page, taken by Eddie in the hospital the morning Nevvie and Mikey were discharged from the hospital following his birth. She smiled.

Family.

Her family.

After a few minutes, the men stepped away from each other and wiped their eyes. Tyler reached for Nevvie and pulled her tightly to him, burying his face in her hair. "I don't know whether to spank you or kiss you, sweetheart."

She smiled. "Either one's fine with me, Ty."

That made him laugh. "Somehow, I knew it would be."

Tyler kept his arm around Nevvie and looked at his father. "Was there ever really another woman?"

Andrew shook his head. Tyler closed his eyes and struggled to maintain his composure.

Nevvie stepped in again. "There's a lot to catch up on, and we can do that while we eat. He's cooked a wonderful dinner."

* * * *

They ate and talked and, with Nevvie's encouragement, Andrew told his story. Tyler silently listened, nodding when he finished.

"I'd always wondered if there was more," Tyler softly said.

"You were only thirteen. Your brother and sister even younger. You can see why I couldn't tell you."

Tyler studied his plate. "I suppose Nevvie's told you about us?"

Andrew nodded. "Your wife strikes me as a special woman. You two are very lucky men."

Tyler smiled and looked at Nevvie. "You've no idea."

They helped Andrew wash the dishes, then Nevvie and Tyler sat cuddled together on the couch. She did most of the listening while the two men talked and caught up. A little after midnight, she yawned.

Tyler gently nudged her. "Love? Are you still with us?"

"I'm sorry."

"I'm not in a hurry for you to leave, but you should probably put her to bed," Andrew said.

Nevvie's eyes flew open. "Crap!"

Tyler flinched, startled. "What?"

"We didn't call Tommy!" She pulled out her phone and dialed.

He answered on the second ring. "Well, I thought y'all'd forgot us."

"No, sweetie, we didn't. I have a surprise for you. And the boys." She heard Adam talking in the background, trying to get Tommy's attention. "Put him on for me."

"Okay." She heard Tommy talking to Adam, probably pulling the little boy into his lap so he could hold the phone for him. Adam had already destroyed three phones by dropping them. "It's Mommy and Daddy."

"Mommy?"

"Hi, sweetie. Are you being a good boy for Poppa?"

"I helped him bath Mikey."

She grinned. "Bath?"

"Yep! Only got Poppa a little wet."

Nevvie could only imagine how that went. "Listen, sweetie, Daddy and I are talking to someone I want you to say hi to."

"Who?"

She met Andrew's eyes. "Grandpa Andrew."

"Who?"

"Grandpa Andrew. I'm going to hand the phone to him so you can say hi." She reached over, encouraged him to take it.

Andrew tentatively spoke. "Hello?"

Adam always yelled on the phone, so Nevvie could hear Adam's excited voice on the other end. She knew she'd have some splainin' to do to Thomas.

"Gwampa Andwew? I din know I had a gwampa!"

Tyler kissed her forehead. "I absolutely adore you, love," he whispered.

She patted his thigh.

"Well, son, I didn't know I had a grandson, either, until your mummy told me."

"When can I see you?"

"Your mummy got me a computer—" Nevvie cringed when she felt Tyler's gaze on her again, "—and taught me how to use email. She said we'll email back and forth."

"You gonna live wif Gwamma Peggy?"

Tyler snorted with amusement. "You get to explain *that* one," he murmured.

She giggled. "Happy to."

Andrew looked a little confused. "No, I live in London."

"Is dat near Savannah or Atwanta?"

Tyler laughed, loud and hearty. Nevvie struggled not to cry again, happy, relieved tears this time.

"I live in Britain," he explained to Adam. "Not in the United States. Your mummy and daddy are here now, talking to me."

"Okay. Poppa wants to talk now. Wuv you, Gwampa!"

"I love you too, son," Andrew said, his eyes brimming.

Nevvie never ceased to wonder how young children could readily accept situations thrown at them without batting an eye.

Nevvie started to reach for the phone, but Tyler beat her to it. Good thing. She heard Thomas' drawl loud and clear.

"Um, Ty? What the fuck is going on?"

"We'll explain later, love." He looked at Nevvie. "Our girl has pulled another rabbit out of her hat, as it were."

"What was Adam talking about? Who the hell is Grandpa Andrew? Isn't that your dad's name?"

Tyler closed his eyes. "Yes," he softly answered.

Thomas went silent on the other end. Nevvie reached for the phone. "Don't swear in front of the kids."

"What the fu—freak is going on, Nev?"

In the background, Adam chanted, "Poppa said a bad word. Momma gonna wash your mouf out wif soap when she gets home!"

"I'll explain later."

"Explain now."

"Can't right now. We'll call you later, when we get back to the hotel."

* * * *

They finally returned to the hotel a little after one. They would go to Andrew's the next afternoon following Tyler's interview. When they were safely locked in their room, Tyler pulled her to him, tightly hugged her.

"I love you, sweet. I love you so much. How can I ever thank you?" He held her at arm's length. "How in bloody hell did you know?"

"I suspected. After what Delores said to me when I called her to tell her about your heart attack, then what she said in the hospital room, then when I questioned you about it later, it wasn't hard to see there were some major pieces missing from that puzzle. I decided to go looking for them."

"And what if it'd turned out my mother's version was correct?"

"I don't think your mother could tell the truth if it bit her on the freaking ass." Because of their pre-emptive publicity strike, Delores never had a chance to sully their name. They hadn't heard from her since, although Tyler's brother and sister were tickled to find out they'd made Delores mad and spoiled her plans.

They called Thomas back and Tyler explained as much as he could over the phone. When he finished, he handed it to Nevvie. "He wants to speak to you, love." Then he went into the bathroom.

"Hi."

"Ahem."

She rolled her eyes. "I'm sorry I didn't tell you. I didn't know if this was going to work out or not. If it didn't, I wasn't even going to tell Tyler about him. I met him first to make sure my theory was right."

He fell quiet for a moment. "Is he really okay? Is Ty handling it okay?"

"Yeah. He is." She yawned. "Now I'm going to say goodnight because I'm exhausted. We'll call you tomorrow."

She put the phone on the table and crawled under the covers.

Tyler joined her a few minutes later. He looked like he'd been crying.

"Are you okay?" she asked.

He curled around her. "I dare think it's safe to say I'm better than I've been in years, love."

* * * *

They spent as much time visiting with Andrew as they could before they left. Before they said good-bye at the airport, he hugged them both, Tyler first.

When he hugged Nevvie he whispered, "Thank you so much. I am forever in your debt, my child."

She smiled when she stepped away. "No problem, Dad. That's what family's for."

Andrew smiled.

Back home nearly half a day later, it was the middle of the night when the limo dropped them off at the house. They left their luggage inside the front door and Thomas awoke as they undressed and crawled into bed with him. This time, he was in the middle as Nevvie and Tyler tightly snuggled on either side.

He kissed Tyler, then Nevvie. "Welcome home, guys."

Late the next morning, Nevvie woke to find herself curled in Tommy's arms. She heard Tyler in the kitchen with Adam and Mikey.

Thomas kissed the back of her neck. "Fucking sneaky woman, that's what you are. Evil Genius Junior, I swear to God."

She laughed and rolled to face him. "He's so sweet, Tommy. I can't wait for you to meet him. I'm going to fly him over here. I'm going to try to talk him into moving here."

"Nev, is this for you or Tyler? Honestly?"

She frowned. "It's for the boys. I want them to know their grandfather."

"Uh huh. Sure. Right."

She smacked his shoulder. "You're just mad I didn't let you in on it."

"Damn straight."

"You would have told him."

He hesitantly nodded. "You're probably right. What if this had backfired?"

"But it didn't. That's the point. Everything went perfectly."

Three weeks later, all five of them were waiting at Tampa International Airport when Andrew's flight arrived. Tyler entertained Adam; Thomas held Mikey. Nevvie had a thought and leaned close to Tommy.

"Do you think Eddie and Pete have any single friends?"

"Oh, fu-freak no, baby girl. Don't go matchmaking."

"Well why not? If he meets someone—"

Thomas glared. "No."

When Andrew finally emerged from the terminal shuttle, Nevvie waved and pointed him out to Adam. "Go meet Grandpa Andy," she said.

Needing no encouragement, Adam ran up to him. Andrew scooped him into his arms. "Well, hello there, young fellow. You must be Adam."

"You must be Gwampa Andy!"

He smiled. "I suppose I must."

Thomas leaned in. "Holy fucking shit! Looks just like him!"

"Don't swear in front of the kids. And yes, I know. Spooky, isn't it?"

He nodded.

Tyler walked over and hugged him, and then tried to take Adam, who refused to leave his new-found "gwampa." They walked over to Thomas and Nevvie. Nevvie hugged him. Andrew nervously smiled.

"Hello. You must be Thomas."

Thomas leaned in and gave him a one-armed hug, both men trying to avoid smushing the boys in their arms. "Nice to finally meet you, Andrew."

Tyler beamed. "Well, let's go home!"

* * * *

Andrew had never been to the States before. After his initial nervousness faded, he quickly settled in. Nevvie stood in the kitchen one afternoon and watched him playing with the boys in the living room. Thomas walked in and noticed her contemplation. He slipped his arm around her shoulders and kissed her neck.

"What're you watching?" he softly asked.

She snuggled closer and nodded toward the living room. "Isn't this great?"

"Yeah, you did good, baby girl. Real good. I'm proud of you."

Tyler emerged from his study and joined Andrew and the boys in the living room.

"This is the way life's supposed to be," she said. "Our family's complete."

He pulled her tightly against him and kissed the top of her head, rested his chin there. "No arguments from me, babe. No arguments from me."

Over the next two months, they flew Andrew to Florida five times, each stay longer than the previous one. Tyler and his father spent a lot of time bonding and catching up. Nevvie enjoyed having a father in her life again. Mikey was a little too young to understand, but Adam adored having Gwampa Andy around.

And she set her sights firmly on convincing him to move to the States permanently, to come live with them. Or at the very least to allow them to buy him a vacation home nearby. Adam emailed Andrew nearly every day when he wasn't with them, and was becoming very adept at using the computer as a result.

Three days after Andrew flew home to London following his latest visit, Nevvie lay curled on the couch with Tyler. She watched TV while he read. With her head in his lap, she knew she could easily go to sleep. Thomas, having a bad day with pain, had taken a couple of Tylenol PM and went to bed early.

"Perhaps we should do a little digging into your past," Tyler offhandedly suggested.

It took her a moment to process his words. "What?"

He glanced down at her. "Your family."

She froze. "No."

"Why not?"

"Because."

He waited for a moment. "You were never curious about your birth parents?"

She shrugged. "Not really." When she was younger, yes, after she first found out. Then she decided she didn't want to know. She was too busy trying to survive on her own to worry about it. And at the time, she carried way too much resentment and anger in her heart to even care.

"There are valid reasons for finding out."

"They didn't want me. That's all I need to know." Old pain threatened to bubble to the surface.

He put his book aside. "Love, that might not be true and you know it."

She remained silent.

"Think about Adam and Mikey. You should know your family history for them if not for yourself."

"That's a low fucking blow." The boys were asleep, so she didn't worry about them hearing.

Tyler remained undaunted. "Love, what if you have any genetic conditions we need to know about? We already know Adam should be screened for cardiac issues, but we know nothing about your history."

She chewed on that, could come up with no valid argument to counter it. "No."

He waited a moment to try again. "Bob could handle it all."

"I would have to get in touch with Mary," Nevvie said. She had trouble thinking of her as "Mom" even though that's what she'd grown up calling her until Nevvie was fifteen and had learned she was adopted. As far as Nevvie was concerned, Peggy Kinsey was her mom, in title and heart.

And while she'd always love and miss her "Daddy," Andrew was now her dad.

"Love, Bob could—"

"I don't want to talk about this right now, Ty," she muttered before rolling over on the couch.

He sighed. "Very well."

Chapter Twenty-Six

A week later, Thomas had a bad morning with pain. Tyler volunteered to drive him to the office. Nevvie had already planned on going out with the boys. The little boys. Because sometimes when her four boys—five if you counted Andrew—got together, it was hard to tell the adults from the children the way the men acted.

They were both good dads. And Andrew was a great grandfather.

She stopped by a florist on the way and then drove to a place she hadn't visited in far too many years. Blinking back her tears, Nevvie loaded Mikey in the stroller and let Adam walk along beside her.

It took a few minutes of searching. She worried she'd have to go to the cemetery office when she finally recognized one of the older headstones, an odd name she recalled from her youth. Her feet remembered the path from that point.

The trees were taller and provided more shade than they had when she was eight and stood by her mother's side at the grave. It'd just been the two of them and a few scattered friends and distant relatives on a scorching hot Tampa summer afternoon. Nevvie remembered the extra misery of the borrowed black dress two sizes too big for her as the blazing sun beat down on them.

Her mother had tightly gripped her hand as the cemetery staff lowered her father's coffin into the ground.

Nevvie spotted the headstone and her feet slowed until she stood before it. Adam stilled his soft babbling and looked at it, then her.

"Are you sad, Mommy?"

She sat in front of the headstone and tucked the flowers against it. Then she pulled Adam into her lap and kissed the top of his head.

"Yes, baby. Mommy's sad."

He laid his head against her shoulder. "Don't be sad, Mommy. I love you. So do Daddy and Poppa and Gwampa." His big blue eyes widened, studying her.

The laugh forced its way through her sadness. He was so much like Tyler, always striving to make people feel better. "I know you do, baby."

He pointed. "Who is that?"

"That's your Grandpa Michael."

"We've got Baby Mikey."

"That's right. Baby Mikey is named after Grandpa Michael, just like you were named after Grandpa Adam."

He turned in her lap so he could study the headstone. "I'm sorry they gone."

She hugged him. "Me too, baby."

"When we gonna see Gwampa Andy again?"

Nevvie smiled. "He's coming over to visit next week."

"I miss Gwampa Andy."

"Me too, baby." She kissed Adam's head and hugged him.

Mikey fussed a little in his stroller. Nevvie reached out and gently rocked it. He settled after a moment. Much like his father, he preferred to be on the move when possible.

Nevvie didn't want anything to do with her step-father, Preacher Jim. While the pain and betrayal of her mother leaving her on her own had haunted Nevvie for years, from the hindsight of motherhood, she could understand why. A woman widowed, with a young daughter to care for, suddenly on her own trying to do the best she could most likely without any financial support from others. Then she'd met Preacher Jim. She'd had two sons with him and when he demanded Mary turn Nevvie over to a cousin's care before they moved out west, she'd probably felt like she had no alternative.

Nevvie hoped if nothing else the woman had found happiness with the asshole.

Nevvie never would have been raped at age eighteen if she hadn't had to work and support herself. Her car wouldn't have broken down, she wouldn't have accepted his ride...

She closed her eyes and tried not to dwell on that. She wouldn't have dropped out of USF and lost her academic scholarship, either. Wouldn't have moved to New Orleans and met Alex and nearly died twice at his hands.

Then again, she never would have met Thomas and Tyler.

Or had her sons. Or Andrew and Peggy and the rest of the Kinsey clan. Pete and Eddie.

It was time to forgive and move on. It didn't mean she wanted to be friends with Mary, but Nevvie knew she needed to heal or she'd never get past it. And she realized she wanted answers.

Needed answers.

Over the years she'd demonized Preacher Jim in her mind. She'd resented his dictatorial ways and fundamentalist religion. He was nothing like her warm, loving Daddy. While she'd always known she didn't quite fit in exactly right, she also realized how much her adopted dad had loved her. Preacher Jim never even tried, yet he had no problem fathering two sons he doted over with Mary.

As an adult Nevvie knew it wasn't her job to psychoanalyze why her mother did what she did. It was time to put on her big girl panties and face her past once and for all, rip the scab off and clean out the wound so it could finally heal for good. Time for her to take to heart the advice she gave to Tyler and Thomas about their emotional scars. She was no longer an abandoned teenager, but a mom with two loving husbands who would never leave her, and a huge extended network of family and friends to support her.

The only family that truly mattered now was the one she'd willingly chosen to be a part of.

And she apparently had a backbone made of steel, even if she never realized it before.

After another twenty minutes at Michael Barton's grave, Nevvie stood and brushed off her jeans. With Adam quietly walking by her side, she returned to the car.

* * * *

Later that night, Thomas had to take a prescription pain pill, his first in a while, and go to bed early. Nevvie put the boys down for the night and found Tyler in his study. He sat behind his desk and stared at his laptop screen.

"Hello, love." He held out his arms and she crawled into his lap. He'd always held her like this, even before they were involved. It made her feel safe and comforted.

"I think I'm ready to go to sleep," she muttered against his shoulder.

He gently stroked her back. "Exhausted?"

"Yeah." Nevvie took a deep breath. "You know what we talked about? About my birth parents?"

"Yes?"

She settled deeper into his lap. "Okay," she softly said. "But I want to be the one to talk to her. I want to see her face to face one last time."

He didn't make her repeat or clarify. He knew what she meant. "I'll call Bob tomorrow and have him start the process."

"Thank you."

They sat there a few more minutes before he gently said, "Let's go to bed, sweetheart. I'm rather worn out, and I'm sure you'd like to get to sleep."

She nodded but didn't move.

Tyler kissed the top of her head. "Where did you go today? You look rather sad."

"I took the boys to visit my dad's grave. I haven't been there in years. I needed to go."

He fell silent for several long minutes. "Are you all right? You know, you don't have to have any contact with them. We can let Bob—"

"No. I need to finish this. I want to see her one more time. I want her to see what she's missed all these years so I can turn my back on all of that for good."

"If it's what you want, you know we'll do it. Anything you want."

"Maybe we can turn it into a family vacation?" It was a question, not a statement.

"You're not asking permission, are you?"

She snorted. "Well, I don't want to just demand it."

He sat her up in his lap. "Darling, you say the word, it's done. You know that."

"Would Tommy be up to a trip like that?"

"I think it might just be what he needs. We could drive, take our time. Lately we've taken damn few pleasure trips, you know. Usually it's dash somewhere for work and dash back home. I think a long extended trip would do us all some good." He nudged her to her feet and took her hand. "How about you let me handle the plans, right?"

Nevvie smiled. It would be nice to step back and let Tyler fully take charge again, like he had in the early days. "Okay."

Tyler's broad smile lit her heart. "Aces. Let's go to bed, sweet."

* * * *

Nevvie put their conversation behind her. She knew Tyler would take care of things without her involvement. She enjoyed her sons and helping Maggie with the business. Between Maggie and Kenny, both Nevvie and Tommy felt comfortable not being in the office every day. It wouldn't be long before he stepped back and let Kenny take full control of everything.

And Nevvie had decided when that day came, she would most likely stay home full time with him and Tyler.

With her family.

Andrew came over for his next visit and stayed with them nearly two weeks. They enjoyed his company and the boys loved spending time with Gwampa. Tyler's emotional healing from reconnecting with his father made him even happier than Nevvie and Thomas ever thought possible.

It was with some surprise that, two weeks later, Nevvie looked up from her laptop one rare, cool Florida spring afternoon where she'd been answering Tyler's fan email. The windows were opened to take advantage of the beautiful weather, and Mikey was asleep in the nursery. Tyler had gone out that morning and taken Adam with him to run errands. The loud rumble in the street, like a large truck, sounded like it came from in front of their driveway.

Thomas walked down the hall, drawn from his study by the noise. "What the hell is that?" he asked, frowning as he walked to the front door. He opened it. "Son of a bitch!"

Nevvie put the laptop on the coffee table and stood to join him. "What?"

He snorted, whether in amusement or irritation, she wasn't sure. "Come see."

Nevvie had never seen the large red and white RV parked in front of their driveway before. Scratch large, it was huge. Her old Chalmette apartment in New Orleans probably had less square footage than this beast.

The side door opened. Adam carefully climbed down the steps and ran up the driveway to them. Thomas scooped him up.

"Poppa! Mommy! Look what Daddy bought us!" Tyler appeared in the doorway, a sheepish grin in his face.

Nevvie knew that look. The "forgiveness instead of permission" look. He knew he'd get chewed out over this.

He also knew damn well the two of them would quickly forgive him.

Stunned into silence, Nevvie walked down the driveway.

"Well, loves? What do you think?"

She couldn't chastise him for spending the money. The movie rights and residuals from his last book would probably pay for ten of these things.

"You bought it?"

"Well, love, they don't let you drive one off on your own unless you do." His grin told Nevvie he already knew she would give him a pass on this. "You did agree to let me make the plans."

Thomas stopped next to her, holding Adam, and stared at the RV. "Holy crap, Ty—"

"Thomas!" Nevvie scolded.

Adam grinned. "Poppa said a bad word."

Thomas laughed and rubbed noses with the little boy. "Holy *crud*, Ty, what the heck did you do?"

"We're going on a road trip, loves."

Adam threw his arms up in the air. "Yay! Vroom vroom!"

Nevvie laughed. "*You* driving this? I'm not sure I'm comfortable with that."

Knowing he was already forgiven, Tyler kissed her, then Thomas. "They worked with me at the dealership before I even signed. They have a huge lot in the back where you can practice. It's quite easy."

Thomas shook his head. "You can barely drive a motorcycle. You expect me to believe you can steer this land yacht?"

Adam nodded. "Daddy did good. Only hit three cones."

Tyler quickly added, "That was just backing up in the beginning. I wasn't used to the camera yet. We have an appointment tomorrow at two to come back for you both to get lessons." He looked at them. "Well? Don't you want to see the inside?"

He gave them a quick tour and explained that the dealership would send someone over shortly to pick it up and bring Tyler's car home. They couldn't keep the RV parked at the house because of deed restrictions—and no room—and Tyler still had to make arrangements to get a spot in their subdivision's RV storage yard. As Nevvie sat in one of the chairs near the front, Adam climbed into her lap.

"Did we do good, Mommy?"

Those huge, blue eyes. Just like Tyler. Just like Andrew. How could she or Thomas ever discipline him? In fact, it was increasingly obvious Tyler was apparently the only one immune to his "look," frequently the one who had to be stern when called for.

"You did great, baby."

"Daddy let me pick the color. Do you like it?" He looked worried, tiny creases furrowing his smooth brow.

She laughed. "It's beautiful, baby. You did good."

"I can't wait! Daddy said we can see the whole country. We can go to Yellowrock and see buffalo!"

Nevvie tried to decipher that and looked to Tyler for clarification.

"Yellowstone," he corrected.

Thomas shook his head. "We need a tow dolly and a car for that. You can't drive this crate around the park. It's too big."

Tyler grinned. "Already taken care of. I went and talked to Rollo."

"Daddy let me pick the color out there too!" Adam chimed in.

Thomas closed his eyes and rubbed the bridge of his nose. "You bought a *car*, too?" Tyler was as mechanically inclined as a banana in a fruit salad.

Nevvie laughed. "Oh, boy. What'd you get?"

"A Pilot. Brand new. It seats eight, and Rollo is coordinating with the RV dealership to get a car hauler for us." Tyler happily clapped his hands together. "I've taken care of everything, loves."

"You? Bought a car?" Thomas repeated.

"Well I'm not a total ignoramus in that department, Thomas."

Thomas and Nevvie both arched an eyebrow at him.

"I bought new!" Tyler defended himself. "It's not like a used one. Thomas, you yourself said Rollo has never cheated us."

Nevvie and Thomas exchanged a look. "Well," Thomas finally said, "I guess we're going on a road trip." He hugged Tyler and left his arm around his shoulders. "So when are we leaving, Evil Genius?"